MOUNTAINS OF THE MOON

CONNIE J. JASPERSON

WORLD OF NEVEYAH

ISBN-13: 9781680630183

ISBN-10: 1680630180

Graphics & Maps © Connie J. Jasperson

Special thanks to Eagle Eye Editors
www.eagleeyeeditors.me

Published by Bard Books
In association with
Myrddin Publishing Group
Contact us at - www.myrddinpublishing.com

A SUBSIDIARY OF MYRDDIN PUBLISHING GROUP

BOOKS BY CONNIE J. JASPERSON

WORLD OF NEVEYAH, TOWER OF BONES SERIES:

Tower of Bones (Tower of Bones series book I)

Forbidden Road (Tower of Bones series book II)

Forthcoming in 2016: Valley of Sorrows (Tower of Bones series book III)

WORLD OF NEVEYAH (stand-alone)

Mountains of the Moon

The Wayward Son (forthcoming in 2016)

OTHER BOOKS BY CONNIE J.JASPERSON:

HUW THE BARD

TALES FROM THE DREAMTIME

This book is dedicated to my husband, Greg, with all my heart and all my love. Your support and belief in me mean more to me than mere words can possibly express.

Sherrie DeGraw, you are more than merely a sister; you are my best friend in this life. Your wise reading shapes my words.

This book wouldn't exist without the hard work and sincere efforts of Maria V. A. Johnson, Carlie M.A. Cullen, Irene Roth Luvaul, Alison DeLuca, David P. Cantrell, Tim Walker, and Mark Kenney.

The hundreds of hours you spent combing it for inconsistencies, errors, and typos were appreciated more than you will ever know.

PART
I
WYNN FARMER
LIGHTNING
MAGE

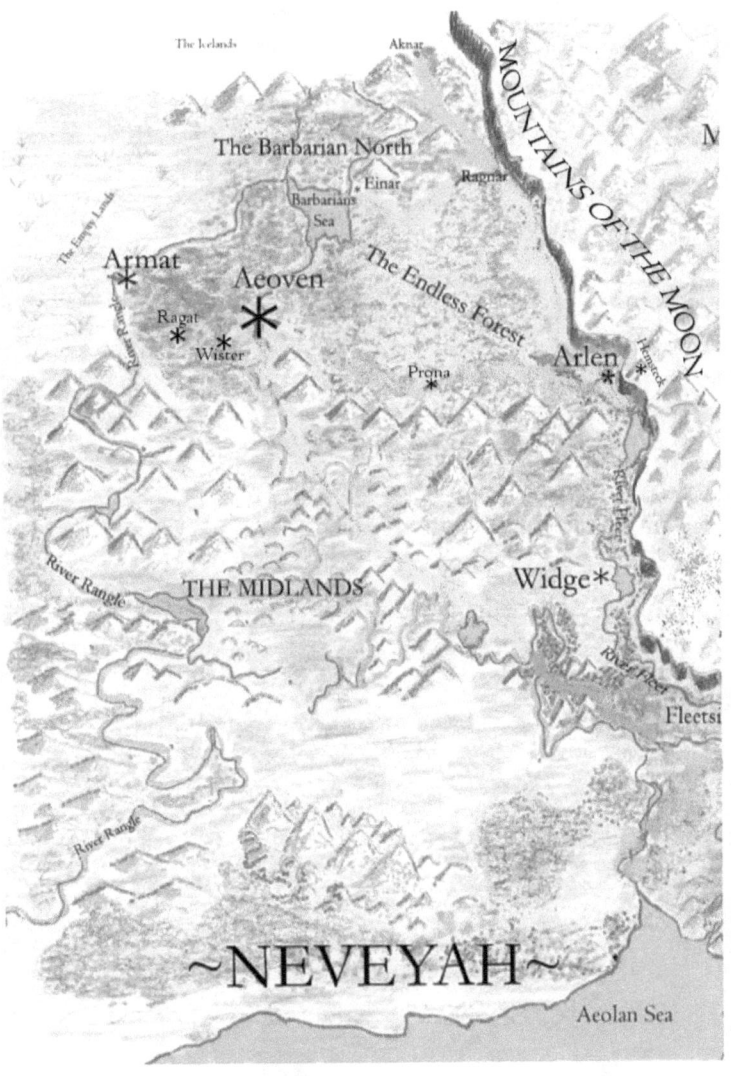

Map of Western Neveyah

Chapter 1

Wynn Farmer discovered his old boots had holes worn in them when he heard the soft, squishing sound, perfectly in sync with every step he took. If he'd known he would be dropped into some strange world when he left the house, he might have planned ahead a little better and slipped some new cardboard in, just until he could get them resoled. But he hadn't known, and now he trudged along a faint path with wet feet, through a dark, eerie prairie, completely lost and shivering in the cold, misty rain.

As he tried to stay warm, he thought back to less than an hour ago when he left the house. He was hot on the trail of a straying sheep, the sun was shining, a beautiful late-summer morning. Wynn's father and mother had taken the wagon to town for supplies, so he'd left them a note explaining about the sheep even though his father would blame him for it somehow. Things that went wrong were always Wynn's fault.

By the time he followed the trail to the old rock ledge at the edge of his family's farm, it grew warmer, and he took off his jacket, tying it around his waist by the sleeves. When he arrived at the outcropping an eerie glow suffused the cleft in the boulders, catching his attention. Wynn leaned down to see what was causing it.

Abruptly, something grabbed him, and he was

1

dragged through the crevice. He endured a strange feeling akin to being funneled through the neck of a bottle, and just as suddenly, whatever had seized him dropped him. Landing on his feet, he looked around in amazement.

As his eyes adjusted to the darkness, he saw no sign of the outcropping.

"No!" His cry fell into the silence. For a brief moment, he panicked, turning in circles, searching for the rocks. His legs gave out, and dropping to his knees, he scrabbled around, combing the area carefully, searching every inch with his hands, feeling nothing but the flat, barren, rock-free soil. "No! No! No!" His shouts of denial sounded flat and muffled in the hushed darkness.

The stones were gone, as was everything he'd ever known.

Standing up, he peered through the gloom, trying to get his bearings, unable to make out his surroundings. His fists balled up, except there was nothing to hit but his own forehead. "Aaugh! Aaugh!" Despite the pain of having hit himself, nothing changed, and if he was dreaming, he didn't wake. Wynn paced back and forth, frustration boiling over as he tried to decide what to do.

"Oh, Goddess. Where the hell *am* I?" Taking a deep breath, he scrubbed at his eyes, wondering what his parents would think when they realized he'd vanished.

The sky was dark except for an angry glow low on the horizon. No stars shone above, making it impossible to tell what time it was. It was cool out, and a fine, misty rain fell. He put his jacket back on, wishing he'd brought a hat.

Now, turning in a slow circle one last time, Wynn tried to see something, anything, to help him find his bearings, but in the dusky gloom, he could see very little clearly. As his eyes grew accustomed to the dark, he could make out a trail leading away from him, as if folks had come *to* this place or *from* this place. Where they went when they got *here* was a mystery, since the trail ended where he stood, and he could see no glowing rocks for anyone to slip back into. "It must lead somewhere," Wynn told himself. "Hopefully not to a beast's den."

Walking quickly, he followed the trail. The mists around him began to lighten as if with the dawn, and he was able to move more swiftly. By now, he was cold, wet, footsore, and completely mystified. He could hear no sounds of insects or wildlife, and the silence worried him. He jumped at the sound of his own boot snapping a twig. He had no idea if he was trespassing on someone's property or not. Hoping to avoid unfriendly notice, he walked as silently as he could, following the path through the tall grass and scrubby trees until he came upon a camp.

To Wynn's eyes, it appeared occupied by the nobility. A great quantity of costly gear was stacked about the fire, indicating wealth and social status. This presented a problem, because Wynn was most definitely a commoner. The few nobles who lived around the exceedingly rural village of Markett tended to be rather touchy about their rank and whom they associated with. Unfortunately, they were given to making their point with their swords.

A low fire burned merrily, and a teakettle sat on a

3

stone nearby. Under a canvas lean-to, a dark-haired, muscular young man sat, leaning propped against his bedroll and reading a well-worn book by the light of a small lantern. Heavily tattooed about the neck and face, he wore expensive-looking red leathers cut in an unusual style, and his kit sat next to him. Another kit and bedroll were piled next to him, along with two sets of fine armor. One was red and the other brown. Both were highly lacquered and appeared expensive. Looking around, Wynn didn't see the nobleman's companion anywhere.

Quickly deciding the man might possibly be gracious enough to tell him where he was and point the way back to Markett, Wynn politely cleared his throat to get his attention. Instantly, the man leapt to his feet, sword drawn. Wynn jumped back, his eyes wide, his long knife in his hand, ready to defend himself.

◆◆◆

Jules had been waiting for someone but had become involved in his book. He wasn't sure who it was exactly, but he'd been told to meet a young, blond man there, and this was definitely a young, blond man. Actually, he seemed younger than Jules had expected, more of a boy than a man. "Oh, it's you, farm boy. Good. We can get out of here and reach the inn at Armat before they close the gates tonight." Jules's sword slid back into his scabbard as quickly as it had emerged. His brown eyes quickly took Wynn's measure, hoping the pretty-boy wasn't as soft and girly as he looked. In his brief glance, he noted the boy appeared to have good reflexes for a lad of fifteen or so. Smiling wryly, Jules thought that even with his hair wet and plastered to his head, the boy looked like a maiden's romantic dream come true, all golden-haired and blue-eyed.

"Um, pardon me, sir knight, but do we know each other?" Wynn hung back, bedraggled, confused, and clearly not ready to trust the man immediately. "My name is Wynn Farmer, and yes, I'm a farm boy, but I'm twenty now, so I suppose I'd prefer to be called a man." Looking slightly self-conscious, he smiled.

"Twenty! I would have said somewhat younger." Jules's grin didn't hide his surprise. "But, as I said, we need to get on the road."

Visibly nonplussed, Wynn stayed where he was. "To be quite honest, I don't have a clue where I am, nor do I know *you*, my lord. I don't think I should go anywhere with you until we're better acquainted, don't you agree?" His smile was friendly, but wary. The long knife was lowered but still in his hand.

Jules apologized for not introducing himself. "I'm an idiot! Jules Brendsson, journeyman fire-mage, also twenty years old. I've come from the Temple of Aeos in Armat to bring you to the city of Aeoven for training in the art of battle-magic. Your father, Liam Farmer, was quite well known here as a water-mage."

"Perhaps you have the wrong person? My father's name *is* Liam Farmer, but he's not a mage. My family's not important—all we do is raise sheep." Wynn sheathed his knife and came into the light of the fire, sitting on his heels as he warmed himself. He looked curiously at Jules and asked, "By the way, my lord, where *is* here? Even though we should be on my family's farm, this place is nowhere I've ever been."

Jules laughed. "You're right! The village of Markett is in the world of Ariend now, am I correct?"

Wynn nodded his agreement, confused by the phrasing and clearly feeling he'd missed something. "Can you tell me how to get back? I've left several things undone, and my folks will be worried when they find I'm gone."

"I've no idea how to return you to your family if the portal isn't working." Uneasiness shaded Jules's voice. Nothing was going the way he'd been told it would. The man he'd been expecting had turned out to be more of a boy, no matter how old he said he was, and obviously had no idea what was going on.

"Portal?" Wynn paled, and his hands trembled. "No…ah…no. I need to get home. My dad is sick and my mother needs me."

Jules rapidly sorted through his options, deciding the best course would be to go forward with his original plan. "I'm sorry to hear that, really I am. But I was sent to meet the son of Liam Farmer, and you're his son. You're here at the meeting place, and I've no idea how to return you to Ariend, so we'll just work with what we have now and straighten it out later, agreed?" At Wynn's abrupt nod, Jules continued. "Anyway, this," he gestured around them, "is the world of Neveyah. Your family lives in Markett, which is in the world of Ariend now, but which used to be in Neveyah. The veil between the worlds is not solid, and like a curtain at a window, it moves occasionally. Markett slipped to a different world when it last shifted. Abbott Dorn had a true-dream predicting you were coming and sent me to meet you."

"I see, I think," Wynn replied, a thoughtful look on his face. "My father has on occasion mentioned a man named Dorn when speaking to my mother about old friends." Worry lines creased his brow, making him look more as if he really were twenty, as he'd claimed. "What you're saying is I'm stuck here." The words came out with more force than he intended.

"I'm afraid you are." Jules raised one eyebrow. "You look doubtful."

"I don't know what to think. And…well, my dad has tattoos a lot like yours, but they're faded blue. My mother also has some, only they're green. They must have gotten them here because no one has tattoos in Markett except sell-swords or my parents, but theirs are quite different from the ones sported by mercs. And they know the same person you know." Wynn's voice trailed off, staring into the darkness. His gaze returned to Jules. "I've never been able to picture either of them as mercenaries, though I've tried."

"They weren't mercenaries. Your mother was a healer, and your father was a famous battle-mage before he left Aeoven. Go on. I'll answer your questions as well as I can."

Wynn burst out, "Why? Why didn't he tell me he's some sort of mage? I've never seen him do any magic, but it could explain the new irrigation system for the vegetable garden. None of the neighbors could figure out how he found and piped it so quickly, although he's amazing at dowsing for water. If there's any water nearby, he'll find it." Standing, he paced nervously. "Everyone comes to him when they want to dig a new well. But he finished the whole system in one day, while I was in the upper pasture with the sheep. You couldn't even see where he'd dug the soil, but when I got home, the water was there, right where it was supposed to be."

"As it should be for as strong a mage as he is reputed to be," Jules agreed.

Wynn looked into the misty darkness beyond the campfire's warm light. "I've been told I was born in a foreign country. My mother is from there and speaks with an accent, but they never talk about it." Wynn was not only puzzled, he was a little hurt. "Why did they leave me in the dark about this? I hate being the last to find out anything."

"I know what you mean. Well, if I remember right, Abbott Dorn told me your mother is from beyond the Mountains of the Moon, a valley called Mal Evol. They do have an odd accent there. I don't know why they didn't tell you about this place. It'll make my task a lot harder," Jules replied, shrugging. "But we have to get you geared up and hit the road, or we'll not make Armat tonight. I've been waiting here for two days as it is."

Unable to see any other option, Wynn decided his best course would be to go with Jules. It turned out the pile of brown armor also contained a set of brown leathers for him. They were made for a slightly taller person, but they fit well enough across the shoulders. "We went by your father's measurements when we drew these from the armory," Jules told him, as Wynn changed out of his clothes and into the leathers. "I think the armor will fit you fairly well too, so you should be fine. I doubt we will run into any beasts out here in the empty lands, but you never know. Your boots will get you to Armat, but you'll need new ones when we arrive."

"I don't have any money for new boots, my lord. I didn't know I was going on a journey. These will be

8

fine. I was planning to have them resoled soon anyway," Wynn replied. "We're almost ready to harvest the apples. I'd have had money for new ones soon enough if I were still home."

"I'm just Jules, not 'my lord.' The Temple provides all our gear and clothes. You'll have new boots at no cost to you, don't worry." He busied himself with packing his kit.

Wynn looked through his own kit, finding all his needs had been thought of in advance. Tucked inside was a change of clothing, including socks and underwear, and a small cloth bag with soap, flannel, and a small towel. A toothbrush, a razor, and a comb completed the set. Also included was a wide-brimmed hat one could roll up and stuff into a pocket, which he gratefully put on over his wet hair.

A sword in a brown scabbard that matched his armor was attached to a belt. "Now, do you know anything about swords?" Jules asked him, in the tones of an instructor about to give a lecture.

"Just what anyone would know, sir," Wynn replied in a matter-of-fact manner. "They're expensive to make, so most people in Markett don't own one. We commoners defend ourselves with the bow or a good long knife. I'm considered good with both weapons." This was said straightforwardly; Wynn was not a braggart. "You've a sword of fine steel, so you must be nobility of some sort. I'm sorry I'm not familiar with you or your house. I don't know which noble house has red for its colors. Truly, I don't mean to be rude."

Jules was taken aback. "I am not a lord or a sir! I'm Jules Brendsson, the son of Brend the farmer, and I grew up much the same as you. Things are different here, I suspect," Jules replied simply. "I'm the arms instructor at the Temple of Aeos in Armat, and my task is to teach you how to use a sword and test you for magic ability. Once we know what type you have an affinity for, we can begin your education in the battle-magics." Wynn's expression of skepticism surprised him, so Jules explained further. "Most mages are taken to the Temple at the first sign of their ability, around age nine, to prevent the madness. Those who aren't found by the Temple go mad, and we must be ever on guard against them to keep the people of Neveyah safe. But you've been in Ariend, so you haven't been subject to the build-up of excess chi, though you will be now."

Wynn looked at Jules warily. "I don't feel magical right now, so don't be disappointed," he remarked dryly, a frank grin crossing his face. "I feel rather more like a drowned cat."

Jules laughed, saying, "Well, how would you know? Magic works a certain way here in Neveyah. I've heard it's not common in other places."

"No one has magic where I come from," Wynn replied, and then added, "except for my father, apparently." He heard the slightly bitter tone in his voice as he spoke and didn't like the sound of his own angst. He qualified it, saying, "My father and I don't get along well. Everything I do grates on his nerves something fierce, so I stay out of his way as much as possible. It keeps peace in the family and makes my mother happier." Wynn smiled a self-deprecating smile and added, "I try not to, but I tend to get him riled up more often than anyone, I'm sorry to say."

Jules grinned and, closing his eyes, held his hands up to Wynn as if warming them by a fire. Opening his

10

eyes, he said, "You have strength in battle-magic, and I can tell right now you'll be strong. What your element might be I can't tell for sure yet, but from what you're saying, I feel sure it's not water, or you'd get on with your dad a bit better." He clasped Wynn's shoulder companionably.

"Ah...if you say so." Wynn was unsure how to react to such a pronouncement. "I think I'm geared up now. Do I have everything on right? This armor is different than what they wear back home, mostly plate, and they ride huge warhorses. I've heard it's heavy, but this isn't so bad." The armor was made of leather with overlapping ribs of steel on the back and breastplate. It was made to be rolled up around the leg and arm guards and stashed in his kit when he wasn't wearing it. Wynn buckled the sword-belt on, placing his long knife just in front of the sword where he could reach it quickly. His bow and quiver were slung across his back, and he stood indecisively, not sure leaving with Jules was the right thing, but not knowing what else to do.

Jules looked Wynn over critically, making sure he could easily reach his weapons, and said, "Well, you seem to know what you're doing. Let's be off. We've a long walk, and we'll be working as we go." He picked up his kit. "I read that most of the larger cities, along with the aristocracy of old Neveyah, were taken to the world of Ariend to maintain the balance when Aeos and the Almighty Father divided the worlds. Plate armor is old-fashioned and far too heavy for the way we fight here, but I've read about it, and a friend of mine has some displayed in his family's old keep. The lords of Mal Evol used it in the old days, but even they use this style of armor now or else wear mail. This is a lot more useful for us because the clergy of Aeos travel on foot unless we must hurry, and then we take the mail coach."

They started off, following the path, traveling east. The sun was apparently fully up, since the gray day had lightened but didn't seem to be getting any brighter. "Is the weather always like this?" Wynn asked Jules. His feet now made loud, squelching noises in his boots. "It was still high summer when I left home this morning. It feels like Harvest here."

Jules laughed and said, "Actually, no. This is usually a fairly dry area, but the Harvest rains seem to have come early all over Neveyah, even though it's still midsummer. The farmers around here are suffering from too much water and not enough sun this year. Potatoes and beans will be good, but it's bad for melons. My folks raise melons, of course. My friend Bran tells me the weather will be improving over the next few days though."

"Ah! He's a weather-witch." Wynn nodded his comprehension.

"Weather-witch?" Jules shook his head. "Is that what you call your healers in Ariend?"

"Healers? Do you mean doctors?" Wynn laughed at himself. "There are more differences between our worlds than I realized at first, but it might just be my own ignorance. Doctors heal people with herbs and leeches, and weather-witches know the weather and can warn you when a storm is about to flatten your crops. Farming is a hard way to make a living," Wynn commented wistfully. "But it's all I know and all I ever thought I'd be allowed do, though I once hoped to be apprenticed to a smith. Of course, I would like to meet the right girl, get bonded, and have my own smithy, but now my path has been changed. It's a strange feeling, almost like I have no roots. I don't like this feeling."

Jules stared at him and then laughed, trying to follow Wynn's convoluted thought patterns and conversation. "The Goddess plucks us from our comfortable existence and gives us a task only we can do. The Temple will be your home here, so don't worry. You'll love it!"

Jules's good humor was quite refreshing to Wynn. His neighbors back home were a dour bunch of fellows, and his father was frequently ill and quite moody. He enjoyed being with such a light-hearted person.

Jules decided it was time to test his student. "Now I want to determine your strength and ability for magic. When we use an element, we 'call' it to us to separate it from the air. So, while we're traveling, you will need to see what you can call and then practice doing it. We will begin with the two easiest today. Do you understand?"

Wynn nodded.

"First, I'll call water to my hand." Jules held his palm up, and it filled with water, overflowing. "It's the easiest of all the elements to summon because it's the most abundant. Nearly all mages can call it. Even most healers can manage small amounts. It is also the most difficult to master. Few mages can grasp all of its many nuances, but your father is accounted by all as the finest water-mage of his generation."

"Amazing." Wynn's eyes went wide. "How do you do it?"

"Well, energies exist all around us although we can't see them. They are the four basic elements—

water, fire, earth, and lightning. Everything in the world is made of these four elements. The air around us is the combination of all four, and a few of us are able to separate them and use them as tools or weapons. This is what a battle-mage does."

Wynn was silent for a moment, thinking about what Jules had just said. Then he asked, "How do I go about separating them out?"

"It takes practice. Hold out your hand and think about water, how it feels. It's cool, and if color can be felt, cool water almost feels blue, wouldn't you say? So imagine your hand grasping cool, blue energy. Your thoughts call it to come to you."

Jules was quiet as Wynn cleared his mind and concentrated on calling water as Jules had described it. His father's constant admonition, "Clearly visualize what you want to do and you will make it happen," surfaced in his memory, and automatically Wynn's mind fell into the old habits his father had encouraged. He pictured his hand filling with water, cool and silky and overflowing. He could sense it in the air, so close, so near. Cool, blue…he could feel it—

Suddenly, Wynn's hand filled with cool, clear water, spilling over. Jules's eyes widened. "You learned awfully quickly! Are you sure you've never done this before?"

Wynn's grin lit up his face. "I just did what my dad is always telling me to do. He's always reminding me, 'Clearly visualize what you want to achieve.' I wish he'd lay off me about it. I understand what he's saying. He doesn't have to keep nagging at me!"

Jules's voice was calm in the face of Wynn's mood changes, but internally, he was shaken by the comment about his father. "Visualization is the basic, underlying rule of magic. It's taught to all novices in the course of their first two years at the College of Warcraft and Magic at Aeoven. Learning to think in a disciplined fashion is essential in order to fully realize your abilities. It is the most critical skill a battle-mage can develop to be effective. Your father was teaching you how to think properly to successfully call elemental-magic, though you didn't know it."

Wynn stopped walking. "But that would mean he knew I might have the ability and I would end up here someday." He shook his head slowly. "He aggravates me so much, always cautioning me to visualize everything." His expression gave away his mixed emotions as he met Jules's eyes. "Now I feel bad for not appreciating him. I was pretty ungrateful because I could see no reason for it."

"Well, you can't change what was, only what is." Jules's common sense comment eased the sharpness of Wynn's regret. "But now, I want you to think about calling earth. It's the same thing, except the energies are thick, and I think of them as being brown. The difference is this: you don't want to call it to your hand. Instead, I want you to call a pile of earth to this spot here. Imagine scooping the earth from here and piling it here," he said, pointing to both places.

Once again, Wynn cleared his mind. Sitting on his heels, he visualized scooping a pile of soil from the place Jules had indicated and putting it in a pile in front of him. A hole appeared in the soil after a great deal of concentration, and a small pile of earth sat in the place Jules had pointed out.

Jules simply nodded, telling him to do it again,

feeling rather bewildered by how easily Wynn understood the concept of calling the elemental-magics. The rest of the day, they walked, and Wynn practiced calling water and earth, filling their drinking containers and digging random holes and filling them in.

Jules explained a mage had to have high reserves of something called "chi" in order to call and use magic and said he could feel Wynn's like heat from a banked fire. "Just keep practicing calling water and earth. Using battle-magic regularly will keep the chi from building up and becoming a problem. In a few days, I'll teach you to summon fire, and if you do well, we'll work on lightning. Those two elements are dangerous and are mainly weapons, although fire can be a useful, domestic magic. Lightning is also used in the armory, creating the finish on our armor. There's no domestic use for lightning. We only teach it when we're sure the student is ready to follow instructions to the letter, which you seem able to do quite well."

"I understand," Wynn replied, with a serious I-am-paying-attention look on his usually blithe face. Jules was hard-pressed not to laugh. "Don't worry. I'm used to following instructions exactly. You know how it is on a farm. My dad was a lot stricter than most, but now I see he just wanted me safe."

Jules said, "My father said we either learned or died, although I'm sure he was joking. Of course, there *were* nine of us. You sound like you're an only child."

"Yes," Wynn nodded. "It was a bit lonely, and I always wished I had a sibling. When I was young, I went to school and had a few friends there. But when I was fourteen, we graduated and went out into the world. Well, my friends did anyway. I stayed on the farm. We don't see each other anymore except at the county fair at the end of summer. But, I have my books, so I'm not really too lonely. Working on the farm gives me plenty to do. Actually, it's too much for one person." Wynn gazed back in the direction they had come, and his voice had a hint of worry. "I honestly don't know how my dad will cope without me."

When they stopped for a lunch of bread and cheese, Jules worked with him to develop his sword skill, mentally cataloguing his student's abilities. Wynn was able to easily block his attacks quite well, despite the difference in size between the sword and the long knife Wynn was obviously well acquainted with. Jules was unable to hide his glee, as he realized the boy would be good, perhaps even better than Rall Ivarsson, who had been the Temple weapons master in Aeoven for two years.

They worked for about an hour, after which Wynn was adept at getting his sword both out of and back into the sheath without slicing himself. He was also able to block well with it and knew all the basic forms, which his father had apparently taught him for use with the long knife. Once again, he surprised Jules with his reflexes.

"I never thought I'd be this clumsy," Wynn remarked as he re-sheathed his sword upon finishing his first lesson with the weapons-master. "I'm actually fairly good with the long knife and bow, but this...I'm not very graceful." His rueful grin lit his features.

"You're doing well and learning much more quickly than most. Obviously, you understand weapons, because you have a respect for the sharpness of the blade in regard to your own fingers." Jules laughed.

Wynn shrugged. "I do well enough to hold my own at barehanded fighting or with the staff, but I've won both the archery and knife competitions at the county fair for the last six years. From as far back as I can remember, my dad worked with me every evening—until recently." His smile had become strained.

Jules looked at him questioningly, and again Wynn elaborated. "When there is a famine, many highwaymen will prowl the king's roads. They often have swords of iron or low-quality steel, so we might have to defend ourselves at close quarters, using our long knife against their blade. My father used to train with me every day. He always says he wants me to live long enough to provide him with grandchildren, but lately he hasn't been well enough to work out with weapons."

They walked in companionable silence, and Wynn practiced calling water and earth.

"Do you have a girl?" asked Jules after a while, thinking Wynn probably did since he had the sort of pretty face the heroes in romance novels all seemed to have.

His face was full of wry humor as he replied, "Since I've not met any girls out there on the farm, it's unlikely to happen any time soon, a fact my father doesn't seem to understand. Except for the county fair and occasional trips to the general store in Markett, I rarely get to town anymore." He laughed and shook his head ruefully. "I've been pretty busy around the farm since I finished school."

"That doesn't seem fair," Jules said, frowning. "What do you do for fun?"

"Fun? Lots of things—I like to tinker around,

building small models of machines, like little windmills and things of that sort. My dad thinks it's a waste of time, so I don't often have a chance to do it. Mostly I read or play cards with my parents in the evening." Wynn caught the look on Jules's face. "I know. It surprises you that at my age I'm still living with my parents. I had wanted to get apprenticed to a smith." Wynn's face grew serious. "The problem is there's no one else to run the farm. Dad's been suffering from kidney ailments lately." He glanced away. "When he's really bad, my mother can't manage the farm by herself and take care of him. They'll have to hire someone, I suppose."

"I am sorry your father is ill," Jules replied sympathetically. "He's considered by all as a great mage. Your father is right about one thing though— knowing how to defend oneself properly in any situation makes a great deal of sense. And you are also right that farming is a lot of work. I was never going to be a farmer. I planned to enlist in the Temple army even before I began showing the signs of being a young fire-mage." Privately, Jules was shocked by Wynn's revelation regarding his seclusion on the farm.

As the afternoon progressed, Jules became more and more confused about his companion. They had a lot in common, yet he'd never met anyone more naïve than Wynn. The two men both read voraciously and enjoyed discussing classic literature. Jules was rather astonished to learn he enjoyed reading romantic poetry. "It's not something a warrior admits to reading, Wynn," he said, laughing.

Grinning sheepishly, he replied, "But I'm not a warrior, Jules. I'm a farmer! No one cares what a farmer reads, as long as he produces the produce!"

Jules grinned at Wynn's play on words. He enjoyed Wynn's company more and more as the day wore on, despite the fact he leapt from topic to topic like a grasshopper in the sun. He often said the most outrageous things. Jules found himself laughing uproariously at Wynn's commentary and enjoyed the walk to Armat immensely.

By the end of the afternoon, both men were tired, wet, and dirty. As they trudged toward the gates of Armat, Jules could think only of the hot bath that awaited him there. But now, despite his wishes to the contrary, the lovely friendly-girls who all adored his tattoos loomed in his mind. *You're a bad man, Jules. Not three days ago, you swore to yourself you would stop being a jackass.* His guilt assailed him as it did every time he misbehaved with the free women known as "friendly-girls." *Aneka wouldn't approve of the way you've been behaving if she were to find out.*

Now Jules had arrived at the place in his mental conversation where he always became confused and angry. *But there's no reason she should care. You aren't hand-fasted yet.* Even to himself, his thoughts sounded pathetic. *Really, Jules, you're a free man, and what she doesn't know won't kill you. But no, you should try to behave. What will Wynn think?*

Jules was miserably aware he would misbehave for as long as he could get away with it. He struggled with his conscience, trying to justify his own weakness. *I'm not weak! I'm a free man. I didn't make any commitment to her.* He forcibly put the face of the girl he'd left behind in Aeoven out of his mind, not understanding why he felt so trapped when he thought about her. Aneka was the perfect girl. He was sure he would settle down with her once he did decide to bond, but until then, he was free, a bachelor in all ways. She'd quite obviously left the option to bond open on the last night they had been together, but Jules had neatly dodged making any sort of commitment. He'd seen his friends fall one by one. *Look at Rall...his life is over. It's not going to happen to me.*

Jules quickened his steps until he and Wynn were nearly running, but somehow, no matter how fast he ran, he couldn't escape his thoughts. By the time they arrived in the rural town of Armat, Jules was feeling quite rebellious, ready to take up on the offer of the first friendly-girl who made an advance on him just to show his ridiculous, over-active conscience who was the boss.

The same state of affairs played out in his head every time he came to an inn where the luscious and, well, just plain *friendly* friendly-girls waited for Jules to liven up their evenings. Unfortunately, they all knew him too well.

Chapter 2

Armat was a small village with a thriving market, a brand-new Temple still under construction, and an inn called The Lying Dog. The sign over the door boasted a faded hound curled in a sleeping position. "The food here is good, and the men's bathhouse is over there," Jules said, pointing across the courtyard to the rear of the inn. "Let's get our rooms, and then you can head on over to the baths while I report in at the Temple."

The innkeeper welcomed Jules back and offered to have his possessions moved out of storage and up to his new room, but Jules said he would most likely leave again after only a night or two, and he wouldn't need them this time. "I may get a new posting soon, so maybe we should move my things to the Temple."

"There's several of the ladies who'll be right sorry to see you leave so soon, Jules." The innkeeper winked at Wynn as he spoke.

Jules's smiling face reddened slightly. "I'll miss them too, bless their generous hearts." He looked out of the corner of his eye to see Wynn's reaction, grinning as he realized his friend hadn't heard a word of the exchange.

Wynn stood absorbed in his own thoughts, oblivious to the whole conversation and staring around the inn. "I've never been in a city this big," Wynn finally remarked. "The streets here are paved with stones. I've read about this but never thought I would see it. I wish Markett had them. Of course, Markett only has one street, but still...it should be simple enough to do." He fell silent, obviously lost in his own thoughts. Jules and the innkeeper shrugged and exchanged glances with eyebrows raised.

Jules and Wynn stowed their kits in their small rooms, stuffing them under their beds, and then met in the hall. Jules gave Wynn a quick summary of what he could expect in the villages of rural western Neveyah. "I've been posted here, assisting Abbott Dorn for about half a year now. It's a good town. This close to Aeoven, there's a lot of respect for people who wear Temple leathers. We'll get boots and whatever else you need from the local Temple. Abbott Dorn will want to meet you tomorrow and explain things to you. We'll probably move on toward Ragat the day after. In the meantime, I have to report in and let them know I'm back, so you just go on out to the baths and get cleaned up. I'll meet you there shortly."

Later, when Jules entered the men's bath, he found a red-faced Wynn Farmer sitting in one of the claw-foot tubs, clutching a large flannel over his lap and politely telling the chambermaid he really, honestly, did *not* need her to wash his back. She hovered over him helpfully, apparently unable to do enough for the farm boy. "No, I don't need any more hot water, thank you. Please, the other customers need you." Wynn's voice had a note of desperation to it. "They want baths too. Jules wants *his* back washed. Please, go help him."

Jules looked at the chambermaid with some amazement. She was a comely enough widow of about thirty years, who had been the bath attendant since the death of her husband several years before. He'd never seen this sort of behavior from her. On the contrary, she was usually a model of grim efficiency.

"Mari! Bath?" He cleared his throat, and she looked up, blushed, and hurried to get his bath filled.

"Now, if you would, please leave us in peace," he said firmly, since she looked ready to help Wynn again. Undressing and getting into his nice, hot tub full of steaming water, Jules stared at him, wondering what had caused such aberrant behavior on the part of the maid. Wynn's face was still pink.

"I'm sorry if I'm behaving badly," Wynn finally mumbled, confused and trying to hide it. "I've never been in a public bath, so I don't know the rules. I didn't intend to be rude to her. I'm sure she was just doing her job, but I haven't needed help bathing since I was a little child. I hope her feelings aren't hurt."

"The maids here aren't usually so helpful," Jules commented. "I've been living in this place a while now, and just getting an extra towel from her usually takes a bit of flattery and charm." He looked at the embarrassed country boy and decided he might need a bit of education regarding the women of the world he'd been dropped into. "Wynn, have you ever met a friendly-girl?"

"Well, all the girls I've met are always awfully friendly and nice, but my dad usually has to get back to the farm before I can say more than hello to them," Wynn said, sinking down into the hot water and enjoying his bath immensely now the maid was gone.

Jules shook his head but kept his thoughts to himself. "Well, here in Neveyah, there are many girls who choose not to settle down and bond. In fact, there are more women than men here, now I think about it. But these ladies like men, lots of different men, and they are quite free with their affections, if you understand me."

Wynn didn't quite understand, having never been

told about the birds and bees. He understood the mechanics of reproduction because he'd been raised on a farm, but it hadn't occurred to his father to explain any further. Wynn decided Jules meant they were pleasant and helpful, so he nodded. "I think I understand, maybe. Like the maid, obliging and nice."

"Um, yes. These ladies can usually be found in common rooms and will often be *very* affectionate with you. They don't want to bond with you or anything. In fact, they don't want to get bonded at all. They all have jobs, of course, during the day, but they just want to have a good time, like a party every evening." Jules nearly laughed at the expression on Wynn's face but managed to keep a serious tone to his voice. "No one looks askance if you spend the evening with a friendly-girl. These ladies can be rather willful in regard to men, so people understand if they see you with one. Many single men are quite close friends with at least one friendly-girl."

"I wouldn't know what to say, Jules. You can talk to them," Wynn said, flushing again. "I don't want to embarrass you with my country ways."

Later, clean and presentable, they entered the common room and found a table in a corner where they had a good view of the bard, who sang a romantic ballad. "I've never been to a common room," Wynn told Jules as they sat down. "My father didn't think it was a good influence, so I've never…Jules, look at those girls. They sure are pretty." Wynn gawked about the room wide-eyed, looking for all the world like a boy who had never been off the farm, which was, in fact, the truth once Jules thought about it.

"The women in this town love me. I'll introduce

you. Getting to know one well would greatly contribute to your education. A friendly-girl will teach you how to make a wife quite happy, once you find one. Trust me on this," Jules said, with a knowing leer as he raised his arm, beckoning the barmaid. She was already on her way over, closely followed by the local friendly-girls. "Ah, my favorite ladies. You have not forgotten...me." His voice trailed off in consternation as the barmaid and all the friendly-girls sailed past him, gathering about Wynn, elbowing each other out of the way and stumbling over themselves, each trying to get his attention.

One bold girl toyed with Wynn's golden hair while he laughed sheepishly and told her it tickled. Another stood behind him, massaging his neck and shoulders. Wynn, the lucky dog, enjoyed every minute of it, red-faced and shy though he was. "Thank you, ma'am. I *was* feeling rather tired. It was a terribly long walk to get here." The women seemed to adore his shyness, ignoring Jules completely. "Jules told me all about you and said this is normal. He also said you ladies would teach me how to make a wife happy, although I don't know what he meant. I'd like to learn whatever you have to teach me. It would be good to know how to make a wife happy."

Jules's eyes opened wide, and his mouth dropped open in horror.

That was all Wynn had to say. The girls were his from then on, all five of them. So was the barmaid. The six women hovered around him as they tried to explain exactly what they could teach him, despite the fact he had just blurted out the most outrageous and rude thing he could possibly have said. Jules would have been dumbfounded if he hadn't been so jealous.

Jules tried and failed to get the barmaid's attention. "Excuse me, Lorna!" he said loudly. The barmaid glared at him. "Could I get a mug of ale and a bowl of stew? That *is* what you do here, right? Serve ale and stew?"

She flounced off but returned almost immediately with two glasses of ale and then again with two bowls of stew. She then continued to ignore the rest of the customers, giving curt, resentful service only when forced to.

Jules, however, received a glass of ale as often as Wynn did, and Lorna was certainly diligent in plying Wynn with ale. He'd become a bit tipsy; in fact, Wynn Farmer had never felt so wonderful in his entire life. "This is rather a good drink," he said happily to his flock of friendly-girls. "It makes you feel very free, doesn't it? I wonder why my father said it was bad for you." The friendly-girls all giggled.

As the evening progressed, the atmosphere in the common room became more and more strained, with every man glaring at Wynn and every woman fighting for his attention. The party at Wynn's table roared along merrily, but unfortunately, the rest of the room was dead.

Wynn, ever the naïve bumpkin, was discovering girls in rather a grand way, apologizing for his country manners and receiving kisses as rewards for each faux pas. With lovely, dark-haired Glena boldly claiming her place in his lap, and Lila and Kisa each hanging on an arm, he was on his way to learning in one evening all the sweet mysteries of life he'd never before encountered. Wynn blushed and stammered the whole time, and the friendly-girls vied for the opportunity to enlighten him on the ways to "make a wife happy," whispering things in his ears that made his eyes dance and his cheeks turn bright red.

Having resigned himself to being completely ignored, Jules was surprised when a rather pretty friendly-girl named Misa, Kisa's sister, shyly tugged on his sleeve to get his attention.

"Yes, my lovely, what can Jules do for you tonight?" He smiled and applied his charm as heavily as he knew how. Perhaps the evening would not be a complete waste after all.

"Do you know this man? Could you introduce me to him?" Her dark eyes shone hopefully. "He's so handsome." She actually sighed, looking at Wynn with dreamy eyes. Absently clutching Jules's arm, she leaned her cheek against his shoulder and stared at Wynn, saying, "Poor thing, he's never been away from home and never met any girls. He must be so lonely."

"I…never mind." Jules felt rather bewildered as he watched Wynn. Blithely unaware of the proprieties, the ignorant lout inadvertently monopolized all the women, not even having the grace to share. As Jules sat nonplussed and feeling rather nauseated by the whole thing, he gradually noticed every woman in the room, even the bonded ones, was staring at Wynn. Surprised, he saw Evangeline, the prim and proper baker's wife, watching Wynn with undisguised lust. Her husband was not happy, glaring from his wife to Wynn and back before abruptly standing up and saying, "C'mon, Vangie. We're going home. Now!" He grabbed her arm and nearly dragged her out the door.

All the women looked at Wynn as if they would

love to roll with him under a table, and the men obviously wanted to kill him. Only his complete preoccupation with entertaining the free women kept the peace in the common room.

It was too much for Jules. He gave up and went to bed early, gently disengaging Misa from his arm. "Sorry, dear, I have an early day tomorrow," he told her. When he got to his room, he thought about writing Aneka a letter, but then realized miserably he'd never actually gotten around to writing her at all since he'd been posted in Armat. *I've never been much of a letter writer,* he consoled himself. *Surely she knows how I am. I haven't even written my folks any letters. I've been very busy. Very, very busy.*

Back in the common room, Misa barely noticed Jules had left, sliding over next to Wynn and nudging Kisa out of the way.

Chapter 3

The next day after Jules awoke, he knocked on Wynn's door. Hearing no answer, he looked inside. What he saw made his eyes pop. Wynn wasn't there, but his room was certainly not empty.

He quickly closed the door and stood leaning against it, feeling entirely out of his element. Friendly-girls never stayed the night. They took what they wanted and left. For a moment, Jules wondered what was going on and then decided he was better off not knowing.

Going downstairs, he found Wynn already up and in an obscenely cheerful mood as he downed a huge bowl of porridge in the nearly empty common room. Jules looked closely at him, trying to figure out what all those women saw in him. Wynn seemed perfectly ordinary to him, albeit rather pretty in a girly-looking sort of way. "Did you have a good night?" Jules could not keep the slight tone of resentment out of his voice, though he tried to be pleasant. "You should be feeling somewhat delicate, with all the ale you drank last night. There are girls in your room. The Temple won't pay for them to sleep here too."

Wynn coughed, turned bright red, and mumbled, "Oh. Sorry." He ran back up the stairs and hastily got the women out the door before the innkeeper discovered them. Then he tidied his room as fast as he could, straightening the bed and picking up several stray garments to return to their owners later.

While Wynn busily hid the evidence of his wild adventure, he refused to examine his conscience too closely. He glossed over the notion that despite what

Jules had told him about such flings with friendly-girls being normal, he'd misbehaved relatively badly. Throwing open the shutters to air the stale perfume out of the room, he had a brief moment of guilt, knowing his father would never approve of his drinking ale to excess or…but what a night. He didn't know why he'd let those girls talk him into such a crazy thing, but he knew he would do it again if he was offered the chance. Wynn's eyes had been opened, and there was no going back now.

Finally, back in the common room, Wynn sat down to finish his now-cold breakfast, pretending nothing unusual had happened.

Jules was not at all talkative, and was not really at his best in the mornings anyway. His angst about Aneka and his own morally bankrupt state had returned with a vengeance upon seeing Wynn's room, and Wynn so cheerful about it all. *I'm not as bad as him, am I? Am I? Really, more than one girl at a time is just plain debauched. I may be a beast, but I'm not debauched.*

Wynn made several unsuccessful attempts to engage Jules in conversation. He didn't understand what could have happened to suddenly change him from sunny to grumpy. He knew it couldn't be his behavior with the girls because Jules himself had explained to him all about them, assuring him their behavior was acceptable. He picked at his food, wracking his brain, but couldn't think of anything.

The innkeeper watched the interaction between the two Temple boys with a knowing smile, thinking it was high time Jules Brendsson had a taste of his own medicine. "That boy's been flying too high for far too long," he told his wife. "Rumor has it there's a lady earth-mage in Aeoven who's gonna kick his butt. From what I hear, she's not too happy with his tomfoolery." He chuckled merrily at the thought, and his wife rolled her eyes.

◆◆◆

After breakfast, Jules and Wynn walked across the street to the Temple of Aeos. It was new, as was most of the rest of the town, and had been built in the same style as the inn. The Temple was a large, two-story complex of buildings with a carriage port and several outbuildings behind it, all built around a large, central courtyard.

A squad of Temple militia was usually stationed there, but it was currently assisting another town eliminate some outlaws, a problem that required extra soldiers. As he slipped back into the role of teacher, Jules gradually loosened up and soon forgot his angst. "Armat is peaceful. Outlaws don't seem to come out this way," he told Wynn. "Of course, there's nothing out here to steal except sheep and turnips."

A large, well-tended kitchen garden took up most of the space in the courtyard. A typical outdoor kitchen for summer cooking and baking was flanked by the usual long table and benches, but much longer than usual to seat the large number of people who ate most of their meals there when the squad of soldiers was in town. Except for its huge size, the kitchen garden looked exactly like the ones found behind any home in Markett.

Wynn was surprised by the similarities to his hometown, and said so.

"Armat Temple is typical of most villages. It's the smallest and most recently built of the new Temples,"

Jules explained, trying to hide his grin at Wynn's naïveté. "Right now, the people assigned here on a permanent basis live in the houses next door. The others, like me, stay at the inn if they're only temporarily posted here. Once the living and guest quarters are completed, all mages will live at the Temple."

He pointed out the storeroom, saying, "A mage or Temple soldier can get everything needed from there at no cost. We'll stop and get some new boots for you later." As they passed other outbuildings, Jules said, "The Temple employs a laundress, a blacksmith, and a stable boy. Many other people are temporarily posted here to fill various positions as needed, but frequent rotations keep people from becoming stale in their jobs."

"I once hoped to be apprenticed to a blacksmith," said Wynn, on seeing the forge. "Now I'm too old—the smith in Markett only takes men fifteen to eighteen years old."

Jules introduced Wynn to Abbott Dorn, who briefly explained to Wynn that he was required to become a member of the clergy of Aeos. The abbott then directed him to a desk in a sunny corner of the study where he handed him a treatise explaining the duties and responsibilities of battle-mages. Dorn placed a stack of paper and a pen at his elbow. "Feel free to take notes, boy. You will be tested." With Wynn fully occupied, he called Jules aside.

"I gather you saw what happens when you take him to a common room." Dorn's expression was a knowing leer.

"How did you know?" Jules still felt the sting.

"I know his father," Dorn replied. "You'd better get used to it, because until he meets the love of his life, that's how it'll be. Young Liam Farmer wenched his way across Neveyah, collecting women like nothing I'd ever seen before."

"Well, I don't like it," Jules asserted petulantly, hating the sound of his own whining. "It's an embarrassment." His bad mood had returned in a big way.

"You've no room to talk, my boy, none whatsoever. Listen up, Jules," Dorn said sharply, gesturing for him to sit down. "It doesn't matter what you like or don't like. You were selected for this."

Mentally, Jules resigned himself to being chastised for being human. Abbott Dorn's ability to shine in the reflected light of other people's efforts and his lack of interest in anything that might require effort on his part were legendary. He'd even managed to get out of explaining Wynn's duties to him just by handing him a book and telling him to sit down and read it.

"Look, Jules. What I'm about to tell you isn't a particularly pretty thing about myself, but when I first met Wynn's father, Liam, I took an instant dislike to him even though we were only novices. He can be moody like so many, really strong water-mages of your own acquaintance. With my being a lightning-mage, well, let's just say we didn't hit it off. We ended more than a few days brawling in the barracks.

"He was like honey to the bees. The fool women simply couldn't leave him alone. It stuck in my craw how the very same friendly-girls who'd only a week before sworn by the love of Aeos that I was the center of their universe were now hanging about him like so many trophies around a barbarian's neck." Dorn exhaled heavily and then admitted, "I was completely jealous and made it clear to the powers-that-be how much I did *not* want to work with him. I despised everything about him. But I was forced to, and rather surprisingly, we did straighten things out." He shrugged, saying, "Well, we had to find common ground, or we'd have failed our mission. Neither of us was willing to risk being responsible for something as unnecessarily stupid as that. Many times, it was just Liam and I in those mountains. Several times, I'd have come to an untidy and disgusting end without him, and a few times my abilities saved his neck. But because of what we went through, Liam and I became as close as brothers."

Jules looked at the bald, portly Dorn out of the corner of his eye, trying to picture him scuffling over women, and failing. He felt quite sure Bertte, Dorn's equally stout wife of many years, would take a dim view of the tale.

Unaware of Jules's scrutiny, Dorn continued his lecture, saying, "Wynn is the image of his father as a young man, maybe not quite as tall, but he's blonde, handsome, muscular, witty, and full of charm. He's every maiden's dream come true. But what you don't see when you look at him is the curse." He looked over at the far corner of the room where Wynn was absorbed in his reading, oblivious of everything else. Jules's eyes widened fractionally at hearing the word "curse."

"The Temple of Aeos has prophecies that tell us from his line will come an important scion, the 'Hero Foretold' or, alternatively, the 'One Who Takes Back All.'" Dorn now had Jules's complete attention. "I see you've heard of them," he said dryly. Jules glared at him, not appreciating the sarcasm. The abbott knew full well the prophecies were the core study area of the senior journeyman, and complete understanding of them was critical if Jules was to advance within the hierarchy of the Temple.

Dorn watched Jules's eyes turn incredulously to Wynn, who was still absorbed in his reading, a shaft of light falling on him and illuminating his halo of golden hair as if he were an angel. The angelic impression was dispelled as Wynn absently chewed his nails and nervously tapped his left foot. Now he looked more like an anxious novice sitting in the headmaster's office. "Yes, Jules, *him*. Now you know why you were chosen as his arms instructor. Since you and Rall have been studying the prophecies so intently, it seemed only fair you two should have the opportunity to meet and quest with him."

"Don't tell me *he* is the one!" Jules suddenly sat up and leaned forward, all traces of his sulkiness gone. "The prophecies…what do they say? Surely it's not the end-time yet. I've seen none of the signs. Mal Evol has not yet been conquered by stealth…Braden Temple is not the domain of the Lost One."

"Relax. We haven't reached the end-times yet, though they're fast approaching. We don't yet know why or when the son of his family will be needed, but the omens now say the time is nearing. Within only a few generations, the need will become apparent. Wynn's grandson or perhaps his great-grandson may be the promised one." Dorn looked at Jules, and a strange, bleak look crossed his face. "When the time comes to pass, I hope I'm gone, for it will be the end of Neveyah as I know and love it. As you know full well, the prophecies are clear that *only* this hero will be able to save us when the time comes."

"But he's so ignorant of life in general. You have no idea, Dorn. He's like a country bumpkin joke come to life. Last night was the first time he'd even spoken to a girl, and he ended up.... Scions of his will be popping up all over Neveyah if he keeps going the way he went last night." Abruptly, his mouth snapped shut.

Dorn laughed at the expression on Jules's face. "Actually, no. Only one girl out there will ever bear his child, and he just hasn't found her yet. The Goddess has a rather heavy-handed approach to ensuring this happens. Aeos has selected a girl for him, but to make sure she falls in love with him, she makes the men in his bloodline irresistible to *all* women. Friendly-girls have no propriety and no desire to maintain decorum, so they're always the obvious casualties of this curse, but I've seen countless, normally well-bred women fall all over themselves to get to his father. Even my Bertte gets into a tizzy around Liam. When Wynn meets the right girl, he'll never look at another woman. They'll be two halves of one whole, and he'll meet her soon, any day now, in fact. When he does, there'll be a bonding registered before you can say, 'Wait, you idiot.' He's twenty, and men in his family are *always* bonded by his age. It could happen as soon as he gets to Aeoven. Two weeks at most, I'd say, because Abbess Lera's most recent true-dream indicated he'll have a son before you leave on your quest, which will most certainly be announced within a year or two. The reason he was called here now is to meet the girl he's to bond with and to be trained in the magic arts."

Jules slowly turned his eyes toward Wynn, completely taken aback by the abbott's revelations. Jules found himself smiling, saying, "Well, he can't help it. What a strange mix he is. And he tries so hard to find the good in things, even when he's inadvertently riled everyone up." Jules turned his gaze back to Dorn. "Wynn told me his father is already suffering badly from the kidney ailments," he said, gently breaking the news about Dorn's friend. Despite being frequently irritated with the abbott, Jules reluctantly liked him. "He doesn't yet know it's the result of his father's intense connection to the use of water-magic. I'll talk to him about it, I promise."

Dorn sat back, tenting his fingers, trying to absorb what he'd just been told, his face sad. "It doesn't surprise me. Most mages of my generation are beginning to suffer the effects of the magic. As you know, only about a third of all mages will survive into their fifth decade."

"Well, does Liam know about the prophecies?" Jules asked dubiously. At Dorn's nod, he then asked angrily, "Then why didn't he tell his son? That boy over there knows nothing of what he's doing here or even of life in general. He's never been off the farm, Dorn! In fact, he'd never seen a cobbled street until we walked into Armat. Until last night, he'd never even seen a common room or actually been allowed to talk to a girl. It's the most unfair thing I've ever heard."

"Liam isn't stupid, Jules—you saw how girls are about Wynn. If magic doesn't work the same way in Ariend as it does here, who knows what else could happen? Liam deliberately sheltered Wynn completely so he'd make it to Neveyah *without* having a wife and child in the wrong world. Believe me, *that* would be a disaster. But I don't know why Liam told him nothing about Neveyah." Shrugging, Dorn added, "Perhaps he wanted Wynn to have an unbiased view of his own importance. Liam's own life was a circus in some ways. His mother's great-great-grandmother was Biann D'Braden, the first abbess of Mal Evol Temple and founder of the city of Braden and the Temple there. His paternal many-times-great-grandfather was none other than Aelfrid Firesword, the founder of the College of Warcraft and Magic and the founder of Aeoven. They were among the most important mages in the history of Neveyah."

"I've read both of their histories," Jules murmured, taken aback. "Their exploits helped to found modern Neveyah. They were the greatest heroes of all time."

"Everyone expected great things from him, which, of course, he did do, but the fame and constant scrutiny were too much for him. Liam just wanted to have some privacy, which he could never have in Aeoven. If he went to the common room for a glass of ale, it was all over town by morning.

"What I'm about to tell you is not known outside of the highest Temple clergy, Jules. Even Wynn is unaware of this, as far as I know." Dorn paused while Jules laid his hand over his heart, signifying it would remain a Temple secret. "Liam was posted to the Temple at Mal Evol City. His wife's family is prominent there, and they spent a lot of time at her family's country estate. When Wynn was about two years old, a family servant whose mind had been tampered with kidnapped him."

Jules sat back, plainly shocked.

"Liam, our old friend Kaye, whom you know from the armory in Aeoven, and I were able to rescue him before the kidnapper made it across the valley to the portal to Serende, but it was a close thing. Soren Torsson was the healer who went with us since Arla, Wynn's mother, was too distraught. Soren was convinced the kidnapper had no idea what she'd done, and I assure you, he is an adept at mind-magic. The woman's mind had been wrenched away, and she was never normal again. Mother Relynne was the abbess in Mal Evol City at the time, and she felt sure Tauron had a hand in the kidnapping somehow. The Bull God fears the bloodline of that family."

Jules agreed. "It's clearly stated a scion of his blood will right the balance of the worlds and end Tauron's reign.

Dorn nodded. "But, because of that incident, Liam suddenly retired and moved the family to a farm in the obscure western village of Markett. At that time, it was still on this side of the veil, but right after he moved his family there, the veil slipped. It became part of Ariend, and that area of Neveyah became the Empty Lands."

"I always wondered why that happened," said Jules.

Dorn personally didn't understand Liam's choice to keep his son so completely ignorant of his family's connection to Neveyah. "He used to say we were too hidebound when it came to using and understanding magic. He felt we don't fully make use of it because we refuse to see the possibilities, seeing instead only the rules and restrictions. He believed the rules originally developed to protect us actually hold us back in many ways."

"Well, he has a point, but I totally disagree with his solution to the problem." said Jules, glancing at Wynn. "You know what I think about that subject. We've talked before about the limitations of magic. But why did he feel so strongly?"

"I believe it was a result of our quest. While we were still novices, Mother Relynne, who was the Armsmaster in Aeoven at the time, had a vision that indicated Liam would need an ensorcelled sword to accomplish the task he was given. The smiths created a masterpiece named Scorpion, a sword that turned magic back upon the caster, thus enabling Liam to use his enemy's own strength against him. The unique sword was our edge in the last battle we fought against Bregat. It enabled us to persevere against terrible odds, but the abilities it conferred on Liam increased his doubt. He always wondered why mages who weren't Temple-trained frequently have skills we don't and can sometimes do the impossible. Of course, without augmentations, they're completely mad with the excess chi. But still…perhaps he wanted his son to see things from a completely unbiased perspective. And Wynn wouldn't have suffered from the madness in Ariend because only in Neveyah does it become a problem."

Jules was appalled. "But Wynn is an adult! For all he looks and, in some ways, behaves like a fifteen year-old, he isn't! He's twenty years old and has exceedingly strong abilities. He should have been sent to the Temple eleven years ago. How will he learn what he must know of magic if he's the only adult in the novice barracks?" The very notion disgusted him.

"Wynn Farmer won't be going to the novice barracks, Jules. You'll be teaching him weaponry and will continue working with his magic until you get to Aeoven. Mother Relynne is sending Rall Ivarsson to meet you in Ragat since he needs to get away from Feia for a while."

Jules rolled his eyes, nodding. "Do you blame him?"

Dorn ignored his comment. "Rall will be teaching Wynn shielding. Another mage will assist the two of you in his education regarding magic, but Abbess Lera will decide who that mage will be once she meets Wynn and his element of strength is determined.

"In the meantime, Wynn must be augmented, so you'll have to spend a few more nights here. Once you get to Aeoven, he'll receive the second augmentation. And now, I need my tea." Abbott Dorn stood, signifying his lecture was over, and began to head toward the kitchen. Jules followed him closely.

"Abbott, please. A moment more of your time, if you will," Jules begged. "Why is he being pushed so hard? Yes, his abilities are strong, but I've seen no sign of madness from the buildup of excess chi, and I've been working him with water and earth to avoid such a thing. He still needs testing in fire and lightning. I wasn't going to rush him."

"When he's fully augmented, he'll be more colorful than Rall Ivarsson. Mother Relynne tells me it must be complete before winter solstice for him to be ready for his posting. It gives us little more than five months to get it done in small enough increments. If we don't get started as soon as possible, we could have a problem with him. A mage of his anticipated ability could go mad with augmentation reaction, and we don't want *that* to happen again now, do we?" Dorn's expression was grim and rightfully so. Jules mutely agreed with Dorn, mentally shuddering.

Only a year before, a promising fire-mage from the rural South, whose abilities had gone unnoticed for several years longer than most, had been given the first, second, and third augmentations in one sitting and had gone mad with the excess chi, not knowing how to bleed it off or smooth the flows. He had burned down the Temple at Bannoc, killing himself and the healer who tried to help him in the process.

"Have you explained about augmentations to him?" Dorn stood waiting for the answer he knew was coming.

"No, of course not. I've not had the chance. I assumed he wouldn't get them until we arrived in Aeoven, so I thought I'd have plenty of time." Jules shoved his hands in his pockets to prevent himself from choking his boss. "He only arrived at the meeting place yesterday morning. I waited there for two days."

"Well, he looks just about done with my little treatise on the duties of the clergy, so now is your opportunity. Colorist Sylvi and his journeyman, Nolen, will be here with the mail coach, so you have an hour or two to prepare him. He has to have at least attempted to call all the elements, so you'd better get on with it." Abbott Dorn walked away, leaving Jules stunned and feeling somewhat like a landed fish.

"Dorn," Jules hissed, and the abbott turned back. "He's a lightning-mage. I'm sure of it, and *you* should be mentoring him. At the very least, it should be *you* teaching him to call his first lightning! This is your responsibility!"

"Handle it, Jules! I'm behind on my reports, and I

want my tea." The door shut firmly behind the stout abbott.

Chapter 4

Jules stared as the door shut behind the abbott. "Oh, for the love of Aeos!" Pulling himself together, he crossed the room to stand next to Wynn, who looked out the window. "So, Wynn, you may have noticed I bear some rather colorful tattoos."

Wynn nodded. "I noticed Abbott Dorn has also been tattooed, and some other people. Is it a common thing around here?"

"Yes, actually it is. All mages have them because it allows us to store and use excess chi for battle-magic. These tattoos are called augmentations, and without them, we couldn't cast a major working. Without chi, we have to rely completely on our swords. Finding yourself without chi is not optimal, especially when facing an elemental beast, as swords are useless against water-wraiths and such. I'm telling you this because today *you* must be augmented." Jules felt that bad news should be delivered quickly so the recipient could absorb it and move forward.

"You're older than the other novices, so today you'll most likely receive both a lightning bolt on one of your cheeks and a small body augmentation, perhaps on your arm. The color of the lightning bolt will indicate the element you're strongest in. This will give you the opportunity to get used to the feel of your augmentation and learn how to access the chi by the time we arrive in Aeoven, where you'll receive another one."

Wynn's expression changed from mild interest to one that indicated his nervous desire to run far, far away. "Thanks for the offer, but I don't really want one.

I understand they're quite painful to get, what with all those needles and all. And they're permanent—if you don't like them, you're stuck for life." Wynn demurred as politely as he was able, edging toward the door. "I mean, yours are really well done, and you look awfully dangerous...but I've never pictured myself with tattoos." His intention to bolt was clear in his frank, blue eyes. "I'm not really a tattoo kind of guy."

Jules's anger at Dorn boiled over, and he had the urge to strangle Wynn simply because he needed to choke someone, but he restrained himself.

Barely.

A vein throbbed in his forehead, and he said firmly, "You have to do it. You don't have a choice."

Wynn's jaw jutted out, and it was apparent he was going to argue about it.

Jules's irritation with the situation overcame him. He spoke sharply, "You'd better get used to it, lover-boy, because apparently the colorists are going to be here in a few hours." He rolled his eyes with exasperation. "Now come on."

Wynn said nothing. He nodded his head, and the whipped-dog look was back on his face. "After reading that book, I thought I'd have some choices, but it's no different than home. I hate feeling like I have no say in my life."

Immediately, Jules felt bad for speaking so harshly. "I promise you it wasn't my idea to spring this on you so quickly. Please believe me. You absolutely must be augmented. Your sanity depends upon it, and without tattoos, you won't be able to cast large spells more than once."

"My sanity?" Wynn looked shocked.

"Remember? I told you about mages who go mad. It will happen to you if you don't get augmented. The chi will build up around you, and something about it breaks your mind."

"I don't really understand, but I believe you," replied Wynn, seeing the conviction in Jules's eyes. "If I really have to, then I will, although I don't like it. This whole place is confusing to me."

"I know, and I'm sorry."

Dorn took that moment to poke his head into the room and point at Jules, motioning for him to get Wynn outside for his magic lesson.

Immediately, Jules's irritation with Dorn's refusal to tutor Wynn in lightning ballooned again. Forcing himself to remain polite, Jules said calmly, "I suppose while we wait for the colorists, we can see if you are able to call fire and lightning. Let's go out to the courtyard and practice there." Inwardly, he verged on giving in to an unprofessional fit of howling and tearing at his hair, because he couldn't remember ever feeling so unsettled and angry. As he pushed Wynn toward the door, Jules attempted to calm and center himself with only limited success. He was the iconic fire-mage, normally sunny and happy, sometimes hotheaded, always passionate, and always completely ill-equipped to deal with other people's problems.

"I can only try." Wynn shrugged. "I read what Abbott Dorn wanted me to. Being a priest of Aeos is a serious job. People depend on you. What if I mess it up?"

"Oh, pish-posh. You're a grownup now despite your baby face." Jules urged Wynn toward the door again. "Honestly, I don't mean to push you around.

We've much to do and not enough time, is all."

Wynn obediently hurried through the open doors to the garden. "Things just seem to happen *way* too quickly here. I can't keep up."

"Some things are just beyond my control." By the time they arrived at the cobbled square near the outdoor kitchen, Jules had calmed down. He began by first demonstrating how to summon fire. "Fire and lightning are the two battle elements that are most difficult to call and contain—and the most dangerous. We don't teach them to young novices until they've demonstrated some maturity, age twelve or older. You're an adult, you listen well, and you visualize clearly. I'll teach you what I can today, but don't feel bad if you can't call these elements. They're extremely difficult to entice."

Jules placed a lantern on the cobblestones. "Now you must remember to imagine the fire *inside* the lamp, lighting the wick. It's warm and I always imagine that it feels red, but you don't want to touch it since it *will* burn you quite seriously. Remember, visualize your flame lighting the lamp." Jules demonstrated for him. He then extinguished it. Raising his fire-shield, he stood back and waited for Wynn to make the attempt, ready to cast water if he set himself alight.

"What a useful trick." Wynn's eyes were round as he thought about all the things he could do with the ability. "I hope I can call fire." After two tries, Wynn had the lamp lit with a cheery, little flame.

Of course, he picked it up with no effort at all. What am I even doing here? Dorn could teach him this by handing him a book. Jules continued with his lesson, trying with moderate success to keep his sour attitude to himself. "The principle is the same any time you call fire. You absolutely must have a particular place in mind for it and a proper container, or you can cause some serious damage."

Unaware of Jules's inner troubles, Wynn kept practicing doggedly. "I can see how it would be dangerous to use fire in an uncontrolled way. This must be a terribly effective weapon," he replied seriously. "But there are all sorts of good uses for it. I think you could get even wet wood to burn with this spell. Every morning the house would be warm, no matter what."

Pleased at Wynn's comprehension, Jules agreed. Then, reluctantly, he decided Wynn understood how to call fire well enough, and it was time for lightning. This was the trickiest of the elements to test him on, and he'd been dreading this moment. He'd been accidentally zapped before by novices with a lot more experience than Wynn and he wasn't looking forward to it. Even he should have some difficulty with lightning since he was so new to the idea of calling magic. *I have good shields. He has equal strength in water, earth, and fire, so he should be quite good when he does finally make lightning work for him. The only mage I ever heard of who called lightning on the first attempt was Feia, and she managed to zap herself with it. But even if he can't do it just now, he'll have made enough of an attempt to ensure he can be augmented.* With his neutral expression masking his thoughts, Jules reclaimed Wynn's attention away from his newfound skill with fire.

Raising his basic shield, followed by his strongest lightning-shield, Jules prepared to speak, but Wynn interrupted him with a surprised look on his face. "What is this?"

"What is what?" asked Jules, confused.

"This," said Wynn, as he gestured around Jules. "It's like...like the air is different. But it feels like magic. You did it before too."

Jules found himself gaping at Wynn. "I raised my shields. You'll learn about those when we meet Rall in a few days. He's a master at them. I'm not going to teach you how to raise them because it's important you don't have any bad habits when it comes to shields. Your life will depend upon how well you understand them."

"Oh," replied Wynn, accepting the fact he wouldn't get a complete answer to his question. He'd never had a question fully resolved in his life, so he didn't really expect it. "All right then, what do you need me to do next?"

Whoever heard of an untrained mage sensing something as gentle as a shield? Jules forcibly calmed himself. "Now, this is the most difficult of the elements to separate out, so don't feel badly if you fail completely at calling it. New mages, even new lightning-mages, are unable to call it until their third year in the novice barracks because it constantly twists away from you, and you must have an excellent ability to visualize and contain the elusive element while holding it away from you. It's as if the lightning is a wild creature. You must tame it to make the element come when you call it, and then you must be sure to make it go where you want it to *without* letting it touch you."

Jules showed Wynn something called a cat-zapper. "Now, this is the basic novice form. It can be deadly, so do exactly as I tell you and nothing more."

Wynn nodded, listening intently to Jules's instructions.

Standing all the way across the courtyard on the opposite side of the kitchen garden from a somewhat largish boulder, Jules raised his right hand and fired off the low-level bolt. The large rock had obviously had similar treatment in its past. The bolt struck it with a satisfying flash and bang. A tiny bit of steam rose from the small puddle of rainwater that filled the hollow on the top of it.

Wynn jumped back wide-eyed and said, "Ah...I felt it before you did it. I felt a pressure, like you were building something, and then suddenly, there it was." He was completely enchanted with Jules's new trick. "Can I try?" The look on Wynn's face reminded Jules of a puppy.

"You felt it building?" A stab of some unfathomable emotion assailed Jules. *It figures....* He found himself suffering an unaccustomed moment of professional inadequacy, which wasn't helped at all by his experience of the previous evening. "Sure, you can try. What's the worst that could happen anyway? If you accidentally zap me, I have good shields."

As usual, Wynn didn't understand Jules was asking a rhetorical question, and he blithely answered it. "Well, you said it was called a cat-zapper, which sounds uncomfortable for the cat." Wynn smiled rather timidly, and in spite of his bad mood, Jules laughed. "And you said it was only good as a weapon. I could probably hurt myself, couldn't I...I could even hurt you if I visualize it wrong?"

"I have shields, but yes, you could hurt yourself," Jules replied slowly, suddenly realizing he'd been almost hoping Wynn would do exactly that, because everything just came too easily to him. He felt his face flush. *What's wrong with me? I owe him more than this. He can't help what he is. He didn't ask for any of this.*

Jules pulled himself together and then said, "Remember, you want to visualize it clearly on the rock because this element is a weapon, and we're pretending the rock is the enemy. This is the hardest of all the elements to call, and before you ask, we don't know why." Jules put as much encouragement as he could into his voice, trying to make up for his earlier bad mood. "When you do have it, it feels like you're trying to grasp an ice-cold wire that tries to wiggle away from you. I always think of it as white, for some reason." He checked his shield, making sure it was firm and then said, "Try it now."

"Put white, icy wire on the rock," Wynn said. He closed his eyes and visualized a bolt of lightning like Jules had cast. Raising his hand, he tried to picture it as clearly as he could. He thought he could feel icy wire and concentrated even harder, but it refused to form in his mind, and nothing happened. He opened his eyes and looked at Jules and shrugged. "I'll try again. I'm finding it hard to concentrate. So much has happened to me since yesterday, I'm feeling quite distracted."

Once again he failed.

On his third attempt, Wynn visualized his lightning bolt as clearly and as large as he could and tried to put as much effort into mentally grasping the icy wire as he was able. Suddenly, he had it and released it, picturing a gigantic bolt striking the rock with as much force as he could muster. Just as he let go, he heard Jules yell, "No! No! Not so big!"

With a deafening crash, the boulder shattered. Although they were across the courtyard from it, the concussion knocked Wynn and Jules off their feet and onto their backs. Thunder rattled the doors, and flying shards broke windows all along the courtyard. Wynn's ears rang, and he couldn't see well. Something wet stung his eyes, and numbly he wiped at it, his hand coming away with blood. He sat up and saw Jules lying on his back with his eyes open and staring, bleeding from multiple wounds where shards of rock had lodged in his body. Stars flashed before Wynn's eyes, and he felt exceedingly nauseated, barely managing to keep from throwing up.

He crawled over to Jules's mangled body, using his own rather bloody shirt to staunch the blood oozing from his friend's forehead as best as he could. He checked his pulse, picking the shards out of Jules's face and clothes. As far as Wynn could tell, he was just stunned but was covered in gouges from the shards. Absently, Wynn noticed he was himself also covered with wounds, and his face began to burn. The stinging immediately escalated to agony as the courtyard slowly spun.

Jules lay stunned, staring at the sky and feeling like his skin was on fire. As he regained awareness, Abbott Dorn and a man in green leathers raced out of the backdoor of the Temple.

"What happened? What did you do?" The abbott shouted, but Wynn could barely hear him. The courtyard spun faster and faster. "I felt a major-working in progress out here."

"I...cat-zapper.... Oh Goddess, it hurts." A black curtain came down over Wynn's vision, and everything went away.

The next thing Wynn knew, he was lying on the ground, staring up at an older, red-haired man wearing green leathers, who leaned over him, talking. "There now. Can you hear me?"

"Jules...." Wynn struggled to sit up. "He needs a doctor."

"I'm fine." Jules's voice sounded normal. "You just knocked me ass-over-teakettle, is all." When Wynn turned to look at him, he was no longer bleeding, and except for being rather pale, he looked completely uninjured, although his clothes were bloody and shredded. "Bran healed me, and he's just finished healing you."

"Thank you, Bran." Wynn's voice was full of gratitude and wonder. "I don't know any other doctor who could heal as well as this." He blushed and looked down, overcome with remorse and embarrassed for causing such a terrible accident.

"It's my form of magic. I have healing-empathy," Bran explained. Then Wynn noticed the green stars and crescent moons tattooed on Bran's forehead and cheeks. His hands were covered with green vines that disappeared up his sleeve, and a crescent moon crossed the palm of his right hand. "Your wounds were quite minor, just surface injuries, although they did look spectacular. You both managed to throw your arms up and shield your eyes, so we were lucky there."

Abbott Dorn stood with a perplexed look upon his face, gazing from the shattered rock fragments to Wynn and back. Finally, he said, "Son, I'd say you cast a 'curtain-call,' which is a devastating spell, very useful

54

against a single enemy. But even *I* can't blow up a boulder with that spell, and I'm a damned good lightning-mage." He thought for a moment and then said, "Of course, there was a puddle of water in the top of it, and the cracks were probably full of water too, so that might have had something to do with it...rapid expansion of the steam and all...." Dorn looked closely at Wynn, holding his hands up as if to a fire. He sat hunched over, hugging himself for comfort. "But look at you. You're completely out of chi. Are you feeling nauseated? Spots before your eyes?"

Wynn slowly nodded. "I'm a little better now."

"Well, you came close to burning out your gift." Abbott Dorn stood thinking for a moment and then spoke to Jules. "It will have to be Feia who works with him, no matter what Rall wants. He can't run away forever. He's still going to have to teach Wynn shielding even if it does mean he'll have to work with her. This animosity of theirs is ridiculously inconvenient for me."

Bran and Jules both rolled their eyes. "How rude of them to be so unhappily bonded," Jules murmured sarcastically. "I'm sure it was intentional."

Dorn glared at Jules, who didn't care. Wynn thought about leaving quietly to let them just get on with their quarrel, but Bran gripped his shoulder, holding him in place, and shook his head.

Turning to Jules, Bran said, "Well, you're in for a rough time of it if you have to work with both Rall and Feia. We healers were hoping to get them out from under the same roof to sort of ease the situation, but now...well, it must be her. She's the only one with anything near Wynn's strength and who *also* has the inclination to be an instructor." He looked meaningfully at Dorn, who shrugged. "In the meantime, you must work with Wynn only in the other elements."

Then he turned to Wynn saying, "You understand that because of your ability and lack of control, you're absolutely *not* to attempt to call lightning until Feia is able to work with you. It could be at least a week or more, depending on when you get to Aeoven. I can place restrictions on you if you feel you might be tempted."

"I understand completely, and don't worry. I won't use magic again, ever. Jules, I'm so sorry." Wynn suddenly felt homesick for the nice, safe farm where nothing ever exploded. "I don't think I want to do this anymore. I should probably go home now. My father needs me. He hasn't been well lately, and no one's there to help him." He stood up, looking for the gate to the street.

"You won't be going home for a while, Wynn, and you *will* use the gift whether you want to or not. The Goddess has claimed you for her own, my boy." Dorn's attempt at sympathy didn't really help, but Wynn nodded and politely thanked him anyway. "Trust me, son. Your father knows exactly where you are and has been expecting you'd be called here to learn to use your gift." Dorn clasped his shoulder comfortingly.

"Wynn, I know you didn't do it on purpose. You only did what I told you. I didn't realize your father had trained you so well." Jules turned his heated glance to Abbott Dorn. "Don't worry too much about us, Abbott. We'll muddle along somehow, so please don't feel compelled to be helpful." Jules spoke, once again forgetting to temper his words in his frustration.

Dorn gave him a sharp look. "Jules, sometimes things aren't what they appear to be. I've a reason for putting you in charge of this." After scowling again at Jules, he looked closely at Wynn and asked, "Are you feeling better now?"

Mutely, Wynn nodded, too overwrought to speak.

Dorn smiled happily and patted his shoulder, saying, "Well, that's all right then. Jules, I'll leave you to get on with it." He turned and went back into the Temple, calling over his shoulder, "I'd better get a note about this little display ready for Mother Relynne. The mail coach should be here any minute, so you'd better explain to Wynn about how they do the augmentations so he's not too surprised!"

Jules stared resentfully at Abbott Dorn's back, thinking *Lightning-mages. They're nothing but trouble, every one of them, and now we're going to have to play nice for Feia. Goddess help us all.* He rolled his eyes again. "I swear he's the laziest man in the Temple. He's lazy even for a lightning-mage. I've been told he's brilliant, but I haven't...." Gradually Jules realized Wynn was staring at him, and snapped his mouth shut.

Bran clearly read Jules's mood, finding humor in his dissatisfaction with the abbott's style of leadership. "Dorn has a good reason, trust me. You're the only person for this whether you believe me or not." Privately, he thought perhaps Jules had been posted at the lonely end of the trade road for too long, thinking he might do well in Widge, Braden, or even in Aeoven until he was needed in Armat again.

He decided to send a note of his own to Mother Relynne, and hiding his thoughts, Bran tried to divert Jules from his frustration with Dorn. "So now you must deal with Rall and Feia. Well, I certainly would never have let my village arrange a bonding for me, even if it did end a blood feud," he murmured thoughtfully. "I suppose the two of them felt compelled to obey their elders' wishes. It *has* made traveling in the far North much safer over the last two months. But it's made things difficult for the rest of us." He shrugged. "Oh, well. At least the town of Einar is still celebrating."

Turning to Wynn, Bran's eyes twinkled as he said, "I knew your father rather well and gained a lot of experience when we were novices, healing him from his own foolhardiness. Although for him, it was fistfighting with Dorn and the other bullies as often as not, rather than blowing himself and his friends up." Wynn reddened and looked down. "Don't feel bad. Jules here set his own shirt on fire with his first successful fire-spell. Magic is a dangerous toy."

Wynn shivered, oblivious to Jules's wounded look at Bran. "I'm completely sure it's not a toy, sir." Wrapped in his own misery, he hadn't even heard the healer's jab at Jules's expense.

"Well, I need to get back to the infirmary. My new journeyman isn't too sure of herself yet, so I should get back and help her." Bran spoke in a soothing tone of voice. "Why don't you two get some new shirts from the storeroom and have a snack before the colorists get here? Those are nothing but rags now. You'll have to wait until you get to Ragat or Wister to get new leathers. These are a little worse for wear, being somewhat pockmarked, but they're still good enough. You'll only need them when you're traveling anyway." At Jules's questioning look, Bran elaborated. "We've leathers, but nothing big enough for either of you two boys in the storeroom today. The squad outfitted two new soldiers before they left."

Jules nodded. Then he led Wynn to a storeroom where he selected two shirts from the pile that lay folded on the shelves and two pairs of dark blue trousers. The shelves held all sorts of clothes: shirts, several plain brown sets of leathers and armor waiting to be issued to those who might need them. In fact, everything a person traveling on Temple business might need, from kit-bags to spyglasses, could be found in the storeroom. "We may as well get your boots now too," said Jules. On one of the lower shelves, he found Wynn a pair that fit him perfectly.

They both checked off what they had requisitioned and signed a sheet of paper attached to the clipboard hanging on a nail near the door. Jules locked up behind them. "Let's get ourselves cleaned up as well as we can," he said and showed Wynn to a small bathing room just off the armory and smithy. "We can get a quick shower here, but this time of day the water is probably cold. Sorry about that."

The water wasn't too cold, but they bathed as quickly as possible so they could get some lunch before the mail coach arrived.

"You might want to think about cutting your hair," suggested Jules, as he watched Wynn pulling a comb through the long, damp strands. "It would be easier to take care of."

"I wear it in a braid usually, so it's not a problem. But I suppose I could," Wynn replied doubtfully. "I put the braid down the backplate of the armor yesterday, so it was out of the way. My dad is always after me to cut my hair, but I'll probably keep it long."

His hair was probably the only form of rebellion he was ever allowed, thought Jules. "You don't have to cut it. About half of the men wear it long. Rall does, but he's a barbarian, and claims the men of his village never cut their hair for any reason," said Jules. "I probably shouldn't have said anything since I suspect you've already had enough changes thrown at you."

"I do feel somewhat out of step with everyone else right now," replied Wynn, trying not to look as upset as he felt. He pocketed the leather thong he usually tied the braid back with and left his hair, which hung over his shoulders and past his waist, to finish drying.

"Well, at least the food will be good today since it's Bertte's day to prepare it," said Jules. "We take turns making lunch here for the whole group. I'm not very good at it, but Bertte usually helps me out." She was a model of efficiency and usually did everything that needed doing, but Jules didn't say so.

Chapter 5

After Jules and Wynn were once again presentable, they went to the communal kitchen and had a pre-lunch snack of bread and cheese, sitting quietly while Abbott Dorn's plump wife, Bertte, laid into Jules about the broken windows. "You of all people should know better, Jules!" She was an earth-mage with a red lightning bolt on her right cheek and thorny vines in red, blue, and yellow twining from the back of her hands to just above her collar.

Unfortunately, the damage had made her less susceptible to Wynn's charm. Besides, Bertte had known his father *very* well. She was the headmistress of the Temple school in Armat, and now she dished out a lecture on discipline with the food.

Looking at Wynn, she punctuated her commentary with brandishes of a wooden spoon. "Control is everything, young man." She shook the spoon. "Without control, you're no better than a rogue-mage." She stabbed the air as if the spoon was a sword. "Did you know you look just like your father? Now there was a mage who understood control!"

"Yes, ma'am. I know, ma'am," muttered Wynn dejectedly, each time Bertte took a breath. Like a bull heading for the barn, she just kept plowing over the same old ground, lauding his father's abilities and pointing out Wynn's failure. By the time she was done, he felt like the lowest creature ever to crawl on the earth. He sat at the table, nearly unable to eat, miserably saying "yes ma'am," and "no ma'am."

Finally, unable to watch Wynn taking any more abuse, Jules stood up and said, "Enough, Bertte. He's brand new to the Temple and has never cast lightning before. He *has* no control, so get off your high horse and stop berating him for not using something he doesn't have. That paragon of virtue you admire so, Liam Farmer, did *not* send him to the novice barracks when he was nine as he should have done. Instead, he kept his son caged up on the farm, rotting away in Ariend. He only arrived here yesterday." Bertte's mouth hung open in shock. Jules paid no attention to her indignation, telling her firmly, "Now lay off him and let him eat. He's nearly burned out, and on top of everything else, he must be augmented today. Do you understand?"

She did understand.

"Oh, you poor thing!" Now Bertte couldn't do enough for Wynn, apologizing over and over for her irritability, hugging him to her ample bosom in an excess of motherly exuberance. "I'm just a grumpy, old earth-mage. Pay no attention to me. Jules, how could you let me be so cruel to him?" He rolled his eyes as she kissed Wynn's cheek. She insisted on feeding them some delicious egg-and-potato salad, and brought out some fresh bread and cheese for them both, clucking like a little red hen over them the whole time.

"Did you know you look just like your father? What a gorgeous man he was, oh, my goodness. But he did cause some trouble, what with him being the most handsome thing for miles around and all." She winked at Wynn. "I'll bet you're just as wicked as Liam was with the friendly-girls." He nearly dropped his sandwich in shock. "No wonder poor Jules is grumpy. He probably has to behave himself for a change, the naughty, randy boy." Jules's eyes popped out of his head, hearing her say such a thing.

Fortunately for Bertte's safety, Jules heard the clopping of horses in the courtyard and the uniquely squeaky sounds of the mail coach. Standing up, he immediately began easing Wynn out the door to the main hall. "Um…thank you, Bertte, for all the wonderful food, but the mail coach is here, so Wynn must go and be augmented now." He unceremoniously shoved Wynn out the door.

"Thank you, ma'am," Wynn called over Jules's shoulder. "The lunch was wonderful."

"Oh yes, poor dear. Don't worry. I've some wonderful herbal remedies to help with the pain."

Jules quickly shut the door behind them. *Gah! Bertte, don't tell him "pain!"* He leaned against the door, smiling brightly, hoping Wynn hadn't heard her. "So, let's go meet the colorists, shall we? We mustn't delay them because they have to return on today's mail coach. The driver will have his lunch and a small rest, so we only have until midafternoon to get this done."

"Pain? What pain?" Wynn asked nervously. "I think I've had enough for one day."

"It's nothing. You'll be fine," Jules said briskly, pushing a reluctant Wynn toward the visitors' study. "If the abbott thought this would be bad, Bran would be scheduled to help you, but this augmentation should be minor, so no worries. They want to do this gradually."

"Um, if you say so," Wynn replied nervously. His hands shook, and he felt like running away but steeled himself to endure whatever was planned for him.

"Are you all right? You seem pretty jumpy." He thought Wynn looked like he was going to bolt, and didn't blame him.

"I'm tired of surprises, is all. It's been one thing after another since yesterday morning. I'm fine." Wynn didn't really convince himself.

The colorists, a wiry lightning-mage in his mid-thirties named Sylvi and his journeyman assistant, Nolen, unloaded their equipment and baggage from the coach. Sylvi had a yellow lightning bolt on his left cheek and two tiny green stars on his throat just above his collar bone. He also bore many tattoos. All the colors except green were equally represented.

While they were setting up the special folding table and unpacking their tools and inks in the empty study just off the meeting room, Jules explained about augmentations, delivering the same lecture almost word for word he'd given many times to young novices. "Warriors have vines with thorns, or they may have dragons colored to represent the elements they're strongest in. You've seen mine, so you know what to expect when you've been completely augmented, which will apparently be sometime around winter solstice. If you're to also be an armsmaster, you'll have runes for strength and skill, which, as you can see, are both woven into and around my dragons. Assassins will have runes for stealth and luck, but this is rather rare and only happens later.

"If the battle-mage has some small, healing capabilities, a small star or two may be augmented on his hand or cheek, but this too only happens later in life. Battle-mages *never* have more than exceedingly minor healing skills because the two magics conflict. The *only* element healers ever have is water, which they're unable to use as a weapon. The two disciplines, healing and battle-magic, are incompatible and cannot exist together with strength in one person."

"How do they conflict?" asked Wynn, fidgeting nervously. "It seems like magic should be magic."

"It isn't though. Healing is building and life. Battle-magic is destruction and death," Jules replied firmly.

"Ah. That actually makes sense," said Wynn thoughtfully. "What's the difference between healers' tattoos and yours?"

Grinning at Wynn's use of the word "tattoo," Jules said, "Well, the color of a healer's augmentation is green. The symbols are stars, crescent moons, and flowering vines, with runes for true-sight, compassion, and strength. Healers may also have blue flowers if they have some water affinity. Healers are *never* augmented with the stealth rune because it's the assassin's rune. It allows him or her to go in secret. Many healers are unable to kill even in self-defense."

Wynn nodded numbly, not understanding at all.

"You'll have time to learn all of this, I promise." Jules felt a surge of pity for him. "The rest of the day will be simple, don't worry. I must warn you, though. You'll have to be naked to get your augmentations because the magic chooses where it will manifest on your body, and while some things like the lightning bolts on the cheek are usual, no one knows for sure ahead of time. But don't worry. The colorists have seen every mage in the Temple naked, including me, so you won't be the first or the last."

Wynn had a wide-eyed, dumbfounded look to him.

Frankly, Jules felt a bit dumbstruck himself. *Oh Goddess. He looks like a terrified friendly-girl. No wonder his father wanted him to cut his hair!* He resisted the urge to laugh at Wynn's expression.

Soon the colorists were all set up. Wynn lay stark-naked on the special padded table, covered by a sheet that he nervously clutched to his chin, while Sylvi and his assistant, Nolen, prepared the colors for the augmentations.

Sylvi explained how the tattoos were created magically. "What you receive today will be determined by the type of magic you will be strongest and most adept in. We have a saying, 'the magic chooses,' meaning *my* will has nothing to do with the design, only the will of the Goddess Aeos. She will guide us in making the first of the augmentations that will enable you to fulfill the tasks she may set before you. Are you ready, son? You seem awfully nervous." Sylvi was somewhat perplexed, as he didn't usually have first augmentations on children as old as Wynn appeared. Thinking the boy was about fifteen years old, he decided a sleep-spell was in order.

Wynn nodded nervously, saying, "I've had a bad couple of days up until now. I know I'm jumpy, but I can't help it. This was a surprise, and I've had too many shocks today already." As he finished speaking, he felt himself completely relax. He then dozed off, sleeping deeply. Unbeknownst to Wynn, Sylvi had cast a spell for calm on him and had then followed it with sleep.

Colorists were a rare breed of mage, somewhere between healers and battle-mages, usually of the lightning persuasion, with great artistic talent and some minor healing ability, able to cast very minor healing spells such as sleep and calm if they were in close proximity to the subject. They were often highly respected artists, creating beautiful pieces when they were not working. Sylvi was quite well known for his surreal, hauntingly beautiful landscapes done in oils, and his assistant, Nolen was a talented portraitist.

Soon Sylvi and Nolen were fully tranced, and the augmentations were underway. They placed a yellow lightning bolt on Wynn's right cheek. A thorny vine equally represented in yellow, orange-red, red-brown, and blue was wound about his right bicep, spiraling in four turns from elbow to shoulder and up his neck. Then the colorists placed two runes, one for strength and one for courage, over his heart. Finally, tiny runes for luck and strength were woven into the vines about his arm.

Bran was called in before Sylvi woke Wynn, as the augmentations had been a little larger than they had initially believed, but not dangerously so. Sylvi asked Bran how a fifteen-year old had escaped being augmented and was shocked to hear his actual age. "I would never have guessed he was so old. He shows no sign of the madness. How can such a thing be, I wonder?"

Bran told Sylvi who he was, who his father was, and gave him a quick rundown of Wynn's adventures. "He a bit of an anomaly, I would say," Bran finished up.

"I thought he looked familiar, but I didn't know Liam well. He was already a journeyman when I was a novice. Well, this explains the completely shattered state of nerves he was in when we began the augmentation," Sylvi replied wryly. "I couldn't imagine why he was so overwrought." He smiled broadly, saying, "So Jules got a dose of his own medicine last night. Well, well! I'd say it's about time. He's had it all his own way far too long." He and Bran exchanged knowing smirks. "But blowing up a boulder—even Feia hasn't done such a thing, and to hear her talk, she's the hottest lightning-mage in the history of the Temple. She needs a taste of humble pie to sweeten her disposition, I think."

"You and many others," Bran agreed with a satisfied smile. He wasn't proud of it, but he couldn't change the way he felt. "I'll wake our newest brother now. He's already gaining chi. Can you feel it? It looks like a red halo to my healing-sight."

Sylvi nodded, holding his hand over Wynn. "I do feel it, though I can't see it as you do. The boy will be as good as his father was, I think."

While the two older mages talked, Nolen and Jules caught up on each other's news. Nolen tidied up, packing their tools and dyes as the two spoke.

"You've been creating quite a stir back in Aeoven, Jules," said Nolen, greeting his old friend.

"Oh? I live a pretty quiet life out here in the wilderness. Are you sure it's me who's been having adventures?" Jules couldn't think of anything he'd done worth commenting on in Aeoven's hotbed of gossip.

"Oh, they're talking about you, for sure! Everyone's heard rumors about you and your exploits with the women in every town in the West. You've become a bit of a legend." Nolen spoke with the frankness that was a trait of lightning-mages. "You're considered a manly sort of a man since only Rall Ivarsson can kick your butt in the practice yard. Now the older novices and first-year journeymen all want to be just like you, wenching and partying when they're not saving the world." He didn't notice the sudden, stricken look on Jules's face. "Rumor has it you'll be asked to return to the college to teach weapons since Rall is going to be Mother Relynne's permanent assistant. All the young warriors want to be your student and go out on the town with you on Sunnaday night."

"What do you mean 'everyone' has heard of my adventures? I mean, it is just a rumor, right? I lead a pretty modest life here, you know." Jules wasn't pleased to hear his indiscretions were the topic of conversation in the dining hall at the Temple college. "I lead a *very* quiet life, early to bed and all. Why would anyone be interested in talking about me?"

"Gosh, I'm sure I don't know. Everyone talks about your girls and the way you love them and leave them. I mean, even Aneka didn't catch your interest for long, and all the men want to court her. Why, not long after you left, the earth-mage, Devyn D'Mal, went down on one knee in the dining hall, begging her to be his wife. She told him rather sharply that one man was not likely to interest her for any length of time ever again and to get off his knees. She's never going to settle down. She's less interested in that than you are. But on the way here, we stopped to stretch our legs in both Wister and Ragat. The friendly-girls all pestered us, asking when you were coming back. They were *very* glad to hear you'd be returning soon," Nolen replied helpfully.

Chapter 6

Before he woke Wynn, Bran healed his augmentations, which usually wasn't necessary, telling Jules the uproar of the day made it a good idea. "His nerves are shattered and so are yours. You don't need to worry about them healing properly. They're done now, so all you have to do is keep him on track with his other lessons until you meet up with Rall."

Before he went back to his infirmary, Bran showed Wynn how to bleed off his excess chi and smooth the flows so he didn't experience surges. Now, in the men's bathing room at the Temple, Wynn stood looking at his reflection in the mirror that hung over the basin. He wasn't sure how he felt about the yellow lightning bolt on his cheek, but he couldn't really hide it. "I suppose I'll get used to it," he told Jules. "I hope shaving doesn't bother these tattoos. I don't have much of a beard, but I don't like how it feels when it grows out."

"They're augmentations, not tattoos, remember? And no, shaving doesn't affect them. Even if you're injured and seriously scarred, they sometimes come back." Jules leaned against the door, waiting for Wynn to finish looking at his face. He was hungry but didn't really want to deal with the common room at the Lying Dog after the day he'd had.

You may as well face it, Jules. If you didn't know you're going to spend the evening sitting alone in a crowded room, you would already be over there taking whatever comfort was offered. You'd do it despite the fact you really want Aneka, not some friendly-girl looking for a night of pleasure with the next cute boy who enters the common room. His face reflected his grim thoughts, but soon his expression turned to one of shocked mortification. *Oh Goddess. Aneka! Maybe she's been out of town.... If she's heard about my recreational adventures here, she'll be done with me forever.* His stomach churned as he realized he could be in big trouble. *Jules, you're an animal...a disgusting, lustful beast. Aneka is going to kill you.*

"You don't look well, Jules," said Wynn. "Maybe we should go back to the inn and get an early night's sleep. Today was a long day."

"I wonder what they're serving for dinner tonight." Jules tried to sound enthusiastic, failing miserably.

"I really didn't mean to almost kill you, Jules," Wynn said glumly, assuming Jules's bad mood was his fault. "I was just trying to do it right. Call the lightning, I mean."

"It's not you, Wynn. It's me and me alone. I've got a girlfriend who is going to give me hell when I get back to Aeoven." Jules heard his own voice and couldn't believe he'd just spewed the truth. He smacked his forehead. "I talked to a friend of mine today, and apparently, rumors of my transgressions have filtered back home."

"You have a problem with the friendly-girls too?" Wynn looked away and then back, blushing. "My parents wouldn't be happy with my behavior. But I can't help it if these girls like me. Maybe it's because I'm new in town. They're all so nice and welcoming."

"I know, Wynn. Believe me, I know. But this is my problem." Jules figured he'd better tell the whole truth since he'd started. "I have sort of an understanding with a girl who really means something to me. She's an earth-mage, and I've not been honest with her since

71

I've been stuck out here at the edge of the world, alone and bored. Now we're going to Aeoven, and she's there waiting for me."

"It's a problem because you're basically an honest person and you're not proud of yourself."

Jules was surprised. Wynn had just seen through to the meat of the matter, though he appeared blithely ignorant of everything around him.

Wynn continued, "Have you both agreed to see only each other?"

"No, but...." Jules didn't know what to say because until Nolen had mentioned it, he really hadn't considered that Aneka might have other men in her life. She'd been willing to settle down with him, but he wasn't ready to commit to something as permanent as bonding and had managed to avoid talking about it right up to the day he'd left. In his mind, he saw her, regret he was leaving written across her face. "She's waiting for me. I'm sure of it."

"The girls here in Neveyah seem to have minds of their own, Jules. At least the ones I met last night certainly do." He blushed again but continued speaking, "You're free and she is too, so it's all right. You didn't ask something of her that you're unable to do. You haven't been unfaithful because you never promised you *would* be." Wynn spoke supportively. "Cheer up, Jules. You're worrying too much."

"You mean she could be seeing other men?" Jules's voice held all the horror he felt at the thought. *Oh, no! What did Nolen say? "All the men want to court her." Devyn D'Mal...he's a bloody prince, and he's been hanging around my girlfriend!* He felt like his heart had stopped.

"Of course! I'm sure she'll understand you've been lonely and bored," Wynn said, grinning cheerfully. "She's been bored and lonely too." He clasped Jules on the shoulder companionably. "You're worrying about something that isn't a problem."

Sitting in the common room, Jules was subdued. His mind staggered at the thought of his sweet Aneka having other men in her life. His ability to think coherently had flown out of the window in the face of this catastrophe. Now he sat helplessly wondering what he should do to solve his problem.

Somehow when Wynn was hauled away again by all the friendly-girls, it just didn't matter as much as it had the night before. "Don't forget to bleed off your excess chi" was all he said as they dragged him off.

◆◆◆

The next morning, Jules and Wynn sat at their table with bowls of porridge before them when Dorn came huffing and puffing over to them. "The sun isn't even up yet, Dorn. What's happened?"

"You two have a mission to accomplish as soon as you're done with breakfast. The miller's son didn't come home last evening, and his parents can't find him anywhere. We can only hope he's simply strayed too far and gotten lost, rather than something more dire. Get out there and find him as soon as you've eaten." The abbott's face was red with exertion. "With the squad gone off to Beckett, we don't have anyone else to do this."

"Right," Jules replied, trying not to talk with his mouth full. "Do you know where he was last seen?"

"His father has the mill just outside of town on the River Rangle. It's located at the falls just downstream from the south gate, perhaps half a league. They say he often plays along the banks of the Rangle, but there's no sign of him there. Bertte, Bran, and I just got back from searching all night, but we couldn't find any sign of him in the dark. Bran searched the water with his healing sense and tells me the boy's not in the river, thank the Goddess, but brigands and who knows what else are out there. It's a wilderness here at the edge of the world." Dorn turned and left as quickly as he arrived.

They finished eating and then went upstairs to gear up. Jules glanced into Wynn's room, but his girlfriends had all left, and the room was quite tidy, with the window thrown open for air. He grinned. "You're a fast learner, Wynn. Always hide the evidence of your indiscretions."

Red-faced but ignoring Jules's jab, Wynn checked his quiver as he strapped it across his back along with his bow. Then he belted his long knife to the front just left of his sword. "I'm not at all useful with a sword yet, so relying on it wouldn't be in my best interest right now. Do you agree?"

"Yes, it's probably not a good idea." Jules was pleased by how quickly and efficiently Wynn geared himself up. "Good. Every one of your weapons is near to hand, even your long knife. You've done this before, I take it."

"Not with armor, but this is easy to put on. Animals and people go missing sometimes." Wynn's calm reply belied his quick movements.

"You're right about your skills with the sword, though most men would never admit to being less than proficient with any weapon. I'd hoped to work with you this morning, but it'll have to wait." Jules looked Wynn over. Finding him well geared up, they left the inn. "If we find the boy this morning, we can practice this afternoon."

In no time at all, they were heading out of the south gate of Armat, taking a rutted lane that followed the course of the River Rangle. The sky began to lighten as they passed various farms. "This area looks a lot like home," Wynn told Jules wistfully after they had walked for a while. "Every one of these farms could easily be the place I grew up on, except they're so close to town and close to each other."

Soon they arrived at the mill, and after speaking to Davey's frantic parents, they took the path where the boy had last been seen playing. Wynn automatically assumed the role of tracker, leading Jules to believe he'd done a lot of it.

"Many people have been down this way looking for him," Wynn told Jules. "Any tracks the little boy might have left have been pretty well erased, but I'll find something to follow."

"Have you done much tracking?" Jules asked Wynn, who was examining the muddy ground between the path and the river. "I haven't done as much as I would have liked because I was sent to the Temple when I was nine."

"Yes. I do a lot of hunting, but I prefer fishing." His rueful grin lit up his face as he looked closely at the damp earth by the bank of the river. "Chicken or a nice catfish is on the Restday menu at home more often than not!"

Wynn examined the path and shrubs for signs of the missing boy, sure of himself and completely in his own element now. Jules watched as he found the trail he was looking for, searching for signs of the child, and could see no trace of insecurity in his student. He decided Wynn had simply had too much thrown at him in too short a time.

"I think we need to go this way," Wynn said finally. "There's a faint game trail here and some strange tracks. I've never seen anything like these. Do you recognize them? What sort of large creature leaves slime like this behind?"

Jules heart sank as he looked where Wynn pointed. "It's the track of a water-wraith. This is bad. The boy may well be dead now," he replied grimly. "Wraiths poison their victims to put them to sleep, since they...ahem...they don't eat dead meat." Jules didn't know how to phrase it so it would be less shocking.

Wynn's eyes widened. "I see," he said and turned immediately back to the hunt. "This way." He was already on the trail, silently following it along the edge of the river. "What is this water-wraith you speak of? I've never heard of them." His low voice didn't carry, and Jules could barely hear him. Speaking in a low whisper and trying to walk quietly, Jules explained what he knew about water-wraiths and their more common and much less dangerous relatives, water-sprites.

"They're creatures some say were created by the beast-masters, people who are rogue-mages and have some magical control over beasts. I've also heard they came here from the river world of Danus before the gods and goddesses closed their borders to Tauron. I'm inclined to believe that story because the beast-masters are not gods. They can't create something, only alter what is."

"What are they like, these wraiths? What are their habits?" Wynn searched as he slowly moved down the trail, seeing everything around and ahead of them while Jules watched behind.

"Well, they're not wraiths as are the ghosts of the dead. They're elemental creatures with physical bodies like any other beast, yet different from other animals of our world. The water-wraith is the strongest of the lower water elementals. They're unbelievably fast and nearly impossible to see in the mist. They also have excellent shielding abilities, which, I'm sorry to say, you don't have yet, and this makes them hard to kill. You've no skill with magic and no ability to shield yourself from magical attacks, so once we find this creature's lair, you must stay completely away from it or you *will* be killed." Jules's complete certainty of the outcome of such an encounter convinced Wynn to follow his teacher's wishes. "They *always* fight magic with magic, so if you have to battle one and have no shields, your best bet is to hack away at them until they stop healing themselves."

Wynn was quiet for a moment, and then he said, "It's too bad I'm too new at this to be able to use my lightning ability to help you, but we'll do the best we can. I did make a promise." He turned back to tracking the water-wraith. "Why are they difficult to kill with weapons?"

"Their bodies absorb the blows, and any slices they receive are immediately healed. The other thing I must warn you about is you must *never* cast water at a water-wraith because if you had by some miracle managed to injure him, the water will help to heal him. You'll have wasted all your chi and you'll die." Jules hoped Wynn was paying attention, because that peculiarity was a common feature of all elemental creatures. "This is why the rogue-mages who are also beast-masters go to great efforts to find and use elementals. The element that heals the beast is the one they're named after, and you must *never* use it against them. It's the element that will also be their best magic weapon, and they have high reserves of chi and strong magic at their disposal."

"I see." Wynn did see and what he saw disturbed him. "So what are these beast-masters you speak of?"

"Very few are left to plague us now, thankfully. They're rogue-mages, healers who have never received the training and augmentations and haven't taken the vows to serve. They go mad with the power and are acolytes of Tauron. The really strong ones are nearly unstoppable because they have covens of battle-mages in their thrall. They've been known to take over whole villages and their surrounding areas, creating small countries of their own, treating the people whose homes and lands they usurped with the greatest cruelties. Some seek out and kidnap children with the talent, the ones who are so young the Temple hasn't found them yet. They turn these children to Tauron, raping them of their magic and destroying their minds in the process," Jules whispered in a low voice.

The thought made Wynn feel ill.

"Only the combination of discipline, augmentations, and our vows keep those of us with the talent focused on doing the best we can to serve Neveyah. Before the founding of the College of Warcraft and Magic and the creation of the clergy of

Aeos, mages who survived the learning process often made life a misery for the rural people." Jules saw he had Wynn's full attention now. "You know the Temple serves Aeos, the Goddess of Hearth and Home."

Wynn nodded slowly. "I was raised to serve her also."

Nodding, Jules said, "Aeos's great enemy is Tauron, the Bull God. Tauron imprisoned and murdered Aeos's husband and even now tries to convince her to wed him. He works against her by subverting those of her people who are weak and untrained, which is why we search out the children who show the signs of being a budding mage. The first time a child uses his or her magic to harm another, Tauron claims them. The Dark God uses them to whittle away at Aeos's rule here in Neveyah, even though the borders are closed to him and he can't send his children here anymore."

Wynn's surprise was evident. "I've read the Book of Life, so I know the story of *Ariend and the Crystal Spear*. I've also read the tales of Aelfrid Firesword and his battle against the evil wizard Daryk. I didn't actually think of those stories as being real though."

"They are real. Too real."

"I understand now why it's so important for me to become a member of the clergy." Once again, Wynn bent down to examine something and then noiselessly moved forward. They both fell silent as they followed the faint trail. Soon it became more pronounced, and they were able to go more quickly, although the ground was somewhat mushier.

They followed the path until the sun had fully risen. As they rounded a corner, Wynn stopped suddenly, his arm out to hold Jules back.

"There's a large burrow high in the sandbank just up ahead. Some creature has been going in and out of it lately," Wynn said. "Something heavy was dragged into it in the last day or so. It may be the child we're looking for. But there are a lot of tracks here for just one beast. I'm sure there are two of them."

"I have to go in and get the boy out if he's in there and still lives. We don't dare take the time to go back for Dorn and Bertte because if I don't do it now, he won't be alive for long." Jules spoke heavily. "I'll return as soon as I can. If the creatures are in there, you'll definitely hear the fight. If I don't come out, go back and get Dorn. He's an accomplished lightning-mage, and he'll know how to kill this beast and protect the community." Clasping Wynn's shoulder, he moved off and soon had climbed the bank and disappeared into the den.

Wynn crouched just out of sight of the burrow, mulling over the situation. *I'm fairly useless at this point. What if the water-wraith wins, but Jules is only injured and not killed? How could I save him?* He suddenly felt cold. *Poison—what if I could poison an arrow?* Wynn looked about him, seeing the vegetation that grew lushly near the river. *Are they susceptible? Jules never said. Most creatures are vulnerable to some form of poison.*

Wynn recognized several plants as being poisonous, but while they might produce a bad rash or diarrhea, nothing would cause death except in a child or a badly-weakened, older person. But if he could get one of the poisons inside the creature, he might at least incapacitate it. He saw poison oak growing in small thickets along the riverbank.

The rash that occurred from contact with poison oak was terrible, the itching unbearable. Wynn had gotten into some as a young boy. Applied internally by an arrow, it might at least keep the beast occupied while he went in for Jules.

Wynn looked carefully at the area the trail wound through, noting the beasts had avoided the poisonous plants and wondering how to coat his arrows without getting it on himself. As he knelt, trying to solve his dilemma, a terrible noise erupted from the den. "Hurry up, fool. Just do it." Gingerly, he took four shafts and wiped them on the oily leaves of the plant, turning each and coating them as well as he could with the poisonous oils. Carefully, he hooked a bit of leaf to help with the grief he hoped to give the wraiths. When they were coated as thoroughly as possible, he crept back to the den. Placing the arrows on the sand where he could quickly reach them, he knelt and waited, his bow at the ready with the first one nocked.

Wynn could feel Jules and the beasts trading many spells back and forth. By the feel of the magic, he could tell Jules had fired off a large lightning spell, but apparently the beast had shielded against it. The noise reached a crescendo and then was cut off. Dead silence reigned in the clearing.

Then Wynn heard a strange shuffling noise. Suddenly, the monster emerged from its den, filling the entrance. It was a horror, a gigantic, silvery-grey creature, human-like in form and obviously male, but no intelligence lived behind those terrifying eyes. The water-wraith stood half again as tall as Wynn and had gelatinous skin that shone wetly. Instead of hair on its head, strange worm-like extrusions waved, each moving as if brushed by a breeze of its own. A phosphorescent radiance surrounded the beast.

Wynn stood mesmerized by its grotesque appearance until he abruptly realized the beast was building a spell. Suddenly, icy water drenched him, startling him into action. He shot two poisoned bolts that struck the creature squarely and lodged deep inside it. Both arrows disappeared completely, shaft and all, into the wraith's barrel-like chest.

With a hoarse, whuffing sort of bellow, the water-wraith clutched its chest, clawing at itself as if trying to dig the arrows out. The creature began screaming, a high-pitched screech, deafening Wynn. It collapsed to its knees as it fell out of the entrance to its den. Wynn knocked another arrow and fired it off, wishing with all his heart he could use a lightning bolt. It struck the wraith squarely in the chest but didn't disappear as the first two had.

With another earsplitting shriek, the beast began to melt, his flesh hissing as great gobs of jelly sloughed off and dripped down the bank before the den. The creature screeched a dreadful harmony to the hissing of its flesh.

Quickly, Wynn shot two more arrows, one an unpoisoned bolt, both lodging in the horrific, quivering, soupy mess that was the water-wraith. The howls slowly died away until dead silence reigned in the clearing. Stunned, Wynn moved forward, eyes wide as he looked at the disgusting remains of the creature. The stench of the thing was overwhelming as he climbed past the goopy corpse, getting some on him as he entered the lair.

Wynn found Jules lying unconscious but alive next to a boy who appeared to be sleeping deeply on a heap of debris in a corner of the fetid den. With relief, Wynn saw his friend still breathed, but a large lump had formed on his forehead. "Jules! Jules...oh, no...this is bad." Wynn lifted Jules's shoulders and supported his head, trying to think of what to do. "Jules, don't die on me. We have to get out of here! Jules," Wynn said urgently, "I think more than one of these things lives here." He cradled his friend, wishing he'd been born a healer, wishing Bran was with them. "Please—you have to wake up."

"Let go of me, you big oaf," Jules mumbled weakly into Wynn's shoulder. "I'm not one of your friendly-girls! Aaugh...my shoulder hurts."

"Jules, I didn't know what to do." Wynn helped him sit up. "You've been hit on the head so don't try to do too much."

After a few moments, Jules regained his wits and said sharply, "What are you doing here? I told you to get Dorn if I got into trouble!" He sat up and began pulling his gear back into place, wincing as he moved his right arm. "Help me with this. I can't get it on right." Wynn got Jules's breastplate straight and took off his own shirt to make a sling, easing the pain somewhat in Jules's shoulder.

"It came out and cast a spell at me," Wynn said, looking at the entrance nervously. "I think it has a mate, so we have to get out of here."

"You're going to have to carry the boy," Jules said. "I'm pretty useless right now. You get him and I'll get myself out." Wynn reached out to help him anyway. "Go!" Jules's voice was sharp.

The child was large for his age, and the den was cramped. With a great deal of difficulty, Wynn got the boy out, getting covered in the process with the disgusting-smelling gore in front of the lair. They were all fairly covered in slime by the time Jules dragged himself one-handed to his feet and then slid down the bank through the mess.

Standing in the sunlight of the entrance and looking at the reeking remains of the water-wraith, Jules glared at Wynn. "It smells like lightning! You were told not to use it."

Highly offended, Wynn replied rather sharply, "I didn't. I used poisoned arrows. See? There they are." Wynn pointed at the shafts sticking out of the unrecognizable, jelly-like mess. "I keep my promises!" He laid Davey down on a sandy area. "I don't lie!"

"I believe you. Please don't yell. My head is killing me." Jules looked at the mess. "This is a good opportunity for you to practice building a larger spell in a situation where you can work on your control. Visualize scooping a hole under the corpse and then put the soil on top of it."

Wynn complied, and Jules was satisfied he'd done the task as well as he himself would have. Then he had Wynn collapse the den.

Once those tasks were done, Wynn settled the unconscious Davey over his shoulder, and they began trekking back to the mill along the muddy river path. The trip back was difficult and took longer because of Jules's injured arm. The unconscious boy was a heavy, ungainly burden despite the fact Wynn was used to carrying heavy loads. The difference was he was usually shifting bales or heavy bags from one place to another, not hauling them for long distances over rough terrain.

At last, they struggled into the courtyard of the mill where the boy's parents were waiting. "Thom—hurry and get the wagon!" The boy's mother was frantic when she saw the lifeless child. "We have to get him to the healer!"

Soon Wynn and Jules found themselves in the back of the wagon, rattling along the southern road to Armat. Jules could find no relief for his shoulder no matter how he positioned himself. When they arrived back at the Temple's carriage port, the healers both came running out.

Bran immediately asked if they knew what had poisoned the boy. "Water-wraith," Jules said, gritting his teeth against his own pain. "Wynn shot it full of arrows. He managed to find some poison to smear on them. Whatever it was he found killed the thing as well as lightning does and just as messily. He says it has a mate, but we didn't see it."

"Well, the boy should wake up in a day or so then," Bran said to the worried parents, as he checked him over. "It should wear off, but don't worry. We'll keep him here in the infirmary and make sure he's not having a bad reaction to the wraith's poison." Then he turned to Jules. "I need to see to your shoulder. Your head wound isn't too serious, which is a blessing."

Dorn took the worried parents off to one side at that point. He had a weak stomach for healing and never watched it if he could avoid it.

"Good—your shoulder is only dislocated, Jules. I can take care of you now. Whoa, look at Wynn!" Jules turned to see what Bran was pointing at. Maribeth, his assistant, grabbed and held Jules firmly, and with a deft movement, Bran put his shoulder back in place. She winked at Wynn.

Jules cried out, and as soon as Bran released him, he leaned over, emptying his stomach, nauseated from the pain and angry at being tricked. "You could have warned me, Bran," he said, wiping his lips with the back of his hand. "But thanks, I think." His head ached and he still hurt.

Casting a spell for pain relief, Bran said, "You would have tensed up and it would've been worse. Now you need to get to the baths, both of you. Those leathers will have to be cleaned because we don't have any to replace them, but everything else should be burned. I'll send someone to take care of them. You'll be here an extra day, I'm afraid. That stench is quite difficult to get out of anything it touches. When you're done bathing, Dorn wants you to come back here. We'll eat, and you can tell us all about this morning's little party." Bran turned to leave. "It's my day to prepare lunch, so we'll see you in about an hour."

"Bran, may I speak to you for a moment?" When Bran turned back, Wynn said, "I hope I have the opportunity to repay you for all the healing you've done on me and my friend lately. He's not ungrateful, truly he isn't, and he doesn't mean to be grumpy. He's just had a very bad day and was knocked unconscious too." He surprised Bran with his astonishingly honest smile, "I've no money to pay you, but if you ever need me, just let me know. I'll be right there to help you, no matter what."

"Thank you, Wynn. But healing is what we do, and it costs nothing because it's a gift from Aeos to the people of Neveyah." Bran smiled kindly at Wynn. "Now go! You two smell like you've been rolling in dead water-wraith. *Not* a good thing!"

Chapter 7

Wynn and Jules sat at the table in the sunny garden behind the Temple, attempting to enjoy a late lunch of bread and cheese, accompanied by a green salad, fruit, and a large serving of humble pie dished up especially for Jules.

"You always take so much on yourself, when you ought to remember your place. What were you thinking, dealing with a water-wraith by yourselves?" Bertte was well into her rant. "You should have come back and gotten us. It takes at least two full mages to handle a major elemental. You're supposed to be teaching this poor boy properly and...."

Jules's patience snapped. "Enough, Bertte! Only last week, a farmer down the Rangle told you he'd seen the tracks of a water-wraith crossing the road. 'No, it's just hysteria talking,' you said. 'They're extinct now.'"

Bertte started to interrupt him, but Jules shushed her, her eyes popping then with outrage at his temerity. "You said it. Don't deny it. When we came upon the beast's den, we were a full hour's walk from Armat Temple, traveling as fast as we could." Jules's voice dripped with sarcasm. Being a fire-mage, he had a flaring temper when pushed too far. "I do assure you we did *not* kill the damned thing just to ruin your day!"

Bertte's face was livid, and in her anger, she lost her words.

Rolling his eyes, Jules turned away from her, fixing his glare on Abbott Dorn. "And what do *you* want to know about this whole debacle?" He'd quite forgotten to pretend to have some respect for his boss.

Smiling innocently, Dorn replied, "Oh, nothing

much. Maybe you could tell me how big the thing was, if it had a mate...just the usual." He'd rather uncharitably enjoyed seeing his wife get a well-deserved dressing down and felt rather forgiving at the moment. He turned his deceptively mild gaze to Wynn. "And you killed it with poisoned arrows. That's an unusual way to deal with them, but apparently effective." His pen was poised to take notes. "What sort of poison?"

"Poison oak, sir." Wynn was a bit uncomfortable under Dorn's scrutiny but told the story of what had happened, stopping only to answer Dorn's questions. "And when that thing emerged from the den, he cast water at me. I shot two arrows into him. They completely disappeared into his chest!" His face still showed shock and disbelief. "He tried to claw them out, so I fired several more. Finally, his skin started hissing. Then he melted."

"You know, hissing and melting isn't usually how a poisoned water-wraith dies. It's the way lightning kills them." Abbott Dorn scrutinized Wynn's face. "You both reeked of fried water-wraith when you got back."

Indignantly, Wynn said, "Sir! I swear I didn't use my ability. I promised I wouldn't, and I don't break my promises. I admit to *wishing* they were lightning bolts, but I assure you they were only arrows." Wynn sat back, clearly wondering if he was in trouble anyway. "Then I buried the beast using earth-magic and collapsed the den." He exhaled heavily, saying, "I really did wish those arrows were lightning when I got a look at that thing."

"I imagine you did." Abbott Dorn smiled wryly.

"I'd have felt the same under the circumstances. But I'm sure you'll understand if I ask Bran to truth-read you."

Wynn nodded. "I understand. You don't know me well, and I could be lying to you. But I'm not. I don't tell lies."

Centering himself and opening his healing-sight first to Jules and then Wynn, Bran scrutinized them with his empathy, truth-reading the two, and what he saw surprised him more than anything else had over the last two, rather astonishing days.

"They've both told you the truth as they know it," Bran said, desperately trying to think of a way to phrase it so what he was about to say would sound like a normal occurrence, which it most certainly was not. "Like most untrained mages, Wynn used his magic but doesn't realize it. With my healing-sight, I can tell he did cast lightning today, but he's truly not aware he did so. Jules couldn't tell he had because he was knocked out—you know how head injuries affect your ability.

"Wynn's use of earth-magic depleted his chi nearly completely, and with his new augmentations, it shouldn't have, unless it wasn't the only spell he'd cast. He feels like lightning to my healing-senses—the way you do after a major working, Dorn. He's nearly recovered now, and he truly did have the chi to do both spells. He must have inadvertently infused his arrows with lightning, though he didn't know it."

"I should have let you fix me so I couldn't use it," Wynn muttered, his face scarlet. "All I did was *wish* the arrow was a bolt of lightning...." He was suddenly frightened. If he'd done such a thing unintentionally with only a wish, what other mayhem would he be capable of? And then there was the issue of his broken promise. Grasping Bran's arm, he pleaded, "I've never broken a promise before, never in my life. You must fix me—today! I don't want it to happen again. What if it happens in my sleep?"

Bran looked at Wynn, surprised by the intensity of his distress.

Jules didn't feel too sympathetic at the moment. "If it happens in your sleep, there'll be a pile of dead friendly-girls in your room," he said, rolling his eyes. "That could be tough to explain to the local constable."

As usual, Wynn didn't hear the sarcasm in Jules's statement. "Exactly! How would I explain such a thing? Even worse, how would I explain it to my father?"

Dorn and Bertte both stared at him and then burst out laughing so hard they nearly fell off their bench.

Bran's mouth twitched in an effort to contain himself, but he too succumbed to the urge to howl at Wynn's plight. "Oh Goddess. He's even worse than you were, Dorn!"

"See? This is what I've been dealing with for the last three days," Jules muttered, red-faced as he too began snickering. "And you all wonder why I'm ready to bite someone."

For a moment, Wynn wasn't sure what he'd said that was so funny, but after he thought about it, his face burned and he looked away. "I'm an idiot. I'm the bloody village idiot," he mumbled. Eventually, the hoots of laughter at his expense subsided.

In the end, Bran took pity on him, patting his shoulder. "Don't worry, lover-boy. I'll set the restriction on you so you can't sense or use lightning. Someone will remove it when you get to Aeoven." He spoke with hardly a trace of a giggle. Wynn breathed a huge sigh of relief as a feeling of warmth settled over him. "All done. You won't have to worry about it anymore." Bran's reassurance comforted him.

Abbott Dorn had been scribbling and now checked his notes. "Untrained...we just don't see too many of them nowadays." Just as Bran had hoped, he nodded his head sagely. "Every child knows the famous story of the mage who was able to imbue his weapon with magic, though it was a sword of fire, as opposed to lightning-arrows. One of your early great-grandsires, Wynn. It's a true story and led to the founding of the college. Aelfrid and his sword of fire." He made some more notes and then said to Wynn, "Well then, if you can remember how you did it, you'd have a useful trick in your arsenal. Lightning-infused arrows would be quite useful against every water-elemental you'll likely meet and not a few other beasties. Except, of course, waterdrakes. Arrows just bounce off them. But we never see them nowadays, so.... Well, you two need to head off to Ragat the day after tomorrow. It's a two-day journey, Wynn. Rall will meet you there, and he'll give you some instruction in shielding." Dorn turned to Jules, "How is he coming along with the sword?"

"He hasn't cut himself yet," Jules replied. "I suppose I can work with him this afternoon after our lunch settles. His father also trained him to use blades properly, although he didn't have access to a sword. My right arm isn't feeling up to it, but I need to work out with my left hand anyway."

As lunch progressed, the others became engaged in a hot debate over something Wynn couldn't quite follow involving someone named Feia, and coming along on top of all that had happened, their bickering overwhelmed him. Wynn suddenly needed to go someplace private and think about things. He thought longingly of his room at the inn. Quietly standing as the argument heated up, he tried to slip away, hoping to make himself as unobtrusive as he could.

He'd nearly made it past the abbott when Dorn's hand shot out and grabbed his arm in a surprisingly steely grip. "I'm a lightning-mage too, Wynn. I know exactly what's going through your mind right now. You feel like running, don't you? You need to get off by yourself and calm down, right?" Wynn nodded mutely, the look in his eyes reminiscent of a hunted deer. "The urge to flee from petty quarrels and silly drama is normal for a lightning-mage. We all feel the same way in situations such as this. I know it's too much for you and your nerves are shattered, but you have to stay. I need to talk to you about your arrows and what you were thinking at the exact moment you fired them into the beast. You may have a career in the armory. I'll talk to the master armorer, Kaye, about this." He gestured for Wynn to sit beside him at the table.

The others nodded approvingly. "Good idea, boss," Jules murmured, making Bran's lips twitch in a smile again.

"I intended to get apprenticed to a smith when I was younger, but my dad got sick and needed my help, and now I'm too old," Wynn replied, his desire to escape completely forgotten. He sat down next to Dorn, wholly interested in hearing what the abbott had to say. "How can I get an apprenticeship with this armory?"

"You'll see when you get to Aeoven and are measured for your armor," said Dorn. "Probably the day after you get to town."

After Wynn had answered every question twice, the abbott rose from the table and suggested to Bertte they discuss their plans for hunting for the water-wraith's mate. "We'll have to get the constable to find a good tracker to help us since the squad is out of the Temple right now. Can't let it roam loose now, can we? Jules and Wynn have to leave, so it's just you and me, dear. Besides, we've killed a few of them before, remember? You shake them up with your earth-magic, and I zap them back to hell where they belong." They both giggled as they went back inside the Temple.

After the door shut behind them, Bran looked at Jules. "You were out of line earlier. You need to work harder at pretending some humility, Jules. I don't know what's gotten into you, but you've got to hide your dissatisfaction better."

"I know, and thank you. I've just had a rough couple of days, Bran. You can't imagine what it's been like. I'm sure Wynn is at the end of his rope too. He's been having all this fun right alongside me and he's not used to the way things work here." Jules smiled tiredly at Wynn, who just nodded. "It's just so frustrating dealing with Dorn and Bertte. How are they ever going to…never mind. Take care of them if you can." He looked out of the corner of his eye at Wynn, who felt completely bewildered and looked it.

"You need to look beyond what they let you see, Jules. They'll take care of the beast's mate, and it'll be done by the time you return—*if* you return," Bran assured Jules. "You may find yourself posted elsewhere soon. Just because they're plump and lazy doesn't mean they aren't capable. Bertte is the quintessential earth-mage and is damned good at her work, for all she clucks around here like an old hen. They fought Bregat and won, don't forget."

Jules struggled to look convinced and failed miserably. "*He* should be instructing Wynn now, not waiting for Feia the Magnificent to bestow her presence upon us. It just feeds her ego. She'll be even more convinced she is irreplaceable."

Bran grinned maliciously, saying, "Believe me, Jules, in a mage-duel, Dorn is perfectly capable of zapping Feia into a corner and leaving her to lick her wounds if he chooses to. However, Dorn is brilliant as a lightning-mage, but he is the worst instructor and he knows it. Feia is an excellent teacher despite her other failings. And, just so you know, Dorn may claim to have never blown up a boulder but only because he never saw a reason to exert himself. What he *does* excel at is finding young mages, and his administrative skills are without peer. Everything that's been done to get our Temple and facilities here in Armat built so quickly has happened because *he* made it happen." He paused, thinking. "I traveled with the three of them, Liam, Kaye, and Dorn. They escorted me to Widge for my first posting, and a dangerous trek it was in those days, taking nearly a month. Trust me, Dorn isn't as incompetent as he pretends, and Bertte's magic is as sharp as her tongue. They'll kill their water-wraith and do it effortlessly. It's just the way they are, brilliant and lazy. Mother Relynne knows their frailties as well as their strengths. She gave them this particular post because they're the only ones who could get the task done this far out in the wilds."

Wynn heard nothing Jules and Bran were saying.

He sat gazing at the sky, wondering at the horrible turn his life had taken. He was quite subdued for the rest of the afternoon and didn't really perk up even when they worked on his swordsmanship, although he paid close attention.

However, once they arrived back at the Lying Dog, had their dinner, and a few ales had passed his lips, Wynn soon forgot his troubles. He enjoyed the companionship of the friendly-girls, leaving Jules to play a game of stones with Bran until the common room closed for the evening. Jules wasn't really surprised and had become somewhat used to being ignored by the fickle women of Armat, although it didn't improve his attitude, as Bran sourly pointed out.

"You've no reason to be judgmental about him, Jules. You're in for a surprise of your own when you get back to Aeoven, you know." Bran picked up the stones and board, preparing to depart for his own home after having whipped Jules's butt at his favorite game. "You're so distracted a mere healer just kicked your arse!"

"What surprise?" asked Jules suspiciously, ignoring Bran's taunt. "What's been going on behind my back?"

"Oh, no. I'm not spoiling it! But I will ask you this—what makes you think you have the right to act like a pleasure-boy in every common room you come to and then sit in judgment on Wynn for doing exactly the same thing you've been doing for the last six months?" Bran headed for the door and turned back. "My daughter, Lorana, is quite good friends with Aneka, as you may remember. She, Aneka, and Seri are like sisters. The three of them talk about everything, Jules.

Everything. My daughter is a kind girl and regularly writes to her widowed father, telling me the gossip of the old town.

"So here's a little something you need to know— Dorn is not the only person who travels to Aeoven regularly. He has been surprisingly reticent about your behavior, even defending you. But there are many who are not as fond of you as he is and who would love to see you humbled. You might want to think about your good fortune having a friend like Dorn."

When Jules went up to his room, he was unable to fall asleep due to the churning of both his stomach and his conscience. *Bran is right...I'm a jackass.* He sat at his little table writing and rewriting letter after letter to Aneka, but even to him, each attempt just looked like a pathetic attempt to curry favor and just ended up in the wastebasket.

About the time the friendly-girls were saying their wistful goodbyes to Wynn and tiptoeing down the hall, Jules fell asleep, exhausted and as miserable as he'd ever been.

◆◆◆

They spent all the next day working on Wynn's magic and sword abilities while they waited for their leathers to be cleaned and returned to them. Jules developed a real fondness for him, despite the changes he had brought to his comfortable existence, and they laughed often as the country boy tried to learn the ways of his new world. That evening went the same way as the previous night, with Wynn happily monopolizing the girls and Jules brooding about having destroyed his chances with Aneka.

The morning of Wynn's fifth day in Neveyah, they

walked out of Armat's east gate, taking the trade road. They marched as quickly as they could through the gradually lightening dawn.

Each time they stopped, Wynn called the water for them to drink and used his earth-magic to dig the privy pit. Then he called fire to make their tea, and when they made ready to leave, he filled in the privy pit and smothered the fire, again using earth-magic. He did the same when they made camp at dusk. He was relieved to find he couldn't even sense lightning and applied himself to his other lessons with a will.

Jules instructed him in sword techniques as they walked, and often they would stop and he would show Wynn a particular move. Privately, Jules felt he was a serious contender as a battle-mage. *He's going to shake things up when he gets to Aeoven, in more ways than the obvious.* A crafty smile crossed his face as he thought of how he could use Wynn and his skills to the best advantage. *Rall and I might be able to make a little money off of him, backing him in mage-duels.*

Betting on mage-duels was not officially sanctioned, but status within the elemental-magic side of the clergy was often determined by the outcome of a battle. At the highest level, known as the "clash-for-coins" group, money changed hands at every privately arranged match. Dueling was the way the clergy entertained themselves.

Early in the afternoon of their second day out of Armat, they entered Ragat. Just inside the western gate, a wooden building leaned over the cobbled street, and a nearly illegible sign swung in the breeze over the rickety steps. The paint was peeling and faded. After looking at it long enough, Wynn could just barely make out the words "Murfee's Public House" over a picture of an ale keg. Wearily, they walked up the steps of the inn and settled their kits in their rooms. To Wynn's relief, Murfee's Public House was much nicer on the inside than on the outside, surprisingly clean and tidy, and Mr. Murfee was quite welcoming, glad to have their business.

Chapter 8

One of the four baths was already occupied when Wynn and Jules entered. Lounging in a steaming tub and dozing was an unusually striking man with white-blond hair. A blue lightning bolt and several runes for strength and wisdom stood out on his face. Multiple Temple augmentations completely covered his torso, arms and neck. He opened one moody blue eye and said lazily, "Where have you two been? I've been here since Restday." The man was huge, much larger than anyone Wynn had ever seen. His heavy braid trailed over the edge of the tub and coiled on the floor.

"Rall! I thought we would have to wait for you, now that you're a bonded man and all," Jules said, with a wicked glint in his eye. "Why are you here early instead of spending the extra days practicing making babies?" The two men undressed and got into the steaming tubs the attendant had filled for them.

Rall abruptly sat up and poured more hot water into his tub from the little kettle that sat on the table next to his heavily tattooed, muscular arm. "What? Are you daft?" He rolled his eyes. "She tried to knife me on our wedding night. There's seldom a truce in the bedroom for us, I am afraid." He slid back down and put his flannel over his face, pretending to sleep. Lifting the cloth and glaring at Jules, he said, "*We* will not be having any children, I guarantee you. She wants to grill me slowly over an open fire for having referred to future offspring when the seneschal assigned us our house. That's why I left two days early—she needed to cool down a bit." The cloth dropped back down over his eyes. "I've stayed busy here. I sent a youngster back to Aeoven on this morning's mail coach. The girl will be a fire-mage, I'm sure of it. I set the restrictions on her."

"Whatever made you refer to possible children? Feia's the sort who eats her young," Jules replied. Wynn just looked from one to the other, somewhat nonplussed by their conversation.

"It was a moment of temporary insanity. The seneschal pointed out a room for a nice nursery, and I agreed politely. She took it to mean I was expecting her to be a broodmare." Rall spoke from under his flannel.

"Why did you bond with her anyway? You didn't have to. No one has arranged bondings anymore," Jules said in an exasperated tone. "You just *had* to go and do it in the Einar Temple too, in front of everyone, you bloody idiot. It looked like a feast day, you had so many witnesses."

"Shut it, Jules! I don't need your sarcasm. For Einar, it *was* a feast day. Perhaps you don't remember the blood feud," Rall muttered into his flannel. "Try going against the wishes of an entire village sometime. The bonding settles the feud, end of story." He sounded like a man who had told the tale one time too many. "Of course, I did what they wanted me to do. It's not like I ever had a choice, once I took the vows to protect Neveyah. At least, because of the way she felt about me and our situation, I managed to put it off for two years. But now I'm a tenured adept, so I had no excuse." He took the flannel off his face and changed the subject, looking at them with a wry grin on his face. "So what took you and pretty-boy so long to get here?"

"They made pretty-boy here get some decorations on his beauteous self before we could leave Armat."

Jules told the story as sarcastically as he could. "But first he had to sleep with every girl in town, and then he felt compelled to blow up a boulder, which was fun, although we all had to bleed profusely over it." Rall raised an eyebrow. "Then we had to stay an extra day to rescue a boy from a water-wraith, a task that involved arrows infused with poison oak and accidental lightning. And last but not least, Wynn had to make love to every friendly-girl in Armat three more times, but first he had to get Bran to set restrictions on him so he didn't accidentally zap them to heaven in a moment of unguarded passion. It all took time."

Wynn choked and turned red.

Rall stared at Wynn.

"Ah…. I don't really feel too pretty right now. Tired and dirty, but not too pretty," he said, with an apologetic smile. "My name is Wynn Farmer, and yes, the girls in Armat are quite friendly, and it's true I don't have much control over anything, *especially* girls or lightning yet." He reddened again but continued, "I'm glad to meet you, Rall, despite your troubles. Unlike Mr. Grumpy there, I *do* understand duty. It sounds like you did the only thing you could under the circumstances, although I don't know your whole story. I've heard you're one of my teachers."

"Grumpy! Anyone would be grumpy after what I've been through over the last six days," Jules replied with mock disgust. "I'm quite miserable here, so let's have some sympathy."

Rall sat looking from Jules to Wynn. His attempt to glare at Jules was ruined by his tendency to laugh. "What an amazingly complicated jumble of events you spewed there, Mr. Grumpy. And whether you admit to it or not, Wynn, you are quite pretty for a warrior. Can you fight?"

"When I have to, I guess. I don't like fighting," Wynn shrugged. "When I was still in school, I had to sometimes. Well, a lot actually. It wasn't ever my idea, but for some reason, guys just want to fight me. I don't know why." A stubborn look crossed Wynn's normally agreeable face. "I don't let them win."

Rall nodded and slid back down in his tub.

"He did kill the water-wraith with an arrow, but other than that, he hasn't had much opportunity to show off his skills." Jules's offhand remark was calculated to get Rall's attention, and it did. "But wait 'til you see him in action in the common room. He hogs all the women and won't share. It's disgusting."

Wynn didn't know how to respond, so he just lathered his hair and ignored Jules. *I didn't realize I was taking Jules's girls. He must be mad at me, but he never said.*

"I'm a bonded man. Friendly-girls don't concern me," Rall muttered piously. "It does explain why *you* are so grumpy and why guys like to fight him for no reason." He looked at Wynn, both eyebrows raised. "How the hell do you kill a water-wraith with an arrow?"

Jules cut in. "Like I said, first he wiped the arrows on a poison oak bush, and then he imagined they were bolts of lightning. Soon his water-wraith was melting and stinking to the high heavens." He smirked at Wynn.

Wynn rolled his eyes and shrugged, saying, "I don't really know how it happened. I didn't mean to do it. I swear I only wished my arrows were lightning when I saw the thing come out of its den." He ducked his soapy head under the water and sitting up, he wiped his face with his flannel. "I keep my promises, Jules. Anyway, I made Bran fix me so I can't accidentally do it again. And I won't take all the friendly-girls. I didn't realize I was hogging them."

Rall burst out laughing and so did Jules, saying "Ah—I'm swearing off friendly-girls now. You can have them for all I care. I have enough explaining to do when I get back to Aeoven as it is."

"Oh, yes, indeedy-doo, Jules, my friend! You have a *lot* of explaining to do, from what I hear." Rall looked from him to Wynn and back again, still chuckling at Jules, who winced and sank down in his tub, feeling nauseated. Seeing his chagrin, Rall laughed wickedly.

Later, Jules and Rall sat listening to the bard sing a rousing epic tale, quietly discussing their student, who had been dragged away by the pack of eager friendly-girls.

"I have to admit I've never seen anything like it," Rall said, perplexed. "Once they saw him, they had absolutely no ability to see anyone else. Even the bonded women couldn't keep their eyes off of him. The friendly-girls swarmed him. I hope he has plenty of stamina, because they certainly have plans."

"Apparently he's more than up to the task. The women in Armat are still weeping over his departure. He's somewhat legendary there," Jules muttered. "Did I finish telling you what happened when I tested him for lightning? You remember the boulder in the garden that Bertte was always nagging at us to move?"

Rall nodded, sipping his ale. His notebook lay open, his pencil at the ready.

"Well, it has definitely been moved," and Jules proceeded to explain what happened.

"Now you've met him, you see what I mean. I warn you, don't say anything around him you don't want to have made public at some later time, because he's quite likely to blurt it out at an inopportune moment. Some of the things he says without thinking first are pretty hilarious. It's a trait that might have irritated his father if he's always been like this, since his dad is a water-mage. I understand they don't get along well, but he loves him fiercely and is worried about him and their farm. The old man is in bad health, and from what Wynn says, it's kidney trouble." Jules looked pointedly at Rall. "It sounds to me like the curse of the water-mage, though his father seems too young to be as bad as Wynn says he is. But they don't have healers there, only herb-doctors. Wynn's mother is ill too."

Uncomfortable with the topic, Rall nodded. "I hear what you're trying to tell me. We have no choice but to do what we do, and no one knows how to prevent it. Besides, fire-mages have their own troubles to look forward to, so take care yourself when casting your element, my brother." Rall changed the subject, making notes as he talked, a habit he'd developed since his first journeyman appointment. "So he comprehends the basic principle of focus and visualization and uses it instinctively, but had never heard of magic before coming here. He was fully trained in the use of blades, despite the local prohibition on peasants owning swords."

Setting his pencil aside, Rall stared into his ale for a moment. "For myself, I wish Feia wasn't involved in this, but I can see she's the only one to train him in his element. She's a dedicated instructor, and he'll learn more from her than he would from anyone else." He sighed morosely. "The problem is, I can't seem to appease her at all. I'm trying to stay out of her way, hoping she'll forget she hates me if she doesn't have to see me too often. She's the angriest person I've ever met, and it's all directed at me because she had no say. Do you understand? The elders chose me for her. If we're apart often enough, she can be cordial when we *do* see each other."

"She didn't have to bond with you," Jules said quietly. "She could have told them where to shove the whole thing, and frankly, I'm surprised she didn't. Maidenly compliance is not like our Feia at all. She was always the angriest person, even when we were novices, and *you* were always the cause because of that stupid arranged bonding hanging over your heads."

"She's not as bad as she wants us all to think she is," Rall said, with some defensiveness. "She's actually a rather traditional person and is proud of our heritage and what it means. Honor is everything in our culture, which is how the whole blood feud began. When we became journeymen, we took the vows to place the welfare of Neveyah ahead of our own wishes, and we both meant them with all our hearts. Like me, Feia feels if our bonding will bring peace to our village, it's worth the sacrifice. So many innocent people from both sides have died over that ghastly, obscene feud, Jules."

"But still...forcing you to bond with someone, just to make the village happy...I don't see how that could happen, even if you *do* each represent the two most powerful clans." Jules couldn't comprehend it.

Rall groped for his words, trying to explain. "You didn't grow up there. You can't imagine what it was like. Revenge murder after revenge murder, and no one ever feeling truly avenged, because of the retribution from the other side that was sure to follow. All those deaths couldn't stop the feud, but our bonding has settled it once and for all. We don't even have to live in the same house if she doesn't want to. I didn't insist on the geas of fidelity—she's free to do as she wishes. I've made it clear to her that I won't protest if she has 'friends' as long as she's circumspect about it and word doesn't get back to Einar. For her, nothing has changed."

Jules caught the slight emphasis on the words "for her." "But it sounds like everything has changed for you." Jules looked closely at Rall and saw uncertainty and pain, but couldn't help him. "Unlike me, you don't even miss the company of our favorite friendly-girls."

"Yes, well, I meant the bonding vows when I made them," Rall muttered. For a brief moment, the emotional storm raging within him showed starkly in his eyes, surprising Jules by its intensity. Rall immediately buried it again under his usual serene exterior. "I did what I had to do, and I'll stick by it. Some days it's worth it, Jules, and those days make all the difference."

He looked at Jules out of the corner of his eye. "Your exploits in Armat have gained you a somewhat legendary status among the younger journeymen in Aeoven. But don't worry. Aneka hasn't been lonely either. Between them, she and Seri have cut a wide swath through the journeymen. Neither lady is seen breakfasting on Restday mornings with the same lucky man more than once. But you know how Seri is, she'll never settle down. According to Feia, she's waiting for some knight in shining armor to sweep her off her feet, as if that's really going to happen. But you've lost your chance with Aneka, my friend. You've messed it up beyond saving."

"Who? I'll fry them!" Jules spoke too loudly. Everyone turned to see what he was talking about. Embarrassed, he tried to tone it down. "Who's been playing up to my girl while I've been gone? Devyn D'Mal—it's him, isn't it? It's always him, trying to steal my girls. He was my friend, and...." He was suddenly seething with jealousy and several other nameless emotions he was not equipped to deal with. "Tell me who."

"I'm not naming names, you idiot," Rall replied, enjoying Jules's discomfort immensely. "You have to work with them. You'll do something stupid, and then where will you be? You should have asked her to be your wife before you left town. She would gladly have agreed to it then, but you have missed your opportunity. She's had nearly as many lovers as you since you left. How will you measure up against the competition? Arne Severnsson daily begs her to be his bride, and he's not even once been seen breakfasting with her. Aneka is leaning toward accepting his proposal, I think. Quite honestly, Jules, in comparison to Arne, you look like a selfish moron who is only out for yourself and what you can get." A wicked smile crossed his face as he added, "She refused Devyn quite publicly, which I must admit I enjoyed watching immensely. But you have no room to talk, my brother. You're considered every bit as much a jackass as Devyn D'Mal is."

Jules's face went white with rage, but he forced himself to sit calmly while Rall told him the ugly truth. Finally, he had himself under control enough to be civil to his oldest and dearest friend. "Devyn was a brother to me, even if we didn't live well together. All right, so he threw me out. I survived. But I trusted him, and now I find that the minute I left town, he cozied up to Aneka. I can still rectify my mistakes and, believe me, I will, just as soon as I see her again." The now-familiar feeling of shame and dread mixed with fear soured his stomach. "Seeing the way the friendly-girls are around Wynn has made me realize exactly what a jackass I've been."

◆◆◆

The next morning, the three mages left Ragat, once again traveling in the dark hours before dawn. As they walked, they discussed shielding, and Rall began teaching Wynn how to raise the battle shields that would save his life.

"Many creatures that aren't really dangerous will strike at you with an elemental spell if they're startled or disturbed in their nests. And there's always the occasional rogue-mage to deal with, though we hope to have them completely eradicated soon. You must have the ability to raise battle-shields quickly and accurately."

Rall demonstrated to Wynn the correct way to erect a basic, all-purpose shield. "This by itself will protect you from most magic-wielding creatures. Just picture the air making an invisible barrier over you. You must clearly visualize the air forming a shield. You will layer your elemental shields over this."

Wynn did as he was instructed, managing a wobbly

but fair shield. Rall prodded at it magically and then said, "This is a good beginning, but you must have no gaps whatsoever."

Wynn gasped as a sharp zing from Rall's magic prod broke through. The whole shield disintegrated. "Ah…sorry. Let me do it again," he mumbled. "It's slippery, isn't it?"

Rall laughed and agreed, though he'd never thought of it that way. Once Wynn had become proficient at building the basic shield, Rall showed him how to raise a water-shield by calling water, just a scant palm-full, showing him how to make the small amount into a shield that would repel attacks. "The first shield you will learn is the water-shield because it's the easiest element to build with. Most mages learn to toss one up fairly quickly, as long as they've become good at keeping the basic shield up at all times." Rall watched while Wynn struggled to make it, not at all surprised he learned the skill on his second try.

"This brings us to the difficult part of shielding. You must maintain the basic shield at all times, *and* you must watch your chi because the shield is a slight but constant drain on it. Also, if you're not careful, the basic shield will fade and you will be caught without. It takes precious time to put a full shield up from scratch, so it's important to never let it fail." Rall grinned wickedly as he added, "For the rest of your life, I will be testing your shields randomly, even when we're not actually working together. You'll never know what to expect or when to expect it, so be prepared."

After a while, Rall decided to throw his student into the river, so to speak, feeling that nothing was more educational than cold, wet knowledge. "Each time you feel a mage begin to call water, you must raise this shield as quickly as you can, because speed is the only hope you have of avoiding being suddenly drenched or worse, being knocked off your feet with a large-spell attack. I'll demonstrate a few for you here, and we'll test your shield against a small-spell, such as a minor elemental might cast. Water-sprites are the sneakiest because you can stumble onto their nests with no warning. They're harmless but annoying, and they don't like lightning-mages."

Using an unsuspecting sapling as his victim, Rall showed Wynn the four main attacks in the water-mage's arsenal from novice to adept level. "Each of these spells varies in intensity from mage to mage, but I can assure you they're quite effective in compromising your enemy's mobility and confusing a group of attackers so that you or your party can sweep in with weapons and defeat them.

"Your father was quite well known for being able to cast large, multiparty spells with great effectiveness. I too am rather effective when I put my mind to it," Rall said with a smile. He negligently dropped what seemed a river's worth of water on the poor sapling. Wynn's eyes were as wide as any child's, causing Jules to laugh at him.

"And Rall is known to be humble in regard to his abilities too!" Jules mocked. Rall just shrugged and grinned.

Wynn despised the magic jab that accompanied his failures, hating it so much he quickly learned how to avoid it. Privately, he suspected Rall enjoyed dousing him with icy water but didn't hold it against him, accepting the surprisingly cold reprimand for what it was.

The day approached noon, and Wynn had grown used to being somewhat wet and bedraggled. They stopped at a roadside campsite, intending to have a quick lunch of bread and cheese. Rall was occupied rooting around in his kit, digging out their food, when a group of four raggedly-dressed half-men ambushed them, seemingly out of nowhere.

Wynn had barely pulled his sword out of its sheath before Rall and Jules had taken care of two of them. He managed to kill one, feeling a small sense of surprise that the skills his father had taught him were so easily adapted to the sword. He didn't want to slay the creature, but it kept attacking him, though it had suffered grievous wounds. Finally, he was forced to kill it because the maddened thing left him no choice.

"Who are they?" asked Wynn. "I've never seen anything like these people." They were half his height, almost like humans, but with ratlike faces. They were all male and had no weapons but the vicious claws on their four-fingered hands. They were dressed in clothes that had been worn to rags and the disorganized, chaotic way they behaved during their attack indicated they were not in possession of their minds.

"I've never seen anything like them," Jules said, kneeling by one of the bodies. "They seem familiar, but I'm sure I've never seen people like them before." He looked up at Rall, whose face had gone white, as if he'd seen a ghost. "Rall? Are you okay?"

"Ariend's children," Rall said, as his shocked, blue eyes met Jules's dark ones. "These are the God Ariend's people. Their ratlike appearance and madness are part of what Tauron inflicted on the men of their society. But this is an impossibility! What they could be doing here on the plains of Neveyah is beyond me. The air down here is too thick and heavy. To breathe it is like drowning for them. But if we were to go to even the lowest of their towns, we would die from the thinness of the air."

Rall knelt beside Wynn and looked closely at the dead creature. "Something has changed them. Their hair has begun to fall out, and look at their claws— they're blue-tinged." Rall's amazement was shaded by a deep sadness. "These men could never hold a pen with their hands deformed like this. They're scholars and scientists, a gentle people who completely shun violence—they don't even eat meat." His blue eyes looked off toward the east where snowcapped mountains reared into the sky. "I fear this change. The Bull God is able to manipulate Ariend's children because he took nearly half of Cascadia when he imprisoned their god. Those people whose mountains are now a part of Serende *can* be changed by Tauron. Through them, he can affect all of Ariend's children."

"Imprisoned? I always heard he *murdered* Ariend," Jules said with surprise. "How can Tauron affect us here? His people can't cross the veil between Mal Evol and Serende."

Rall rose and walked away, beckoning Jules to follow him.

"Ariend's children can and do cross the veil between the two worlds." Rall spoke softly so Wynn couldn't hear. He felt almost sick at the realization. "They cross in the highest reaches of the Mountains of the Moon because their land exists in two worlds, Neveyah and Serende. They have remained in contact with the far villages, and young men are often sent to be husbands on either side of the veil. They are very few in number, thanks to Tauron's decimation, and worry greatly about inbreeding. Their head-women have remained in contact with each other and carefully work to ensure their people are not weakened by such."

Jules whispered to Rall, "Why am I only now hearing that Ariend is imprisoned? We're taught that the tale in the Book of Life is an allegory. The Temple teaches that he was murdered."

"He lives but is imprisoned. Think about it, Jules. What could a rogue-mage do if he got his hands on Ariend's prison? He or she could take Neveyah for the Bull God." Rall looked at him expectantly. "Consider the actual teachings in the Book of Life. Of course the truth is a Temple secret. It must be held close—my wife doesn't know this secret, nor can you share it with yours, should you ever be so fortunate as to have one." Shocked, Jules laid his hand on his heart, swearing himself to absolute secrecy.

Still speaking in a whisper, Rall glanced over at Wynn, who still picked through the pockets of the dead, completely absorbed in his own thoughts and not hearing a word they said. "You're on the high road to an abbacy, though you don't realize it. You need to know what you're fighting for." He met and held Jules's gaze. "And you need to know *what* you're defending with your life. This is why you were chosen for this task." Rall gestured toward Wynn. "The other half of this equation is the secret that lies in the Keep of Mal Evol and the *other* bloodline we're sworn to defend with our lives."

Jules ignored Rall's comment about the abbacy,

intent on the problem at hand. "Tauron wants nothing more than to gain custody of Ariend's prison," he said, finally. "He uses the broken minds of our rogue-mages to wear away at Aeos's rule here in Neveyah." In his mind's eye, Jules saw the Keep of Mal Evol, slightly rundown and standing solitary among the vast vineyards of the royal family in an out-of-the-way corner of the great valley.

The sudden understanding of what lay hidden in the old keep that stood in the lonely, rural north of Mal Evol brought Jules to his knees. "Oh, Goddess...the Throne of Stone and Bone. Ariend's prison." Comprehension of what Rall was attempting to discreetly tell him dawned in his eyes. "Devyn's brother, King Daxyn. In the prophecies, the Lords of D'Mal are always referred to as the Keepers. Now I understand why. They guard the secret with their lives and their children's lives." Both men's eyes turned toward Wynn, who closely examined the fingernails of one of the dead. A silent acknowledgement regarding his heritage passed between them. "Abbott Dorn explained to me that Wynn was taken out of Neveyah for his safety and that in the prophecies, his bloodline is referred to as the Vine That Was Planted." Jules's dark eyes were filled with uncertainty. "*Now* I understand what the primary task of the clergy is. We're *not* here simply to chase down rogue-mages. We do what we must, but those duties are secondary to our true purpose. We have two very important families to protect, and we must ensure the Throne of Stone and Bone remains hidden in obscurity." His mind spun for a moment. "But now you must tell me what you know of what's happened here." He indicated the four dead men.

"You've met their kind in the high reaches—I remember hearing some of what happened. Dalis, Vere, and Rylen died on that quest, and you nearly did too."

Rall nodded. He hated the mention of his first quest because it had gone so horribly wrong. "Fortunately for Ariend's Children, Tauron's minotaurs can't survive in the high altitudes either, so the mountain people remain relatively unmolested."

Rall walked back to where Wynn still examined the corpses. He knelt next to the body of the first attacker he'd killed, picking up the bloody hand, feeling inexpressibly sad. "Unfortunately, Tauron has dominion over those who remain on his side of the veil that divides the worlds. Through them, he has a foot in our door. Now something has changed, something that affects the balance of power, and I don't like it." He stared into the distance, seeing nothing, his mind completely occupied with the conundrum of the dead men.

Wynn's voice pulled him back. "I've found some things of interest in their pockets." Spread on the ground before him were a small book written in a foreign language, several unfamiliar coins, and an assortment of snails and small pebbles, things a curious child might have in his pockets. "Though these people are strange to me, I can tell these men were prosperous and educated. I don't believe they were highwaymen. Judging from their behavior when they attacked us and from what I've discovered by searching the bodies, I would say they were in the grip of some form of madness. Perhaps they ate some of the wrong mushrooms by mistake, the sort that send you mad before you die." He spoke seriously, with the voice of sad experience. "They're all young males around our age. Their clothes are expensive and finely made, but they've been worn day and night for weeks, to the point of being rags now." He lifted the arm of one of the bodies so Rall could better see the sleeve with its tiny stitchwork and elaborate decorations.

Turning the dead face toward Rall, Wynn said, "They're starved. See how thin they are? And look, their lips are bluish, and so is the skin under their nails where the claw begins." Wynn opened the eye of one of the men so Rall could see red spots on the whites of his eye. "These people were struggling to breathe, as if they suffered from some sort of pneumonia. They would have died, perhaps within hours, if they hadn't gone mad and attacked us."

Rall replied, "I don't know much about them, but they certainly behaved as if they suffered from some madness, though what caused it, I've no idea. They're too young for it to be the curse that affects their old men." Grimly, Rall looked at the emaciated bodies. "Running into one of them could be considered an anomaly. Four is too much of a coincidence. Yet here are four very young men, far from their mountain home, where they should never be able to breathe, any more than I can breathe submerged in a river. We must bury them with some respect. They were strangers in our land."

◆◆◆

They were a somber group as they trudged through the gates of Wister, but Jules began perking up immediately as the Lion's Share Inn came into view at the far end of the long boulevard. "The baths here are a joy to end all joys," he told Wynn. "Hot springs to soak in and the best food outside of Aeoven—this is what I've been waiting for all day."

"You're right," said Rall, as his steps began to quicken. "The baths here are the best in all of Neveyah!"

"Ha! You value a good bath more than you do anything else, Rall!" Jules walked even faster, pretending to be trying to get there first. "You'd spend your whole life in one if they'd let you."

"Wait up, you two!" Wynn found himself almost running to keep up with them. "I like a good bath as much as anyone but not enough to run myself to death for it! Slow down!"

"Last one to the porch buys the first round of ale," shouted Jules over his shoulder at Rall, walking as fast as he could.

Rall immediately quickened his steps to get ahead of Jules.

"Wait! I have no money, remember? Oh, heck, no one is listening to me." Wynn took off running, passing both Rall and Jules, who immediately gave chase. He easily beat them to the porch and stood there waiting.

Rall arrived at the porch with Jules hot on his heels, who stood gasping and out of breath. "What was that all about?" Both men were red in the face and breathing heavily. Jules gasped, "What made you decide to run down the street like your boots were on fire?"

"Well, you said the last one here has to buy the first round of ale. I don't have any money, remember?"

"It was a joke, you idiot! It was a joke." Jules leaned against the porch railing, trying to get his breath back. "The Temple pays for everything. I don't have any money either!"

"Oh. So I didn't have to hurry after all. You're a little out of shape, Jules," Wynn said solicitously. "You should probably run more often."

Jules's eyes bulged, and his face turned red as he tried to think of a smart remark and failed.

Rall leaned against a column, laughing so hard his sides hurt. "Don't kill him, please! You did say the last one here had to pay!" Jules glared at him. Tears streamed down Rall's face as he slumped with his back against the column, hooting. Finally, Jules had to laugh too, while Wynn was left to wonder what he'd missed.

Chapter 9

Only one room was available for the three of them. Wister was the nearest town to Aeoven, and a lot of people were traveling on Temple business. Indeed, the innkeeper seemed quite harried when he assigned them their room. Quickly stowing their gear, they soon found themselves soaking blissfully in the men's baths.

At last clean and in a much better mood, they entered the common room, finding it quite full. They stopped at the bar to get their ale. Rall saw that a few tables toward the back were still open, so they made their way through the throng. As they worked their way to the empty tables, the crowd gave way before Rall. His height and massive, muscular frame proclaimed his barbarian heritage. Beaded feathers were braided into his exotic, white-blonde hair, left loose over his shoulders to dry and hanging nearly to his knees. Although he wore Temple leathers, to Wynn's eyes he looked foreign and quite intimidating.

Both Jules and Rall were intent on enjoying the evening, but as they rounded a pillar their good mood faded upon seeing a lovely, dark-haired woman wearing red and brown leathers. She waved to them, beckoning them to come over to her table. Rall and Jules both stiffened. Jules muttered, "Oh Goddess. It's Aneka. And guess what? Your wife is sitting there with her. We're both in for it now. I'm probably a dead man."

"You certainly are," Rall said, without moving his lips, "Oh heck. I see her." He forced himself to remain outwardly calm. "She hasn't seen me for more than a week. She might be in a better mood." He smiled warmly at the ladies as they made their way through the throng. "It could happen."

"You're such a dreamer," Jules answered, smiling widely.

As they approached the table, Wynn saw that the woman who had beckoned was seated with a stunningly beautiful lightning-mage. She had abundant, curling hair of deep mahogany and flashing dark eyes and wore white leathers with red and yellow accents that gave her an exotic appearance. A third woman sat at the table, a healer wearing leathers of several shades of green.

Despite the flamboyant beauty of the two darker-haired mages, the woman who caught Wynn's attention was the healer. Long, honey-colored hair and warm, brown eyes sparkling over a shy smile captivated him. Her eyes met his, and suddenly Wynn Farmer was speechless. The room disappeared, and a bell rang through Wynn's mind and soul as he locked eyes with Seri Aronsdottir. The bell echoed, connecting them and consuming them with an exquisite joy, divinely blessed. The joyous ringing was inaudible to the others, who remained unaware of the earth-shattering event Wynn and Seri experienced as they first set eyes on one another. Without speaking a word, each one knew beyond a shadow of a doubt that for them there would be no other ever again.

Wynn boldly inserted himself next to the healer as if he belonged there. Startled, the other two men took his cue, seating themselves accordingly. He was oblivious to the look of surprise on the others' faces as he slipped between Aneka and Seri, nor did he hear the mahogany-haired lightning-mage say waspishly to Rall, "Hello, husband. I suppose this is your student?"

Jules quickly seated himself between him and

Aneka, with a glare at Wynn's temerity. Absently, Wynn shifted closer to Seri at Jules's prodding.

Rall simply nodded and said pleasantly, "He is indeed, wife. Jules can tell you all about him. I only just met him two days ago myself." He then addressed himself to his mug of ale.

"I suppose for the sake of appearances you must move your things to my room." Feia tossed her head and looked away from Rall.

"If that is your wish," Rall agreed blandly.

Jules finally got Wynn's distracted attention and introduced everyone.

The pretty girl in red and brown leathers was Aneka, an earth-mage. She said, "We're escorting Seri back to Aeoven, and then in a week or so, we're to escort her to her post in Arlen. She's being transferred from Wister to Arlen and needs protection from the brigands who seem to haunt the roads in the area." Aneka spoke with a lilt and a slight accent, proclaiming her as from the most southern part of Neveyah, the area around Farmington. The look she gave Jules was enigmatic, and he seemed slightly uncomfortable under it. "They're preying on healers since they don't fight back and usually carry valuable medicines. Feia and I volunteered since we're between postings."

"She'll be well protected then." Rall shifted in his seat, unsure of his footing with his wife. "Jules tells me a pair of water-wraiths has been bothering folks on the Rangle south of Armat. He and Wynn killed one but didn't see its mate, though Wynn said the tracks indicated the beast wasn't alone."

Jules nodded. "Dorn and Bertte have most likely taken care of it by now." After a derisive snort from

Feia, who had a low opinion of Dorn, a moment of silence fell around the table.

Wynn stared raptly at Seri, unable to speak. His ribs suddenly received a jab from Jules. "Oh, ah…my name is Wynn Farmer. I'm rather new, so…." His wonderstruck eyes found their way back to Seri, and he fell silent again.

Meanwhile, the friendly-girls had found their way over to the table and were all standing behind Wynn, who didn't notice. The only woman he could see at all was sitting next to him, looking back with the most beautiful brown eyes he'd ever seen.

One daring beauty glared at the ladies at the table and boldly asked Wynn to dance, tugging on his hand.

"No, thank you, ma'am," Wynn said, absently pulling his hand free and turning his rapt gaze back to Seri.

Jules and Rall exchanged a meaningful glance, eyes wide and mouths hanging open.

"Shoo, silly girls! These men don't need your services," Feia said sharply. "Hunt elsewhere!"

Jules was about to make a smart remark when Rall's elbow caught him in the ribs. Instead he said, "Hello, Aneka. How have you been?"

"She's just fine and doesn't need you anymore, so forget her." Feia's voice grated, and Jules cringed at the sharp tones. "She has much better prospects than a womanizer like you, Jules Brendsson! You'd be amazed at the number of decent, hardworking men with bright futures who, unlike you, daily beg for her hand. They value her as you never did."

Jules looked at her, feeling like she'd gut-punched him. The pained look on his face surprised her.

"Oh, lay off him, Feia." Aneka smiled lazily at Jules. "I've missed you, Jules." He brightened and smiled his charming best. She continued, "But not enough to overlook some of the things we've been hearing about your exploits off in the lonely west. Perhaps a letter would have been nice, back in the beginning."

Jules's smile faded, and his stomach nearly turned over. "Um…I know. I'm really bad at writing letters. I didn't even get around to writing to my own mother."

"Now, why does that not surprise me?" murmured Aneka, looking at him out of the corner of her eye. "But you've been awfully busy. Or so we hear." Jules's face turned red, and he was at a complete loss for words.

Feia had all the words Jules lacked. "I should hope you would *not* overlook his behavior, Aneka," she said in her superior way. "Jules, you are nothing but a pleasure-boy, I swear! Your trousers come off for any woman the moment ale passes your lips!" Jules choked and started to make a retort, but she plowed right over him. "And just who is this bumpkin gawking at Seri like he's never seen a woman before?"

"Oh, trust me, he's seen women before," Jules muttered, red-faced. "*He's* the pleasure-boy at this table!"

Wynn was unaware of Jules's comment. In fact, he was oblivious to everything except the girl next to him.

A determined friendly-girl tapped on Wynn's shoulder, and again he brushed her hand away.

"Will you leave us?" Feia's eyes snapped, and her voice was loud enough that heads turned in their direction. "Take your hand off him. He's obviously not interested!" The woman glared at Feia and moved off.

Soon the bar was lined with friendly-girls, all of whom stared at Wynn with hot, hungry eyes. He didn't seem to notice. "Have they never seen a country lout?" Feia's irritation was apparent, but even her gaze as she looked at Wynn was openly appreciative, as was Aneka's.

Both women sat staring slightly slack-jawed at Wynn and pretending not to. "I must say, he is rather handsome in a country sort of way." Aneka's comment drew an angry hiss from Jules. "Oh, my. This man does have some charisma!"

Feia also sat smiling faintly with a speculative look in her eye. "He's quite pretty to look at," she said absently, unaware she'd spoken at all.

A sudden stab of pure jealousy pierced Rall's heart at her comment, and he looked down at his mug, gripping it as if he would crush it. Jules noticed the whiteness of his knuckles and shifted nervously.

Wynn and Seri stared raptly at each other, completely ignorant of the hostile climate at their table. Indeed, they appeared unaware they were even *at* a table with other people. Wynn offered her his hand to shake, intending to introduce himself but forgot what he was going to say. Seri took it, staring into his eyes.

"Seri, what's your new posting in Arlen?" Jules attempted to get the conversation rolling at their strangely awkward-feeling table. Unbidden, the memory of Wynn saying, "Guys just like to fight me for some reason" came to mind.

Seri gazed at Wynn, not hearing Jules's question.

He tried again. "Seri?"

She looked blankly at him and then back to Wynn.

Both Feia and Aneka blatantly ogled Wynn, each one pretending to be taking his measure. "Hmmm,"

Aneka said in an offhand way that didn't fool Jules at all.

"He doesn't seem at all warrior-like. Is he a fighter?" Feia unconsciously rested her chin on her hand as she looked admiringly at Wynn.

Jealous hostility openly seethed in Rall's gaze. His pewter mug hit the table. All pretense of civility was forgotten. Icy blue eyes glared at Wynn, who only saw the girl with honey-brown hair.

Abruptly, Jules rapped on the table, trying to get the waitress's attention. Everyone looked at him except for Wynn and Seri. "Over here," he beckoned wildly. They gave their orders to the waitress, and then he said sharply, "Oh, do stop drooling, Feia. He's not pretty. Aneka—he's obviously in lust with Seri. You aren't interested in him. He looks like a badly-dressed friendly-girl, and he's as stupid as a stump to boot—Rall, how about a song?" He dropped his head into his hands. "Aeos, help me. This is like trying to round up water-sprites."

Dimly sensing hostility nearby, Seri automatically raised her hand and cast "calm" toward Rall without taking her eyes off Wynn. As the spell took effect, Rall stared at her in shock and suddenly flushed as he realized he'd been displaying his jealousy for everyone to see. Jules breathed a sigh of relief.

Wynn, of course, was completely absorbed with looking at Seri, who only had eyes for him. "You have the most amazing eyes, ma'am. I could fall into them forever." He now held her hand as if it were the most precious object in the world.

Again, Jules tried to gain control of the situation. "Feia, Wynn can actually fight rather well. He did kill a water-wraith with only his bow, and he's already reliably casting water, fire, and earth after only four days of instruction." With a wicked glint in his eye, he said, "He had to get augmented in Armat, so Dorn had me attempt to show him how to call a cat-zapper in the courtyard of the Temple with rather surprising results."

"We ran into Nolen. He was spouting nonsense about some new mage exploding a boulder," Feia said, reluctantly tearing her eyes away from Wynn. "It's ridiculous. No one can do such a thing, especially a novice. I assumed Fat Dorn was exaggerating as usual to make himself look better."

"Oh, Dorn isn't so bad. He's quite good at what he does, and in this case, you've assumed wrongly." Jules knew he sounded snide but felt an obstinate desire to defend Dorn to the impossible woman. "If you look closely at our leathers, you'll see the holes where the shards got us, and we were clear across the garden from the boulder. Bran spent much of his chi healing us." As he knew she would, Feia stood up and looked closely at their clothes to see they did bear the marks of the incident.

She made a rude noise. "It takes a special person to teach visualization, and *you* are not the one for the task, Jules," Feia said in superior tones. "You don't teach magic like sword fighting. Magic is an art, with specific rules and parameters. It takes delicacy. We do not randomly bludgeon things to death with it."

"Oh, goodness me! You are more than welcome to test your theories on Wynn Farmer, and I hope you're prepared for it." Smiling broadly, Jules spoke in the most agreeable tones he could find. "I know my own limitations, and I'm definitely in over my head with *this* student. But all is not lost, Feia, my friend—*you* have been selected as his instructor in magic once he arrives in Aeoven. My task was simply to keep his chi balanced and to get him to at least try to call every element so they could get him augmented. But now with you here, I can relax and concentrate on working on his sword-arm, while you get on with teaching him magic." His eyes danced, and he smiled winningly at her.

She looked at him suspiciously. "Why? What's wrong with him? What makes you unable to teach him? I'm far too busy to take on students you're too lazy to teach." Feia glared briefly at Jules and then went back to staring at Wynn.

He fought down the urge to blast her with his best fire-spell. Rall laid his hand on Jules's arm in warning.

Fortunately, their food arrived just then.

Deciding to steer the subject to safer territory, Rall said, "Perhaps we four can play a game of stones tonight. I am sure *they* won't be too interested in joining us." Rall indicated Wynn and Seri with a jerk of his head. They had progressed to introducing themselves to each other, stammering and blushing all the way, still oblivious to the rest of the table. Their food sat untouched before them. Seri still held Wynn's hand, or he held hers. It was hard to tell.

"Oh Goddess, here we go," Jules's voice was low. "You know what Dorn said about him. I don't know how, but he knew. He told me it would happen immediately, but I didn't believe him. Dorn as much as told me Liam had kept Wynn hidden on the farm so he would make it here without a wife and child in Ariend, to meet the girl Aeos had selected for him."

"You may be right," Rall muttered. "Abbess Lera told me his parents were bonded practically the day they met."

"According to Dorn, this is the way it always is," replied Jules, stunned at seeing Dorn's assertions proven before his eyes. "The Goddess created them for each other. They'll be bonded as soon as we get to Aeoven. Dorn told me so."

"You're right, my brother. They have definitely found each other. But he stirs up trouble with absolutely no effort on his part." A look of chagrin crossed Rall's handsome features. "Oh Goddess. A few minutes ago I actually wanted to—never mind," he said, as Jules looked knowingly at him, commiserating with his baser urges. "I'm still just a barbarian after all." Rall gazed at Feia with an inscrutable look.

Feia and Aneka both shook their heads, confused and looking wonderingly at Wynn and Seri, who only saw each other. "She's done for," Feia muttered. "I suppose she'll be his next victim. Or he'll be hers. She has absolutely no morals. She's worse than Aneka...ow!" She rubbed her leg where Aneka's delicate boot had kicked her. "Well, it's the truth. You behave worse than friendly-girls, both of you."

"On the subject of Wynn and Seri, I will disagree with you, wife. She will be the love of his life," Rall told her, certain now of what he was saying. "We have just seen a prophecy fulfilled, history in the making. I will explain it to you somewhere less public." He indicated the crowded room, and Feia nodded reluctantly, understanding he was going to impart a Temple secret to her. He *never* threw words like "prophecy fulfilled" around lightly. She wasn't used to seeing this aspect of Rall. Actually, she avoided seeing any aspect of him if she could, but…he seemed quite sure of himself.

Against her will, Feia was intrigued.

Chapter 10

Jules passed the door to Rall and Feia's room, following Aneka into hers although she'd not invited him, closing the door behind him. They had left Wynn and Seri in the common room, and the love-struck pair had not even noticed.

Although Jules had followed her into her room, Aneka clearly had not decided yet if he was going to stay there or not. She said, "Did you see what I saw down there in the common room tonight? I swear those two fell in love the minute they laid eyes on each other. You could almost hear their hearts beating." She crossed to the window, gazing at the full moon. He stood behind her and eased his arms around her. A nearly overwhelming sense of having come home swept over him. Instinctively, he tightened his embrace, overwhelmed by an intense desire to bury his face in her hair, closing his eyes against the feeling.

Twining his fingers in her long, dark hair, he repeated what Dorn had told him about Wynn's lineage and Aeos' approach to matchmaking. Aneka just said, "Lucky them, to be able to fall in love and have no need of a geas of fidelity to ensure their happiness."

The needle hit home. Not wanting to face that sore spot, Jules turned his thoughts to the trip Aneka, Seri, and Feia were to make from Aeoven to Arlen. A surge of protectiveness took him by surprise. "Be careful on your journey." His voice caught in his throat, and he held her close. "Something big is about to happen, and it involves Wynn Farmer or he wouldn't be here in Neveyah. I don't want you caught up in it with only Feia to guard your back. She relies too heavily on her magic and her sharp tongue. The silly woman refuses to learn any real weapons skills, and she'd pick a fight with a firedrake. Those sharp knives she's so fond of are no match for what's out there, Aneka. Some strange, bad things are happening right now." He held her as if he could somehow guard her. "I don't want to lose you. I couldn't take it."

A derisive laugh burst from her. "Hah! Don't be ridiculous. You've nothing to worry about—you did that a long time ago." She couldn't believe Jules felt anything other than friendly affection and simple lust for her. "Besides, Feia's bark is worse than her bite, but she'll die before admitting it. Wynn and Seri...I saw the way those friendly-girls hovered over him all evening, no matter how many times Feia told them to move on."

"They can't help it. The free women won't leave him alone."

Aneka's voice had a note of wonder to it. "I thought Feia was going to bring out her knives there toward the end of the evening. I can't blame the friendly-girls, really. They have little sense of propriety, and they were just doing what every girl who sees him wants to do." A note of appreciation colored her voice as she added, "He really is something else."

Jules's voice displayed his envy despite his effort to keep it neutral. "You should have seen him in Armat and then again in Ragat. The friendly-girls, all of them, swarmed him, and he made close friends with them all."

"Well then, he'll be able to keep up with Seri. I swear the girl has no conscience, but I've never seen her like this, ever," she said, slowly shaking her head. "She keeps them at arm's length, not letting them stay close to her for more than a mere moment's dallying and perhaps, if they're really fortunate, a night."

"Two weeks ago, Wynn had never been off the farm and was completely ignorant about women. But he got educated in a big way when he walked into the common room in Armat. And don't pretend you weren't gawking at him just like all the rest of the women, prim and proper Feia included. You were ogling him blatantly," Jules said sharply. "I meant it when I said he behaves like a pleasure-boy." He sounded pious, even to himself, and didn't care.

Aneka, however, didn't like his tone of voice. "So what if I was ogling him? I'm a free woman, as you well know! After all, *you* made sure of that. Wynn is nice to look at, but he's completely smitten with our Seri. I don't get involved in others' affairs." She turned and looked up at Jules, seeing undisguised jealousy in his face.

Smiling at his discomfort, she turned back to look at the moon again. "You're jealous of him, you disgusting hypocrite. I began hearing about all your girlfriends in Wister and Ragat almost the day you left—and then I was told about the women in Armat. I heard the details from multiple sources, so don't you dare criticize Wynn and his lack of morals." A sharp stab of satisfaction shot through her as she felt him cringe at her words. "Your own morals are completely lacking." She was overreacting and knew it, but somehow she couldn't stop.

Jules gaped at her, feeling somewhat like a landed fish, a sensation he'd begun to have quite often lately.

"Spare me your shocked disbelief. I know exactly what your problem is. Because of him, you've been without a woman for more than a week." She turned in his arms and looked up at him. "We both know the reason you're trying to make up with me, and now *you* know I'm not under any illusions about you," she said, with a mocking smile.

He pulled away from her with a look of surprise and consternation on his face.

"What's wrong? Are you suddenly too tired for romance tonight? What's happened to the man who claims to be the world's most passionate lover?" Aneka turned to staring out the window again, her back to Jules. "There's a crowd of friendly-girls in this town who would gladly jump on you just to work off their lust for Wynn."

"I don't want friendly-girls." He stood, dismayed and unable to think of a graceful way out of his predicament. Finally, he opted for the truth. "You're right, I've behaved badly. And you're also correct that I am totally disgusting. Believe me, you have no idea just how disgusting I am. And you're dead-on that I am completely jealous of Wynn, never more so than when I saw *you* staring at him as if you wanted to leap on him in the middle of the common room." He turned her to face him. "Do you really want to know my passion? I'll show you passion! You love me despite my failings, don't you?" He kissed her. "Don't you?" He smiled as her arms went around him, feeling a deep sense of relief. Hope shone like a beacon in the night.

Confused by her mixed feelings, Aneka said derisively, "Oh, no, Jules. I'm not stupid enough to fall in love with you again. I know you far too well to be fooled by your glib tongue."

Her words silenced him, as if his heart had stopped.

"No. No, you're lying to me." He stroked her hair, looking into the darkness outside the window, seeking an answer from the moon, though he received none. Her words did upset him, far more than he wanted to admit. In fact, they made him burn inside, a seething combination of fear and jealous anger. "You love me—I know you do. You just want me to suffer because I hurt you so badly."

Jules's lack of communication and neglect of her after he'd left Aeoven the previous winter rose in her memory, as raw and bloody as if it had just happened, making Aneka glad she'd hurt him. Her slight accent grew thicker, and her voice became harsh from her pent-up pain and anger. "You never want what you have, Jules Brendsson. You had *me*. With all my heart, I loved you. But you weren't satisfied, no! You wanted to have all the other women in Neveyah too. I loved you, Jules. I loved you, and you kept me dangling all winter until I finally got over you. I know exactly what you're up to now—I won't let you into my heart again."

Jules felt frozen. Neither his mind nor his lips would work properly. He'd expected her to be angry, but he was unprepared for this depth of resentment and pain. He'd stupidly believed they would agree he was a jackass and then kiss and make up. Somehow, he thought they would decide to start over, and then everything would be fine. He'd had no idea of how deeply she'd been hurt by his ignorant inability to just be a man and settle down with the one woman he'd ever loved.

She continued tearing him down. "I *like* you despite your past cruelties toward me. You will always be dear to me as a friend and coworker, or perhaps even occasionally as a lover. I'm just not going to fall for your lies again, is all. You need to be honest about this. What you and I have is a loose, open-ended relationship, just the way you like it. There are no strings attached, and certainly, I'm happier this way." There was acid in her bitter tones. "I have you to thank for my attitude toward men."

Jules had no way to express what he was feeling at that moment.

Smiling at his dismay, she said deliberately, "I confess I do enjoy you in bed though, more than any other lover. You're good at what you do. You apply yourself to the task with a will and rarely leave your lucky partner unsatisfied." She enjoyed hearing his sharp intake of breath.

"Other lovers," he said, and stopped, unable to continue. He'd been told, but deep-down, he'd not believed it.

"Of course I've had other lovers, you silly man! I'm a woman, and I'm not made of stone! However, not every man is as diligent in matters of the bedroom as you are. That's why I didn't turn you away downstairs." She was lying—she'd let him into her room because she was an idiot, and she knew it, but seeing him suffer at her words made her feel so good. "Lovers with knowledge and technique are rare. And I too have been alone for the last few nights. You may stay if you wish, but let's be honest about what we have between us. You want to make love to me, and yes, I admit I want to make love to you. But then, just like a pleasure-boy, you'll return to your room, and we'll pretend it never happened. It will be our dirty little secret. Otherwise, the friendly-girls are waiting for you, and there will be other lovers for me."

"What other lovers?" he asked sharply, his worst fears confirmed. "No, don't tell me. I'll be so much happier not knowing. And I will *not* leave before dawn as if you were dirt! Besides, you're done with sampling the men of Aeoven as if they were so many sweets on a tray. You've not been any less promiscuous than me. I too hear stories!"

"So what?" Aneka started to speak, but he silenced her again, laying his fingers on her lips, making her gasp with outrage.

"Aneka, no, listen to me, please! I know it's my own fault for not being completely honest with you and for being unfaithful. I know you would never have turned to anyone else if I'd only been truthful with you in the first place and committed to a permanent bonding. But we can start over tonight and begin fresh the way we should have done. I swear you are my only lover from this night onward. I promise. And in return, I am your only lover from now on, Aneka." He kissed her gently, his hands stroking her. "Tell me I'm the only one!" He kissed her throat in such a way she found herself leaning to meet his caresses. Jules felt the quickening of her pulse as she responded to his passion and pressed his advantage. "Tell me I'm the only one!" His lips found their way to her earlobe and back to her shoulder. "Say it was a lie. Please, say you do still love me."

At her silence, his heart sank. "Tell me your silence is only because you want to hurt me for all the pain I've caused you." Jules's low voice took on a note of pleading. "Please, Aneka. Tell me I am the only one for you."

Suddenly, the rage and the remembered humiliation Jules aroused in Aneka became too much to take. She tried to push him away, but he wouldn't let her. The ache in her voice hurt him. Her voice rose with each word until she was shouting. "You left me, and you didn't look back, Jules, you bloody beast!" Her fists pounded on his chest, and he gasped at the intensity of her rage. "Not a letter, not even a weekend trip home on the mail coach! You left me and hurt me, after everyone had warned me that I was just another notch on your belt, and I didn't believe them! So I got over you in the only way I could and still hold my head up. I filled the void with empty affairs, looking for something, anything, to replace you. Better men than you, Jules! Men who *want* to treat me well for the rest of my life, despite the fact I'm every bit as despicable as you are. I can't trust them, and I certainly can't trust myself. And by taking *you* back, I'm getting everything I deserve, believe me."

Jules felt as if his heart had stopped, and his arms tightened around her, afraid she would pull away from him again.

"All right, Jules, yes. I *will* let you into my heart again." Jules relaxed, his lips caressing her shoulder, but she shrugged him off. Her voice turned as hard as stone. "If I take you back, you had better be completely faithful to me, Jules Brendsson, no matter what the circumstances, or I swear I'll bury your body deeper than even Abbess Lera can find with her second sight. And you know I have the magic to do it!" She pulled away from him and dropped onto her bed, barely able to contain her rage.

Lying on the blankets next to her, Jules's kisses

clouded her judgment exactly as they had always done. Abruptly, she pushed him away. "I don't doubt your passion, Jules. Passion rules you. What I doubt is your convenient love for me. Tomorrow, will I wake up and find you gone? If that happens, then all I'll have is the memory of how you lied in order to spend the night with me, and I believed you despite my own best judgment. I swear I'll never forgive you if that happens." She turned away from him, facing the wall and dashing her angry tears away, her hand shaking with the intensity of her fury.

The ringing silence was harsher than her words had been.

Finally, Jules pulled his wits together enough to try to pick up the pieces of his life. "No, Aneka. I'm never going to treat you with anything less than the love and respect you deserve. I swear I am a changed man," Jules vowed with absolute conviction. "I will be there every morning for the rest of your life. I swear by everything I hold holy, I will never hurt you again."

Her storm of anger had subsided. Aneka sighed miserably and said, "Don't say such things. I would prefer you had just said you wanted to keep it casual. Then at least I could pretend I don't care when I hear about your randy adventures with each and every one of the bloody friendly-girls in every Temple town in Neveyah!" Her voice had become loud again. Warily suspecting she had gone too far, she wondered if he was just going to leave her now instead of waiting until after he'd gotten what he wanted. Hot tears poured down her cheeks.

After a long moment trying to pull himself together, Jules knew what he wanted to tell her, wanting her to believe him with all his heart. "Aneka, please look at me. I'm trying to be honest with you." She turned and saw raw emotion on his face—regret, love, and fear all clearly written on his handsome features. "I should never have left our relationship hanging like I did. Rall is right. I've been a complete jackass, and if I've truly lost you over this, I have only got myself to blame." Jules's voice was rough with his own guilt. "Please give me a chance to prove I'm serious when I tell you I love you."

He closed his eyes in frustration, not knowing how to express his true feelings. "Of course, I intended to make love to you tonight. But that doesn't matter anymore. What does matter is I love you, and I want to be your husband. I want us to have a life together." He smiled a sad, hopeful, worried smile that touched her despite her fervent wish to keep him at arm's length emotionally. "Even before Wynn came and showed me what I looked like, I had realized how much I do value you, so much more than I ever thought possible. When I imagine my future, I see myself with you, as your husband."

Unwillingly, Aneka saw naked honesty in his eyes.

"You can't possibly know how much I hoped you would *not* find out about my behavior, because somewhere along the line, I discovered I missed you, loved you, and couldn't get you out of my mind." His voice caught as he admitted, "But by then, it was too late for me to change what I'd already done. I will never be the same if I lose you over my own gross stupidity."

Aneka stared into the dark, not sure what he meant by his torrent of words. During the entire previous summer they had been together, Jules had never once uttered "I love you" or "I want to be your husband," and now he'd said both those things in one sentence.

She knew she shouldn't trust him. She wanted to believe him, but there was too much pain between them.

Finally, she said, "Why don't we sleep on it tonight and see if you still feel the same way tomorrow." Her voice said she doubted he would. "Just hold me. That's all I really want from you tonight."

"I love you, Aneka. I'll prove it, you'll see," Jules said, holding her hand and willing her to believe him. "I'll make you believe me, tomorrow and every day after, I promise. I swear it."

"That is exactly what I'm afraid of, Jules. I'll believe you, and you will have gotten what you wanted. Then your next away-posting will be the end of us again," Aneka said bitterly. "Don't make any promises to me."

Jules held her as she sobbed her anger and heartache out. Lying on the bed fully clothed, he tried to comfort Aneka as she cried herself to sleep, leaving him lying awake in the darkness, alone with his thoughts and self-blame. He continued holding her as she slept, unable to let her go and unable to sleep, sick to death of himself and the ruin he'd made of his life. Just after she drifted off, he heard the sounds of Rall and Feia making love in the room next door. Their passion didn't touch him; he was lost in the labyrinth of his own mind. Somehow he had to salvage the mess he'd made of things but was at a complete loss as to what he could do.

The answer came after hours of soul-searching and

self-recrimination. *I know what we have to do,* he thought, just before he dozed off. *I just have to convince her to do it.*

◆◆◆

The muffled sounds of a bitter argument coming from Aneka's room next door had finally subsided. Seri's room was silent. Rall carefully sat on the edge of his side of the bed with his back to his wife, reading over the notes in his journal, making sure he had written everything down exactly as it had happened over the last few days. He added a footnote about the history of Wynn's family and what he'd witnessed when Wynn and Seri locked eyes for the first time. His pencil made a slight scratching noise.

He most carefully did *not* look at his wife as she undressed. They'd already had the usual extremely polite conversation about his being an oversexed barbarian who would remain on his side of the bed, and he had agreed with everything she said, in an effort to keep the fragile peace.

"Tell me again what Jules told you about Wynn's father," Feia demanded, as she brushed her hair. "Wynn cannot possibly be so far advanced with his ability to visualize what he wants the magic to do. Jules is far too easygoing to make an effective teacher, and no one has seen Liam Farmer in years. From what I heard, he disliked teaching. He turned down the offer of an abbacy so he could retire to raise sheep somewhere in the wilds." She turned to see if Rall was looking at her despite her admonition never to watch her as she undressed (he wasn't) and resumed her rant. "He turned his back on his vows by leaving Neveyah."

"He didn't actually leave Neveyah. The veil shifted

after he took his family back to Markett," Rall said blandly, not wanting to start a fight right before sleep. "Dorn feels Aeos and the Almighty Father intended to separate their family from their fame so they could be relatively unknown and perhaps more effective." He paused politely so Feia could make a rude noise expressing her opinion of Dorn's opinion and then continued. "Liam apparently felt the college at Aeoven was too hidebound in its teachings. I don't know why. Dorn quested with him when they fought the rogue-mage, Bregat." Rall was careful to phrase his remarks in as non-threatening a fashion as possible.

"*Fat Dorn* was their lightning-mage?" Feia's voice was incredulous. "They rescued a kidnapped girl and took down a waterdrake, or so Pallia told us." She snorted her derision. "He must not have been so fat then, eh?"

"As you say, he must have been much more slender," Rall yawned. Without asking if he was done journaling, Feia extinguished the light, the signal he could lie down and go to sleep. *I'm mortally tired,* he thought, as he shut his journal and placed it on the stand by his side of the bed. The light of the moon shone in through the window, lighting the room well enough for him to see his way around. As he lay down and pulled the blankets over himself, he yawned again. "Happy dreams, Feia."

He was just dozing off when he felt her breath on his ear as she whispered, "I wonder what Jules and Aneka are doing right now, husband. Perhaps I could show you...." Her hand caressed his chest, and he felt her nakedness as she pressed herself along the length of his body.

Wide awake now and fully aroused, Rall turned to meet her, his hands stroking her back. He kissed her throat, caressing the silky mass of her hair as it tumbled over her shoulder, and she responded, rising to meet his kisses. Without reservation, Rall gave himself up to the moment, relishing the knowledge she hungered after the over-sexed barbarian that lurked within him every bit as much as he yearned for her.

Toward dawn, Rall lay utterly spent in Feia's arms, marveling at the many facets of the woman who was his wife. He never knew from one night to the next if it would be a knife in his ribs or a night of passion with Feia, but he prized her to the point of obsession and always had. Her anger, her spite, her temperamental ways, it was all worth it just to have one night with the real woman who lay hidden underneath her mask of arrogant resentment, the armor that protected her from the world.

Of course, if he was stupid enough to tell her he loved her passionately and had since the day they were sent to the Temple as novices, she *would* stick her knife into his ribs. He fell asleep, smiling.

Feia too lay smiling, unable to hide her triumph, savoring the way their skin felt, slick with sweat and smelling of sex. Her mind replayed over and over the moment and the feeling of power as his release had roared through them both. Her desire for Rall was her one weakness, the chink in her armor. Feia thought she might be in love with him despite all her efforts to the contrary. She didn't know how it had happened, but somehow she would have to deal with it. She loathed admitting she desired the man she'd been forced to accept. It was a vulnerability, and she couldn't allow herself to appear weak. Still, she thought it was worth it for a night like the one they had just experienced. She sighed in contentment as she drifted off to sleep.

♦♦♦

Wynn sat in the common room holding Seri's hand. The others had gone their separate ways, and the two of them knew they should also get to sleep since they had an early departure planned for the next morning. "I don't want to say goodnight." The longing in Wynn's voice expressed his reluctance better than his words. "It's already nine o'clock, and we have to be up early. But now I've found you, I know what I've been waiting for my whole life. Tonight, everything fell into place. The rest of my life is mixed up—I'm without a home, and I don't know what waits for me in Aeoven. The only thing I know for sure is that tonight all the pieces of the puzzle came together, and I can face whatever comes along. Now I know why I'm here."

"I feel the same way." Seri's voice was soft and melodic. "It never occurred to me I would actually meet someone like you. I always dreamed of it but never believed it would really happen!" Wynn found her laugh exceedingly attractive as she confessed, "I've been like a ship without a rudder. Mothers warn their sons to stay away from girls like me, girls who don't know what they want and flit from one man to the next, always looking for the prince who will sweep them off their feet." She blushed and looked down. "To be honest, even though it doesn't reflect well on me, I've always been attracted to danger and pleasure-boys."

"I'm glad you're honest," Wynn said wryly. "It's too good to be true, hearing you feel the same way that I feel about you. But you're not alone being attracted to

145

the wild side of life. Jules has been frank in his disapproval of my behavior over the last few days, and I've earned it."

Seri laughed, saying "You must be quite the bad-boy if Jules, of *all* people, disapproves of your behavior. He's not at all well-behaved himself!"

"I did take his friendly-girls, but it was an accident. And then he found them all in my room," Wynn admitted awkwardly, blushing. "You don't even want to know."

Pretending to be shocked, Seri said, "That *is* naughty. No wonder he was so prim and proper this evening! He was jealous!"

Hand in hand, they went up the stairs, hearing low voices as they passed first Aneka and Jules's, and then Rall and Feia's room. At the door to Seri's, he leaned down to kiss her without even thinking about the proprieties of it, and she responded by kissing him like he'd never been kissed before, leaving his knees weak. His voice shook as he said, "I should leave you. We have to get going early, and you don't know me. How would you know if I'm a scoundrel or not?"

The sounds of Aneka and Jules having a bitter discussion came through the walls, sounding clearly in the hallway, Aneka's tones scathing and Jules's voice pleading.

"I'm a healer, Wynn. I know these things." Seri took his hand. "Why should we be the only ones sleeping alone tonight? This is about so much more than pleasure. Come and talk to me. Tell me everything about you and how you came to be here."

"You won't believe me when I tell you this because it sounds like a clumsy lie, even to me. It isn't

146

for pleasure I want to stay with you, though I admit I do want you in that way. I just want to *be* with you and never part from you again." Wynn's honest reply took her breath away. "But I don't want to use you the way I have the friendly-girls. I'm embarrassed and sorry for the way I've behaved toward them."

"I understand friendly-girls quite well," Seri admitted. "Feia frequently says I'd spend all my nights behaving like one if I had the chance. But now I could never go back to my old ways. I can never even think of anyone else in that way again."

"Friendly-girls are only searching for true love, I think. They're sure the next boy will be the one, like me thinking the next friendly-girl would somehow be the right one," said Wynn. "Jules was right. They used me as a pleasure-boy, and I encouraged them." He suddenly felt mortified, although why he was embarrassed by it, he didn't know. "I don't want to use you. I love you."

"I've left a lot of wreckage behind me, good men who really wanted to make a life with me," Seri replied sadly. "But I couldn't settle down. I tried, but now I've been seen breakfasting with too many men for anyone to take me seriously, and you'll have to work with them all when we get back. I will tell you who I've not been seen breakfasting with. Rall and Jules are not former lovers of mine. I never poach on another girl's territory."

"Breakfasting?" Wynn asked, confused. "Who watches you eat breakfast?"

Seri giggled as she replied, "I thought it was strange too when I first came to the Temple. Unbonded journeymen all eat in the Temple dining hall because no one in the bachelor quarters has a kitchen or time to cook," or she told him. "To be seen breakfasting with someone implies you have an understanding with them, and others assume you're sharing a bed and they don't interfere."

"We don't have any customs like that where I come from. If you're together for a year and a day, only then can you be bonded," replied Wynn. "But we all have kitchens." Seri laughed at him, and he held her closer. "You do know if you are ever a healer in Armat and Ragat, you will most likely meet my friendly-girls. Be kind to them when you do. They're good people."

"They're frequently my patients, Wynn. I know them all. I'm glad you understand them too." She inadvertently yawned and quickly apologized.

"No, you're tired. We both need rest," said Wynn, laughing. "I promise to behave if you do."

Fully clothed, they lay on top of the blankets in each other's arms, embracing in the dark and talking frankly about their families, their childhoods, and their lives. Toward dawn, Wynn covered them both with the quilt. He lay wide awake listening to her breathing as she began to drift off to sleep.

His mind spun with the possibilities, but one thing was clear. He knew without a doubt what he had to do. He drew her closer, whispering into her hair, "Will you be my wife? You'll have to give up your lovers. I don't share well."

"Of course I will, silly man. But you're done entertaining friendly-girls." Seri's voice was sleepy. "I won't share you either!"

"I was done with them the minute I laid eyes on you, Seri. I've been waiting all my life for you," he murmured. "I'll just stay away from the common rooms, if that's what it takes." He laughed, feeling somewhat chagrined. "Now I know why my father avoided them."

"I trust you, Wynn," Seri replied. "I can tell with my healing empathy you'll be a good and faithful husband." She smiled contentedly, and her voice trailed off as she said, "Feia will never believe we didn't make love." Her breathing slowed, and she drifted off to sleep.

Neither will Jules. Wynn thought. He smiled wickedly, sure Jules was not sleeping alone either. He lay there luxuriating in the deep contentment that suffused him, wide awake and enjoying the sounds of the birds as they began their dawn chorus. Through the window, he watched as the stars faded and the sky gradually changed color from a deep rosy pink to a brilliant blue with the light of the rising sun.

◆◆◆

The three men met in the bathhouse, where they brushed their teeth and gave themselves a quick wash. Jules found himself staring at the bites and scratches on Rall's body. He was about to mention them to him with some mocking comment but jumped when he received a jab from an elbow in the ribs. Catching Jules's eyes meaningfully, Wynn shook his head. Realizing the farm boy had a point, he pretended not to notice the visible evidence of what he'd inadvertently overheard the night before.

In the women's bath, Feia was quite disheveled and spent a great deal of time repairing her hair. She was unwilling to admit she'd enjoyed every minute of her reunion with her husband, but whenever she forgot to school her expression to a frown, she would find herself smiling.

Aneka was exceptionally quiet and refused to meet her eyes, which, of course, Feia didn't notice.

Seri was completely preoccupied with the momentous thing that had happened when she met Wynn and saw nothing at all odd in her friends' demeanor. All three women were pale and tired-looking as they finally arrived at the table for breakfast. The men looked no better, with the exception of Wynn, who looked like he just had the best night's sleep in his life.

Rall had an inscrutable look about him. He knew Feia had enjoyed their lovemaking. He'd made it his business to ensure her pleasure several times before he had finally sought his own release in her arms. Just remembering her passion aroused him again, and he had to think strongly about other things to control his errant body, as his leathers were just a little too revealing. Still, he found himself smiling faintly.

Regardless of what had passed between them in the dark of their room, Feia pointedly ignored him, just as he had expected she would, and displayed her usual temperamental self to the others. For some reason, her behavior just made him smile even more widely.

Wynn and Seri held hands at every opportunity, unable to stop themselves, causing Feia to roll her eyes and mutter, "Good grief! Is he that good in the sheets? She can't take her hands off him! This is not like her at all. She usually boots them out before dawn."

Their food arrived, and Seri said, "We have a favor to ask. We're going to register our bonding this morning before we leave Wister. Will you be our witnesses?"

The table was silent as the couple's companions stared at them.

Jules looked from Wynn to Seri and back. "Wynn, two weeks ago, you'd never even talked to a girl. Then you spent six nights with I-can't-count-how-many friendly-girls. Normal people don't have that many fingers." Wynn blushed, nodding, but let Jules continue. "Now you want to bond with Seri after sleeping with her for one night? Be reasonable. You just met her. Seri is our friend, and we don't want her hurt, understand?" Aneka glared at him sharply. Jules flushed and looked down at his hands. "Please, trust my judgment in that regard."

"We need each other more than I can explain," replied Seri. "I love you all for caring. You'll never know how much it means to me, Jules. I know you care for us both, but Wynn hasn't been alone in his bad behavior. People will be looking at me with harsh, judgmental eyes when we get back to Aeoven. But we intend to be bonded this morning, and we want you to be with us."

Wynn squeezed her hand. Turning to Jules, he said, "I understand what you're saying and why you're concerned. I don't appear at all mature to you, do I? You're right to point out how disgracefully I've behaved since I arrived. But this is the right thing to do. This is about so much more than I have words to express. We're ready to make a life together—that's why I'm here. I can feel it in my bones." His clear, blue eyes and honest face conveyed the certainty he felt. "We didn't make love at all last night. We've been talking all night long. Sex is not the important thing here, though we both agree we want to. Not until we're bonded though, so we want to do that this morning. Tonight we will make love."

Jules choked, and Rall dropped his spoon, blushing bright red as he picked it up. Aneka looked everywhere but at Jules, and Feia's eyes went wide, and her mouth dropped open.

"What are you two thinking? You only just met yesterday afternoon!" Feia's voice trailed off, looking at Rall with an oddly confused look on her face. "Oh, well," she said pointedly, determined to maintain her pretense of misery in her own bonding. "I guess you can dissolve your contract in two years if you find you are completely wretched. Seri, are you sure this is what you want?"

"Feia—you've continually wondered why I could never settle on one man. I told you I would know the right one when he came along," Seri told her, calm and serene despite her lack of sleep or perhaps because of it. "Now he's here beside me. This is the right thing to do. Aeos will bless us."

As Seri spoke those words, Rall faintly heard a bell tolling along with her words. *Aeos's bell! This is her will.* Feia must have heard it too. Her eyes widened, and she looked at Rall. They were both taken aback and wondering, but no one else had heard it. "Of course we will be your witnesses." Rall recovered his composure. "We would be honored."

Jules glanced at Aneka, who had refused to meet his eyes since she'd tried to slip out of the room without him. "This will work out perfectly. I was planning on us registering our bonding today anyway," Jules said into the silence. "The registry will be open soon, so we can do it on our way out of town."

Aneka's shocked eyes turned toward Jules. All of her confused thoughts were clearly written on her face, ranging from fury to unvarnished glee and back. Reluctantly, she nodded her head in agreement, obviously fearing she was making the worst mistake of her life.

"I meant what I said, Aneka. I love you, and I'm not going to lose you again over my own stupidity." His voice was firm in his conviction.

Wynn's broad smile indicated his approval, and he clasped Jules's shoulder companionably. "See? It's easy to give up acting like a jackass once you find the right girl."

After a moment of shocked silence, Seri, Aneka, Feia, and Rall burst out laughing so hard everyone in the common room turned to see what was so funny. Red-faced, Jules nodded, laughing weakly at himself. "For once you're right, pretty-boy!"

Chapter 11

The six mages walked as fast as they could and arrived in Aeoven in the late afternoon, entering through the western gate. Bonded mages lived in a section of town adjacent to the college, on several streets lined with tightly packed row houses, with more under construction.

Jules explained the layout of the city as they walked. "The north side of the Temple square is where the journeymen's quarters are, and the novice barracks are on the south. Beyond is the building that houses the armory. Every working mage must maintain his or her skills with weapons." He exchanged a sly look with Rall behind Wynn's back. "You'll have many opportunities to spar with the other mages working in Aeoven at one time or another. Don't worry."

Rall knew exactly what Jules was thinking and grinned wolfishly, anticipating their profits. His own thought was that by winter, Wynn would be dueling regularly, earning him and Jules a tidy sum in wagers.

Feia, Aneka, and Seri walked ahead, discussing something they didn't share with the men, laughing and casting looks back at them.

Lagging behind with Rall and Jules, Wynn found himself gawking at the shops and houses as they walked to the college and their respective homes. "I never imagined a city could be so big. It makes me feel very small," he said. "I'm embarrassed to think how large and fine a city I thought Armat was when I first saw it."

"You should see Mal Evol City or Braden," said Rall. "They make this town look like a collection of mud huts. But they're the heart of Neveyah and have a much longer history. We're still in the wilds out here."

"You'll land on your feet just like you always do," Jules told Wynn firmly. "At least you don't have to decide whose apartment you'll sleep in tonight. Of course, mine is probably still a bit of a wreck. I didn't leave it in very good shape, and I've been gone for a long while."

"Why does that not surprise me?" replied Wynn, laughing at him. "But you might want to let the competition know that Aneka's breakfasting with her husband from now on. Seri tells me being seen breakfasting with someone of the opposite sex here indicates you have an understanding, even if only temporarily. I certainly intend to make it clear about Seri and me right from the start. But I guess I'm the jealous sort!"

Jules's eyes bulged, and he started to say something and then fell silent. Rall laughed at him. "Well, you'll have to pick up your dirty socks soon enough, Jules, because you'll be moving. You'll both be assigned a home soon. Housing is tight in the bachelor quarters, so they're building another wing. The seneschal's office will want your apartments immediately. I guarantee it. They took both our apartments before the ink was dry in the registry book when we were bonded." The group strolled by the many shops, eyeing the various and sundry wares the craftsmen offered as they passed.

"Will we get a house so soon?" Jules had been expecting to have to stay in the bachelor quarters until one was available. "Here—this is Temple Boulevard. The Mages' Quarter is this way." They left the main market square and turned down a broad avenue lined with small shops and even a common room, The Mages' Rest. Residential lanes branched off the street at regular intervals.

"They just added three new streets of row houses. Soon, the whole area originally designated for housing the clergy will be built." Rall noticed Wynn's raised eyebrows. "We had to make sure the supporting staff has adequate housing first, and we had to make sure the shops were properly set up for the merchants before we could really worry about adding mage housing. The Temple can't function without the supporting staff, and the market is the source of funding for Aeoven. This whole town is under construction."

Stone structures, the size of small outhouses, open at the front and facing away from the direction storms came, stood at the end of each street. In each, a boy or girl about twelve to fourteen years of age was seated at a desk. Some were writing as the travelers passed, some waved, and others were occupied with reading or doing decorative needlework on items of clothing. "What are these little houses, and who are the people sitting in them?" Wynn asked.

"They're messengers," Jules explained. "In this city, everyone is in the employ of the Temple and could be called out at any moment on Temple business. They stand ready to deliver messages and also serve as the fire watch. It keeps the novices busy and out of trouble once they've proven they're reliable, giving them an important task to do while they finish developing their mage or healing skills."

Soon, the group came to a lane with a sign that read "Primrose Street." Rall and Feia turned and made their goodbyes. "So, as soon as we put away our things, we'll be over to your place, Seri. We have a lot to explain to Wynn tonight since he will most likely be visiting the abbess tomorrow. We're now in the second house down on the right," Rall said. "Number three."

"You will visit us this next week," Feia commanded. "Rall will cook you a meal to die for." Suddenly realizing she'd just inadvertently praised her husband, she shut her mouth with a snap, a comical look on her face.

Rall looked momentarily shocked at her praise but quickly recovered and blandly nodded, saying he would do his best, pretending he had not heard praise fall from her lips. Everyone else agreed they would enjoy any meal he cooked, and they parted ways.

"He does cook amazingly well." Jules turned to Aneka, speaking loudly and well within earshot of the messenger at the end of Rall's street. "I'll just get my books and dirty laundry and move them to your place for now until the seneschal assigns us a house. Now that we're bonded, we should live together to prevent misunderstandings. That way no one will have to die at my incredibly jealous hands." He smiled brightly.

Aneka rolled her eyes, knowing exactly what he was up to. "Establishing your territory?" she asked him.

"Yes. That is precisely what I'm doing," Jules replied, grinning broadly.

As she heard Jules's words, the bored messenger perked right up and began to make a note. "Sir! Ma'am! Congratulations on your bonding!" she called to Jules and Aneka. Soon, the news was traveling across town exactly as Jules had intended.

Wynn and Seri smiled widely, holding hands as

they walked, her staff making clicking sounds on the cobblestones. She had told Wynn that healers only carried a staff for defense because most were unable to kill. Good staff-work could disarm and disable even the best of swordsmen long enough for the healer to put the offenders to sleep with a well-cast spell.

The four remaining travelers arrived at the bachelor quarters where a messenger sat on duty near the foot of the stairwell. Seri reported to her that they had arrived safely, and since they had registered their bonding in Wister, Wynn Farmer would be staying with her. Smiling, Seri asked her to take the message to Abbess Lera. "And could you please ask if a meal for six could be sent up to my rooms? Rall, Feia, Jules, and Aneka will be eating with us up there in a working meeting. We have to complete the reports on our journeys for submission tomorrow morning."

The little novice healer congratulated them, her eyes as big and round as dinner plates, and prepared to leave her post to deliver Seri's messages. Aneka stopped her and asked her to tell the abbess she and Jules had also registered their bonding in Wister and were now safely home. "Oh, my goodness! Congratulations! It's so romantic!" The girl ran off.

"I'll be right up with my things, wife. Five minutes at the most," Jules said loudly as he continued to his apartment on the first floor. Aneka rolled her eyes and smiled as she and Seri led Wynn up to the third floor.

Seri's apartment was tiny, with no kitchen. It had two small bedrooms, a somewhat larger sitting room, and a small bath chamber between the bedrooms, with hot and cold running water. "This is modern," Wynn commented on seeing it. "Back home, we only have a hand pump, but some of the neighbors have plumbing like this."

Seri agreed. "My mother's house had a hand pump, and we heated the water on the stove for baths." She looked around the apartment critically. "I've never tried to make this into a home, really, because I've been posted away so much. The only things I own are clothes and books anyway. But now I have this urge to fix up a place for us. When we're assigned a house, we'll have a day or two before I have to leave. We can...." She broke off as Wynn kissed her.

"We'll be too busy to decorate much, starting tonight!" He hugged her possessively. "And tomorrow and every day from now on, you will be seen breakfasting with me!"

Wynn's comment made Seri laugh.

Just then, Jules and Aneka knocked on the door, followed by Rall and Feia, and then the trays from the kitchen arrived. While they ate, everyone explained to Wynn as much as they could about what he could expect the next morning and over the next few months.

A messenger knocked on the door just as they were finishing their meal, bringing a summons for the six of them to a meeting in Mother Relynne's study at nine o'clock the next morning. "I rather expected it," said Rall. "Two bondings, a water-wraith, an exploding boulder, and various other things seemed to have been inspired by your advent into our world, Wynn Farmer. She's definitely curious about you!"

After their meal and the completion of their tasks, they made their polite goodbyes, and Rall and Jules carried the trays back to the kitchen, leaving Wynn and Seri to enjoy their first night together.

After they closed the door on their friends, the newly bonded couple made a point of tidying up. Then laughing, Wynn and Seri fell into each other's arms. "We've waited so long for this." Wynn whispered, "I've waited all my life for you."

◆◆◆

"What a crazy last few weeks I've just had," Jules told Rall, as the two men carried the trays and dishes back down to the main kitchen. "I can't even begin to tell you how bizarre it's been!"

"Well, I've got to admit I've never seen you so grumpy and easily upset as you've been lately," replied Rall with a smile. "Usually nothing upsets you or catches you off-guard."

"I've been on pins and needles since Wynn came through the portal," admitted Jules. "It's like the minute Wynn Farmer fell into our world, he started a crazy chain of events. I've found myself saying and doing things I had no intention of until he came along." He laughed ruefully. "He says the most peculiar things, things shockingly truthful! Yet you can't feel angry with him because you're laughing so hard. I'll tell you this, Rall—our lives will never be boring again with him around shaking things up! I think the fun has only just started!"

"Having seen him in the common room, I suspect his father was hard-pressed to keep a tight leash on him until he could be safely returned to Neveyah," Rall said thoughtfully. "He's a catalyst. If you take two perfectly ordinary people or situations and add Wynn to the mix, you end up with something that can easily veer out of control."

"That's why I'm worried about Feia," Jules said

seriously. "He's unbelievably good at visualization—you know how he is. She thinks I'm an idiot, but he has the strongest affinity for lightning of anyone currently working in the Temple, and he has the best visualization skills. That's a dangerous combination in an untrained mage."

"She can handle it. She'll be surprised a few times, I'm sure, but she'll adjust to his needs. While you were gone, Feia developed into an excellent teacher." Rall's posture said he would hear no criticism of his wife. "She takes too much pride in her work to pass up this challenge."

◆◆◆

Mother Relynne met them, along with Abbess Lera. The Holy Mother was a fire-mage, and at first glance, she appeared to be a cozy, grandmotherly sort of woman.

The abbess was a woman who, at forty, was in the prime of her life. Her brown eyes were warm, and her burnished coppery-brown hair was worn loose in a style similar to Feia's and gleamed in the sunlight that entered through the large windows. Like Aneka, Feia, and Seri, the abbess was physically fit and obviously able to use the sword that hung in its scabbard on the back of her chair.

Abbess Lera was striking, but on a closer look, Wynn realized the Holy Mother was formidable.

"You six have been busy," Mother Relynne said, in her deceptively soft voice. "I'll read your reports later, but perhaps you could give us a brief summary of what's been going on." Her hair was mostly white, and she wore it pulled back into two plaits, wound around her head like a crown. Her smile warmed them and made them feel at ease, as if they could tell her anything and she would understand. Yet, though she sounded like a doting grandmother, she radiated a strength that made you feel as if she would move heaven and earth to destroy whatever threatened Neveyah.

She sounds soft, but she's made of steel, Wynn thought, as first Jules and then Rall told the story.

When they got around to the sudden bondings, both the abbess and Mother Relynne laughed knowingly. "We're familiar with this phenomenon in your family, Wynn. That's the way you all do it." Mother Relynne grinned at him.

"But Jules, how precipitous of you! Perhaps you've finally begun to show some maturity." Abbess Lera's eyes twinkled at his look of shock. "So, what are we going to do about this situation?"

Wynn cleared his throat, and everyone looked at him. "I didn't intend to wreck your plans, ma'am," he said, with his startlingly honest smile. "We'll abide by the schedules you've already set for us. I know I have to be trained so I'm no longer a danger to anyone." A shadow crossed his eyes. "I know Seri is leaving soon. We're content to abide by your wishes, though we'll miss each other. It'll only be for a short time." He tried to look as content as he claimed but failed.

Mother Relynne said, "Ah, but your bonding does change everything, Wynn. Aeos is the Goddess of Hearth and Home, and we're her servants. It would look bad if we didn't allow you and Seri some time to start your life together, and the same goes for Jules and Aneka. Things are quiet right now, and nothing much is happening, so changes in scheduling are easy to arrange, and we've many capable mages who'd like to get out of Aeoven for a while." Her eyes flickered toward Jules. "In fact, under the circumstances, it might be best to send Arne Severnsson to serve in Arlen for a while."

Jules nodded, unable to hide his satisfaction.

"After you've all had time to begin your lives together, we'll reconsider your postings, sometime after the Winter Solstice." Mother Relynne and Abbess Lera exchanged brief glances, but only Rall and Feia seemed to catch the look. "In the meantime, I've need of your services here in Aeoven, so fear not. You will be busy."

Abbess Lera had been sent many true-dreams regarding Wynn Farmer, including two recent prophecies concerning him. She *knew* the next big event involving him would occur sometime near Winter Solstice. Several years would pass before whatever loomed on the horizon presented itself, but by then, Wynn would be ready to meet the challenge. Two more important things had to happen before his true mission would be known, and Lera's true-dreams had revealed exactly what they were.

"In the meantime, I'll see you after this meeting, Wynn, to explain your duties, but first, we must get your houses assigned. Your bondings couldn't have happened at a better time. We can free up three apartments by moving you four into family housing today," Abbess Lera said, making notes as she spoke. "This is perfect—we've five novices who're more than ready to become journeymen. This gives us exactly the right number of bachelor apartments for them to live by themselves. Things always get ugly when journeymen have to share quarters. You and Devyn didn't do so

163

well as roommates if I recall, Jules. I'll notify the seneschal right now, so pack your things up, children. You're moving house today."

Jules rolled his eyes at the mention. "Devyn just didn't appreciate my relaxed sense of style," said Jules.

"He didn't appreciate your slovenly housekeeping habits," said Feia, sharply. "No one did, not even Rall."

Rall, the traitor, actually nodded his head in agreement with her assessment. "You're a mess, Jules. Aneka will have her work cut out for her, getting you housetrained." Everyone laughed while Jules tried and failed to think of a smart retort.

"And now, I think Wynn should make his vows so he can collect his pay packet," Mother Relynne said, with her eyes still twinkling at Jules's red face and obvious discomfort. "Are you ready?"

"Yes, ma'am, I think I am. I'll do my best to prove I'm worthy." He colored slightly at being the center of attention. "I read the book Abbott Dorn gave me, and Jules explained what the clergy does. My father also told me how the Bull God, Tauron, works to conquer the people of Neveyah and that the clergy of Aeos stands against him. So I know what I'm getting into. I'm honored to serve Aeos and through her the people of Neveyah." Wynn's candor shone in his easy smile. "I don't accept this task lightly—I know it's a lifelong commitment and that I might be called upon to give my life in her service."

Relynne was momentarily taken aback by the resemblance of his smile to his grandfather's smile as a young man. Calling her errant thoughts to order, she explained in detail what she was about to do in administering the vows, which was really the setting of spell called a geas, that bound the mage to a strict protocol of behavior in the use of his talent. Then, satisfied that he did indeed understand, Relynne prepared herself to perform the ceremony. "Think only of your wish to serve Aeos with all your heart."

Wynn cleared his mind of everything except his willingness to serve the Goddess, repeating the vows after her holiness. As he spoke the vows, the Holy Mother cast the spell of binding. The weaving of this spell sealed him to the service of Aeos. A comforting feeling of warmth settled over him, as if he were standing in the midday sun.

"Wynn Farmer, you are now a journeyman lightning-mage in the service of Aeos."

◆◆◆

Wynn and Feia remained in Abbess Lera's study. The others had the day off to get settled or moved, and were eager to get started, promising to meet for lunch. The abbess explained the workings of the Temple to Wynn and signed him up to the firewood-cutting crew that met every Sunnaday morning. Every person in Aeoven donated a day of labor on various tasks to provide the resources that kept the city self-sufficient, from mass-producing the simple shirts and trousers everyone wore to making quilts, canning and preserving food, or cutting firewood. The work parties were fun, and Neveyah as a whole benefitted from them, as the extra food, garments, and blankets were distributed to the far corners of Neveyah for the poor. The abbess said, "We support ourselves well, but the clergy of Aeos serves Neveyah. The fruit of our labor clothes and feeds those whose lives are hard."

After Abbess Lera was finished with them, Wynn

and Feia went to a sheltered garden, where she tested him to determine his strengths, and despite his trepidation, she led him in calling a cat-zapper successfully and safely. For the rest of the morning, under Feia's supervision, he demonstrated all the magic he'd been taught. She was, however, more than a little shocked at how quickly he grasped the concepts she had to teach him. His habit of innocently answering rhetorical questions and instantly obeying commands that were actually sarcasm had her quite disconcerted by lunch.

They met up with the others in the huge dining hall for a meal of bread, cheese, and fruit. Jules took one look at Feia's flustered disarray and smiled widely at the comical distress she tried so hard to hide.

"Jules!" The sharpness in her voice grated in his ears, and he winced, wondering what he'd done wrong now. "I owe you an apology. You did well with your student. I should never have doubted you."

Jules tried not to look as astonished as he felt. "Thank you, Feia, but I must be honest and tell you his strength and visualization skills are definitely beyond my abilities to cope with as a teacher. You're going to be far more able to help him than I was, I think."

Now it was Feia who looked like a landed fish.

At lunch in the crowded dining hall, a tall man with gray hair stopped by their table. "My team has two houses on Rose Street ready for you to move into," he said cheerfully. "They're in the new section, and you'll be the first tenants in them. The cleaners have just finished. They stocked the kitchens with dishes and utensils and made sure you have towels and bedding and a few amenities. It's a bit of a walk, but I like the way these houses are laid out better than some of the older homes closer to the college. It's only two streets farther. My crews are at your old rooms right now, loading the carts with your baskets and things you had packed. They'll leave your possessions in your new sitting room for you to unpack as you wish. They should be done by the time we get there." With a fatherly smile, he strode off to the buffet table to help himself to some food.

"He's Aljer Kerikson, the seneschal. He's the single most important person in Aeoven," Feia told Wynn, her voice indicating admiration for the man. "He's not a mage, yet he works more magic than the rest of us combined. All the Temple bows to him. He makes sure we all have a roof over our head and furniture to sit on. He even provides us with pots, dishes, and linens for the beds. Of course, you might want to buy your own things as you go along, but in the meantime, you'll be able to live in your new house."

After lunch, Wynn and Seri walked behind Aljer, who chatted with Jules, Aneka, and Feia. They turned down Rose Street, one street beyond Rall and Feia's and the one with the new construction Wynn had seen the day before. The left side as they walked was lined with narrow row houses, each with tiny back gardens. The right was identical, only still in varying stages of being built. Twenty-four houses sat on each side of the street. Just after numbers twelve and thirteen, a wandering path bisected the center of the entire Mages' Quarter like a creek, connecting and crossing all of the streets in the neighborhood and ending at the college, where all mages posted in Aeoven would be working. On the other side of the connecting path were twelve more houses, with the street ending at the wall that ran along the river.

The entire town was easy to get around. Each neighborhood had a central path leading directly to the Temple and the market district. Also, each had a large, central garden where children could run and play under the watchful eye of their parents.

"You're in number two," Alger told Jules and Aneka. "It has a lovely, south-facing back garden. You'll like it, I'm sure. And you two," Aljer said, looking back at Wynn and Seri, "are in number four, right next door. You'll all have to put up with construction for a while because the plan calls for Rose Street to be completed by Winter Solstice, and then construction will begin immediately on the next one over, Lilac Street. The entire Mages' Quarter of Aeoven, out to the walls, will be complete by the end of the next year. With the number of young mages and healers being found before they go wrong nowadays, we'll double our clergy in ten years. When this section is complete, there will be eight streets of row houses for the Temple clergy. They aren't fancy, but they're well-built and adequate to raise families in."

"They look wonderful—much nicer than the place I grew up in," Seri said, smiling as she looked about the street and the rather plain houses lining the sides. "I heard you designed them yourself!"

"I did, and a bit of work it was on this slope. We want to cram as many houses as we can into each neighborhood." Aljer was justifiably proud of his team's accomplishment. "I think we managed to make some fine homes here."

"Well, you've done magnificently," Jules told him,

as he gazed around appreciatively. "This will be a wonderful place to raise our children." Aneka gave him a flat look but said nothing. "When we're ready for children, of course," he said, qualifying his statement. She looked relieved and nodded agreeably.

Their homes were simple but pleasant, slate-roofed row houses built of sandstone, with the front doors opening onto the cobbled street at varying places. Staggering the placement of the houses allowed each to have good-sized windows in every room despite shared walls.

Seri surveyed her new home, nearly unable to believe the turn her life had taken. She sat on the bench that ran under the coat hooks, looking at the way the rooms were laid out. It occurred to her that perhaps her inability to settle down had masked her desire to have a real home, but until Wynn came into her life, she hadn't understood it.

Now she wanted nothing more than to make a happy life and raise their children there. "My mother would have loved a home like this," she said wistfully. "But Dad died young, and Mum was never able to do more than just scrape by. She died just after I came to the Temple." Wynn squeezed her hand supportively, sensing her sadness.

"My family's not exactly rich either," replied Wynn. "My father tries, but he's not really good at farming. Most years, we'd have starved without his ability to locate wells." He wandered through the house, examining every corner.

In the kitchen, ceramic tiles with blue geometric patterns in the same design as on the fireplace hearths in the other rooms covered the front of the wood-fired stove that was built into the wall. A brick oven was also built along the side of the chimney, and a large ceramic-tiled water heater in the corner of the chimney completed the modern amenities. One fire in the kitchen would heat the water heater, the stove, and the oven. "This is very efficient." Wynn looked at the arrangement with approval. "We'll use much less firewood with this system."

"That's the idea," replied Aljer, grinning at Wynn's interest in the mechanics of the house. "Right now, the sun heats the water tanks on the roof, so there's no need to have a fire in here at all, since you'll be cooking in the garden anyway. We'll come around and switch each house over to the kitchen water heater when it's time, so you don't have to worry."

Wynn saw a small door at waist height in the wall near the sink and opened it, finding a metal-lined cupboard with two shelves. "What sort of cupboard is this?"

"It's the cooler," replied Aljer. "The cold water coming into the house is piped around it, cooling the metal and making a perfect, chilly place to keep food fresh for a day or two."

"I would never have thought of that." Wynn was surprised by how modern the plumbing was and told Aljer so.

He laughed and said, "With all the water-mages in Aeoven, the plumbing is the easiest part of building homes here. Fitting houses into the least amount of space and still keeping the bits of garden livable is the hard part."

Wynn stood on the back steps, already planning a late-summer vegetable garden and a chicken coop. The backdoor opened onto a screen-enclosed sun porch with a large sink for doing laundry and lines to hang it on. The standard outdoor oven and stove for summer cooking were flanked by a picnic table and benches. A shed for tools and storage stood along the back wall. A gate opened onto a narrow alley wide enough for the refuse and wood delivery carts to travel.

Across the alley were the houses that lined Primrose Street where Rall and Feia lived. In fact, Jules and Aneka's house was directly behind theirs, with their back gates opposite each other. Though the houses on each street were staggered in such a way every room had a large window, Wynn and Seri's chimney wall was shared with Jules and Aneka's, and a neighboring house shared some of their opposite walls. All in all, the houses were built to be good family homes, although they weren't at all fancy compared to those of the more well-to-do farmers, merchants, and other wealthy people throughout Neveyah.

Wynn asked why all the buildings in Aeoven were built of stone. Aljer laughed. "We have the good fortune of having a lot of journeyman earth-mages hanging about with nothing to do, so we put them to work quarrying stone and building. The houses go up fast with their help. You'll have a job that will require your magic too."

Jules and Aneka were just as delighted with their house, although they would never admit to it out loud, not after Feia said Wynn and Seri were "just so cute" about it.

Chapter 12

Four months had passed since Wynn fell through the portal and into Neveyah. The entire group had settled into their new lives. Wynn had indeed developed well as both a mage and a duelist, exactly as Rall and Jules foresaw, but was unaware of his outstanding ability.

Holy Month, the thirteenth month of the lunar calendar, had arrived. A month that belonged to no season, being between Harvest and winter, it was set aside for travel and for preparing for the largest feast-day celebration of the year. On the day of the Winter Solstice, Holy Day, every family would celebrate with gifts and gatherings in their homes. All over Aeoven, people secretly looked for small presents to give their friends and loved ones.

Late in the afternoon of the first Sunnaday of the month, a knock sounded on the door. Wynn answered it to find his nearly unrecognizable father standing there in old-fashioned, faded-blue leathers that hung quite loosely on him. Belted at his side was a sword unlike any Wynn had ever seen. Liam's kit was slung over his shoulder, and he leaned against the door jamb, terribly thin and worn, looking more ill than Wynn had ever seen him. Grief was deeply etched on his face. He looked like an old, old man, though he wasn't. Illness and something else had taken a terrible toll on him.

"Dad! Come in! Where's Mom?" Wynn was unable to disguise his shock at his father's appearance. "What happened?" He put his arms around his father, holding him gently, dismayed at feeling the uncontrollable tremors in his father's frail body. "Sit here. Let me get your boots off." He helped his father onto the cushioned bench by the door. "Is Mom coming too?" Seri closed the door behind them.

Liam sat, shaking his head, trying to find the words to tell Wynn what had happened. Finally, he said, "She passed away just over a week ago, Son. She developed a cough at the beginning of Harvest that wouldn't go away. I tried to get her to come to Armat to be healed, but she refused to leave the farm. Then it was too late. I failed her, Son. I failed her." He broke down, sobbing. "I should have made her come back here. I should have made her do it! How will I live without her?" All Wynn could do was sit down beside him, and holding his father, he tried to absorb what he'd just been told.

Seri touched Liam's cheek, casting a small spell to calm him. "Right after the funeral, I closed up the house. Then the dog and I brought the sheep to Armat. We got there the day before yesterday. I gave them to the Temple farm. I left old Duke there too because he didn't want to leave the sheep. Bran wouldn't let me come here unless he and Dorn made the trip with me, so we rode the mail coach here. Apparently, he thinks I'm on my last legs or something. They practically carried me to your door, but I made them let me do this on my own. They should be up at the Temple by now." His breath caught in a sob, but he managed to keep himself pulled together. "I didn't know what else to do. I couldn't bear to stay there, where everything reminds me of Arla."

Liam leaned his head back against the wall, tears streaming down his face unheeded. "Everything shouts that she's gone, and I don't have the heart to care for the farm anymore. I don't know if you want me around

173

after what I put you through, but I had to tell you first. I owed you that much. Lera will find me a place to live."

"What do you mean? Why wouldn't I want you?" Wynn sat back, shocked that his father would think he wasn't welcome. "I've been worried—I knew something bad was happening there. I knew it! I should have gone back when I was still in Armat." He couldn't comprehend the loss of his mother, but the frailty of his father concerned him. "I didn't mean to let you down, Dad. I couldn't find the rocks when I tried to go back. I tried, and they were gone!"

"You have to be in Neveyah, Wynn. The portal won't open for you until you're done here. It's our bargain with Aeos. You can't leave just yet." Liam struggled to comfort his son. "I knew why you were gone and so did your mother. It will be the same when the time comes for your son to take his place here."

Seri said firmly, "And now your place is here, Father." She delved him, and speaking quickly to hide her alarm at the sight of him, she said, "We're a family, and we've more room than we'll ever need here." As she spoke, Seri searched him with her healing senses, finding seriously damaged kidneys. She cast a healing spell on him, though she had no expertise in ailments of that sort. Some of the grayness left his cheeks, but he was still very ill. She embraced him, sending as much comfort as she could. "You will remain with us. That's all there is to it!"

Liam smiled bleakly at her firmness. "You don't know how hard I was on him, Daughter." His lips trembled, and he had trouble keeping his voice level. "He may not want me in your home. I was too hard on him, trying to prepare him for coming here."

Overwhelmed with concern and grief, Wynn said fiercely, "We didn't always get along, but I never doubted you loved me, Dad. You always did your best for me. Where else could you live but with your family?" His voice caught, and after a moment of trying to pull his thoughts together, he sighed heavily. Tears filled his eyes, but he ignored them. "We have plenty of room, more than enough, really. We need to take care of you and get a healer to see you." He stood and picked up his father's sword belt and kit, starting up the stairs with them. "I've missed you, despite our differences." Tears sprang to his father's eyes again. "I've nothing but gratitude, Dad."

The look in Liam's eyes broke Wynn's heart. "I love you more than I have words to say, Son. I am so proud of you." His body began trembling again.

Wynn's worried eyes met Seri's, and an unvoiced agreement passed between them.

"Come on, Father, let's get you up to your room," she said comfortingly, casting calming and easing spells again. "We'll get you settled in the front bedroom. It has the best light. I'll just check on supper and send a message to the Temple that you'll be living here."

While Wynn helped his father upstairs, Seri scribbled a note. She ran up to the street corner and sent a messenger to Abbess Lera and also to the infirmary. An old friend of Liam's, a senior healer named Duran, was on call for the evening, and in her note Seri begged him to come over immediately. "Go to the infirmary first," she instructed the messenger. "It's an emergency! My father-in-law is a water-mage with kidney failure! He's at my house." Nodding, the novice raced to the infirmary.

Duran soon arrived, bringing with him a kit stocked with potions and teas that were specific remedies for kidney failure. He delved Liam, and with Seri assisting, he cleansed Liam's blood. Duran saw to it she understood how to help her father-in-law each day.

"It's because he's a water-mage, isn't it?" Seri asked him later as they sat in the kitchen, while Liam slept upstairs with the aid of a sleeping spell and the potions.

Duran nodded sadly. "It's the penalty for being a great mage." He explained to Wynn, "Water-mages are prone to kidney ailments, earth-mages suffer from bad lungs and congestive heart failure. Fire-mages frequently have crippling joint ailments, and lightning-mages often develop strange cancers. The deeper the mages' connection to the expression of their main element, the more likely it is they'll suffer the consequences. I've treated your father tonight as well as I'm able, but he must be seen by Dillon."

"I know who Dillon is," replied Seri. "But I've never worked with him. I've always specialized as a midwife."

"Dillon has skills that will enable Liam to live normally for a while yet, maybe even years. But we'll talk about this later, in a few days or so, after you've had a chance to get him over his loss and devastation somewhat. It feels to me like Bran healed him several days ago, so tonight I just continued what he started."

"I'll work with him daily," she promised Duran. "He'll be much better soon."

The next day, Liam sat in their cozy sitting room,

surrounded by friends. Thanks to Duran's treatment of his illness the evening before and Seri's tender care, he gradually emerged from his shock and deep depression. His old friends, including Bran, Dorn, and Lera, were there to support him. All of the senior mages currently in Aeoven stopped in all day long to pay their respects. Mother Relynne came and held Liam's hand, comforting him.

While Wynn and Seri helped him get ready to receive company, Jules and Rall fed the chickens and did the few chores Wynn normally performed on a Restday. Then they remained, acting as hosts so he and his father could grieve properly. Jules and Feia served food and tea, tidying up between waves of guests, while Rall and Aneka stayed in the kitchen preparing the food. Many people brought casseroles and pies, so the work wasn't arduous.

Later, Rall and Jules sat at the picnic table, keeping Wynn company under the chilly sun of late afternoon. The house was crowded, and Wynn felt like he was going to fly apart, but Jules had brought him outside, thinking a breath of fresh air in the winter-bare garden would calm his friend.

With his father in the care of his friends, Wynn finally began to deal with the fact he would never see his mother again, feeling the pain of her loss quite keenly, regretting the fact he hadn't been able to say goodbye. He sat silently at the table, unable to fully articulate how he felt, other than saying he was grateful for his friends and that at least he still had his father.

♦♦♦

The house finally settled down late in the evening, and after tidying up, Jules and Aneka went home, leaving through the backdoor and walking up the alley to their gate, followed by Rall and Feia. Feia had hugged a surprised Liam and told him how sorry she was for his loss, and then she said, "But you still have your son and Seri, and you have all of us! We are here for you too. Don't forget it!"

"The poor man," Feia said, as they parted, her stormy eyes dark with sympathy and something akin to fear, as she secretly glanced toward her husband. "He loved his wife so much. But at least he and Wynn can enjoy the time they have left. That's important, don't you think?" Jules and Aneka looked at her and then at each other but simply nodded their agreement.

Once they were safely in their own kitchen, Jules said with a sardonic smile, "I fear our Feia has fallen madly in love with her own husband. How will she handle this turn of affairs?"

Aneka laughed and said, "She'll continue to make his life a misery, but her heart won't be in it." Standing in the shelter of her husband's embrace, she said, "I feel the same need to hold on to the happiness we have today."

Jules silently agreed with her, his arms tightening around her. "Seeing the greatest water-mage of his generation brought so low as poor Liam is has made me think about things too. We have to make the most of every day we have."

* * *

The same evening, Mother Relynne met in her study with Dorn, Bran, and Lera. They sat trying to decide just what Liam's unexpected reappearance might portend for Wynn's future and the Temple.

Relynne rubbed her hands together. "We're once

again living in interesting times. The father has returned to live at his son's hearth, as the prophecy said must happen. Several more events must occur, one in particular, and when it does, we'll know the time for action is upon us. Soon you will tell us what Aeos requires of us, Lera. The Goddess will speak through you as she always does."

"It hurts to see him so ill. He's only my age, but he looks so old—his hair is completely white! His illness is far more advanced than it should be. What could have caused it to be so pronounced in him?" Lera's pensive mood was contagious. Even Dorn was affected by it. "I wonder why some of us succumb and some survive. What's the difference between one mage and another that one becomes sick from the magic and another doesn't?"

"We may never know the answer to that question, Lera," Mother Relynne gently told her. "I've seen so many of my dear friends gone before age forty-five. Liam's father, Iain, passed on at forty-seven. Yet here I am at sixty-five and doing quite well, thank you. It's the price we must pay to serve the people of Neveyah."

Dorn said, "It broke my heart when he suddenly appeared in Armat looking like death walking. I think the only thing that kept him alive was the idea that he had to tell his son what had happened."

Bran nodded. "You may be right. I can't explain why he was still tottering, when he should have been dead."

"But even my Bertte's not as well as I could wish. She has been struggling to breathe these last few months and has lost so much weight. She's far too agreeable and hasn't scolded our new journeyman once." Dorn's eyes were troubled, and a permanent sadness had taken root in his once cheerful heart. "When we hunted the female water-wraith last summer, I had no idea it would be Bertte's last hunt. It's happened so suddenly I'm afraid to leave her for too long. Bran here tells me it's only a matter of time." He saw Lera and Mother Relynne looking closely at him and smiled wryly.

"I know he's told you of my own problem too," Dorn confirmed. They nodded compassionately.

"You still have some years before the cancer will become unmanageable. It's early days yet," Bran said. "We were lucky I caught it so early."

"I should last long enough for Jules to take over in Armat when he returns from saving the world from whatever crisis looms on the horizon with that crazy boy of Liam's. I've seen to it, whether he likes it or not." They all laughed knowingly. "A few years of boredom as the armsmaster here will sharpen his desire to use his very fine abilities as an abbott. I'll retire then, and Bertte and I will come back here where Jeran is." Dorn's eleven-year-old son, Jeran, was a novice earth-mage. His eyes said he knew his wife would not make the journey back to Aeoven with him.

"It seems so unfair sometimes," Lera murmured, looking out of the window into the darkness. "Yet we do it anyway. At least the healers are able to do wonders for lightning-mages these days."

Dorn's face gave away none of his feelings as he answered, "And so Bran has done for me. What else can we do but spend our magic and our lives for Neveyah? We're the first line of defense for the people of this world. The Temple clergy must do all we can, or

Tauron will win." His face darkened, and he said, "We know the Bull God is behind all of the rogue-mages and bizarre elemental beasts we've dealt with since the borders were closed to his children. Bregat was surely enamored of him, if you remember, Lera. The dark god is up to something now, regardless. I feel it in my bones."

Mother Relynne and Abbess Lera agreed with him, both unwilling to admit they were worried the end-days were approaching.

We can't do anything about it, Relynne thought philosophically, as she prepared to go home. *It'll be for our children and their children to worry about. What I must do is make sure they have the tools they need when the time comes.* She closed her eyes, praying silently.

◆◆◆

After Liam's return to Aeoven, Wynn and Seri fell into a routine. The infirmary began sending her home by two in the afternoon, and Duran told her she would receive a permanent posting in Aeoven as a full midwife. "Liam needs you here. He's looking better every day now he's receiving proper treatment, but the damage has been done. Dillon tells me we must take it one day at a time with him."

Liam, quite surprisingly to Wynn, was pleased with everything his son had done, from bonding with Seri to building his "chicken palace." "This is the finest coop I've ever seen, Son. They must be very special chickens to have flowers in window boxes and all." He laughed, but he was quite impressed with Wynn's craftsmanship. "You've done well for yourself, boy. I'm proud!" Liam looked at his visibly shocked son and smiled sadly. "I know you find it difficult to believe. I was too hard on you. Arla always said I was, but I just wanted you to be able to think beyond what they teach you. I meant well but was wrong in how I went about it."

Wynn's loyalty came to fore. "You prepared me for everything I had to know to survive here, Dad. I didn't understand it at the time, but I do now. I always knew you loved me, so I was sure there must be a reason for things that made no sense, even if it did make me feel frustrated sometimes." His dad nodded. "After I fell through the portal, I worried about you all the time. I knew you two wouldn't be able to handle the farm without me."

"I wasn't able to work, but it's my own fault. I need to be honest with you. It didn't have to happen. In Ariend, there is no magic. If you use your gifts, the chi comes directly from your life-chi." Liam's eyes filled with tears as he told his son the sad truth of why he was so ill. "I couldn't stop using the magic when we were taken there, and neither could your mother. We should have quit when the veil shifted. If we had, we'd have been fine. But we couldn't let go of it." He gripped Wynn's shoulders, his voice urgent. "Don't let the magic become too important, Son. You must be able to let it go when you go back to the farm, or it will kill you."

Wynn embraced his father. "I don't think I'll be leaving here anytime soon, Dad. Maybe never. There's nothing there for me now," Wynn told him. "My whole life is here with you and Seri."

"Well, if you should ever decide to return, the farm will be waiting. I put a water-shield on it that's keyed to you or me. Folks won't even notice the place, so it'll be safe." His face had taken on a yellowish tinge. Wynn encouraged him to rest on the sofa, placing a cushion behind his father's head and covering him with a blanket. He then poured Liam his tea, which had medicines in it to help him sleep. He knew it, but obediently drank it anyway.

"You're so good to me. I always knew you would be a lightning-mage. I knew you were lightning. It's why I stressed visualization so much...critical for lightning-mages to visualize well...." Liam drifted off into a troubled sleep. "You always made me laugh so hard...you were such a funny boy...so funny...."

Wynn sat holding his father's hand, watching as he dozed, thinking about the many things he'd never understood but that now made perfect sense. "I love you, Dad."

◆◆◆

The Holy Day celebration in the Farmer household began in a somewhat subdued fashion. Liam woke up to the knowledge he was spending it without Arla, and the prospect of living without her was more than he could bear. Seri and Wynn tried hard to cheer him, and he attempted to hide his grief for their sakes.

They began by going to the community breakfast at the Temple with all of their friends. Later in the afternoon, they dined at Rall and Feia's artistically decorated home. Rall had found several bottles of an excellent wine that had come all the way from the fabled vineyards of the Valley of Mal Evol to accompany his elegantly prepared meal. Even Liam was able to feel merry.

Chapter 13

Feia fought to keep up with Wynn's abilities. She'd been struggling for several weeks to find things to teach him. On the first day of the New Year, she marched into Abbess Lera's study. "I can't teach Wynn anything more, although he is teaching me new things. His control is excellent, and even when startled, he is accurate and conservative with his spells. His ability to raise all of the elements with strength surpasses any mage I know of currently in the Temple. He has the second best shields in the clergy." (She didn't mention whose shields she thought were better, Lera noted.) "He is a far more talented lightning-mage than I am or even than Abbott Dorn. He should be tested and then posted somewhere or be given a task in order to develop his skills."

"Jules tells me the same about his weapons skills, as does Rall," Lera replied. "Abbott Dorn feels he would make an excellent armorer, given his ability to infuse arrows with lightning. Do you agree?"

Feia smiled broadly. "He's adept with all sorts of tools and often mentions his hope of being assigned to the armory."

Lera called Wynn before the winter conclave of the Abbacy that was meeting in Aeoven, where he was tested along with several other promising, older journeymen. Wynn was raised to the level of adept, and given the task of assisting the master armorer, a senior fire-mage named Kaye. She was a fiery-spirited woman who had once quested with his father.

Eagerly, he settled down to learn all of the secrets of creating the incomparable Temple armor and weaponry. General armor was made by regular smiths, and was considered the finest available for the standard soldier. However, the armor created for the mages and healers came from a one-of-a-kind forge run by an exceptional group of smiths with unique skills. Just as with augmentations, the magic chose the design and color of each set of armor. All aspects of creation, from the first concept drawn on paper to the finished product, were done in ritualized trances and guided by the Goddess specifically for the intended recipient.

At first, he trained as an apprentice, working with Killan, a lightning-mage who'd known his father well. Killan was glad to have a student, as he'd planned to retire, but none of the other lightning-mages was suited to train as his replacement. "Young ones with the gift of control are rare," he told Kaye, the master armorer. "This boy has more discipline than anyone I've ever met, and he learns fast. I never have to show him anything more than once. He'll be one of the great ones."

Wynn's attention to detail and affinity for lightning were invaluable in the creation of the lacquered finish that made Temple armor impervious to rust and corrosion. The finest touch applied to each layer of the special enamel was required to chemically alter it into its final, impervious state. Killan taught him many ways to use his magic to cut the steel, shaping it into the ribs. The work at the forge helped Wynn develop the most narrowly focused lightning bolts of any mage in the Temple, although as usual, Wynn was unaware of his ability, simply loving the work and the feeling of having a craft he could be proud of.

Kaye frequently stopped by to see Liam, sitting in

the garden, talking as they had always done. "That boy of yours is something else," she told him. "I'd heard stories, but I thought it was just a hoity-toity lightning-mage blowing her own horn."

"Aw, Feia's not so bad. She's just a bit prickly is all," Liam replied, with a wry grin. "She's quite a good teacher. Wynn thinks he's found his career, working with you."

"He'll be going on a quest sooner or later. The boys in your family all do eventually. There'll be a place in the armory for him when he comes home," Kaye replied. "I'm more than happy to have him around until then. It's hard to find lightning-mages who aren't either too lazy or too arrogant, but Wynn goes against the norm for that element. He seems driven to work me into the ground. I think he'll really benefit from the control he's developing right now. His ability to focus is unusual in a mage as young as he is, and he's only just begun."

"I know he'll have to go off sometime. It worries me. I feel like we should be the ones doing it. Inside of me is a young mage with no limits who wants nothing more than to go off on a grand quest again and get some of the glory days back." Liam's ironic smile charmed Kaye despite his poor health. "But I can't swing my sword with enough strength to fight my way out of bed anymore," he told her sadly. "My body is just giving out around me."

"I know how you feel," she replied. "I'm losing the mobility in my fingers, more every day. My arms are strong, but I have little ability to grip my sword or hammer now. I'm fortunate to have the young ones like your boy who will follow directions well and someday take over the trade."

"That reminds me—I need a trade," Liam said, musingly. "I'm bored to death hanging around waiting for a grandchild. I'm thinking about asking the seneschal if I can help him out with repairing some of the small things. If Aljer will let me puddle around, fixing loose shutters and such, it will free up a young strong one for the heavy work. I can't really use my magic anymore if I want to be around to see my grandchildren, or so they tell me."

"How do you feel about that, Liam?" Kaye looked at him closely. "I can't imagine you taking it well. Your connection to the magic is deeper than anyone I've ever known."

"I should have let it go when I realized what it was doing to me, but I couldn't. Arla wore herself out trying to heal me, using her own magic when she shouldn't have. She just *had* to use it in the garden and the orchard too. Like me, she couldn't give it up. It killed her, and it's killing me. Bran told me I had to stop using it altogether, and so I have. But in the meantime, I must have a job of some sort."

The look of raw loss and suffering that passed across Liam's face cut Kaye to her heart. Moved by an unfamiliar desire to comfort him, she said, "Well, I think it'll do you a world of good." She thought for a minute and then said wickedly, "I know how you are. You'll just find ways to get into trouble if you don't have something to do. We can't have you hanging about in the common rooms, creating a scandal now, can we?"

Liam laughed, but his heart wasn't in it. "I've no interest in the common rooms. Not since Arla. You know how I feel." His face had colored a bit, which is what Kaye had hoped. "I don't have what it takes anymore, anyway. From what Dorn tells me, I can assure you I'm no longer the man my son apparently is. I may never have been." They both laughed knowingly.

"Some of things he says without thinking are a real hoot, Liam. Has he always been this way?" Kaye's grin lit up her weathered features.

"Oh yes, although he's toned it down quite a bit from what he was like before. He's actually matured since he came here," laughed Liam. "At least now he usually thinks about how it'll sound before he says it. I say usually, but you and I both know he won't ever completely change. He's a lightning-mage. They're always a riot to work with. Remember Dorn and the baker's daughter in Morton before we met up with Bertte?" Laughing, Liam mimicked the young Dorn, "'My goodness, those are some plump loaves you have rising there, ma'am!' It still cracks me up!" He and Kaye both laughed, remembering the day so long ago.

"Well, she did wear her blouse cut low, just to show those very 'plump loaves' off, so she shouldn't have been offended that he mentioned them. They were in his face, after all!"

"Yes, and I thought he was going to end up with a loaf of bread up his arse, the way she took it!" They both laughed again and soon slipped into an animated discussion of the old days, passing the afternoon companionably.

Seri looked out of the window over her kitchen sink, smiling as she watched the two old friends. Seeing her father-in-law so destroyed when he first arrived had shaken her terribly. He looked so much like an older version of Wynn, and seeing him leaning against her door jamb, physically ill, broken with grief, and unsure about his welcome was almost more than she could bear. She couldn't imagine not having him in their lives.

A wave of dizziness passed over her. She hadn't been feeling well for several days. Her stomach was upset in the mornings, and most of the time, all she could think about was taking a nap. She had a strong suspicion she wasn't actually ill but needed confirmation before she said anything.

Along with another plate of scones, Seri took the steaming teakettle outside to refill the pot for Liam and Kaye, telling them she would be out for a while. "Lunch is in the cooler if you want it later," she said cheerfully, hiding her exhaustion behind a smile. "I have to run over to the infirmary for a bit, but I'll be back soon."

◆◆◆

Wynn sat in stunned disbelief. "A baby? We're having a baby?" He knew he was repeating himself but couldn't help it.

"It happens to people who sleep with each other, his father said, smiling broadly. "I meant to explain it to you, but somehow I never got around to it."

"I figured it out," replied Wynn. "This is a surprise. I hope I'm ready."

Liam laughed at his son's disconcerted expression. "I hope so too, because it's happening whether you're ready or not!" He clasped his son's shoulder, saying, "Don't worry. You're a good husband and you'll be a fine father." Liam looked around the kitchen, suddenly feeling more energetic than he had in years. "Why don't we fix supper tonight? Seri could use the rest and a little pampering."

"It's our turn to host a game night tonight, too. They'll be surprised," said Wynn. "Somehow, I thought Rall and Feia would be the first to have a baby since they've been doing it longer than we have."

Liam abruptly choked and burst into laughter as Wynn turned red. "They've been bonded longer! That's what I meant to say, Dad. They've been *bonded* longer than we have."

"I know, Son." As his urge to laugh subsided, Liam pulled his thoughts together. "Well, if we're having company later, we need to make some snacks too. What do you think? Some apples and sharp cheese? That would be good with cider."

"Good idea, Dad. I'll make omelets for supper. I'm actually good at those, and you make the snack plate. But we should let her sleep until dinner. She looks tired." He cast a worried glance toward the stairs.

"Don't worry. This is normal. She may even be unable to hold her food down for a while, but it'll pass."

◆◆◆

Lera sat in Mother Relynne's office, reading the note from Duran, informing the Holy Mother that Wynn and Seri were definitely expecting a child. "This could be the omen." She put the note aside and raised her eyes to meet Relynne's. "Remember the prophecy I was sent at Summer Solstice? *'The hero returns to the land of his birth, bonding with the chosen bride. The father seeks forgiveness at his son's hearth. The anvil rings with the sound of the hero's hammer and the scion grows strong. Green leaves return to the verdant valleys, trouble stirs in the Mountains of the Moon. Send forth the heroes four to stay the hand of Tauron.'* I take this to mean we must be prepared to mount a quest."

"I don't know. It may be we have only a month or so to get ready, or it could be next year or even the year after, which I think it will be. I've heard of nothing unusual happening up there right now. We'll say nothing about it until we actually receive word of trouble in the Mountains of the Moon and a request for help."

"There'll be a fourth, an earth-mage. Who it is will most likely be revealed in a true-dream soon enough," said Lera, yawning as she began to pick up her notes. "Gah! I'm tired, and I still have to meet Denys at the practice yard to work out."

"I practice first thing in the morning. I have more energy then." Relynne looked out the window into the twilight of the early evening. "I wish I could go with them. I haven't killed anything fun in years, not since the last pair of thunder-lizards we came across, Iain Farmer, Rande Pierson, Pallia Albersdottir, and me. What a fight they put up. They aren't really too big, maybe fifteen feet long for a really big one, not like a waterdrake. But Holy-Mother-of-All, they're quick."

Lera smiled at Relynne's well-known love of a good battle. "I do think Rall must be told of the prophecy since he'll lead the quest, whatever it turns out to be. It disturbs me that they had to kill those young children of Ariend last summer. Whatever could have happened to drive them down here? They must have suffered terribly." Lera's worried eyes sought comfort from Mother Relynne.

"I know. It's been worrying me too. I'm sure Rall is correct, that it's an omen of some sort. He's always right about portents, rather like you. For such young men to be out of their villages at all is worrisome because the old men who have suffered the madness Tauron wrought on their people prey on them. The head-women are usually much more protective of their young males." Mother Relynne sighed, an unusually melancholy mood possessing her.

"The destruction of Cascadia and the ruin of Ariend's children must someday be avenged," said Lera, feeling the gloom. "I know the universe will right itself one day, and then we will be free from Tauron and the threat he poses to Aeos and Neveyah."

Relynne firmed up her resolve, trying to project confidence. "All we have to do is keep the knowledge alive and let Wynn and his bloodline do what they must to secure the future until the advent of the end-times."

"I fear we're seeing the warnings now," muttered Lera. "The omens are so dark nowadays."

PART II
MOUNTAINS OF THE MOON

Chapter 14

Two years passed, and the three families had each expanded. With the babies weaned, the women had been traveling a lot, guarding Seri on her healing journeys. One early spring evening, Wynn was out on the laundry porch washing nappies, when a messenger delivered a summons for him to report to Mother Relynne's study the next morning at nine. Liam took the message and thanked the boy.

"I'll have to leave work to go there, I guess," said Wynn, when his father read him the note. "I'm sure Kaye will understand." He pegged the last nappy onto the line and dumped the rinse water, turning the washtub upside down to drain and mopping up with a rag. "I wonder what it could be about. I'm pretty happy with my work in the armory. I don't want to change jobs."

"Well, don't worry about it until you hear what it is," suggested Liam. Privately, he suspected Wynn was finally going on a quest but didn't say anything since he wasn't sure. Off and on over the previous few months, Liam, Kaye, and Lera had been working with Mother Relynne on something special, and now it looked like it was time to put her plan into motion. *Wynn will be unhappy when he finds out I've known about this for as long I have. He hates surprises, but I can't do anything about it. I'm sworn to secrecy.*

♦♦♦

Jules and Rall were waiting in Mother Relynne's study when Wynn arrived. Now the three mages sat quietly as they were briefed about the mission they would soon be sent on. The Holy Mother was somber as she explained the situation.

"So, in short, what we do know about Grakken is slim, but he's a mindbender. Of course, it's not his real name. It's a minotaur name, so he's definitely an acolyte of Tauron. No one we've interviewed can describe him, and no one knows for sure where his base is located. All we have are vague rumors. This lack of information indicates to me that a mindbender with some control over his madness is at work in the shadow of the Escarpment. Why he's chosen to roost in the Mountains of the Moon is a mystery, one your team will have to unravel. Mindbenders usually work in cities where they can blend in and corrupt as many of the local population as possible.

"Several people have vanished while traveling north of Widge, and while we can't be sure what has happened to them, we suspect they were either kidnapped or murdered. Baron Ivan Hemsteck himself hasn't been seen for two seasons. That's all we know for sure, as the spies we sent to check on him four weeks ago haven't returned. We suspect they're dead. We've sent someone else to find out what happened. He left five days ago, so we'll know soon enough.

"Over the last two months, the numbers of wild beasts preying on people traveling in the region have increased to alarming levels. The Temple militia has been forced to build a stockade around the remote trading post of Arlen to keep the more exotic creatures out of the village. This suggests Grakken is also a beast-master, which makes him extremely dangerous.

"In two weeks, you three will leave for the Hemsteck Valley. We'll round out your team with an earth-mage who's on his way back to Aeoven as we speak. Rall and Jules were novices with him." Mother

Relynne looked at her notes, "Devyn D'Mal. I always get his name confused with his uncle Derwyn. It must be a sign of my incipient senility. His uncle Derwyn was quite the ladies' man too, or so I recall." She winked at Wynn, who grinned sheepishly.

Lera smiled and shook her head slowly. "Senile! Your mind is as sharp as your sword. Don't think we don't know your tricks!"

Mother Relynne chuckled. "He's been posted in the South, building irrigation systems in some of the more rural farms and villages, and won't be back in town until Frosday. You'll be able to renew your friendships and get to know each other again. I've some comprehensive training planned for you, which will take about a week, so you'll have time to get your affairs in order before you depart on your journey."

Judging by the looks of consternation on Wynn and Rall's faces, Mother Relynne's soft, grandmotherly voice had just ruined their lives.

Wynn didn't want to leave the forge and especially not his family but figured he should just get it done. "I knew this was going to happen. Dad told me I would have to go on a quest someday, so now is as good a time as any. Best to get it over with so I can get back."

Rall too had been envisioning his career going up in flames, but that minor issue now faded into the background. He'd just heard a name that sent a stab of emotion through him, and it wasn't a good one. It was a name that had once been mentioned briefly in connection with Feia before their bonding. A mixture of dread and jealousy materialized in his consciousness, numbing him to the conversation around him. Anger blossomed in his heart—hot, wild anger he could barely control. "I'll kill him."

Wynn stared at Rall, not sure he had heard him correctly. Jules heard but locked in his own misery, the comment didn't register.

"No, you won't. I have a use for him," said Mother Relynne.

Rall suddenly flushed, realizing he'd spoken aloud. "I meant, ah...I'll embrace him. We haven't seen him in a while."

"Right," said Relynne, smiling innocently. Her sharp mind put two and two together. "You were close friends. This will be a wonderful renewing of your friendship." She knew exactly what would inspire her most trusted assistant to such a comment and resolved to settle it in her own way.

For a few brief moments, Jules had been thrilled beyond all comprehension at the thought of going out and doing something worthwhile again. He missed his frenetic days as Dorn's assistant, though he couldn't tell Aneka of his wistful longing for his old job. She would think he'd become bored with her and fatherhood. Even though such a thing would never happen, he was still careful of how she perceived him.

At least Jules was thrilled until he heard who the fourth mage was. *Oh, Goddess. Please not him,* Jules thought, as a roiling mixture of hurt and anger surfaced in him. *What an arrogant jackass. This trip is going to be hell. Oh well, I can ignore him most of the time.* "Yes. Seeing Dev again will be wonderful. Just...wonderful."

Once, Jules and Devyn had been the closest of friends. But when they became roommates as young journeymen, their friendship had soured. The two men

hadn't parted on good terms when Devyn had begged
Aljer to move Jules in with Rall and move their other
friend, healer Arne Severnsson, in with him instead.
Devyn's desperate plea that rooming with Jules was
like living in a privy had wounded him deeply. "Decent
people don't live like this, Jules," he had said, as he put
Jules's possessions out in the hall. "I refuse to put up
with this for even one more day."

*I'm a little disorganized, but he had no call to turf
me out.* They'd been as close as brothers, and the insult
had hurt. Now, just the thought of Devyn's foreign
mannerisms grated on Jules's nerves. To top it off, he'd
courted Aneka while Jules was posted in Armat, and
they hadn't spoken since.

In the midst of his sour ruminations, Jules suddenly
became aware the abbess was speaking.

"…once you four have taken care of that problem,
you can return," continued Abbess Lera.

He would *be assigned to this quest*, thought Jules
bitterly. *This stinks like a day-old fish.*

Each man hid his disturbance from the others,
pretending he was fully committed to the quest. The
morning wore on as the trip was planned and lists of
supplies and gear were reviewed and discussed.

◆◆◆

Later the same day, Wynn and his father sat in the
freshly scrubbed kitchen, watching his son, John, play,
waiting for Seri to return home. A fine dinner, courtesy
of Liam, simmered in covered pots, and four fat loaves
of bread rose on the work table, waiting to be baked.
"At least we have a week together before I have to go,"
Wynn said for the seventh time. "But Seri was hoping
we could just be together for a while."

"She knows what it's all about, being in the service of the Goddess," replied Liam. "Cheer up, Son. You can't do anything about it, so you may as well get on with it and do the job right."

"Oh, I intend to, Dad. Don't worry," agreed Wynn. "It's just that ever since Johnny was weaned, she's been traveling. Rall, Jules, and I all feel like single parents sometimes. We haven't been together much for the last two months, and I miss her. But we'll deal with this and get home as soon as we can." He lurched after his son who had taken several steps near the stove. "No, Johnny. That's hot."

"Da." Johnny twisted and wind-milled his arms until his father set him down. Pointing at the stove, he said, "Hot."

"Yes. Hot."

Just then, a knock sounded on the backdoor, and Jules entered with his fussy daughter, who frantically chewed on her hand, crying fitfully. "Liam, could you help me for a moment? I can't get Gayla to settle down, and I still have things to do before Aneka gets back. I'm at my wit's end." Jules's red face and agitation were comic. "She can't be hungry. I just changed and fed her!" She chose that moment to fart loudly. "And carrots don't agree with her."

Wynn laughed. "Leave her with us—she can help keep this one busy with his blocks. Then we can all have dinner here when our wives get home."

"Boks." They all looked at Gayla in amazement.

"Aw. I wanted her first word to be 'Dad.'" Jules sighed.

While he watched the babies playing, Liam sat thinking about Mother Relynne's secret project and his part in planning it.

Relynne and those companions of hers, who were that rare breed of mage over sixty-five and still healthy and actively serving the Goddess, would do the real work. They were strong, old mages like Relynne—hard as nails, wily, and shrewd. They would be implementing the part that required magic. Taj was younger and had been in Liam's group of novices, but Pallia and Rande had been novices with Liam's father, Iain.

Liam smiled at the prospect of what was in store for the four unsuspecting young mages, looking forward to seeing how they each dealt with it. *The element of surprise is the hardest thing about undertaking quests,* he thought. *They always seem to involve more surprises and disappointments than anything else.*

◆◆◆

The group all sat in the dining room at Wynn and Seri's house, while the three toddlers snoozed in the sitting room, snuggling together in the large crib Liam had built for them. "This soup is good, Liam," said Feia, as she broke off a chunk of bread to dip into the broth. "Very tasty!"

"I've learned a lot from watching Rall cook," he replied, pleased with the way his meal had been received.

"I can tell!" replied Feia, forgetting to pretend to disregard her husband's accomplishments in her happiness at being home. In response, Rall acted as if he hadn't noticed, as did everyone else. They had become quite good at that. Little Kalen had come into the world two weeks after Johnny, indicating to the world that Feia was not as cold to her husband as she feigned. Gayla, Jules and Aneka's daughter, had arrived two weeks after Kalen.

The three women were full of gossip from Armat.

"Dorn is doing well and starting to get over Bertte's death," Seri reassured both Liam and Jules. Jules had been surprised by how sad he'd felt when he was told she had passed away. "Dorn is still immersing himself in work but with his own particular twist. He felt the need to reorganize the storeroom by himself, to Bran's dismay. No one can find anything now." Everyone laughed. Surprisingly, Dorn and Feia had got along quite well once he put her in her place in his own unique way.

The welcome-home party progressed to the dessert stage. Sweets were a rare treat, and Liam had made blackberry tarts. "So what's been happening around here?" Aneka glanced at the men with a teasing smile. "Something's going on—I came home to a clean house. It makes me very suspicious!"

Everyone laughed at Jules's wounded expression. "I missed you. Gayla missed you. I didn't want a dirty house to get in the way of our reunion. It's been a long two weeks."

"We did miss you three," said Rall, making the effort to be diplomatic. For some obscure reason, he had chosen to wear a leather necklace, thickly strung with rather gruesome beads carved from bone in the shape of animal skulls, and had woven several elaborately beaded feathers into his long warrior's braid. While he often wore feathers, these were unique, much larger and more intricately beaded. The combination made him look rather barbaric.

"Well, you three *do* look like you're hiding something, so spill the beans." Aneka looked from face to face and back to Wynn again, knowing he was the weak link. "Wynn. Tell me the truth."

"I don't know what to tell you—nothing interesting ever happens around here, as you all probably know. Of course, we found out just this morning we're leaving on a quest in a week or two to take care of some rogue-mage or other who's been kidnapping and murdering up in the Mountains of the Moon. We'll be gone for who knows how long, but other than that, nothing's going on." Wynn shrugged and bit into his tart.

Suddenly around the table breaths were inhaled

He continued. "We aren't hiding it. We just wish we didn't have to go. An earth-mage will be with us, but I don't know him. He's been out of town for several years. We have to go to some place called Arlen, and then from there, we'll travel up into the mountains to an abandoned town. The mage is thought to be holed up in an old castle. It's pretty bad—he might have murdered the real owners and taken over their property. We just have to get rid of him, and then we can come home again. It's pretty standard stuff for these sorts of quests, or so I hear."

"Oh? Who is the fourth?" Aneka looked around the table. "Who?" she asked sharply. She knew of only one earth-mage of the caliber of the three men now sitting at the table. Jules just stared at the wall, a neutral expression on his face.

"His name is Demill," replied Wynn, swallowing the last bite of his tart. "He's quite strong, very highly regarded, and is from Mal Evol. I've read about that valley—it's a strange place, created by Tauron but

202

protected by Aeos. My mother was from there."

"It's D'Mal.... I know about Mal Evol," said Feia faintly, feeling a little queasy at the thought of Devyn D'Mal, the lecherous toad. She shuddered and promptly dismissed him from her mind. "I taught you about it, remember?"

Seri and Aneka too both felt surprised at hearing the name, for a variety of reasons. The table suddenly became rather quiet.

"I remember. Well, anyway, he's been posted in the far South for a while, but he'll be here in Aeoven on Frosday," said Wynn, oblivious as usual to the change of climate at the table. "We'll begin working with him on Lunaday." He finally mentioned the part that did worry him. "We have to quit our regular jobs to prepare for the quest. What if there's no room for me at the forge when we return? There are a lot of lightning-mages in Aeoven, and any one of them could do my job."

"Don't worry," said Liam, sensing the edgy feeling rippling around the table and guessing D'Mal was the cause of it. "Kaye will definitely have a place for you. She likes your work." He could also see that both Jules and, more surprisingly, Rall, felt surges of jealousy at the name. Liam had only one small healer's star on his left arm, and his skills were limited to farm magic, improving plants, but some water-mages were highly sensitive to the moods of those who surrounded them, and he was one of them.

For once, Feia saved the day, saying in her blunt way, "Perhaps Devyn isn't such a jackass as he was. He is strong with earth-magic, and he's not lazy, so he's a good match for you three." With one of her abrupt changes of direction, Feia asked, "Do you think Kalen has grown in the last two weeks? I could swear he's bigger. I feel like I've missed something in his life." The rest of the evening was spent on subjects that underscored their relative domestic bliss, a thing that also did not escape Liam's attention and made him smile.

◆◆◆

The days flew by far too quickly for Wynn. On Frosday, he made his goodbyes to his fellow smiths, relieved to know he would have a job to return to. The whole of Restday was spent with his little family, enjoying every minute with them while he could.

Lunaday morning dawned cold and rainy, as early spring mornings were wont to do. The three families walked the babies to the nursery as they always did, after which the group went on to the dining hall for breakfast, again just as they always did.

Jules looked rather grim, as if he had an impertinent student he intended to take apart. Rall looked even grimmer, what with his recent attachment to the trappings of his barbaric heritage. Still, both men were pleasant, publicly kissing their wives goodbye, much to Feia's surprise.

For some reason she couldn't fathom, Rall had taken to marking his cheeks with three black slashes in the style of Einar and braiding his warrior's feathers into his hair. He'd always done so when dueling but not usually for day-to-day business. Feia completely approved of his renewed pride in their tribal heritage. Those feathers had come from the nest of an eagle on the day he'd passed his tests and became a warrior. As Rall's bride-to-be back then, it had been Feia's task to

204

decorate and bead them, and they were exquisite examples of the northern art forms.

He'd also recently taken to wearing his trophy necklace. Although he would never be allowed to display real heads, each bead was created whenever he killed a beast or an enemy. Carved from the femur of his first kill, they were small replicas of the dead foe's skull. Feia was proud of her husband's trophy necklace, as it held more bead-skulls than most warriors twice his age, which reflected well upon her. She assumed he was preparing mentally for the quest and quite liked it, telling him it was good for Kalen to know his true warrior heritage.

Looking rather startled as Rall's lips brushed her cheek, she went to her classroom wondering what had gotten into him, not quite sure what to make of it. She was fully absorbed in planning her curriculum and had completely forgotten who her husband was to begin working with that morning. Had she remembered, she wouldn't have given it another moment's consideration. She touched her cheek and unwittingly smiled as she hurried to her waiting group of young journeymen.

Aneka's stomach was tied up in knots. She knew exactly what had brought on all the extra attention from Jules, even though Devyn's name hadn't been mentioned once since the dinner party at Wynn and Seri's house. Her husband had, however, been exceedingly attentive since her return, and she'd not had much sleep. She smiled, thinking that she liked him in a jealous snit. She just didn't want him to do something stupid like trying to kill Devyn, because the man had never meant more to her than a dear friend. She'd treated him badly when he was only trying to salvage her reputation. At least he'd forgiven her for being so awful to him.

Wynn, of course, behaved normally. He always kissed his wife goodbye publicly, so Seri wasn't surprised. She wasn't worried at all about how he would react if he found out Devyn had briefly been her lover. She hadn't been used to drinking wine and inadvertently became more than a little drunk. They woke in her room, and neither one could remember exactly what happened. Feeling somewhat chagrinned, they agreed whatever it was, it never happened. They were close friends, and neither one had the slightest wish to ruin their friendship. She'd been horribly ill with a hangover and didn't go down to breakfast. So as far as she knew, besides she and Devyn, only her cousin Lorana knew about the incident. Still, even if Wynn was to find out, he wouldn't have a problem with it. He simply didn't care about what happened in the past because in his mind their real lives only began the moment they met.

However, Seri could see the others hadn't forgotten who would be working with them. She did wonder how the morning was going to play out, since both Rall and Jules were seething masses of jealous angst. She squeezed Aneka's hand and cast ease on her as the three men left for the practice yard. "Don't be so worried. They'll work it out."

"I know, but Jules is…I've never seen him like this."

Wynn kept finding himself walking faster than the others, as they seemed to be dragging their feet. Finally, he said, "What's the matter? Are you two ill? Neither one of you looks well today."

"It's nothing," said Rall tersely. "I feel fine." He then began walking quickly.

"Nothing's wrong with me," Jules said, right behind Rall. "I feel fine. Just fine."

Wynn had to walk faster to keep up with them.

Chapter 15

Wynn, Rall, and Jules entered the men's dressing room, finding they were the only ones there. Relaxing a bit, the three of them geared up and went into the practice yard.

"I wonder where D'Mal is," muttered Jules. "It's not like him to be tardy."

A grandmotherly voice answered him. "He'll be here soon—I sent him to the armory. His new armor is ready. Thank you for your efforts, Wynn." Mother Relynne stood waiting, fully geared up. "You three are mine this morning and every day until you depart. After lunch, the four of you will meet your destiny for the week." Both Rall and Jules wore stunned expressions. "Wynn, have you maintained your training despite your descent into fatherhood?"

"Yes, ma'am. People always seem to want to duel with me, so I can't let myself slide or someone could win," replied Wynn promptly. "Jules and Rall are kind enough to spar together against me before lunch most days, which helps me stay alert. I have to work hard to beat the both of them when they team up against me, which is good since I don't like to lose."

Relynne smiled at Wynn's spate of information.

Jules and Rall both looked innocent, pretending they knew nothing.

She looked at them. "So. You two have been training up a secret weapon. I've heard you're picking quite a bit of gold off the journeymen by staging duels with your handpicked winner. Good planning, eh? Wynn was never a novice, so no one really knows him, and they fall into your carefully laid trap." She chuckled at their discomfort. "Then they're all so embarrassed at losing to a mage nobody ever heard of, they don't spread it around. Good for you. Know your enemies' weaknesses and use your tools wisely." Jules and Rall exchanged guilty looks, while Wynn looked slightly confused.

"First things first. Today, I will discover your strengths and weaknesses. Wynn—you and I will duel first this morning," she said. "Then Jules and then Rall, just to see how you two have developed since I last saw you in the arena. Devyn should be here by then, so he will go last." She looked at Wynn and said sharply, "We will use all the elements. Don't even think of going easy on me, boy. If you don't give me your best, I will cut you to pieces. Then I'll call for someone to heal you and I'll do it again. Am I clear?"

"Yes, ma'am. I always thought you were far too busy running things to worry about teaching me anything." He stepped across the practice yard to face her, bowing and raising his shields. With a slight sense of disorientation, Wynn found himself squaring off against the last person he had ever thought he would face.

The only word to describe Mother Relynne was formidable. Wynn immediately found himself tossing up shield after shield against her elemental volleys and defending against her aggressive sword attacks. Soon he forgot who he was dueling and became fully involved in the moment. His body moved automatically in the forms he'd been trained to use, and he too began spell-casting once he discovered the rhythm of her attacks. Somehow, he met and turned aside her every advance, his shields firmly in place no matter how quickly she changed elements. Soon he began copying her style of throwing random elements one after another, enjoying the feeling of having an opponent he didn't have to worry about hurting.

He was just starting to get warmed up when she suddenly called a stop to their duel. Immediately, he raised his sword and lowered his shields, bowing to her.

"Good! I was working a little there at the end, so you'll do just fine. I have to save my strength though in order to give these two layabouts some instruction." Relynne walked across to a table with refreshments. Drinking a little water and eating a bite of cheese on a cracker, she rested and told Wynn exactly what his weaknesses were. "But don't worry. By the time you leave here next Lunaday, you'll be cured." She set her mug down and walked back to the center of the practice yard.

"Thank you, ma'am. I don't usually get to use any element but water when I spar. I wish I could work out with you every day," replied Wynn. His expression made her think of a novice who was sure he would be denied a treat but was asking anyway. "Would you consider working with me again sometime?"

The thought that he could easily have beaten her in a true duel raced through her mind, a notion she wasn't prepared to test. She replied, "Of course, Wynn. Unfortunately, this week I'm pretty busy. But don't worry. I've arranged for a special tutor. The finest swordsman in all of Neveyah will be here just to work with you. You'll meet him this afternoon." Feeling as exhausted as she'd ever done but determined to hide it, Relynne pulled herself together. *Never let them see you weak,* she counseled herself. "Jules! Haul your sorry arse over here and show me what you've got."

As she finished with Jules, a small, thin man with lank, dark hair and dark eyes, wearing red and brown leathers, entered the practice yard, carrying new armor that Wynn instantly recognized, as it had been the most recent creation to leave his forge. Both Jules and Rall instantly bristled, reminding Wynn of lazy cats suddenly faced with a strange dog.

The mage was introduced as Devyn D'Mal, earth-mage. He geared up, and then nodding a polite greeting, he sat next to Wynn while Rall faced off against Mother Relynne. Then he took his turn against her.

After she had beaten each of them soundly, the group sat in the empty dining hall and listened to her plans for them. "I've spent the entire weekend bringing Devyn up to speed with his sword, and I'm sure he won't let it languish again."

He shrugged and grinned wryly. "It shall be as you wish, Mother. My bruises are healing well, and they remind me to heed your wisdom."

"So. Now Devyn is here, we can begin your real education. I've arranged a special week of intense training for you four lucky boys. I will be the rogue-mage."

The four men wilted. Through the mind of each ran scenarios of what she might be capable of inflicting upon them.

"Just for you, I've assembled a team of senior mages who will be my evil minions. I've also assembled another panel of senior mages to devise situations you might find yourselves in. They will set up the scenarios, and we will act them out." Wynn was surprised by the wolf-like expression that crossed her face. "My team will implement those plans, acting in the roles of your adversaries. Every mage involved in your training has fought and defeated some of the most well-known rogue-mages.

"We are going to try to murder you. In return, you are going to attempt to assassinate us. I don't like to lose either, Wynn, so you can be sure you'll be working like you've never worked before. My gut feeling is that by the time Frosday arrives, you boys will be a tightly-knit team." Relynne looked at the four men who, with the exception of Wynn Farmer, sat around the table in various stages of disgruntlement. She decided to shake things up a bit. "But first, we have some baggage that needs to be dealt with."

Rall and Jules looked sharply at her, and Devyn tensed, wondering what she was up to. She'd warned him something was festering like a boil in regard to him, saying she was going to lance it. He hated not knowing what he was walking into and consoled himself that at least the others were in the dark too.

"You three have wives. This man is suspected of having slept with each of them long before they were bonded to you. Any problems with this?" Relynne looked around the table.

"Yes," replied Rall instantly. "I do have a problem with it." His eyes glittered like ice as he gazed at Devyn.

Jules said, "I know he was involved with Aneka. It was my own fault. I was off being a jackass and didn't deserve any less." Jules glared at Devyn, who glared back. "However, we hear he is *still* as much of a jackass as I ever was." Jules sounded prim, and he knew it but couldn't stop the way he felt.

Everyone looked at Wynn, who shook his head, smiling his open smile. "I didn't even know Seri then, so why should it bother me now? When we met, we were completely honest with each other about how neither of us was a virgin. We did not, either one of us, name names because there were just too many to go into." Devyn's jaw dropped, as did everyone else's. "They don't mean anything, anyway. I'm bonded to her, and we're in love with each other, which is all that matters, right?" He turned his grin on Devyn and said, "I'm sorry, but I can't picture her with you. You're not her usual type at all, judging from most of the ones I've met."

Rall and Jules both grinned widely at Wynn's remark.

I knew I could count on Wynn to throw D'Mal into a spin, thought Mother Relynne smugly. *He cracks me up.*

Devyn didn't know how to respond. Rall's hostility he could understand. Jules's jealousy he could accept. Wynn's casual disregard interested him. "You intrigue me, lightning-mage. I thought I had instructed most of the older novices and younger journeymen. I wonder how it is we've never met? In regard to Seri, I would have said the same about you." Hoping to needle Wynn for his indifference, he added, "You appear quite young and pretty for a warrior."

Wynn laughed, surprising Devyn even more. "People always say that, as if I were trying to be something I'm not. I'm sure I'll look older someday." He shrugged. "I'm not a warrior, and I've never claimed to be one. Everyone knows I *hate* fighting. I'm an armor smith." He leaned forward companionably.

"Actually, I helped make your new armor. Do you like it?"

Devyn nodded, wondering why so young and apparently empty-headed a journeyman had been selected for the armory. "Yes. It's exceptional, as I expected it would be."

Wynn cocked his head and said, "Did you know you sound just like my mother when you speak? She was from Mal Evol too."

Devyn's head spun as he tried to keep up with Wynn's conversational diversions but nodded as if he had passed a test, smiling back at him. He felt Rall's eyes boring holes into him and looked up.

"Perhaps we could interest you in a duel with him," offered Rall. His eyes were alight with some unfathomable emotion.

Wynn was surprised at Rall's demeanor. With the black slashes on his face, his trophy necklace, the feathers in his white-blond hair, and those icy blue eyes, he looked more dangerous than Wynn had ever seen him.

Devyn met Rall's gaze. "Wouldn't you rather fight me yourself?" He held his ground, uncertain of his footing but not backing down in the least.

"Of course, I would. I'd love nothing more," Rall grinned, but it was an evil smile if ever Wynn had seen one. "I'm not allowed to though because I have this burning desire to kill you and wear your shrunken head around my neck as my trophy. In my village in the old days, I might have done just that. However, Mother Relynne has a use for you, so I'm sorry—I'll not be permitted to square off against you."

"Why do you feel like that?" Devyn returned his

hard gaze.

"We were friends, D'Mal. Friends! And you dishonored my wife. I do not see me getting past it." Rall's gaze held the depths of winter, and his northern accent had become quite pronounced now he was finally venting his rage. "If I were to find myself facing you, I would enjoy every moment of killing you. I cannot be trusted to stand opposite you with a sword in my hand."

Wynn was surprised to see this side of Rall. The others, however, weren't, having witnessed him losing control of his intense jealousy since they were novices.

"Have you never asked Feia what passed between us?" Devyn's gaze was curious now, with no hint of animosity. "You must have known for several days that I was selected for this. Did you ask her what happened?"

"No! And I will not dishonor her further by doing so." His fists were clenched, and each word was forced out through gritted teeth. "I will *not* offend her."

"Well, I'll tell you exactly what happened," Devyn said. "Nothing."

Rall looked up, his blue eyes piercing in their intensity, opening himself to the man, truth-reading him—the secret trick he thought no one knew he had.

"She refused me—rather vigorously, I might add." He raised his shirt, exposing a thin, white scar on his ribs. "My punishment for having dared to steal a kiss. She quite sharply told me only one man would ever have her, that only one man was worthy of her, making it clear that was *not* me. She was promised to you at the time. I had misunderstood her previous ranting about your and her situation as meaning she intended to be a free woman. She did not mean such, not at all. Indeed, she bonded *you* quite willingly."

Rall sat silently, thinking about the implications of what Devyn had just told him. Finally, his head dropped into his hands. "I'm a jealous fool. I owe her a debt of honor." His uncertain gaze wandered back to Devyn, who was still unsure what to expect. "You did nothing wrong. I apologize for wanting to kill you, not that an apology makes it any better."

Devyn subconsciously breathed a sigh of relief. Rall was dangerous to anger because on the rare occasions he lost control, it came out with a vengeance, and no one could guess how it would manifest.

Wynn was relieved the trouble had passed. "Rall, Feia most likely doesn't even know you've been in a jealous snit for the last week." Rall's mouth dropped open, and Devyn burst out laughing, as did Mother Relynne. "She's just like me. She never notices anything unless it involves her personally."

"You really are still the consummate barbarian, despite all our efforts training it out of you, aren't you, Rall?" Relynne smothered her grin. "Everyone forgets this about you because you're so sophisticated and polished. But, buried beneath the shell of the elegant water-mage lurks a simple, jealous barbarian who thinks with his sword, no matter how hard you try to keep him hidden. *This* is why I'm going to miss having you as my assistant." She patted Rall's arm comfortingly. "I loved the touch about the shrunken head, by the way. I wish I had been born a barbarian."

Devyn shuddered.

Rall's face grew red with chagrin. "Sadly, I am what I am, your holiness. I was born and raised in

Einar, so the barbarian will always be lurking inside of me, causing me trouble." He looked at Devyn and sighed. "I meant it when I apologized. I'm embarrassed to think I believed the worst of you when we were once friends. It was my perception you had disregarded our friendship that made me so angry. I owe you a debt of honor, and I will repay it." His eyes held a fleeting bleakness, which disappeared almost immediately. "I know she was loud in her anger at our betrothal. I can't blame you for misunderstanding her."

"I'm glad you're happy in your bonding," replied Devyn, with a wistful smile, "I've not been fortunate enough to find a wife."

Jules had been shifting restlessly, impatient to have his chance at telling Devyn exactly what he thought. "Well, I'm just going to say it straight out. I don't like you," said Jules, glaring at Devyn. "I don't hate you, and I've no desire to kill you, but I just want it made clear, I don't like you at all. But I can work with you."

"Good, because I don't like you either." Devyn glared back at him. *Jules* he could handle. "You were a pig of a roommate, always stealing my clean socks and never picking up after yourself. And since we're being honest, I'll just say you're a complete jackass. But regardless of how you treated her, Aneka chose you." He was just warming up. "You publicly humiliated her, and she reacted badly. She was throwing her life away, and it was because *you* rejected her. You'll never know how it hurt me to see Aneka, a true friend whom I have cared about and respected since I came here as a novice, brought so low by someone who was closer to me than my own brother!"

Jules visibly winced.

"*I* may be a jackass, but I have never treated a girl in as shabby a manner as you did her. I felt a debt of honor was owed on your behalf, so I offered her respect and an honorable bonding contract. She refused me. It was her right and her choice, even though I would gladly have accepted the geas of faithfulness. I would have been a devoted husband to her even without it. I don't understand why she took you back after you humiliated her so publicly." He refused to look at Jules. "I did accept it, though. I hear you've treated her well since you were bonded and that you are a good husband to her."

Red-faced, his eyes bulging, Jules appeared to be on the edge of an explosion. Rall and Wynn exchanged glances. Relynne shrugged faintly, and the three watched the confrontation as it unfolded.

Suddenly, Jules deflated, looking at his hands. "Well, at least you and I agree on one thing. You're absolutely right—I wasn't worthy of her then. My actions nearly destroyed her, and I was so self-absorbed, I had no idea. Next to *you*, I was the least worthy man she could possibly have chosen. However, she did choose to forgive me, and I thank the Goddess every day." Now he raised his steely gaze to Devyn. "But don't pretend you're any better than I was, because you're not. Your exploits are no less notorious than mine ever were, and from what we frequently hear, you've been enlarging upon them. What about the lady from Dervy just last Harvest?"

Now Devyn winced.

Jules was on the attack, exploiting his opponent's weakness. "You say you don't treat nice girls the way I did Aneka, but rumor has it you stole this girl from

Morvin, just another notch on your belt. But, as soon as your post was up, you were gone and you didn't look back, leaving her dangling. You were too busy entertaining the free women in Moriston. And after you finished with that, it was Minea, the fire-mage, who, so we hear, was rather angry with you. We've all heard how she took you apart on the practice field for it." Despite the fact that Jules had moderated his tone, his words were loud in the dining hall. "So, if you think you're going to get between me and my wife, you can think again. I won't allow it."

"Have some faith in your wife!" Devyn's exasperation at the situation got the better of him, and his voice became sharp. "And, surely you know me better than that after all this time, Jules. Or is it yourself you're worried about?"

Jules's eyes narrowed dangerously. He sputtered, inarticulately grasping for his words.

Devyn ignored his rage. "Since you're curious, I'll tell you about Giuliana of Dervy. She pursued me, and I was quite flattered by it. Like a green fool, I took her up on her offer. Of course, being new in town, I was unaware she had an understanding with Morvin. I was the last to find out, and then it was too late to salvage our friendship. And then, it turned out, as it so often does for me, that she had only been interested in my family's position and my brother's throne." His eyes flashed, and his voice turned bitter. "Once she found out that, since I'm a member of the Clergy of Aeos, I'll never enjoy the money or the position to which I was born, she found other, more lucrative fish to fry. Did you even ask Morvin what really happened, or is all this information through the grapevine? I'm often a jackass, but I don't pursue women who are attached."

Jules started to say something cutting, but Rall put his hand on his arm.

Devyn's firm voice belied his churning stomach. "Also, you obviously know nothing about Minea—she makes Feia look like the soul of reason. First, she made me think I was the center of her universe, and then she dumped me like I was trash. She threw me over for a burly, young officer in the Temple Guard." Devyn shrugged. "And, yes, she did kick my butt all over the practice field at Bryton Temple."

Jules easily fell back into their old rapport, forgetting he'd been enraged only a minute before. "But that's ridiculous. You should have been able to defeat her easily. She has no real strength of magic—she's vicious but predictable with her sword. I know for a fact you could easily have beaten her in a mage-duel, so what really happened?"

"She set me up. I had just trounced her new lover in a fair sword fight, and she was not at all pleased with me at that moment. I should never have let him goad me into it, and she made sure I was sorry I had. That's how I knew she'd set us *both* up. She wanted me exhausted from fighting him so she could best me in a so-called mage-duel. You're right about one thing—she did beat me black and blue—but only because I refused to raise a blade against her. So she threw fire at me until she ran out of chi. I have excellent shields, so her tantrum did her no good."

"Fire! In a duel? What was she thinking?" Jules was plainly shocked, as were Rall and Wynn.

"Fortunately, she can barely light a campfire." Devyn rolled his eyes and shrugged.

"Minea has always been trouble," Rall agreed. "I don't think she'll ever make tenured adept because she's at least thirty years old and is still a rank journeyman. Her temperament holds her back. She's inhibited about the magic and never really learned to visualize well."

"So now you know why my adventures have since been confined to the friendly-girls and free women. They're uncomplicated and have no hidden agendas." Devyn forced himself not to shrug again, as it was a habit that annoyed Mother Relynne. "Besides, I build irrigation systems and damned good ones, if I may say so. In doing my work, I'm always posted to out-of-the-way farming communities for months at a time. Despite my wishes to the contrary, there's no reason for me to think about anything permanent when I'll be away from home all the time."

"Minea cut a wide swath through all the journeymen of her group. I'm surprised you of all people fell victim to her, D'Mal!" At Devyn's embarrassed grin, Mother Relynne softened her harsh tones. "Although you're probably too young to have known about her since she's a decade or so your senior. She stirs up trouble everywhere she goes." Relynne snorted. "Just so you know, that little snit got her sent to an all-female squad and stationed permanently on Serende Wall. I won't tolerate that sort of behavior among the clergy, and she'd been censured before."

"I admit I was lonely, and Minea can be quite entertaining. But enough of my failures." Devyn leaned forward, saying, "Aneka forgave you, and I forgive you. So what is the problem here, Jules?"

Having had the chance to vent, Jules was over his

anger. He easily fell back into the old feeling of kinship he'd always had for Devyn before their rift. "Gossip is often inaccurate, but you know how it is. Scandal is the main source of entertainment in this town. I believed the worst of you because I was angry." His face reddened as he admitted, "In my case, the rumors were correct, sadly. I owe you an apology. I think I'm still hurt over the way you tossed me out when we were sharing an apartment, but I understand a little better now, since Aneka has been house-training me."

Everyone laughed, and Jules rolled his eyes, shifting in his seat again. "So, since you've asked, my problem is this: our quest will be my first posting away since we were bonded. Aneka has been traveling, but I've always been here with the baby. She hasn't come out and said so, but she doesn't trust me. To be fair, she *wants* to, but as Rall and Wynn will both tell you, she'll have that undercurrent of doubt, that niggling fear I'm misbehaving, for the whole time we're gone. I understand, and given my actions before our bonding, I don't blame her, but I meant our bonding vows with all my heart—I'll swear it upon my vows to Aeos, if that's what it takes to make you believe me."

"I know you love her. I also know how you are about your vows, and so does she, I'm sure." A wave of affection swept over Devyn, the feeling of having regained a brother. "She would never have gone through with registering your bonding if she didn't."

Wynn spoke up, consoling Jules. "Don't worry. If we have to go to a common room, we'll just make it clear we're not interested. Devyn can behave like a pleasure-boy to his heart's content, and we three will remain happily bonded." Relynne, Rall, and Jules all burst out laughing. Confused, Wynn tried to figure out just what he'd said that was so funny.

Devyn looked every bit as shocked and affronted as he felt. "I'm not a pleasure-boy. I'm popular." Wynn laughed and apologized. Devyn added gloomily, "Besides, I haven't been to a common room since I left Bryton. They don't interest me anymore."

Wynn clasped his shoulder. "I know," he said. "That life is exciting for a while, but when you're done with it, it's easy to walk away."

Once she stopped chuckling, Mother Relynne turned brisk. "Well, now we should get some lunch. We have a lot to cover before we head back to the practice yard and you meet my special crew of evil minions."

Smiling at her jest, they stood up and had just about made it to the buffet table when Mother Relynne said loudly, "Wynn!" He turned back to her. "You'll be dueling against *my* handpicked champion after lunch." She rubbed her hands together. "I've a small wager riding on you, so don't let me down."

Surprised, Wynn nodded, his sudden, hangdog expression nearly comical.

To Devyn's eyes, he looked like a novice sent to the headmistress's study for an error in judgment. He said in low tones to Rall, "Look at him. He's so young—and he just made it clear he doesn't like to fight. Why is she tormenting him?"

Jules and Rall smiled, wondering who was slated to be Wynn's next victim.

It occurred to Rall that an opportunity to score off his friend's ignorance had just presented itself. Seeing agreement in Jules's eyes, he put his arm about Devyn's shoulders, whispering confidentially so Wynn couldn't hear him. "We don't know why the Holy Mother has it in for Wynn—maybe she's trying to toughen him up. He was her first victim this morning." Rall managed an ingenuous smile. "So you're aware of how young he is. He idolizes us since we're his instructors. If Jules and I support him when he's in this sort of situation, it gives him confidence, so we always *do* back him monetarily. He's awfully good for a boy his age." He sighed, saying, "If you're set on wagering against him, of course, we'll have to take you up on it. It's only what we owe him as friends."

Chapter 16

Wynn stood alone in the practice yard, stretching and warming up, waiting for his opponent to finish gearing up in the men's dressing room. Jules, Rall, Devyn, and Mother Relynne sat in the viewing area along with Lera, Dorn, Kaye, and Liam. They comprised the team of mages who would be planning and setting up the training conditions beginning the next morning. Also sitting with them was an older water-mage named Rande, introduced to Wynn as the abbot of Nola Temple, and a lightning-mage named Pallia, the abbess of Braden Temple. A late arrival was a senior healer Wynn had seen around the infirmary when he went to meet with Seri for lunch. He wondered why all the famous mages were there.

"I hope pretty boy is as good with his sword as you two seem to think he is, but I think I'm stealing your money. Look at him. He knows he's in trouble," murmured Devyn to Rall. "The poor kid. Is he even eighteen years old? Taj will grind him to dust. To my knowledge, he's never been beaten."

Overhearing that remark, Liam grinned wickedly. "Oh, yes! Taj has been beaten. I regularly kicked his arse twenty-five years ago. I didn't know he was still fighting. Oh, and pretty boy isn't really all that young. He just turned twenty-two."

"Really! I wouldn't have guessed he was my age," Devyn looked surprised. Looking at Rall out of the corners of his eyes, he said, "I wonder what else I've been misled about." He leaned over and introduced himself to Liam, clearly wondering who the old mage was. "I'm Devyn D'Mal, earth-mage."

"Liam Farmer, retired water-mage and Wynn's father," replied Liam, smiling. "My late wife was your mother's cousin, Arla D'Vyllyrs."

"I know of you, sir. I've studied your exploits." Devyn's thin face lit up, clearly pleased to find he had family so far away from his home. "So Wynn is my kinsman!"

"Sssh!" said Jules, intently focused on the pair of combatants, as the older mage entered the practice yard. "Watch and learn, Devyn. Watch and learn."

As soon as Taj stepped into the practice yard, Wynn's attitude changed. Unconsciously, he assumed an aggressive stance, the change in his demeanor making him appear more his age. He sensed his opponent was a fire-mage, and he was a giant of a man, taller even than Rall. That Wynn didn't know his opponent wasn't unusual, as he'd never met most of the people he faced. But this man was easily the strongest mage Wynn had ever met. His confident moves as he ran through his warmup exercises left no doubt in Wynn's mind that this adversary knew his way around the traditional mage-duel extremely well.

After five minutes, the man bowed to Mother Relynne. "I am ready." His voice was deep and his speech heavily accented with the sounds of Mal Evol.

The two combatants bowed to the crowd and to each other.

"Champions—in this duel, all the usual restraints are off. You may use any element you have the ability to call, short of killing your opponent." Mother Relynne's voice rang out. "Begin!"

Raising his basic shield, Wynn waited with his sword at the ready for his opponent to attack, completely focused, watching his style and the way he moved. The older mage saw that as a weakness and rushed toward him. The battle was engaged. Wynn forgot everything but the challenge of meeting his opponent's attacks and making his own. His adversary began by calling water, an effort to deceive Wynn about his intention, but instead, he immediately switched to fire. Wynn's nervous sensitivity to the magic others raised was sharp, and his shield switched and held firm, never faltering.

Now Wynn rushed his foe, and they parried vicious blows. Their practice swords clacked, and their stamping feet echoed in the yard as they battled. They separated and circled, looking for an opening and launching vicious spell-combos at each other. Pressing forward, their swords flashed in a display of skill that left the onlookers breathless. Wynn met and blocked each of the rapid-fire blows, parrying and evading, then pressing forward again, neither man landing a blow in the opening minutes.

"Amazing," muttered Devyn. "I've perhaps bet on the wrong mage." He heard a strange, rumbling sound next to him. It was Rall, unable to contain his gleeful chuckle. Devyn rolled his eyes. "I'm such an idiot. I should have known better. I always fall into your little traps, barbarian."

"I know," said Rall, laughing wickedly. "That's what I like best about you." Deep chuckles occasionally burst forth, as he attempted to stifle his mirth.

Wynn gasped as he was stung on the thigh, and he savagely reposted, striking the man's ribs. For each blow an opponent inflicted on him, Wynn always tried to give two, but he struggled with this foe, barely able to return bruise for bruise. The dust raised by their feet hung in the air like a smoky haze as the battle raged back and forth across the practice yard, the combatants pressing attack after attack, interspersed with random spells. Wynn gleefully used the spell-combos he'd learned only that morning from Mother Relynne, causing his opponent to slow, thinking about his defenses.

They were equally matched, and the battle stretched on far longer than most duels Wynn had fought, but at last, his opponent began relying more and more on magic, which meant he was tiring. In response, Wynn pressed his sword attacks even more aggressively, hoping to fatigue Taj further. Fire sheeted off Wynn's shield, followed by lightning, combos that were devastating, but Wynn's ability to rapidly change elemental shields never faltered. Wynn also began to tire but pushed himself, searching for a way to break the man's shield. He cast his own fire, followed by water, followed by lightning, and again he pressed his sword attack, forcing his adversary to backpedal across the yard. Even so, the mage's shield held firm and didn't waver or buckle, no matter what Wynn threw at him.

Exhaustion rapidly crept up on him, and Wynn struggled to stay nimble, barely meeting his adversary's attacks, concerned he might lose after all. *Need to crack his shield...need to break his shield.... His shield is strong as steel...steel.... That's it! Steel!* He fired off a steel-cutting bolt, finely focused into a white-hot needle of light and energy, aiming for the place where everyone tied their shields off. The spell was what Wynn used when making armor.

The bolt cut through the ties and broke his opponent's shield. Immediately, Wynn doused his opponent with icy water and then swiftly followed up with the sword, forcing the older mage to retreat while furiously struggling to raise his shield again. With his adversary's back to the cordons, Wynn broke his new shield and again dumped icy water on him, landing him on his back. Water was the only element duelers were allowed to use on an unshielded opponent.

"Enough! I yield!" Suddenly, the battle was over, and his opponent knelt before him, conceding the fight.

Numbly, Wynn dropped his shield and bowed, trying to get his breath.

The onlookers erupted into applause, and Wynn held out his hand, helping his foe to his feet. "Hello. My name is Wynn Farmer. Where did you learn that wicked little sidestep and strike? And also your trick feint is quite distracting! You nearly had me there at the end."

"I'm Taj B'Jornas," replied the huge man, smiling widely. "I should have known you were Liam's boy. You looked familiar to me, but I couldn't place you. Your style of swordplay is completely different from his. I'll be working with you this week, along with a few other old timers who've already encountered what you're about to face, but there's little I can teach you about dueling," said Taj, his expression rueful as he wiped his face with a large bandanna. "I was warned you were good. You're better at dueling than your father, and he was the best."

"I've heard Dad was quite good before his illness," replied Wynn, with a proud grin. "Unfortunately, he's unable to use his magic now, if he would preserve the life he has left. Are you friends? Here he is." He gestured toward Liam, who was approaching, a wide smile on his face.

While the three men talked, Mother Relynne collected her winnings. "C'mon, Rande, pry open your purse! Pallia already paid up, so fork it over, you old tightwad. Thank you, Soren—I warned you, but you didn't believe me."

Devyn silently handed Rall and Jules their winnings.

"Just like old times, eh, Dev?" Jules laughed at his resigned grin. "I'll tell you a secret because we're stuck with each other for the next who-knows-how-long, and you may as well benefit from it too. As tired as he looks right now, we could put Wynn in the arena again tonight, and he would win. He faced off against Mother Relynne this morning in a duel twice as long as what she put you, Rall, and me through, and *she* called a halt to it, long before he'd even warmed up!"

"I've never seen anything like him," muttered Devyn. "Did you see what he did to Taj's shield? No one's ever broken his shields. I know it for a fact. Why does he claim not to be a warrior? If he isn't, then who is?"

Shaking his head, Rall replied, "Wynn Farmer honestly believes he is just a simple farm-boy-turned-smith who hates to lose. But something about him changes everything just because he is involved. Take a look at his augmentations and count the luck-runes sometime."

Jules clasped Devyn's shoulder. "He doesn't try to manipulate things in any way. He's not the sort of person who would. But you'll find yourself doing and saying things around him you had absolutely no intention of. When you just go along with it, you'll find it was the right thing all along!" He grinned widely, adding, "How do you think I finally saw the light? It was Wynn who showed me I was in danger of losing Aneka forever."

As they stood talking, Wynn came over. "My father tells me we're kinsmen—please, come and have dinner at our house tonight. I'll send a messenger to Seri, but I'm sure she'll be glad to see you again. She was pleased when she found out you were questing with us. Anyway, Taj will be there tonight visiting my father. They were novices together."

"I'll be glad to, cousin, if you're sure Seri won't mind a surprise guest."

"She's used to it, and this is special—I've never had a cousin to dinner." Wynn's smile reassured Devyn. "In fact, you're the only one I have!"

◆◆◆

The next morning, the four questers went directly to the large, fallow field south of the practice yard where the Temple militia usually drilled. At the southern end, a grandstand had been set up with a long table and four chairs on a dais, shaded by a canopy and protected from the weather, where Liam, Kaye, Dorn, and Lera sat. Stacks of paper lay before them, and their heads were bent over something, conferring and making notes. Duran and a pair of journeyman healers sat to one side with medical kits at the ready. A sense of urgency and purpose filled the air.

Many support personnel ran around, getting things ready. Piles of equipment stood waiting and ready for use as needed. Wynn felt intimidated, as he hadn't realized just how big a deal this week of training was going to be.

"What are they doing here? My dad never said anything about this and neither did Kaye!" Wynn said, anxiously. "Look at this place! It has to have been planned for a long time. They couldn't have just thrown this together yesterday. Dad and Kaye must have known about this for a while, but neither said anything." He cast several dark looks in their direction. "Taj was over for dinner last night and didn't say anything either, did he, Devyn?"

"No," Devyn just shook his head, feeling the now familiar sense of being one step behind. "But her holiness loves to see me twisting in the wind."

"How we handle the element of surprise is a large part of this, I'm sure." Jules watched the commotion, saying, "The abbacy has to have known for at least a year that something would happen requiring a quest."

Devyn nodded, but Wynn shook his head, clearly not understanding at all.

"When the Goddess speaks, she often does so through Abbess Lera," explained Jules. "I'd guess Aeos long ago made clear to her and the holy mother through true-dreams and prophecies exactly what will be required of us and how to go about teaching us the skills we'll need."

"You're right," said Rall, a look of complete mystification crossing his face. "But they kept it a complete secret from me. I'm her assistant, so how she did it, I will never know."

"She is one crafty woman, the holy mother is," asserted Devyn dryly. "She's just full of surprises." His bruised body still ached from the torture she'd put him through over the weekend, trying to get him back up to speed with his sword-work.

The field was newly mowed. White lines were drawn with powdered lime, similar to the lines of the kickball field. Boulders had been placed randomly, and small evergreen shrubs and trees now dotted the landscape. It was apparent that several earth-mages besides Abbess Lera had been employed in preparing the field for the training. Each side of the field was set up in the same way. A blue flag waved over the west tent, and a purple flag waved over the east. The side of the field with the purple flag, now rising in an extreme vertical incline as if it were a steep hillside, was elevated much higher than the side with the blue flag. A number of places had been created so the purple team would have good footing and would be shielded from the downhill side. The blue team had a few sparsely placed boulders and shrubs to shield them. They were definitely at a disadvantage.

"Blue is Aeos' color," Devyn said, when Wynn wondered why those particular colors were selected. "Amethyst is Tauron's color."

"So they're telling us this is really about Tauron and Aeos," Wynn mused. "I don't know why it surprises me to think our quest would be about the war of the gods."

"I'll tell you something most people don't know. Quests that involve our families are *always* about Aeos, Ariend, and Tauron. Whenever we're involved, it's because the goddess is countering the Bull God's move." Devyn grinned at Wynn's astonishment. "Do your research, cousin. I'll send you the book you need."

"I'll take it with me because I do enjoy reading,"

Wynn replied. "I'd thought to bring a book of poetry, but that will be interesting."

Wynn's partiality for poetry surprised Devyn. "Who is your favorite? My preference is for Aldo L'Rwyn, but he's fairly unknown in the West."

"Seri and I just finished reading his book, *Leaves and Shadows*," replied Wynn. "We enjoyed it very much. My preference right now is for Rovyn S'Ryll— I'm fond of romantic poetry. Jules teases me no end over it. We read plays quite often too, Seri and I."

"It'll be nice to have someone to discuss the wonderful literature of Mal Evol with, for a change," laughed Devyn. "Jules is partial to epic tales of improbable derring-do, and Rall is only interested in the great philosophers. We'll have much to share on this journey."

The four questers were told to gear up and rest in the tent with the blue flag, supplied with plenty of water and ration bars. A worktable with four chairs around it stood in the center, along with a stack of paper and pencils. Four cots lined the perimeter.

A note on the table read, "Welcome. This is your home until you defeat the rogue-wizard Relynne. You will be released to your families when and *only* when you have utterly defeated your opponent. Just winning a battle will not be enough. You must prevail outright in this war, and you will stay here until you do."

"I wonder if the amethyst team's tent is set up somewhat the same way." Rall fidgeted, pacing and examining everything they had been given. "I suspect they have better food and more medicine. It's the rogue wizard Relynne's lair, so I'm sure they're quite comfy." He was not quite able to disguise his bitterness about so large an undertaking having been organized under his nose and being kept completely in the dark. "In fact, I bet they have Soren Torsson over there, along with his best journeymen healers." He looked out the door, and sure enough, Soren was just slipping into the amethyst tent, followed by Amalea Olesdottir.

Jules saw her too. "Poor Amalea—at least *we* don't have to put up with him. He's not good company when he wants to be somewhere else, and you can bet he doesn't want to be here when there are patients who need him more."

"Soren will be projecting Mother Relynne's seemings," said Devyn. "The man is quite good at them, or so my Uncle Derwyn told me."

"So we won't know what's real and what's not," replied Wynn. "I've read about them. We'll have to assume whatever we see is real because they've gone to a lot of trouble for this. It won't all be seemings because I saw a crate full of water-sprites. They always seek me out, the pesky things."

Jules snorted. "You're a lightning-mage—of course they seek you out. You make their skin itch." He set aside the map he'd drawn of the layout of the field and began a separate list with the words *water-sprites* and *seemings*. Then he returned to looking his map over. "I think I have all the boulders marked." He ducked back outside for another quick look around.

"At least in Markett, I could go fishing without having icy water dumped on me out of nowhere." Wynn loved fishing, and he'd been disgusted to discover the River Stowe that flowed through Aeoven was infested with water-sprites. "They're quite interesting but very annoying."

Rall snickered. "Just wear your armor when you go fishing. It's bespelled against water attacks." He broke into guffaws at Wynn's affronted expression.

"You're hilarious, barbarian."

Rall was still chortling when Jules reentered the tent, adding more notes to his map. He settled down as they looked through the gear that had been left for them and put on the blue tabards over their armor. They saw the sense in wearing them, since the armor worn by each side tended to look a lot alike. Fire-mages had variations on red, water-mages were blue, earth-mages brown and red, and lightning-mages were white and yellow. If things got too thick in a melee of the sort apparently planned for them, it would be hard to tell who was on their side without the team colors prominently displayed.

Soon they heard a horn blast. "Time to go," said Jules, reading from the slip of paper he found resting on his cot. "We're to line up in front of the dais and hear what the panel has to tell us." They followed Rall out through the tent flap, Wynn's nerves as taut as harp strings.

Chapter 17

The sun was setting. The four questers had fought six difficult battles that day, each ending in a standoff, but they had not succeeded in defeating their opponents.

"This could take days," muttered Jules, as he rooted around in their supplies, finding only ration bars to eat. "I bet they have food catered from the kitchen over there."

Jules, Rall, and Devyn huddled around the table in their tent, exhausted and filthy. Wynn sat in a corner, improving their wooden blades, carefully shaving the edges with his belt knife until they were sharp enough to cut paper. Once they were as deadly as he could make them, he mended their armor, getting used to using the tools he would be working with on the road. The other three tried to plan for the next battle while he quickly got their gear ready.

"What do you think the scenario for this next one will be?" Jules asked Rall.

"Whatever it is, it will be more difficult. Both our exhaustion and the lack of light are going to be big factors." Rall's reply was muffled as he rooted around in the medical kit.

"Very true," muttered Devyn. He held a tin cup of medicinal tea with one hand and a compress to his forehead with the other. "They're being healed between each battle and partially healed during each fight. Apparently, Duran is only posted on the dais in case one of us is actually dead. He hasn't stirred his bones all day—instead, he's been having a party, laughing and joking with Wynn's dad, Kaye, and Lera, but doing nothing else. Mother Relynne has both Soren and Amalea in her tent." Dutifully, he sipped the tea, grimacing at the flavor.

"That's the point, though." Rall examined Devyn's head wound again. Closing his eyes, he cast heal, though his curative ability was limited. Devyn sighed as the throbbing diminished. "A few more times of using this skill and I might be able to actually heal a cut or scrape," Rall muttered, unable to tell if his magic was working or not. "I think I was able to stop the bleeding. Yes…there is a small improvement. Not a lot, unfortunately, but now it looks as if it were a day old. If I apply some more ointment, it should improve quickly. At least they gave us the best medicines."

"Thank you. Every time you use your talent, small though it may be, it takes away most of the pain. You've been trained as a field medic, so your skill will help some." Devyn leaned back, resting his head while Rall tended to it, willing the tea to work its magic. "I suspect the star on your hand will be useful on this journey."

"Not as much as we'll need. Grakken will have several untrained battle-mages in his thrall, and he'll be guiding and healing them both during and after any battle. In return, they'll shield him from our attacks. I can't figure out how they're able to do this, and believe me, I've tried." Rall finished re-bandaging Devyn's wound. "Anyway, for healing, we'll have to rely on ointments and potions because my pathetic ability is not good enough. I'm better with plants."

The combination of the pain-relieving tea and Rall's limited healing eased Devyn's discomfort. He sat up, focusing his attention on the problem at hand. "I'd say we'll face some sort of elemental this next time."

Jules said, "I agree. Grakken might use them against us. There's been an influx of beasts along the northern trade road, and rumors are rife, but no one knows for sure what his skills are. Since Mother Relynne hasn't yet pulled a major elemental beast that we're unfamiliar with out of her pocket, I suspect the rare elemental is up next." He passed around rations and poured water for everyone. Wynn quickly ate and returned to his tasks.

"We need to talk to Wynn about elementals," Devyn said, looking over at his cousin's disheveled profile. "If he's as new to Neveyah as he claims, he may not have seen too many of them. And trust me, they're rampant the Mountains of the Moon. Many strange beasts haunt that area."

"He's the only person I know who ever killed a water-wraith with arrows," replied Jules. "He accidentally infused them with lightning, and they took care of the beast. I was unconscious at the time." He shrugged. "I had warned him not to cast any magic at the wraith because he had no shields, and he'd accidentally blown up a boulder the day before, so he wasn't supposed to be using lightning at all." Devyn's eyebrows rose until they disappeared under his bandage. "But when Wynn saw the wraith, he wished his arrows were lightning, and with his visualization skills, that was all it took."

Devyn nodded. "I can see him doing something like that accidentally. Today has been interesting, working with him. He does have an unusual style," agreed Devyn, shaking his head carefully to keep it from aching again. "So he fully understands about what *not* to do with elemental beasts?"

"I think so. You noticed his style," needled Rall, with an evil grin. "One thing Jules and I forgot to tell you—Wynn follows instructions exactly, so you must be precise when you tell him to do something."

"I've noticed your omission," agreed Devyn, rolling his eyes. "You also forgot to tell me he doesn't appear to know the difference between sarcasm and instructions."

"Don't worry. With a proper haircut, you'll look just fine. Once the singed part is trimmed off, you'll be your usual debonair self!" said Jules, also grinning. "At least you didn't get zapped. His cat-zappers are something else." He smirked at Rall. "Just ask Feia…she wore a perpetually startled look for two months when she first had him as a student."

Rall laughed, enjoying an uncharitable moment at his wife's expense. He looked at the list he'd gotten from the planning team. "This time, we're to meet the enemy in the forest. If you can call those scrubby shrubs a forest."

Wynn looked up from his work and said, "I repaired your sword belt, Rall. It won't fail there again, though I wish I had more leather. And your shoulder piece is good, Dev. Here you go." He handed over their gear. "I've been thinking. I could make better swords if I had the opportunity. But we're stuck with these, and I won't have the chance. Anyway, I've made them a little sharper, so we'll inflict some pain. Mother Relynne's team needs to suffer a bit, I think. They have far too many advantages in this fight." Just then the warning horn sounded.

The others looked at each other and thanked him as

they reclaimed their now-sharp, wooden blades. "Better practice-swords?" Devyn asked Jules quietly, as they followed Wynn out to the dark field. "Better practice swords would be swords, wouldn't they? They would be weapons, not practice swords!"

"Wynn is like that," replied Rall, shrugging. "He is always looking for ways to improve things."

"Did you see his chicken coop?" asked Jules, grinning wickedly.

"No," replied Devyn, smiling. "We didn't tour that, although I can't think why not."

"Well, it's a palace. I'm proud to live up the alley from it." Jules couldn't stop smirking at Wynn's pained look.

"I couldn't quit once I got started." Wynn reddened slightly. "It's no big deal."

"It's the most famous chicken coop in Aeoven," persisted Jules. "And his chickens are the happiest because of it!"

Devyn smothered his laugh.

"Aw, lay off, Jules," replied Wynn, rolling his eyes. "You're just jealous because yours fell down in the first windstorm." He spoke in a whisper.

"Why does it not surprise me your coop failed to withstand a breeze?" asked Devyn, also whispering.

"But it was so much better once Wynn fixed it for me," replied Jules, undaunted. "Now my chickens lay happy eggs too."

"It's good to know some things never change," Devyn grinned. "You're still the joker you always were, Jules. And it's still always on us."

"He knows you," Wynn snickered, and Jules just beamed even wider.

"Ssshh! Here we go," whispered Rall, smothering his own grin.

The four mages crept out to the scant shrubs that screened them somewhat from the view of the amethyst team.

Wynn and Rall knelt behind a spindly fir tree. As Wynn peered through the gloom, he was startled to see his mother coming down the hill toward him. Shock and disbelief warred with joy as he leapt to his feet. Shoving Rall to one side, he raced to her. Ignoring the surprised shouts from his teammates, he said, "Mother? Is it really you? They told me you were dead...."

A white fog descended on Wynn, and his mother vanished.

◆◆◆

Wynn gradually regained awareness. Disoriented, he realized he was seeing through the eyes of someone who was fighting Rall, Jules, and Devyn. Then he realized it was his weapon and his magic. He fought his own friends but was not in control of his body.

His arm swung his blade, and he found himself casting magic. The three men shouted, but he couldn't hear them. Desperately, Wynn tried to get control of his body and failed. It was as if someone had moved his awareness to a tiny corner of his mind, where he was forced to observe as his talents and his weapon were used against his teammates.

Despite his efforts to regain control, Wynn's magic was being ripped from him and used to batter his teammates. As he fought for command, his sword rose and swung wildly, making him appear drunk.

Now he realized he'd been lured by a seeming of his mother, and someone had taken control of his mind.

Rage that anyone would do something so cruel overwhelmed him, and he heard a chuckle. "I own you now, boy." The corner he was shunted to in his mind shrank, and his vision narrowed. Still, his magic was torn from him. Still, he mercilessly attacked the friends who now battled him with all their might.

Soren...he's using me to kill my friends.... How do I get my body back? How? He's gone mad! Panicked and desperate, Wynn pictured Soren as he'd last seen him and imagined a hundred needles stabbing the man.

There was a shriek from the amethyst tent, and Wynn found himself back in control of his body again. Throwing his sword to the ground, he knelt before Rall in the pose duelists used when conceding defeat in the arena. As he did so, Duran and his team raced to the amethyst tent with their kits. The horn blew, signaling the end of the battle, this time with a desperate sound to it, and then there was silence in the dark of the practice field.

"That went well," said Jules. Blood trickled down his face. "What the hell just happened?"

Wynn tried to explain, and Jules laughed. "Soren's probably bleeding profusely, Wynn. He was locked in your mind, and with your skills at visualization...he's definitely in need of a healer."

Rall and Devyn both chuckled wearily. Devyn looked out the door. "Duran is back at the dais, so I guess we are still stuck here," he said. "I hoped that meant we were done, but I guess not."

♦♦♦

The horn blew again, and the four tired mages trooped out. "Please, Aeos, just make this misery end," muttered Jules. "Heaven only knows what that evil woman has planned for us next."

"That was a real thunder-lizard," said Devyn, horror tingeing his voice. "I can't believe they had a real thunder-lizard. What is wrong with that woman? What if it had gotten loose?"

"It was only a baby," said Rall, sagely. "Even the holy mother's not mad enough to bring an adult inside the city." Internally, he was shaken. "I *hate* fighting those things because you can't use magic against them."

"I thought it was fun," said Wynn with a tired grin. The others stopped and stared at him then resumed walking. "She'll run out of creatures pretty soon." He tried to conceal his disappointment.

"I hope so," said Jules, brightening up. "I can't think of anything she hasn't trotted out yet."

As the four mages reached the slope opposite the amethyst tent, a thunderous roar shook the field and the night was suddenly lit as if by the sun. An enormous dragon emerged from the dark mists, landing directly in front of the group. Flames leapt and danced along the length of its immense back. Waves of heat like that of a large house fire rolled off it, making the questers unable to get close enough to use a sword, had they been so inclined.

They were not.

"Holy…where the hell did she get a firedrake?" Rall, Jules, and Devyn scattered, giving the beast too many targets concentrate on. Fiery breath roared toward them. Blazing claws reached and slashed, first at Jules and then Devyn. The horrific head swung, looking for a victim.

Overwhelmed by the horror that now stared down

at him, Wynn reacted instinctively. Without even thinking, he cast his steel-cutting bolt to crack the creature's shields and followed up immediately with a large ice spell.

The dragon vanished. Mother Relynne stood surrounded by the amethyst team, and she was completely frozen in a thick shell of ice.

"Shit...Soren! Soren! I think they killed her!" Taj picked Relynne up and raced back to their tent, Pallia and Rande on his heels. The dais emptied as all the healers and mages raced to her aid.

Silently, Wynn returned to the blue tent, followed by Rall, Jules, and Devyn. Rall glared at him. "That was stupid! You used magic against an elemental." He was about to say something else but just shook his head in disgust. He looked out the tent flap. "Well, she must be okay. Your dad and Duran are back on the dais."

Chapter 18

Once again, the four questers huddled around their table, trying to figure out their opponents' next move. "Her attacks are just so random," said Jules, tired and cross. "It's hard to figure out what she's going to do next. Some sort of mix between elementals and a physical attack, most likely."

"I was pretty impressed with her firedrake!" said Wynn, shuddering. "Do they really look all fiery? They're a lot worse than water-wraiths."

"From what I hear, pretty much," replied Rall, yawning. "She must have been quite surprised when you encased her in ice." He grinned widely.

"Yes," agreed Devyn, with a wicked smile, "I think she *was* startled. I surely was. You cracked her shield and froze her faster than anything I've ever seen."

"I didn't realize she was inside," Wynn said, still in shock from the ordeal. "I just wanted to put the flames on its skin out before it did any damage. How do those things live that way anyway? Do you think she's all right?"

"Of course she is." Jules managed to sound sarcastic and exhausted at the same time. "She has the finest healer currently working in the Temple, healing her every time we make a dent in her defenses. Firedrakes live in volcanoes. They're native to Tauron's world, Serende." Jules lay on his cot, putting his feet up, trying to get a little rest. "I'm surprised she trotted one of those out for this. I would think they'd have done something we'll actually be facing."

"But we may easily deal with something like a firedrake, and it will be an illusion just as this was," replied Rall. His weariness was evident in his voice. "It'll still be dangerous, though. Some mage in Grakken's thrall will be casting fire, and it'll be as bad as what we just went through or worse. At least we won this round. That makes two."

"Yes, at least we won that battle," muttered Wynn. "I think I'm done now. It's time to go home. My dad and the whole panel of planners are annoying me. This game has become tiresome. Now that I've seen a firedrake, I don't think there's anything fun left for her holiness to show us. It's time to change the rules and settle this once and for all."

"What do you mean?" asked Devyn. Shadows from the fitful light of their lone candle danced around the gloomy tent. The tiny flame barely illuminated the four filthy, tired men. "We have to play this the way it's laid out for us. They're our superiors. They make the rules and we follow them. You know that. They've got a reason for this torment. They must." Jules and Rall both agreed with him, nodding their heads.

"That's ridiculous. Of course we don't have to follow any instructions—this isn't that sort of game," replied Wynn, crossing his arms stubbornly. "Look—I wanted to see a firedrake, and now I have. She has nothing left to show me that I haven't already seen, so they're wasting my time now. Silly rules mean nothing to me, and I don't understand why they matter to you. No real rogue wizard is going to follow instructions, and that's why we're losing. They've been leading us astray all along, but I didn't mind as long as it was fun." Wynn looked at his companions' surprised faces. "Cheating is the only real rule we need to follow."

"I can't believe I'm hearing *you*, of all people,

suggest we resort to dishonesty. What do you think we should do then?" Jules sat up, boots on the floor and arms folded across his broad chest.

Wynn shrugged. "First of all, we can't figure out their next move because the panel of mages planning this little mess gives us a scenario and we act on it based on their recommendations. I feel sure they're an integral part of the Holy Mother's team, sharing everything we do and say via Duran and Soren's link. That's the only reason Duran is posted there. They've told us nothing about the other team's part in this, so they're able to keep springing surprises on us." Wynn leaned forward, sketching a quick map on the back of one of Rall's notes. "We know they're higher up the mountain than we are, looking down on us as we approach them. They can see our every move. There's no way to sneak up on them in daylight. But so far, we haven't been given the opportunity to formulate our own attack—it's all been defensive.

"We get the bare bones of a plan from the team on the dais, the horn blows, we go trotting out, and they spring their trap. We counter it, using one of the suggested plans, right?"

Everyone nodded.

"Well, the plans we're given never quite work because they're designed not to, which didn't matter as long as it was interesting. But now I'm tired of waiting for the horn to blow. We need to attack decisively," said Wynn. "Let's go over there now and collapse their 'cave' on them." As he explained his plan, marking appropriate targets on the map, the others smiled. "Also, I owe my dad and Kaye a little something special for holding out on me and cheating. They're going to get a little surprise too." He drew a large 'X' through the dais.

"This could be fun after all," said Jules, looking at Wynn's solution, glee written on his gaunt features. "Too bad I can't rain fire on them, but I suppose it's bad form to incinerate your elders. I'm fairly strong in the element of earth, so I'll have no problem doing what you want—Rall and I have worked together that way before. Let's go!"

Silently, the four mages crept into the darkness.

Thunder crashed as Wynn's lightning struck the supports that held up the canvas cover of the dais, collapsing it. He then dumped a large water spell on his father's group. At the same time, Devyn closed his eyes and the earth rumbled, leveling the field, lowering the amethyst side by a good eight feet and bringing down the tent. As people crawled out of the wreckage, Rall dumped icy water on everyone and Jules mixed earth in, making it a mudslide.

For a brief moment, dead silence reigned in the dark.

"We win," called Wynn. "I'm going home now."

"Save some hot water for me, son," called Liam. The sounds of his laughter, combined with Kaye and Lera's hooting, filled the night.

Now, shouts were heard, warriors checking on each other and then laughing as they stood up, covered in chilly mud.

◆◆◆

At noon, after they'd gotten a few hours' rest, all of the mages involved in the exercise gathered in the dining hall, minus the healers, to discuss what they had learned. Mother Relynne passed a plate of sandwiches, and Liam poured cups of tea from a giant urn, handing them around.

Since it was only to be a short meeting, the three young fathers arrived, carrying sleeping babies in packs securely strapped to their chests. Devyn found it strange to see Jules and Rall with children, seeing them for the first time as parents. Even Wynn, though he looked so young, had proven he was as capable a father as he was a mage.

Seeing them so settled underscored Devyn's own deep desire for a family, but he didn't know what to do about it. He carefully refrained from sighing. In Mal Evol, everyone sighed as they felt like it, but here in the west, it often gained him sideways glances. In Aeoven, it was considered a melodramatic habit more appropriate to young novice girls in the throes of a first crush. He'd been forced to tone down a great many habits from his homeland. Sighing was only one of them.

"What made you decide to bring the mountain down on us?" asked Relynne, grinning. "I thought we had at least two full nights of fun at your expense before you figured it out."

"Wynn got bored," replied Rall, shrugging. "He thought you might be out of strange new beasts to show him and wanted to go home. He apparently knew all along you were making up the rules as you went." His sideways glance at Wynn was enigmatic, as if annoyed he'd not realized it himself, sooner.

"Well, he was right," agreed Taj. "The first rule of battling a rogue-mage is that there *are* no rules. But Wynn, if you knew all along, why did you let it drag out for so long?"

Wynn was caught off guard. He'd thought Rall would be doing most of the talking for his group. "We're not usually allowed to play so rough, so it was entertaining, testing the limits of what we can do. And once I saw the crate of water-sprites, I wanted to see what other elemental beasts you would bring against us. Of all the big ones, I'd only seen a water-wraith before, so I was curious. The thunder-lizard was exciting, and so was the firedrake." He turned to Mother Relynne. "I didn't mean to kill you, ma'am. It was an accident." Pallia choked, and Rande pounded on her back. "Do you really think this mage has one under his command?"

"Well, if he does, it'll be a dead one," muttered Relynne into her tea, while Taj snickered at her expense. "I still can't get warm." She shivered. The ice had encased her so suddenly that she'd had no time to react. Instantly, she'd found herself suffocating, experiencing real terror for the first time in years, as her shocked team scrambled to get the ice off her so she could breathe. "I admit I was a tad bit surprised."

Beside her, Rande laughed. "We'd only just gotten Relynne thawed out and healed when you four brought down the house and then dumped freezing mud on us as we tried to crawl out." Soon, he was roaring and slapping his knee. "I wish you could have seen the look on Soren's face when you boys doused him and his journeyman with freezing mud along with the rest of us!"

"Yes, the prissy old thing got what he had coming," said Pallia, and giggling, she ruthlessly mimicked the healer, "But I'm a non-combatant." She burst into loud hoots of laughter, and soon the whole group was chuckling at the expense of Soren's dignity.

Relynne explained that for the rest of the week, they would spend six hours each day out at the field getting Wynn used to the various situations and beasts he might be up against. He solemnly promised not to kill any of them now he knew they were really Mother Relynne.

The men had the rest of their evenings and the entire weekend free, with the exception of sparring practice. They were all quite happy, with the exception of Devyn, who had no idea what to do with himself.

Chapter 19

After the lunch meeting, Devyn walked back to his quarters. *It's only Odensday. What will I do when the weekend comes and I have to spend it all alone? I can't spend every evening at Wynn's. Father always said fish and guests both stink after a day or two, and I don't want to wear out my welcome.* He'd always found comfort in the well-worn clichés of his homeland. *I could go to the library since I'll need a new book soon anyway.*

He didn't have his own place in Aeoven anymore, so he was lodged in the guest rooms at the Temple. Although he was at loose ends, he didn't feel like going to any of the common rooms about town. He'd been eating in the Temple dining hall, but it was lonely since he didn't really know anyone there anymore.

After spending the afternoon organizing and rewriting his notes regarding the events of the last few days, he tucked a book of plays into his pocket and headed down to the communal dining hall an hour earlier than his usual time. As he entered, he saw few people he knew other than the older mages taking part in training, and Devyn had no desire to eat with them. They were of his uncle's generation, and he barely knew them. They were seated in a corner, reliving their old days and having a great time. Indulging in a satisfying sigh, he filled his plate, preparing to eat a solitary meal.

Looking around the tables, he noticed a healer, who had been a novice in his group, seated alone, reading. *What was her name?* He wracked his mind. He hadn't known her well in those days because she was quite bashful. Despite her shyness, he'd always thought her attractive, but whenever he'd been at a party she'd attended, she was always in the company of Ryllen. Also, in those days, Devyn had been drawn to the more flamboyant women of the town, all of whom had long ago bonded and settled down, not giving him a second thought.

Lorana, he suddenly remembered. *Lorana Bransdottir. Her father is Bran, the healer who was headmaster of novices when I first came to Aeoven.* Now that he saw her again, he realized she'd grown beautiful in a quiet way. Her hair was a soft honey color, and her eyes a warm, golden brown. *I used to see her breakfasting with Ryllen for most of the first year after we became journeymen. They seemed very much in love, but he died.... That quest was a tragedy if ever there was one. Rall was the only one who came home, and he was ill for a long while afterward.*

"Hello, Lorana," he said as he set his tray down opposite her. "Do you remember me? Devyn D'Mal—I was in the same novice group as you."

Surprised, she looked up, smiling shyly. "I do remember you, Devyn. You were the first person I used my healing sight on. Belina brought you all into the infirmary so we could practice on you lot before we went out and killed any patients."

Devyn laughed. "It all comes back to me now—I was worried you could read my mind and see how nervous I was. I was afraid you would know what a coward I was, since Belina had just finished explaining to us how healing-empathy is the most powerful and dangerous of all the magics. It terrified me that you were going to use it on me, but you didn't take over my mind. Instead, you healed my augmentation. I was so surprised I forgot to thank you."

"I wasn't supposed to heal you. I was only supposed to delve you and see what a healthy person looked like with my healing-sight, but I was nervous. I could feel the pain in your face, and it just happened." She laughed warmly, a pleasant, cheerful sound. "I think we were all afraid of the different magics in those days. My father is a healer, but I was never around battle-mages much before I came to the novice barracks."

"So what have you been doing since we left the novice barracks?" Devyn found he was curious about her. She was quiet, intelligent, and self-assured.

"Oh, I've mostly been a traveling healer, in the north. Most of the farmers along the headwaters of the River Fleet are my patients, as are the folks in the small villages there in the shadow of the Escarpment," she replied with a smile. "My patients are wonderful people. I heal everyone from cows to grandmothers."

"But caring for the people of Neveyah—it's the most important task we have." replied Devyn, with conviction. "We're sworn to protect and serve. I've been building irrigation systems for the communities in the far south of Neveyah for the last two years, so I know much the same sort of people quite well. I usually board with the local farmers. They've become my close friends."

Devyn's heavily-accented speech charmed Lorana, as did his attractive smile.

As they ate, they discussed their work, both enjoying the conversation immensely. Devyn was surprised and somewhat disappointed when the novices began closing the dining room, putting the chairs up on the tables to mop the floors.

"Will you walk with me in the garden?" Devyn hoped she would say yes, surprised by how much it mattered to him. "We can sit by the fountain and talk more."

Lorana looked at him and wondered if she should. He had a reputation as a bachelor who was practically a pleasure-boy. Suddenly deciding to just enjoy the evening, she smiled. "That would be fun. I haven't been to the gardens since I've been back, and it'll still be light for another hour or so."

Rising, he walked around the table and took her elbow companionably, saying, "Have you read the new play by Fel Eriksson? I'm reading it now and enjoying it immensely."

"I love Eriksson's plays," Lorana replied, her eyes sparkling with interest. "I haven't had time to get the new one yet, but I'm looking forward to it."

"I'll gladly lend it to you, if you wish," offered Devyn. "I've nearly finished reading it now."

Devyn found a reason to sit with her for dinner every afternoon and managed to walk with her each evening. Together, they shopped at the local booksellers and strolled in the many lovely gardens of Aeoven. The week passed far too quickly, and he was now loath to leave town.

◆◆◆

On Frosday evening, Wynn and Seri held a little send-off party. Seri had invited several of their friends who were in town, and Wynn, of course, had asked Jules, Rall, and Devyn. They also invited all the mages who had been involved in their training over the week as a way of saying thank you to them.

"I would be honored to come to your party," Devyn told Wynn. "May I bring a friend?"

"Of course," Wynn replied. "We're kinsmen. Your friends are always welcome, as much as you are."

Devyn immediately sent a note to Lorana, asking if she would accompany him. He was quite disappointed when she sent her regrets, pleading a previous engagement, but was inordinately pleased when he read her invitation to dine in her private quarters the following evening at five, if it was convenient for him. He sent her a reply saying he would very much enjoy it and would be there.

Indeed, he found himself looking for her every morning when he entered the dining hall, although he carefully did not sit next to her at breakfast, as he didn't wish to compromise her, greeting her warmly as he passed her table. *My reputation is bad. She knows it too,* he thought wryly. *She hasn't invited me up to her apartment before this dinner. She only sees me in public places and always says goodbye at the foot of the stairs by the messenger's desk.*

To his joy, the first person Devyn saw at Wynn's party was Lorana, standing by the fireplace. She was beautiful in a soft green shirt and a narrow skirt with matching decorations, embellished to match her augmentations. Her hair shone golden in the candlelight, and he was temporarily tongue-tied on seeing her.

"Devyn." Lorana gave a shy, welcoming smile. Once again, she was struck by how handsome he was, and her eyes sparkled as she greeted him. "I should have realized this was the party you meant—we could have walked together."

"Ah. Wynn is my cousin," Devyn answered with a smile that lit up his face and openly revealed his elation at seeing her there. "We are leaving this week on a long journey but plan to be home by the Summer Solstice. Jules and Rall are also going with us, completing our team." *I'm babbling*, he thought. *I don't make any sense at all when I see her.*

Many toasts were raised to the questers, and then Duran announced that another mage of their acquaintance, Arne Severnsson, would be traveling to Widge, having been offered the permanent position of Temple healer there. Everyone raised toasts to Arne too, and it was a jolly gathering.

Over the course of the evening, Devyn made every effort to be circumspect and not monopolize Lorana's company, although he deliberately managed to walk her home, cutting Arne out with practiced ease. Feeling quite bold, he kissed her hand at the foot of the stairs, and bemused, he watched her disappear up the stairwell. "She is so beautiful," he murmured, not realizing he'd spoken aloud.

"Yes, sir, she is," agreed the novice who sat at the messenger's table and who thought Devyn had spoken to her. "And she's one of the nicer senior healers here. I think she likes you. You're the only mage she ever sees, though many ask her to walk with them."

"Really?" Devyn resisted the undignified urge to leap about with joy. He glanced at the nameplate on the messenger desk. "Tell me more, Shandi."

"Yes," Shandi continued, unaware of his unholy glee. "She's been home for three weeks and still won't accept flowers from Arne. She won't even allow him to walk with her anywhere, and he's just gaga for her. Everyone knows it. He sends her notes every day, but she refuses to accept them."

"Well, well," said Devyn, smiling broadly. "This is good to hear." *Poor Arne, he hasn't got a chance with an educated, witty woman like Lorana. He's decent enough, but all he cares to talk about are boils and carbuncles. Arne was easy to live with...but Jules was much more fun.*

Shandi cocked her head and looked up at him. "I don't know why everyone says you behave scandalously. I always tell them they're wrong about you," she said innocently. Devyn abruptly coughed, taken aback at hearing even the novices were aware of his reputation. "You're always so polite and courtly and never try to force yourself on her hospitality. Not like some ignorant louts I won't mention. Too bad Arne hasn't got your manners. He'd be much more likely to find a wife. Of course, everyone knows he's getting desperate now he's losing his hair. He may have better luck since he's been posted to his own Temple." Shandi smiled encouragingly and bent her head to finish writing her essay.

Devyn found himself smiling as he crossed the courtyard to the guest quarters. He was still smiling as he fell asleep.

◆◆◆

The next day, just after the noon hour, Jules and Devyn were to meet at Wynn's house. Devyn knocked on Jules's door, intending to walk with him as they'd agreed. Jules opened it, looking harried, patting his fussy baby on the back. The little girl wriggled restlessly and chewed on her hand fitfully.

"Here, hold the baby, will you? Aneka isn't back yet, and I'm trying to finish the laundry, but Gayla's still teething. I can't put her down or she'll start crying." Jules thrust the squirming baby at Devyn, who awkwardly took the little girl, feeling completely nonplussed.

She looked up at him and sniffed then laid her head on his shoulder and began gnawing on his collar. His arms automatically went around her, holding her more securely.

Surprised by how natural it felt to hold the baby, Devyn followed Jules through his pleasant and tidy home. "I never realized what a good husband you would make. Aneka has really changed you," he remarked, as he stood in the door to the porch and watched Jules finish up. "I had no idea you did your family's laundry. I'm impressed."

"Aneka works hard, and my job as armsmaster doesn't involve using magic as intensely as hers. She's frequently exhausted when she gets home, so I keep her workload down around here as much as I can." Jules laughed. "I never realized how all-consuming the love a father feels for his child is or how much I would care about Aneka's happiness. It's the most amazing thing, as Wynn always says." He finished hanging several small shirts on the line, poured the water from his wooden laundry tubs down the sink, and turned them upside down to dry. He then dried his hands and reached for the baby. "Seri will watch her for an hour or so until Aneka gets home. I'll leave a note so she'll know where we are."

"Can I hold her for a while longer? I've never held a baby before," Devyn confessed, feeling an odd tenderness for the girl. "They're quite pleasant, aren't they? I've just heard that my brother has been blessed with an infant son, but I haven't been home in two years. I didn't even manage to get home for his wedding."

"Most of the time, babies are good to hold," Jules agreed then changed the subject abruptly. "You were fairly attentive to Lorana last night at Wynn's party. I think she likes you."

"Do you?" He blushed. "Gah! I sound just like a novice." Devyn was strangely embarrassed to discuss his infatuation for the healer. "I'm quite taken with her, but apparently my reputation precedes me. Even the novices here seem to have heard stories about me."

"You never used to care what people thought of you. This isn't like you at all. When you want a girl, you usually apply heavy layers of the D'Mal charm and sweep her off her feet."

Devyn awkwardly adjusted his arms as Jules covered Gayla with a knit blanket before leaving the house. Closing the door behind them, they walked down the alley toward Wynn's back gate.

"I don't know what the problem is." Devyn tried to be honest with himself, as much as with Jules. "Lorana has a power over me. I can't get her out of my mind. She's sophisticated, and her conversation is entertaining. She's the sort of woman you treat with respect and hope to...." He struggled, trying to find the words, and abruptly stopped speaking.

"Hope to what, Devyn?" Jules's dancing eyes demanded an answer. "You've dallied with every woman in southern Neveyah. 'Hope' is not a term I usually think of in regard to your approach."

"Ahh...bond with. The sort of woman you hope to bond with," muttered Devyn, red-faced. "I don't want to dally with her. I want to be her husband."

Jules gaped. "Are you serious? Because we're leaving on a long journey in a few days, and Arne has his smarmy sights set on her, and he's not the only one. You need to act boldly if you mean it."

Devyn nodded. "This unexpected complication couldn't have happened at a worse stage, for me. We're leaving in less than a week—there's no time to court her properly, and I don't know whether she feels the same for me. She was in love with Ryllen, and his death was hard for her to get over. We're going to nearly the same place where he died. I've not told her of that part of this quest yet because I didn't want to remind her of her loss, although I'm sure Seri has told her the details of our journey since they're close." Closing his eyes and pulling up every ounce of his courage, Devyn confessed the most difficult part of his problem. "I'm a coward. Rejection by her would be quite painful. What should I do?"

Jules repeated himself, "Be bold. It's a military campaign now, Devyn. You need to steal a march on Arne. Tell Lorana how you feel, ask her to wait for you, and drag her to the registry as soon as you return from our quest."

"I can't believe I'm asking *you* of all people for advice about a woman." Devyn rolled his eyes. "But I think you're right. I'll see her tonight for dinner. I'll ask her to wait for me then, if my reputation hasn't ruined my chances with her."

"You really *are* in love. You didn't back down at all when Rall was ready to string your head on that gruesome necklace and wear it around his neck, but you're shaking in your boots over this." Jules didn't really know what to say to ease his friend's nerves. "She couldn't take her eyes off you last night. I think she'll wait for you if you tell her how you feel. But most importantly, you need to sit your terrified arse down at her table *at breakfast* before we leave town, or Arne will still believe he has a chance with her."

"Really?" Devyn found himself smiling again. "Gah! I'm behaving like an idiot."

"Yes, really," Jules replied, his sarcasm back in force. "And you're right, D'Mal! You're acting just like a novice in the throes of his first crush."

Devyn sighed and reluctantly handed the baby to Jules. He absently noticed his shoulder was wet, but somehow it didn't matter.

Seri and Lorana were in the kitchen when Jules and Devyn came in. Jules explained why he needed to leave Gayla with her, and Seri led him to the sitting room to collect Wynn. Left alone with Lorana, Devyn tried not to gawk at her but found himself staring anyway.

"Are we still on for dinner tonight?" she asked, blushing faintly. "I thought we could eat in my rooms if it's all right with you. I'm actually cooking it myself. Is five o'clock fine with you?"

"Yes! Absolutely! I must train with Wynn right now, but I will be there, most definitely. May I bring some wine? I've received a shipment from my family's vineyard." Devyn shut his mouth before he could make a bigger fool of himself.

"That would be lovely." Lorana's hands plucked nervously at her trousers. "It'll be nice to use my wine glasses. I bought them last fall and then only had one party before I had to leave again."

Just then, Wynn and Jules came through, and the three men left, making their good-byes to Lorana. Devyn smiled back at her as Jules dragged him down the steps.

"Rall will meet us at the field with Taj." Wynn's voice came in through the back door just before it closed. "Taj has some new drills for us. I can't wait." The sounds of Jules and Devyn groaning were cut off as the door closed.

Seri came back into the kitchen, carrying both babies, handing Johnny to Lorana, and the two women continued their conversation where they had left off. "Well, Devyn is definitely interested in you," said Seri, as Lorana blushed. "I've never seen him so attentive to a good girl." The two women giggled.

Smiling, Lorana said, "Remember that solstice party? You, Nolen, and Devyn were roaring drunk. Nolen actually passed out at our table! How you suffered the next day—ever since, I've taken your advice and tried to be moderate when drinking wine." She laughed. "Healing you took all my chi. I didn't know that's why we don't heal hangovers for people." Her laughter faded as she added, "It was the last party Ryllen and I went to before he went on his quest."

"I don't remember much of that night, but I've been told by several different people that I had a great time." Seri rolled her eyes. "I do remember the hangover all too well. I've never let wine get the better of me since then. You've no idea how horrible I felt, knowing you'd wasted all your chi and nearly burned yourself out healing me of my stupidity. The guilt was terribly hard to bear." Seri looked at her cousin, concern in her eyes. "You've been alone for a long time, since Ryllen died. Too long, some would say, but I know you needed to grieve. How do you feel about Devyn? I think he's fallen for you. It's really kind of sweet, the expression of amazement he gets when he looks at you!"

"Do you think so? He's never tried to kiss me or anything. Well, last night, he kissed my hand." She blushed as she thought of the shivers his lips had sent down her spine, unconsciously holding her hand to her heart. "It was a gesture of politeness, some courtly manners from his homeland, but that's all it was, I'm sure. I think he just wants to be friends. He hasn't given me any indication of feeling anything more," Lorana said, trying to keep a neutral tone of voice. "I've heard many notorious tales of his adventures, but he's been the most polite and considerate man I've ever known, so I think the rumors are somewhat exaggerated. I thought for a few moments last night he might be more interested in me, but no. He didn't try to follow me up to my room or anything."

"I've never seen him look at a woman the way he looks at you," Seri told her. "He's trying to behave himself, hoping the endless gossip that circulates regarding him won't scare you off."

Lorana looked astonished. "Devyn owes me no explanations of his past. I've no intention of asking him for any, either. People wouldn't talk about him at all if it weren't for his brother being the king of Mal Evol. We're just friends, and though I admit I wish we were more, I'm afraid it's all we shall be! Anyway, they're leaving, and I too will be going back to the wilds. I'm sure he's just been lonely while he's staying here. Once they're on the road, he'll be running into friendly-girls at every common room they come to." She hugged Johnny. "I'm sure handsome Devyn D'Mal has no romantic interest in the oldest woman still living in the bachelor apartments."

Seri gaped at her. "Trust me, Lorry, if that were the case, he would have spent the last week at the common rooms over in the weavers' district or the market. There are plenty of friendly-girls there, all of whom know he's back in town and wonder where he's been spending his time. I'm their healer, remember? They've asked me about him several times. He hasn't once gone near them, a fact that, I can assure you, has everyone talking. Instead, he's managed to 'accidentally' run into *you* at the dining hall every evening." She laughed at the mixture of hope and disbelief on her cousin's face. "Tonight, you'll see!"

Chapter 20

Practice went much as Devyn expected. Taj had devised several new torments, and Wynn was thrilled to implement them, demonstrating an unhealthy enjoyment of the novelty.

Back in his quarters after having been beaten to within an inch of his life, Devyn filled his tub and soaked for as long as he wanted, soothing his pain with relaxing bath salts. The realization that he was done with Mother Relynne's week of misery was nearly as helpful as the bath in easing his soreness. When the water cooled, he dressed in the only finery he currently owned, which consisted of a white silk shirt with brown and gold embellishments and tight, brown trousers with polished, brown riding boots. His feast-day clothes were done in the style of his homeland, Mal Evol. His mother had sent them to him for Holy Day, and he'd worn them to the party the night before.

Clothes had once been important to Devyn, but since he'd been traveling and living among the rural farmers of southern Neveyah, he'd lost interest in them. He had his Temple clothes, and they were good enough, but tonight, he wished he had a new shirt. He raised his arms, and his pulled muscles pained him. Easing the shirt over his many bruises, he winced. "Wynn does this to me every time," he muttered. "And he looks like such a nice little boy. At least from now on, I'll only have monsters trying to kill me. Those I can deal with."

He went through his jewelry, looking for a particular signet ring, and finding it, he slipped it over a golden chain. He placed them in a small velvet bag that he tucked into his shirt. "I hope…." His mind spun as he wondered exactly what it was he wished for. "I hope many things...too many perhaps. Maybe she'll accept my ring as a token of my intention to bond with her. Perhaps she'll wait for me." Centering himself, he offered a heartfelt prayer to Aeos, asking for her blessing.

♦♦♦

Shandi led Devyn up to Lorana's rooms. He carried a basket that held two bottles of the finest wine from his family's vineyard and a bouquet of flowers. "Don't worry, sir. She really likes you. I bet if you ask her, she'll bond with you," whispered the novice healer as she turned and left. Devyn stared after her. *Am I so transparent even a novice can read my mind?*

He stood hesitantly and finally raised his hand to knock. Shandi stuck her head back around the stairwell door and motioned to him to just get on with it. *Aaugh! Now a novice is telling me I'm a coward.* Feeling like an idiot, he rapped on the door.

The door opened, and Lorana stood there looking lovely, wearing an apron over her finery. "Good! You're just in time." Pleased, she took his cloak and invited him into her sitting room where she had set her worktable for a romantic dinner for two. "Flowers— how lovely. I have the perfect vase for these. And white wine—it'll be the perfect accompaniment to our dinner." Smiling, Lorana took the flowers and put them in a vase.

Handing Devyn the corkscrew, she knelt and stirred something cooking on the tiny hob most residents in the bachelor apartments used for heating water for tea. Whatever it was smelled delightful. He uncorked the wine, feeling a sense of peace, as if he had come home.

"I much prefer my own cooking to eating in the dining hall, but I don't bother when it's only me." They sat in the chairs drawn up before the fire, as the food finished cooking. "I made an onion soup for the first course, a salad of apples and greens with walnuts and blue cheese for the second, and a gratin for the main course. Seri made honey cakes for our sweets."

"I miss the good food of my homeland, but I've found the people I board with usually feed me quite well. Not as well as this will be, if I may be honest. It smells wonderful." While they chatted, Devyn absorbed his surroundings, pleased to discover her rooms were airy and pleasant. With small touches, Lorana had created a graceful home out of her small apartment. "You're quite talented to cook a meal such as this in your fireplace."

"I love to cook. It's my creative outlet." Lorana laughed. "Feia paints, Aneka and Seri do needlework, and I love to cook for others. I enjoy experimenting when I'm home but don't often have the chance. Because I'm not bonded, they send me all over the place, so I'm traveling all the time." She blushed and then added, "I've not eaten in the dining hall so much in years as I did this week."

"Really?" Devyn knew he was grinning like an idiot again but didn't care. "I'm honored you allowed me to monopolize your evenings. You've no idea how much I've enjoyed your company. I wish I didn't have to leave, but the Goddess has our lives in her hands, and we're sworn to do her bidding."

Lorana blushed and replied, "I've had the best week, spending my evenings with you. And I too will be leaving again for a long posting."

Devyn's heart tripped, and he began to believe he had a chance with her after all.

The meal was perfect, both in the quality of the food and the company. Both were completely at home with each other, enjoying an easy companionship.

After their meal, Lorana quickly cleared the table, and Devyn insisted on helping her wash the dishes in her little dishpan, laughing as he saw how she compensated for not having a kitchen. "You're so clever. Your table and fireplace become your kitchen, and you turn out food to rival the cuisine of my widowed mother's chef." He insisted on drying the dishes, wearing her other apron. Laughing and joking merrily, they made quick work of the cleanup. Once everything was put away, they took off their aprons and sat before the fire.

Devyn opened the second bottle of wine, sipping it slowly as they talked about their families and their lives away from the Temple. The windows began to rattle as a rainstorm blew in. The fire lent a coziness to the atmosphere as they listened to the storm. Devyn said, "You've made your rooms into so much more than a bachelor apartment. They're as graceful a home as any manor house."

Lorana laughed. "I've been in these rooms five years. I doubt anyone else has been in the bachelor quarters for as long. I suppose it happened gradually."

Perhaps because of the sense of being at home that had come over him the moment he entered her rooms, Devyn reached for Lorana's hand as if it were the most natural thing in the world. "This is the most pleasant evening I can possibly imagine. I can't remember feeling this sense of belonging since I left home bound for the novice barracks." The contentment in her answering smile gave him the courage to finally ask the question that burned in his heart.

Setting his glass of wine down and reaching inside his shirt, he extracted the little velvet pouch. "Lorana, you know I'm leaving on a long journey. I'll be gone for at least two months, maybe longer."

Wide-eyed and clearly wondering what Devyn was planning, she nodded. "I'll be leaving too, for a two-month posting."

"I would like to ask you…," Devyn flushed, and his words failed him. At last, kneeling before her, he asked, "Will you bond with me when I return? I would gladly register our bonding tomorrow, but it wouldn't be fair to you. I'm leaving on a quest that will take me nearly to the same place you lost your great love. I *must* leave. We can't delay our departure for any reason." He placed the velvet pouch in her unresisting hand. "This is my signet ring with my family's crest. If you agree, I would give it to you as a token of my love and esteem. I swear upon my vows to Aeos, I'll be as constant and faithful to you on this journey as if I were indeed your husband."

Lorana was silent for a moment, and his heart sank. "I know no one will ever take Ryllen's place in your heart, but I've fallen in love with you. I can't imagine my life without you in it."

As his words penetrated her confusion, her face broke into a joyous smile, and she replied, "Yes! Yes, I will gladly bond with you. I confess you've claimed your own place in my heart, Devyn, a large place. I did love Ryllen, and I'll always honor his memory, but you occupy my thoughts at the oddest moments, and I suddenly find myself smiling. I love you more than you know. But I would ask one thing of you."

"Anything. I'll do anything for you." Devyn held her hands enfolded in his as if he would never let her go.

"I've known all along where you're going, and I don't want to waste one minute of the little time we have left. I know about the terrible trouble in the Mountains of the Moon. Something bad is going on. The dear old baron hasn't been seen in two seasons, and now people in the lowlands are disappearing. Bringing that news to Mother Relynne is why I returned to Aeoven. I was given a furlough to rest, and I'm so grateful for the way it worked out, since you came into my life." Lorana's eyes met Devyn's. "But can we register our bonding tomorrow morning after breakfast, despite your concerns?" The love that shone in her eyes touched him deeply.

"Yes, of course. I wish that more than anything." Devyn held her hands, trembling with emotions too numerous and intense for him to identify.

Lorana leaned forward and kissed him, a kiss that confirmed the desire she felt for him and inflamed his senses. "I won't wait one minute longer for you, especially since we're to be separated for so long."

Overcome with happiness, Devyn clasped the chain around her neck, wincing as he raised his arms to do so.

"Oh—you're in pain." Closing her eyes, she delved and healed him of all his injuries. "There. All better."

"You didn't need to waste your chi on me, my dear one," he replied, with a sense of wonder at how much she cared for him. "It's that mad woman, Mother

Relynne. She has decreed that my cousin must school me vigorously at the end of his sword, and he takes delight in doing so."

"Yes, I did need to heal you." Lorana kissed him in a way that left no doubt about her intentions. "You'll need your strength tonight, my love."

Bemused, Devyn responded, kissing her with all his heart and passion, blessing the Goddess for leading him to her. "We must send Shandi to Wynn and all our friends with a message. They should be with us tomorrow when we make our bonding vows." His voice shook, and he caressed her hair, radiating the joy that suffused him. "Let's have them meet us at the dining hall for breakfast. It'll be our bonding party!"

Lorana's empathy caught his joy and magnified it, nearly sweeping her away in a way she'd thought she would never feel again. Filled with both happiness and the sharp knowledge that their time together was short, she helped him write the notes, and together they took them down to Shandi.

The girl was thrilled, firmly believing she'd engineered the whole thing. She enjoyed delivering messages that evening more than she ever had, grinning with delight when she finally returned. "Aeos knew they needed each other," she said smugly to herself as she filled out her log book. "I just boosted things along."

◆◆◆

The next morning was Restday, and the dining hall was full. Devyn drew the surprised attention of all the unattached men by his insistence on serving Lorana fruits and other tidbits from the buffet, and the impromptu bonding party set the whole Temple abuzz.

273

Arne insisted on toasting the happy couple, admitting he was the vanquished suitor and congratulating Devyn and Lorana, sincerely wishing them happiness and a long life together.

Afterward, the group walked to the registry and then over to the guest quarters to help Devyn carry his few possessions back to Lorana's rooms, making a jolly party out of the whole morning. Once Devyn had been moved and his things put away, they went their separate ways, with all but the newly bonded couple promising to meet at Rall's house for dinner. No one looked at all surprised when Lorana said rather firmly they would be staying in rather than going out.

Feia whispered to Rall that she thought they were the sweetest couple since Wynn and Seri. "I love bondings," she said, her eyes far away. "So romantic."

Rall just smiled and agreed with her.

◆◆◆

On Lunaday morning, Devyn put Lorana on the mail coach, helping her up the steps and kissing her hand through the window. "Take care of my wife," he admonished the driver. "She's the joy of my life, my greatest treasure." He ran beside the coach as it began to roll away. "I'll see you when we arrive in Arlen! Two weeks at the latest," he called. As the coach picked up speed and left him behind, he was overwhelmed by the sense of loss, crueler than anything he'd ever felt, nearly physical in its intensity. "Aeos be with you, my love." His words were spoken as the coach disappeared from view.

His shoulders slumped, and he turned to walk back to their rooms, wishing wholeheartedly he could have travelled with Lorana, but it was impossible. He and the others would leave Aeoven the next morning with their string of pack ponies laden with medicines and the cold weather gear they would need once they arrived in Arlen.

At least Devyn could be grateful Soren had sent Lorana on the mail coach for her safety. Healers no longer walked the wild northern trade road, even with guards. The trade road that connected Aeoven and the city of Widge, the northern-most port on the River Fleet, had become unsafe of late, a situation his team would investigate and, if possible, solve as they traveled.

Sighing, he turned again to watch the empty road, vainly hoping for a view of the coach, feeling rather foolish for doing so. A hand clasped his shoulder in commiseration, and he looked up into his cousin's eyes, seeing understanding reflected there. "I thought you might want some company," said Wynn. "It's a hard thing being separated so soon in your life together."

"We knew it would be this way," replied Devyn, trying to find something positive in his situation. "We decided to register our bonding yesterday anyway. I don't mind the pain because I'll see her again soon."

"I know how you feel," Wynn told him. "When Seri and I were first bonded, we thought we would be parted immediately, but fortunately for us, it wasn't the case. We didn't have any quests looming, and her posting was easily changed. At least you'll see her in Arlen for a day or two before we must go up into the mountains."

"Yes, we'll meet in Arlen." With that thought to cheer him, Devyn made it through the rest of the day.

Chapter 21

Rall, Jules, Devyn, and Wynn each led a pony through the eastern gate of Aeoven and down the trade road toward a town called Sevya. A two-days' walk from Aeoven, Sevya was more of a wide spot in the road, as were all the towns east of Aeoven. It was comprised of a tiny general store with a small common room where the storekeeper sold his own brew and a mill where the farmers could grind their wheat and rye. Mail was delivered to the general store, and the storekeeper kept it until people came to claim it. This system worked well all over rural Neveyah. Behind the general store was a Temple storehouse stocked with medicines and goods people could draw on as needed.

"I'm glad we're finally getting this over with." Wynn's comment drifted back to his companions as he set a brisk pace. "I just want to get to the mountains, kill the evil wizard, and get home. I hate adventure."

"But you're so good at it," said Jules, his usual sarcasm in full force. "I can't wait to see what sort of fun you'll bring to this trip, considering the way our last one went." He shuddered. "I thought I'd never be rid of the stink of fried water-wraith."

"It wasn't exactly my fault," replied Wynn, grinning back at Jules. "I was just trying to rescue you." He walked on the side of the road, keeping his pony out of the ruts.

"Well, we probably won't see any water-wraiths until we get up into the mountains," said Rall. "The worst we'll see down here on the flats will be highwaymen who have a young rogue-mage with them. That's one thing I dread. So far, I've never personally had to deal with one of the young ones."

Wynn looked at Rall quizzically, but he didn't elaborate. Even Jules was silent.

Finally Devyn spoke. "Wynn, you do understand we'll have to kill *any* rogue-mage we come across, right? No matter how young or innocent they appear, we have to kill them because if they have taken to working with highwaymen, they've been using their talents to do murder and other evil things. Once they've done that, they belong to Tauron, and they're a danger to the people of Neveyah." Devyn lifted his collar-length hair, exposing a rune behind his earlobe. Wynn hadn't seen that particular one in an augmentation before but recognized it as the rune for stealth.

Both Rall and Jules's eyes widened on seeing it. Jules's expression and obvious pity for Devyn confused Wynn, who waited, hoping for an explanation.

"Not too long ago, as the only representative of the Temple in the area, I was called to take care of a situation in the far southwest near Bramington. An orphaned boy had been adopted by a group of highwaymen when they discovered he was a budding battle-mage. They protected him and acted as his mentors, hiding him from the Temple." Devyn concealed his true feelings as well as he was able.

"What do you mean, you had to take care of the situation?" asked Rall. "He couldn't have been more than twelve." He asked the question for Wynn's benefit, knowing full well what Devyn had been required to do.

"Lenik was fourteen by the time the Temple became aware of him." Devyn shrugged, his features betraying his regret, despite his wish not to. "He was well advanced along the dark path. The boy had spent much of his life on the streets of Mal Evol City. When he was about ten, a highwayman leaving one of the shabbier common rooms came across a pile of burning refuse. The thief discovered a street urchin, hidden in the shadows, trying to hide his newfound talent as a fire mage. Instead of alerting the Temple as he should have, this enterprising outlaw saw an opportunity and a way to use the boy's ability.

"Claiming he was the boy's long-lost uncle, the unfortunate thief took custody of him. Along with his band of henchmen, he trained Lenik to rob and murder people, which, at first, the boy did only at his mentor's behest. As the boy got older, he grew to love his power and applied his talent with the casual brutality children bring to such a thing. He'd grown to enjoy the sense of invincibility he felt when forcing others to do his bidding. His victims were no longer people to him. They weren't even real. They either gave up their possessions or he rained fire on them.

"By the time I was sent to Bramington, Lenik had turned on his mentors, becoming their master, using them with great cruelty. The very ones who'd thought to use him as their tool were now his servants. No longer an innocent child, this boy had done murder many times over, using his gifts. You know full well that once a mage takes the dark path, there is no going back for him. He belongs to Tauron forever."

"I'm sorry Aeos selected you of all people to bear that rune. What did you finally do?" Jules walked his pony beside Devyn. "I don't think I could deal with so young a rogue-mage."

"I did what I had to." Devyn's clinical reply belied the turmoil he'd felt over having to kill the boy. "He was hidden atop a windmill. When he realized he'd been discovered, he tried to trick me into trusting him. He went to great lengths to explain to me how omnipotent the Bull God is and how much I could learn about *real* power if I would only listen. He was quite persuasive, and in his words, I could feel the might he spoke of, as if his god was speaking directly through him.

"Lenik's attempt to convert me failed because I know the difference between brute force and finesse. That's what I see as the difference between Tauron's magic and Aeos's magic. Most importantly, the vows we take protect us from Tauron's soft words.

"On failing to gain my trust, he used his trick of raining fire on me. He was strong, and crafty and unpredictable in his use of it. His style of magic was very different from anything I had encountered before, and he nearly had me at first. He would have made a fine battle-mage had we found him before Tauron did. He used every skill he had, trying to kill me, but he was unable to best me because I have first-rate shields. His own were rudimentary, slightly better than those of a rank novice, but not much. I used a thunder-fist, though it's not my best element. I just wanted to be done with it quickly, and I didn't want him to suffer. I hated doing it because he looked so young, just like a novice."

"That was the kindest thing you could have done." Rall's voice held a somber tone.

Wynn was visibly upset at hearing the tale.

Jules saw Wynn's distress. "Remember the tale of Daryk and Aelfrid Firesword? There's no hope for these mages once they take the wrong path because Tauron, the Bull God, has his hand firmly on their hearts. The only thing these mages desire is to turn you, or failing that, they will kill you." He explained the situation more clearly. "We've never been able to retrain them. They're just traps waiting to be set off whenever Tauron wants to strike at us from within. Thus, we must kill every mage who has gone over to him, no matter how young or old they are."

Plodding along, Wynn stared at the ground, not knowing what to say. Finally, he asked, "Why can't we save them for Aeos? Surely something can be done. And remind me what that rune under your ear signifies, beyond the obvious, please. Feia told me something about it, but I don't recall what."

Jules said, "Only certain mages are ever selected to bear the stealth rune and never more than a few mages at one time. A mage augmented with it is a person whose soul has been judged by the Goddess as embodying both empathy and compassion and who is wholly dedicated to serving her. Aeos wants these tasks done as quickly and painlessly as possible and only chooses mages who would carry out such an onerous duty in the most compassionate and efficient way possible. It is a high honor to be chosen, but one I hope I never receive. The stealth rune is the mark of the Temple assassin." Jules's respect was clear. "Devyn has been selected to carry a heavy burden, and I don't envy him." He turned to his friend. "You've grown strong in more ways than the obvious."

"As have we all, Jules," replied Devyn, grinning wryly. "Even you."

"Wynn—there is a reason these mages can't be saved." Rall had no desire to share this memory, but it was clear Wynn wouldn't understand any other way.

"I'll tell you a true story, one I was personally involved in. When I was a young novice, one of the older journeymen found a young lightning-mage, ten years old, who'd been kidnapped by brigands and put to work for them. The thieves murdered the boy's widowed mother, leaving him an orphan. Talyn rescued the boy, whose name was Dag, and brought him to Hyram Temple, wanting to save him and turn him to Aeos's purposes. The abbott there decided the boy might be salvaged as he hadn't been with the highwaymen very long, only a few weeks, and he hadn't murdered anyone for them. He was sent to Aeoven with Talyn." Rall fell silent, looking at some internal landscape that was obviously unpleasant.

Devyn took up the tale. "Father Jance occupied the Holy Seat at the time. He was a fire-mage himself. He tested the boy, and what he discovered disturbed him profoundly. The boy had a deeply rooted desire to have his magic taken from him. Dag was torn and embarrassed about the physical sensations he experienced when using it, not understanding that it's normal to have such a fundamental connection to the expression of your main element. He'd also developed habits that would have forever interfered with his ability to learn to properly use his magic."

Jules said, "Father Jance decided he couldn't allow the boy to be accepted into the novice program, so Talyn took him into his home and adopted him. They placed restrictions on the boy so he couldn't sense his magic, and he adjusted well, becoming a son to Talyn. Dag was sent to school and trained to be a scribe and a clerk, occupations he enjoyed immensely. As a family, they were quite happy, and all was well for two years."

He glanced at Rall, whose expression gave none of his thoughts away, and turned back to Wynn. "One day Talyn didn't show up at work. They sent a messenger to see if he was ill."

When he spoke, Rall's voice was harsh. "I was the messenger they sent to Talyn's home. I was twelve years old and proud to be in a position of such responsibility. The front door was ajar, so I went in, calling Talyn's name." He paused, grounding and centering himself as memories came back with the full force of what he'd seen and struggled with since that day. When he spoke again, he'd regained his usual clinical, detached tone. "I had never seen anything like the scene in that house. Blood was everywhere. On the walls were crude pictures of bulls' heads, and the name 'Tauron' was written many times, all drawn in what looked to me like blood. I found Talyn and his entire family murdered in their sleep, stabbed to death, mutilated."

Rall fell silent again, immersed in the memory of the scene he'd come upon. The others waited until he continued speaking. "Dag sat in the kitchen, covered in his family's blood, alternately laughing and sobbing. 'I had to give that which I love the most to the one true god,' he told the Holy Father when the senior clergy came to take him away. 'I loved them most, so it had to be them. We have to suffer to know his love. A sacrifice was required, and a sacrifice is only worthy if it is the thing you value most, so it had to be them.'" Rall clenched his jaw. "It was a difficult thing for a twelve-year-old to witness, and it affected me for a long time afterward. I was the same age as the boy who had murdered his family. Perhaps that was the hardest part of it all for me, trying to understand that."

Wynn was silent, as if he didn't know what to say. Finally he said, "I'm truly sorry, Rall. I didn't know."

"How could you have known? It's not really discussed anymore." Rall's shrug masked his turmoil.

Jules said, "Temple records prove we've never been successful in reclaiming a rogue-mage."

"I hope we don't meet any young ones." Wynn's shoulders hunched in apprehension, and he walked a little faster. "The Temple's been finding all the talented ones and getting them into the novice barracks, so maybe we won't have to deal with any. People bring their children to the Temple to be tested, so there shouldn't be any hidden anywhere. It's bad enough we have this one up in the mountains to deal with. I hope he's an adult. Mother Relynne said he would have mages in his thrall, though. What if they're children? This isn't going to be an easy task, no matter what she said."

They were a somber group as they crossed a creek, one barely knee-deep. Suddenly, Wynn found himself squirted in the face with icy water. A little water-sprite stood on her hind-legs, chittering angrily at him. "Did I not tell you?" Wynn's outrage was comical. "These silly, hairless chipmunks just want to drown me!" The little queen gave Wynn an admonitory flick of her silvery tail and disappeared into the bushes that hung over the banks of the creek.

The others fell over themselves, laughing.

"It's because your lightning is so strong," said Rall. "They like to drown Feia too. They feel you approaching, and your lightning makes their skin itch. If you wore your armor, they wouldn't be able to squirt you like that."

"I don't want to wear it until we have to because it makes me sweat," replied Wynn. "Don't give me that look. You're not wearing yours for the same reason. It's a drain, carrying a shield all the time. I'm not going to waste my chi on it."

"Then you'll get wet either way." Rall's callous enjoyment of Wynn's distress broke the temporary melancholy his gloomy memories had cast over the group.

For the rest of the day, they walked and joked as Wynn tried to dry out. Eventually, he saw the humor in his plight and soon took to carrying a water shield at all times despite the drain on his chi, since water-sprites inhabited every bog and creek along the trade road.

"This route isn't as heavily traveled as the main north-south trade road," Wynn commented, as they searched for a good camping place. "The only things traveling here are the mail coach and the trade caravans with their guards. I haven't seen anyone else."

"You're right," replied Devyn. "This road goes east to the Mountains of the Moon and then turns north to the wild Barbarian North or south to the heart of Neveyah. From Arlen, the road follows the shadow of the Escarpment all the way south to Braden and travels through some of the wildest, most unsettled parts of the North. However, it's the closest way from Aeoven to the barbarian lands because it skirts the Endless Forest. Widge is the most northern port on the River Fleet, so all the goods from Braden and Mal Evol bound for the Barbarian North go there. Barges can't go any further north because Ariend's Falls are upstream of Falls Lake, and the river is rough beyond there. That's where the main branch of the River Fleet plummets down the face of the escarpment to the hill country of Neveyah."

"I've always wanted to see those falls," said Wynn. "I've heard they're so high you can't see the top."

"That's almost true, but not quite. It's only on the rare clear day that the top is visible." Rall guided his pony around a wide puddle. "Ariend's Falls are so high that usually one cannot see the top from the immense lake at their base because like the rest of the escarpment, it's frequently cloaked by clouds. The mists of the falls can be seen for leagues. I've seen the falls, and there are no words to describe them properly. Their thunder is an indescribable din—the very ground trembles from it for leagues around. The power of the cataract as it drops down the last step to the lake is humbling. I felt insignificant as I gazed at that sight."

The four mages walked toward the cloud-shrouded mountains that dominated the sky in the east, leading their ponies and chatting companionably.

Chapter 22

The first night, they camped at a place where many people had camped over the years. A fire pit surrounded by logs for seating made it look almost homey. Wynn and Devyn tended to the ponies, while Jules and Rall found enough firewood to last the night.

Devyn said, "I think the last time I was in this part of the world was when I was sent to Prona to work with old Hanse on the dikes there for flood control. It was my first posting, and he was a good mentor." The two men groomed the ponies and made sure they were well-watered.

Bent over, checking their ponies' hooves, Wynn's voice was muffled. "How long will it take for Lorana to get to Arlen?"

"The coaches have two drivers. They alternate so they can run day and night. She'll be there by the day after tomorrow." Devyn wore a silly grin. "I still can't believe I'm bonded. I actually thought she would refuse me."

"Seri told me Lorana was convinced you just wanted to be friends. I was fairly sure you felt a lot more strongly."

Devyn laughed and said, "I'm not usually so rash, but this was something beyond my experience."

"It's not crazy when you understand. I knew the minute I met Seri I would never want to be with another woman again," replied Wynn. "It's pretty clear to me your feelings for Lorana are very deep. People say you were as bad as I was with the friendly-girls, but I can tell you aren't interested in the wild side of life anymore."

Devyn groaned. "Why do people always need to talk about me? Even the novices know I'm frequently a jackass. They'll just have to talk about someone else now. I'm a bonded man and happy to be so."

"Oh, heck, I just realized what I said! I'm sorry. I didn't intend to be rude," said Wynn. "Feia is always trying to teach me to think before speaking, and most of the time, I'm good at it."

Devyn just looked at Wynn with a wry grin.

"Well, maybe not as good as I'd like to be," Wynn qualified. "I've been working on it though."

Jules and Rall had returned with armloads of firewood, stacking it by the campfire. "You did manage to get a lot done this weekend, Devyn, getting bonded and all. I guess she likes you in spite of everything!" Jules couldn't resist needling him. "You were a mess, worrying she would send you packing."

"I know," replied Devyn, looking a little surprised at the thought.

"Arlen is really out in the wilds. There isn't even much of a store there anymore since the mines at Hemsteck closed, more like an inn of sorts with a few supplies and where the mail gets delivered," said Jules. "She'll be boarding at different farms, mostly. The Temple keeps a horse and wagon at the inn for the healer's use because the farms are so far apart. You may not see her there, you know. Will you be able to accept it if we miss her?"

"I'll have to, won't I?" replied Devyn, shrugging. "We'll take whatever time we have together and be happy for it. It's what she told me when she agreed to bond with me, and she was right." He turned to Wynn and added, "Seri may have told you Lorana was to be bonded once before, to a lightning-mage named Ryllen. She loved him very much, but he died well before you came to Neveyah. She didn't want to waste our chance at happiness."

Rall tossed a log on the fire. "Ryllen died of lung-fever at a place that in some ways is not far from where we are going, but in other ways, it's farther away than you can imagine. It's actually less than four leagues from the keep where the rogue-mage we are hunting, Grakken, may be holed up to the place where Ryllen and Vere are buried. The last two leagues are vertical, though, and you must scale cliff faces much of the way. The trail is unbelievably dangerous and difficult. The last stretch was the hardest two leagues I've ever climbed." Rall sat down with the others by the fire. "The Hemsteck Valley, where we are going, is at a high altitude. A few people get sick there from the thin air, but most people have no trouble once they get used to it.

"However, once you begin to go higher up, the thinness of the air kills some people, and you never know if it will get you the next time you go there or not. I couldn't save Ryllen or Vere once they succumbed to the fever." Rall managed to appear calm as he spoke of the deaths of his friends. "So many things went wrong, right from the first week, things we had no control over.

"Abbess Lera was sent a true-dream, so they knew three of us were dead, but they didn't know who or why until I staggered to Hemsteck Keep, out of my mind with the fever. The baron loaded me into his oxcart and drove me down to Arlen. Elam was the traveling healer and healed me as well as he could and took me back to Aeoven on the mail coach." Rall fell silent, suddenly awash with memories he'd kept buried for years. "I can't go above Hemsteck now because I'm susceptible to the sickness." Rall kept his emotions well-hidden most of the time, so the haunted look in his eyes was unfamiliar to Wynn.

Devyn said, "I've been to High-Point, and I know some of what you endured, although I was there in midsummer. I'm well acquainted with the vertical face of the wall down to the last good campsite on this side. But you had only just turned seventeen, Rall. Vere and Dalis were tenured adepts. They had all the experience. It was your first away posting, and I doubt you could have done anything different."

Sitting next to Rall, Jules stirred the fire. "What could you have done? Dalis led your quest. She was the armsmaster at Braden Temple, and I remember her well. She had three stars on her arm and was fully trained as a field medic. If she couldn't save them, how could you—a journeyman just out of the novice barracks?"

"We were caught in an avalanche just before we got to the High-Point camp. We were all swept away. When we finally dug ourselves out and found Dalis, she was dead," said Rall. "She'd suffocated under the weight of the snow." With his mind locked in the past as it had been for much of the day, Rall's mood turned gloomy. "I'll tell you the story, though it's not one I like to think about. I suppose you should hear it from me." He settled himself and began his tale, unconsciously telling it the way the wise, old shaman had told such tales around the fire in the barbarian village where he grew up.

"Ryllen and I had just become journeymen. It was our first away posting, and we were excited that out of all the mages available, *we* were selected to accompany Dalis and Vere on their mission. We left Aeoven the last week of Scorpius. It was bad timing, leaving so late into Harvest, but it couldn't be helped. Because she was familiar with the weather on the trail up to High-Point and knew its moods, Dalis wanted to get up and back before the storms of Saggitus set in. To speed things up, we took the mail coach to Arlen and immediately began our trek from there. We made it to Hemsteck in two days and stayed with the baron for the night. The next morning, we continued up the face of the Escarpment. The trail is steep and alternates between sheer cliffs you must climb and broad, treacherous expanses, where you must cross glaciers, watching out for deep crevasses hidden beneath a thin layer of ice. We made good time because the weather held fine for the first two days.

"Unfortunately, it didn't last. We had just made it up to the first ledge out of Hemsteck when the first storms came early that year. Twice in four days, we were stranded by blizzards, but we all had experience in cold-weather survival. Ryllen and I were both barbarians, raised near the Icelands, so we knew very well how to survive the cold, and Vere and Dalis had each been sent to the heights before. We built ice shelters, and we were well equipped for the notoriously terrible weather. With plenty of ration bars, we were safe and rode out the storms warm and well-fed. When the weather cleared, we were able to continue despite the deep snowdrifts.

"Around noon on the day after the second blizzard, we were crossing a wide, barren slope. We knew this was dangerous, because on the Escarpment, a slope without trees means you're in avalanche territory, but we had no choice. The sun was shining, and the slope was a vast expanse of pure, unbroken snow—incredible, deceptive beauty masking the peril that lurked beneath the azure blue of the skies.

"We were halfway across when the avalanche roared down toward us, faster than anything I've ever seen. We heard the noise and barely had time to register what was happening before we were swept away.

"You can't imagine what it's like, to be so helpless and at the mercy of such immense power. I knew without a doubt I was going to die. Great, hard chunks of ice and snow mixed with trees and rocks battered me, alternately crushing and tossing me about.

"Finally, everything just stopped. Somehow, I had been left on top of the snow. I lay there, stunned in the eerie silence, injured and afraid to move, but I knew I had to find the others. As soon as I got my bearings, I began calling their names. At last, I found Vere when I saw part of a snowshoe sticking out of the snow at an odd angle. I dug him out, and thankfully, he was mostly uninjured. Together, we searched until we found Ryllen's kit partially buried. With only that to go on and hoping he was trapped nearby, we found a long branch that we used to poke down through the snowpack, hoping to find him that way. It took a while, but we finally found him. He was lethargic and turning blue when we got him out, but we were able to revive him.

"As soon as he could stand on his own, we began looking for Dalis. We searched and searched, and at last, Vere saw a Temple-issue glove lodged in some broken branches. Again using a branch, we finally found her buried deeply. The three of us worked frantically, but when we at last dug her out, it was too late. She'd suffocated. We built a cairn for her and went as far as we could toward the summit before we camped for the night.

"We were each of us terribly bruised and beaten up from the avalanche. It was a struggle, but over the next two days, we made the journey to the last camp before the final climb. We broke camp at first light and began the ascent up the harrowing, vertical wall. We found few proper ledges to rest at, and I feared Ryllen wouldn't have the strength to finish, but somehow, he did. The sun was going down by the time we arrived at High-Point camp.

"Vere and Ryllen had begun showing signs of lung-fever before we even arrived there. Ryllen had begun coughing right after the avalanche, as he'd been buried the longest, and his coughing increased in severity with every hour. How he managed to hang on and climb the wall, coughing as he did, I don't know. Unfortunately, I had no potions for healing them, as our medical kit and many of our supplies had been swept away by the avalanche, carried down the mountain.

"Pleide, the child of Ariend whom we had been sent to meet, arrived the next morning. We exchanged the scrolls, and she immediately returned to the heights where she could more easily breathe. She was drowning in the thick air where we were, and we were dying for the lack of it. By the time we began our return trip, both Vere and Ryllen were gravely ill. Vere insisted we had to get down to the camp at the base of the vertical wall, so we did try to get off the Escarpment that day. We were only able to go half as fast as we needed to, and every inch down the mountain was agony for them.

"Still, we kept going. If they had been in better shape, we could have reached base camp before dark, but instead, a one-day journey became a three-day nightmare. Finally, at the end of the second day, I knew we weren't going to make it before dark. We halted on a wide ledge. The wind was indescribable, but it was the only place that afforded us even a small amount of safety. There was no way we could continue in the dark—it would have been certain death. It was a horrible place to stop, and we had scant shelter. I couldn't find enough snow to make an ice shelter because the wind scoured it away before it could pile up there. Behind an outcropping, we lay huddled together for warmth with my ground cloth and bedroll wrapped around us, the weight of our bodies holding it tucked over us like a tent.

"During the night, Vere and Ryllen both became delirious with fever. At first, I was hard-pressed to keep them under the makeshift shelter. Just when I was beginning to panic, they quieted down, and I thought they must be getting better. But it wasn't so.

"By morning, they were gone. First Ryllen and then, just at daybreak, Vere let go of life."

Rall stared into the flames, remembering how alone he'd been, so devastated he couldn't even cry. "I set about trying to build a cairn for them, but there were few loose stones to work with and no soil. I covered them with the ground cloth, held down with what few rocks I was able to find.

"As you can imagine, my grief vied with the bad weather, bringing me to the brink of despair. I doubted that I would survive. I wondered if I was brave enough to die. By the time I began the descent down the last wall, I knew I was ill. I have no idea how I made it to Hemsteck Keep, because I've no memory of anything after the wall.

"I don't often speak of that quest." Rall gazed into the fire, its light casting shadows on the hard angles of his face. "But I confess it's been preying on my mind since I learned we were heading to Hemsteck. I can't shake the feeling we're walking into something bad."

"But now you have the star on the back of your hand," offered Wynn. "Now you can help the potions and salves out a little with your healing skill."

"Not much." Rall tried not to sound disheartened. Discussing his first quest depressed him, planting the seeds of worry in his mind. "Not enough to make a difference in something like lung-fever. If I concentrate really hard, I can cast a sleep-spell on one person. The star is for farm-magic, Wynn. I was given it so I can heal plants. Remember when I assisted Mother Relynne as her farm liaison? It was to help deal with the blight strawberries and potatoes suffered."

Jules wanted to reassure him but was unsure how to go about it, as the man was notoriously prickly about such things. "We're not going nearly as high as your team went. Wynn is an experienced tracker with even more experience traveling in the wild than we have. We're all of us more knowledgeable than you and Ryllen were then. You'd just left the novice barracks, and even though you were raised a barbarian and had passed all your trials, nothing can prepare you for something like an avalanche."

"Jules is right," Devyn said. "Don't forget, I've spent a great deal of time traveling in the high reaches of those mountains on business for my father." He grinned at Rall's gloomy expression. "While you were working at keeping food on our tables, I was asked to assemble a list of gear we would need, although I wasn't told who I would be traveling with. I personally made sure we have what we'll need for the heights. I also have the medical supplies equally divided among all of us so they won't be lost unless we all are."

Chapter 23

Rall's gloomy thoughts of his first quest continued to weigh on him. Wynn's constant rain of comments and his habit of suddenly disappearing and reappearing seemed to grate on Rall's nerves a little more every day, proving the old adage, "Water and lightning don't mix well." That and the unusual number of beasts lurking on the road made him irritable and hard to get along with.

"I don't know what's going on here," Jules commented, as he cleaned his sword. "I've never known this road to be so dangerous. No wonder they're sending the healers on coaches now. It's so bad even the highwaymen are avoiding it." By now, they'd been traveling for nearly a week. During that time, they had encountered many creatures, including an angry bear and, most troubling, thunder-lizards.

"Let's just get back on the road. You too, farm boy. We've no time for you to make yourself look pretty." Rall was already on edge, and with each incident, his nerves became more frayed, and Wynn became the focus of his temper.

"I'm just washing the blood off myself. If you don't, it stinks, and I don't want to smell like rotten meat." Wynn, of course, had no idea what he was doing to earn Rall's displeasure.

He doubled his efforts to be helpful, attempting to stay out of Rall's way by hunting for their dinner and scouting ahead. The thick, hooded cloaks they wore over their armor enabled them to blend into the forest, so when Wynn returned with their dinner, trying not to bother Rall, he sometimes inadvertently startled him, earning a sharp reprimand of "Stop sneaking up on me!"

By the time they reached the town of Prona, Rall's short supply of patience had run out. He was snappish and altogether disagreeable.

The family who ran the common room in Prona had two rooms they kept for Temple travelers, so Wynn and Devyn roomed together. Settling their things under the beds, Wynn said wryly, "I'd hate to wake up dead because I talked in my sleep. Rall might slit my throat."

"The more nervous you are, the more you chatter." Devyn had no idea what would ease the situation. "You just have to ignore his moods. He's a temperamental water-mage, but more than that, Rall is also a barbarian. He requires time alone for meditation, and he's had no opportunity. Stop trying to make it better, because he thinks you're badgering him."

"I know. I keep trying to force myself to be silent," Wynn agreed. "I'll try harder, I promise."

Wynn managed to get through the evening without saying anything much beyond please and thank you. The common room was small, and there were no friendly-girls, which was a relief to all four men, though no one said anything.

♦♦♦

Two days out of Prona found them battling wild creatures once more and not having a good day of it. This time thunder-lizards had ambushed the four mages, creatures that shouldn't have been nesting anywhere near the road, and yet this was the group's third encounter. Two large, ungainly corpses lay at strange angles in the brush, and the four men stood or sat, trying to get their breath back after the harrowing fight.

"The noise of the mail coaches and merchants' caravans should, at the very least, have driven them off," Jules muttered. "These creatures must have been planted along here. It's the only explanation. Grakken is a beast-master. This must be his work, but we're still fairly far away from his territory. He's showing some intelligence. He knows this is the route any Temple mages will take, and he doesn't want to make it easy for us." His dark hair was plastered to his skull with sweat, and blood splatters dotted his face, the same shade of red as his armor.

Looking every bit as bloody and exhausted as Jules, Devyn agreed. "It does seem odd they're nesting so close to the road. These things usually avoid the settled areas if they can."

"Actually, they now live only in the higher elevations here in the West," said Rall. "The local farmers cleaned them out of the lowlands back in the days of Aelfrid Firesword." His hands shook, and his blue armor was as covered with blood and gore as Jules and Devyn. He managed to keep his anger fairly well damped down, although he did cast one or two dirty looks at Wynn.

Wynn's white and yellow armor was now both muddy and blood-spattered. His hair also sported a fair amount of mud and gore. A large gash over his left eye bled profusely, and his head ached worse than any pain he'd ever endured. He suffered from double vision, trying with limited success to get his eyes to focus. Wave upon wave of dizziness assailed him, and he leaned his head on his hands, trying to will away the lightheadedness. He found that when he did so, the world stopped spinning.

"Wynn, you really do have an interesting style," Jules mocked, sheathing his sword. "Pretending to fall down and accidentally decapitating the lizard hidden by the shrubs was a stroke of genius. I would never have thought of doing that." He rolled his eyes.

Wynn looked up and shrugged in answer to Jules's sarcasm. "I didn't know it was there." His words came out in a mumble. "I knew something was stalking us but didn't know what. I couldn't sense it. When I tripped over Rall, it must have been in the way of my sword as I fell." He leaned his head on his hands again.

Rall was unable to keep his anger to himself any longer. "Well, you did just *have* to cast lightning at its mate. Of course, it reflected your magic right back at you. I thought you knew better." He glared at Wynn through his own raging headache. "You deserved what happened to you and more." He'd been caught in the backlash too, and now his general irritation with Wynn had become unendurable. "Thanks to you, I can't even sense my own magic right now. My head feels like someone's used it for a drum."

Wynn glared back. "I didn't cast the lightning at the thunder-lizard! I cast it at the cougar. The beast got in the way," he replied angrily. He'd been enduring Rall's jabs and condescending remarks for days now, and with his head pounding like a smith's hammer, he was done with it.

"What cougar, you idiot? I didn't see a cougar." Rall opened his mouth to say something else when Wynn's long knife suddenly whizzed past his ear. He heard a thunk, followed by a high-pitched yowl.

Everyone turned in time to see the large cat drop to the ground from the tree behind Rall, thrashing about in the dirt for a moment before it went still. There followed a dead silence. Shocked at the speed with which it had all happened, Rall turned on Wynn, saying, "Warn me when you're going to do that!"

Wynn tore his gaze from the cougar's corpse and glared back at Rall. Abruptly, Wynn snapped. Filled with rage and adrenaline, he no longer felt the pain of his injuries. Gripping Rall's vest, Wynn forced him to hear his words, his blue eyes snapping with fury. "I suppose I could have said, 'Pardon me, Rall, but a cougar is about to leap on your back.'" His words dripped acid. "I could have asked, 'Shall I kill it or would you like to play with it?'" He shook Rall once with surprising strength and abruptly let him go. As Rall staggered back, Wynn stood with his fists balled up, ready to fight. "You think you're so damned important, but you're nothing but a grumpy, ungrateful bastard. I'm sick to death of walking on eggshells around you. You've made this trip nothing but a misery for me."

Nonplussed by Wynn's explosion of outrage, Rall backed off a step further, wondering if he'd gone too far. "I don't want to fight you. We don't have to do this."

"Well, I want nothing more than to beat you senseless right now." Wynn knew he was out of control, and for a moment, he didn't care, but gradually he became aware of Jules and Devyn, both ready to move in and separate them. He knelt and retrieved his long knife from the cougar's carcass, sheathing it with hands that shook visibly. "You're impossible to please, do you know that? I'm sick of babying you, fearing you'll have a tantrum." His glance at Rall was contemptuous. "I've been putting up with your rotten attitude for days. Nothing I do is good enough. I'm not worthy of your exalted companionship. I get it." He pressed his hands to his temples as the pain from his wounds came rushing back, and he reeled, his stomach queasy. "Unfortunately, you're stuck with me whether you like it or not, so learn to live with it, jackass. Otherwise, kill me now and put me out of my misery."

Rall gaped as he tried and failed to think of a retort. "Well, you could have killed me. One minute we're arguing, and the next you're throwing a knife at me. What was I supposed to think?" Embarrassed, Rall realized that his words were inadequate and that Wynn had saved his life for the second time that day. "I thought you'd gone mad. And I'm sorry for yelling at you."

"I never miss. If I'd thrown it at you, you'd be dead." Wynn swayed as another wave of dizziness assailed him. He sat heavily on a fallen log. Devyn used the opportunity to examine Wynn's bleeding forehead, cleaning it as best he could.

Jules and Devyn looked at each other with raised eyebrows and shrugged. Jules felt it was about time Wynn stood up for himself but chose not to say so.

Rall didn't know why he was behaving so badly. It embarrassed him because it was unfair and he knew it.

On examining Wynn's injury more closely, Devyn's expression showed his concern. "I don't know much about head wounds, but this looks bad. Can you walk?" Wynn said he could. "We need to go back to the creek we just passed and get cleaned up. We should probably make camp there. This will have to hold you for a while, at least until Rall's vision clears and he can see well enough to have a look at it." Devyn finished bandaging Wynn's forehead, temporarily tying the bandage in place with his bandanna. "Rall's the only one with full field-medic training, although I have a little skill."

Collecting the ponies, they began walking back.

"Um, Rall, I really didn't mean to get you zapped. I'm sorry I didn't warn you I was throwing the knife," Wynn said. His anger had gone, and now he struggled just to walk. Leaning heavily on his pony, he slowly followed the others. "I don't intend to make you angry. I seem to get you as riled as I used to get my dad."

"I know. I don't know why I'm so irritable. You saved my life back there, and I'm grateful," Rall replied, once again forcefully stuffing down his frustration at his injuries. "I can't sense my magic. And my eyes don't want to focus. But you have a head wound on top of having been zapped. What if you're really injured? Are you sure you can walk?"

"I'm walking. I just want to find a place to camp and get cleaned up," Wynn said. "I have a headache. We aren't too far from the creek. The water-sprites tried to get me, remember? I got them though." Earlier, Wynn had cast a little spark at the group of water-sprites, sending them racing off, chittering and yipping.

"Oh, right." Rall's chuckle turned into a wince, and he concentrated on following Jules.

"I cleaned Wynn's wound and put medicine on it before I bandaged it. But do you think you can at least see to suturing it after we've gotten ourselves cleaned up? I want to be sure his augmentation won't be compromised." Devyn tugged at his reins, trying to keep his pack pony moving. The plump little horse just wanted to munch grass. "I hope your luck rune hasn't been affected, because we need all the luck we can get. It's amazing how you managed to decapitate the one that was hidden and all by accident. Jules was right, cousin. It has been interesting traveling with you!"

Soon, they were back at the creek. Devyn shooed the annoying little water-sprites away. He then cleaned Wynn's armor and leathers while Wynn attempted with mixed success to bathe himself. Jules finally took pity on him and helped him sluice his hair. The cool water felt good on Wynn's injury, and he soaked his bandanna in the creek, holding it to his forehead. The pain eased somewhat with the cool compress,

The four mages gathered about the fire, where Jules roasted quail. "Wynn, you're good to travel with when it comes to filling the pot," Jules said, enjoying the scent of the roasting birds. "We don't get to eat like this in Aeoven very often." Wynn had snared the quail just before the encounter with the thunder-lizards. It was a measure of his discomfort that he simply handed the gamebag to Jules once they were camped.

"In Markett, we usually had meat only on Restday, and by Odensday, we were back to vegetable soup." Wynn lay on his bedroll, trying unsuccessfully to get comfortable. "I like vegetable soup. Seri makes it really well. She cooks everything well."

"We're lucky men," Devyn agreed. "I'm looking forward to Lorana's cooking. It's amazing what she does without a kitchen." He was about to start his usual litany of her virtues when Jules spoke abruptly, forestalling him.

"She's a paragon of virtue, Devyn." Jules was quite tired of hearing the cousins raving about their spouses. "In case you didn't know, Rall and I also have wives. We love them too." He clasped his hands under his chin and made cow eyes. "Gah, Dev. It's not bad enough we've had to listen to Wynn for the last two years carrying on about how perfectly happy he is, but now we have to listen to you, of all people. It must be something in your blood that makes you two so sappy."

Devyn looked a bit offended, but Wynn grinned through his pain and said, "I know, I know.... It's just now I have someone who understands, and thinking about Seri makes my head feel better." He raised the compress, and they could see his forehead sported a large lump. The swelling made the cut more painful.

"Oh, we understand. We might even feel the same way, but we aren't about to discuss it with you or anyone else," replied Rall, rather stiffly. "So remember we agreed we don't want to hear about it, please."

"Rall, his head wound has affected his reason," Jules said, determined to head off another confrontation between the two. "Wynn, why don't you lie back down and rest before Rall explodes and makes Seri a widow."

Rall rolled his eyes. "Humph. He's half dead already. It would provide no sport at all to waste my energy finishing him off."

Jules snickered and pretended not to hear Rall's muttering.

Devyn turned the roasting quail. "The birds are nearly done," he announced. He tested the potatoes roasting in the coals. "These are ready."

"Actually, I don't think food is going to stay down right now. I have a pretty bad headache," said Wynn, trying vainly to find a position that eased the pain. "But at least I don't have double vision anymore."

"Wait a minute—you threw your knife awfully close to my ear. Don't tell me you were seeing double then!"

"I had a fifty-fifty chance of hitting the right cat, so it was probably all right."

Rall's eyes went wide, and he futilely groped for words.

Jules burst out laughing. "Oh, Goddess," he said between gasps. "You should see your face, Rall! You're as white as your hair!" Slapping his knee, he laughed uproariously. Soon Devyn was chuckling too.

"That's right. Go ahead and laugh, you fools! It wasn't you this idiot was throwing knives at!" Glaring at them, Rall crossed over to Wynn to have a better look at his head wound.

Wynn lay propped on his bedroll with his eyes closed. His bruises showed starkly against his pallor. "Oh...things are spinning again...I hate this."

"Why didn't you tell me how badly you're injured? We almost got into a fist fight back there, and you're dizzy and nauseated? You're daft, wanting to pick a fight when you've been head-injured." Rall knelt next to him. Taking Wynn's chin, he looked at his eyes, not liking what he saw. "I think you have a concussion. What were you thinking, not saying anything? We could have made camp back there."

Wynn pushed Rall's hand away and settled back again, resting his head. "I was thinking you and I were having an argument as usual, and I needed to hold up my end." He grinned, trying to take the sting out of his words. "It wasn't far, and I leaned on my pony."

"We're going to have to stop here for at least two days. You definitely can't travel like this. And Devyn is right. I need to stitch this up," said Rall. He began digging out the medical kit. "I'm sorry, Wynn, but I'll try to be gentle."

"I've been stitched together before, by my mother. She had to sew me up several times when I was a child, so it's nothing new. Once it's done with, things heal more quickly."

"We knew something would happen to slow us down," Jules said, seeing Devyn's carefully blank face. "That's why we didn't plan to be in Arlen for two weeks, right?"

Willing his disappointment away, Devyn said, "Nothing is more important than getting you healed properly, cousin. Besides, I think there are salmon in this stream. Those *I'm* good at catching, so you can just rest and let us feed *you* for a change."

♦♦♦

Wynn slept for most of the next two days. Periodically, he woke and seemed normal enough, but talking appeared to tire him. As soon as he began to look around for some small task to occupy himself, he would drift off again.

Jules and Devyn became perplexed by Wynn's continual need to sleep but laid it down to his head wound. "We can't move him the way he is. We're never going to be able to leave here," said Devyn, worriedly. "Should he be sleeping this much? I don't think you're supposed to sleep this much with head wounds. Are you sure he hasn't slipped into a coma?"

"He does seem to be sleeping far too much. Head wounds are dangerous," said Jules, a frown creasing his forehead. "How would we know if he's brain-damaged?"

"He's not brain-damaged any more than he ever was," said Rall, using his most persuasive voice. "Don't worry. He's not in a coma or anything. He just needs sleep to give his body a chance to heal. Remember, it's only been two days since he was injured. He can't do too much, or he'll do himself harm. What if he has a cracked skull along with the obvious cut? I can't tell if he does or not, so it's better if he just stays quiet until the swelling is completely gone. You've seen how he tries to get up every time he wakes up. Even though he's still not healed, he wants to finish the quest."

Jules and Devyn agreed that Wynn seemed to be his usual self when he did wake.

"His eyes look much better today than yesterday. Both pupils are the same size now. Every time he wakes up, he says he feels better. He's eating well and drinking plenty of water. I'm keeping a close check on him. It's just that the lump hasn't gone down much on his forehead even with cold compresses, so I know he's not recovered yet. He's just sleeping, and he'll mend much faster for it. I'm casting my healing spell on him as often as I can."

In truth, Rall was terrified Wynn would kill himself with his nervous energy. Only a year before, Rall's father had died when he was thrown during his clan's annual wild horse roundup and sustained what seemed a minor head injury. Now Rall was worried Wynn would do the same. In his desperation, he had accidentally stumbled upon a solution but suspected his secret answer wasn't exactly proper. Thus, he couldn't quite meet Jules or Devyn's eyes when he spoke.

Just as Devyn was glumly thinking it would be several more days before they could continue, the mail coach came rolling down the road, carrying a healer, their old friend Arne, on the way to his new posting in Widge.

Arne gently woke Wynn and delved him, finding him healing well, although he was nowhere near fully recovered. Fortunately, he'd suffered no lasting damage. "Your skull was definitely cracked, but Rall's efforts have nearly sealed it," he said. Grasping Wynn's head, Arne healed him, taking care of his other injuries in the process.

He was quite complimentary about Rall's stitching on the main cut. "His augmentation won't be compromised at all by this. It's already coming back over the scar." While the coachmen watered the horses and shared lunch with the questers, Arne chatted with them. "I'm looking forward to my new post," he said cheerfully. "I finally get to be the lead healer in charge of an infirmary. It feels good to have a permanent posting at last. I've been journeying for much of the last six years, so I'll be glad to settle down in one place, even one as cold as winters in Widge are reputed to be." He grinned at Devyn. "It's been hard trying to court ladies with you four snapping them up right and left, but now you gentlemen are all settled, so the rest of us should have a chance. Perhaps there is a plump farmer's daughter in my future." Everyone laughed and agreed there had been a great deal of competition for the unattached ladies in Aeoven. "But there was a particular reason I hoped I would run into you. When I found out our journeys would coincide, I had the drivers watching for you."

Jules said, "Oh?"

"I wondered if you were told about the way rogue-mages are said to trick the clergy of Aeos into allowing the vows that bind us to serve Aeos to be broken." Arne's wry grin was met with silence.

"Well, Soren trapped each of us at one time or another, and we fought our way out, but no." Rall shook his head. "No one said anything to me about this. What are you talking about?"

"This is different. The truth is Soren doesn't believe it's possible to break the geas, so he wouldn't even consider teaching you what I am going to tell you. He would see it as a waste of time, and you know how he is about that." The others rolled their eyes, and Arne shrugged. "Anyway, you already know the rogue-mage is a healer. He can, as Soren showed you, take over your mind. That's dangerous, but you all know what to do in that event. But if, Goddess forbid, you're captured and tortured, there is a way he can trick you into allowing him to break the bond between you and Aeos." All four mages nodded, listening intently now. "If you allow this healer to insert any form of pain relief loop into your mind, he will have to break your geas to do it. The only way he can break it is if you give him permission. At that point, he won't have to take over your mind. He'll subvert you, and you will become a pawn of Tauron."

"Why…why didn't Soren say something about this when we were working with him?" Rall's face looked like thunder. "Is he hoping we'll die?"

"He doesn't believe it's possible. Soren's not a bad person. He's just a man who only believes what he can see. He's a powerful healer, and no one knows more about healing burns and serious injuries than Soren. His only failing is that he's convinced the Temple is the only source of knowledge in Neveyah." Arne's grin lit up his face. "I was raised by my grandmother. She was an old herb-woman, and you know how the Temple looks down on their lore and knowledge as being nothing but superstition. She told me many useful things that aren't taught in the Temple, and what I just told you is one of them. I just wanted you to be prepared."

"What can we do? It sounds like we're doomed if we fall into his clutches." Jules's consternation was echoed in the faces of the others.

"There is a way. Remember, this rogue-mage is a healer who was *never* trained by the Temple, so he won't have good barriers against your emotions. If you're captured, use your raw emotions against him. Fuel your anger with petty grievances and keep him off balance. You know how nervous and jumpy novice healers are until they learn how to build proper barriers." The others nodded. "This rogue-mage will be affected by your emotions, and he won't even know it. Most likely, you won't ever need to know this, but I couldn't let you all leave without making sure you at least had the knowledge."

"Thank you, Arne." Jules's mind turned over all the possibilities. "I'd never heard that before."

"Arne, you're a true friend, to make the point of telling us this." said Devyn, clasping his shoulder.

Rall agreed. "We all know things could go bad, but until we get there, we won't even know what we are up against. This is another weapon we can use if needed."

"I hope it won't be. Anyway, I'm glad I was able to stop and heal you, Wynn," Arne said, his jolly face turning serious. "You would have been stuck here at least another week otherwise, even with Rall's help. Head injuries are dangerous, but you did have excellent care, so you were very lucky."

"The trouble is I can never tell if my healing has done any good or not," Rall confessed. "I can't sense a patient the way you can."

"It's clear to my sight that your healing did help him. Of course, you being a battle-mage, your talent is minimal compared to a full healer's, but it's enough to stop bleeding and speed the healing. That's critical in field medicine. He's improved as much as if he'd been resting for twice as many days," Arne told him. "Besides, you can heal plants, can't you? I've heard you're one of the best. Water-mages usually are. There's something about having that affinity for water that makes you able to do such a thing, though I'm not sure what it is. I'm not able to sense plants well, though I can usually keep them alive. I can only call enough water to drink. Without you and mages like you dealing with blights and such, the rest of us would starve."

"Yes, but if I kill a plant, I won't have to explain to its wife what I've done," Rall said, and Arne laughed.

"You worry too much. You can't do anything wrong with your talent," Arne assured him. "All you can do is speed healing and ease pain. I think you could possibly cast a small sleep-spell if you tried." He looked at Rall out of the corners of his eyes.

"I've cast sleep a couple of times," Rall admitted, carefully not meeting Arne's gaze. "I really have to concentrate to do it, though, and it takes a lot of my healing chi." In fact, he'd taken full advantage of Wynn's injury, casting sleep anytime he began fidgeting. Once Wynn fell asleep, he stayed asleep, but he insisted on trying to get up as soon as he was awake. And then he wanted to talk. Short of sitting on him, Rall didn't know how else to keep Wynn lying down and resting, although he did suspect that his solution was unethical. And then he'd found himself using it all too frequently and justifying it to himself.

Arne was aware of exactly what Rall had done, and the lines about his eyes crinkled as he stifled his grin. "Well, anyway, tomorrow you can resume your journey. Wynn, I want you to give my healing a chance to work. The restorative energy comes from your body, so you need to rest today. I know you're a lightning-mage and you get restless, but I don't want you hunting or fishing. Tomorrow will be soon enough."

"I'll do as you ask," Wynn told him, as he drifted off to sleep once again. "Thank you for stopping and healing me."

"It's what healers do, Wynn." Arne smiled, as his spell took effect. "There you go, Rall. He should sleep until breakfast, and he'll wake up fully healed and rested. It's wonderful how well you cared for him. I'm sure a strong lightning-mage like him must get on your nerves a bit—but he won't need to take any more extra naps on this trip, right?" Grinning at Rall's red face, Arne climbed back into the carriage, and soon the coach rumbled down the trade road.

Devyn and Jules looked at Rall and shook their heads, their disappointment evident as they turned away from him.

"Why are you looking at me like that?" Rall decided to brazen it out. "He needed to sleep, and I helped him. You heard Arne. It kept him from damaging himself further."

"You could have just told us what you were worried about. He's not stupid; he would have listened. You need to stop treating Wynn as if he's a child, or this won't be a good quest for any of us," said Jules. "Before we left Aeoven, you two were the best of friends. Now, only a week into our mission, you're acting just like Devyn and I did when we were barely seventeen and unhappy roommates. Your attitude has turned sour, and you're behaving like a green journeyman instead of a tenured adept. You're better than this. If you ever expect to advance to an abbacy, you'd better learn to moderate your moods. I wouldn't want to work for you the way you are now."

Stung, Rall replied hotly, "In Aeoven, I had my own house to escape to. We weren't together every minute of the day, and he didn't grate on my nerves like salt in a wound!"

"We aren't in Aeoven now, so get over it. Your nerves aren't that important. Teamwork is what counts here, and you aren't doing well in that regard." Jules walked off and sat by the fire, stirring it back to life.

Rall stared at Jules's retreating back and then looked at Devyn. "I suppose you think I'm out of line too."

"What I think doesn't matter," replied Devyn. "What matters is this: what do *you* think about it?" He went to sit by Jules, opening his book to where he'd left off reading.

Rall burst out, "I was terrified he would die from my lack of ability, just like Ryllen and Vere! I can't take losing any more friends to stupid quests!"

Neither Jules nor Devyn was surprised when Rall announced he was going hunting and abruptly left the camp. When he returned, he had a pair of rabbits and a more serene outlook.

Chapter 24

Two weeks and one day after departing Aeoven, the four men neared the village of Arlen, bloody and battle-weary. They hadn't been forced to deal with any more thunder-lizards, but they'd met an inordinate number of wildcats and small elemental beasts along the road. Most disturbing, they were attacked twice by marauding bands of Ariend's children, young men in their twenties who should never have been down on the flats.

"Tauron has changed something in the high mountains," said Rall as he knelt by the corpse of a dead attacker. "Our meeting one random group two years ago is one thing, but the appearance of these men means the Dark God has found a way to work his will on Ariend's people once again and is now using them as a weapon against us. Men of such young ages should still be in their village, but these have already been stricken with the madness. What this means I can't imagine."

"There must be some way we can find out," said Jules. "If Tauron has managed to inflict the men with the curse at a younger age, he may have done something else to affect the balance of power."

"Even in the depths of madness, these men should not be down here. Something has driven them into the thicker air, and it should be killing them." Rall looked up at Jules. "The histories say they can only go as low as the meeting place at High-Point, and I believe that to be true. The one I met told me she struggled with the weight of the air, feeling as if she were suffocating. Yet we've been attacked by young men who were quite alive and very much in the grip of madness when we were forced to kill them."

"If it wasn't impossible, I'd swear they popped up out of nowhere." Wynn's brow wrinkled in puzzlement. "They left no tracks I can see. I didn't hear them approach, and I have extremely keen hearing. Yet they were able to ambush us. But there's no way they can do such a thing. At least I can't see how." He fell silent, pondering the possibilities.

It was a silent group that entered the walled village of Arlen, each man occupied with his own thoughts. Rall greeted the gate guard, who said, "The healer will be glad to see these supplies. It's been a hard winter, and we're running low on medicine, even with what she brought when she returned." They led the ponies toward the largest building, which had a sign swinging over the broad porch that read "Shady Rest." The wooden gate closed behind them. The new stockade, made from enormous logs, provided protection from the beasts that now roamed the area.

Arlen was very small, comprised of several houses and a small inn that boasted a tiny common room and little else. Every inch of ground not part of the street was covered with vegetable gardens, showing the first green sprouts of spring. Chickens roamed freely down the lone, cobbled lane that ran straight through the center of the village to a closed gate. Several horses were penned in a large enclosure behind the inn, to be exchanged to pull the mail coach.

The innkeeper handled the Temple mail and also had a small general store in a room off the front porch of her inn, where she sold a few of the basic necessities. Things were done this way in all the small towns along the trade roads. The only reason the village of Arlen was still alive was because it was the logical place for drivers and passengers to briefly rest, have a hot meal, and change horses.

"I'm glad to see you mages. The baron has vanished, poor, lonely old thing." The innkeeper, a large woman named Merylee, took their ponies and helped them offload the supplies. "Something bad is going on around here too, and maybe it's all connected. I don't know. Strange animals that shouldn't be living here are coming down out of the mountains and eating our livestock. Deranged rat-people have taken to roaming the shadow of the Escarpment. Now, on top of everything else, we hear folks on some of the outlying farms have disappeared."

"Rat-people? Do you mean the children of Ariend?" Jules was slightly taken aback by the term.

"Is that what they are?" The innkeeper seemed surprised. "All I know is, over the last month or so, folks traveling on the trade road have been attacked by these half-sized people who look like rats. They appear out of nowhere, and suddenly you're fighting for your life."

"Who else besides the baron has gone missing?" Rall opened his notebook. "We intend to take care of whatever the problem is, but we need as much information as you can give us."

"The healer went out to check on the Leradi family," replied Merylee, with a worried look on her plump face. "They were gone, leaving no trace. Their place was empty, and their livestock was gone. There've been Leradis on that farm as long as my family has been here. The wool from their pacas was some of the finest, softest wool in the North, and now that bloodline is gone, to the last animal. That's a shame, a crying shame, to lose generations of breeding stock like that."

"How many families get mail here?" Rall made notes as she spoke. "It would give me an idea of how many people we need to account for."

"Maybe two hundred families," replied the innkeeper, trying to picture the shelves in her mailroom. "I put the mail in baskets for them, and when they come for supplies, they take it back with them. I could have Bettina count the baskets."

"Why don't you do that," agreed Rall. "We'll also talk to the healer. She's bonded to Devyn, the earth-mage on this expedition." He gestured toward the corner where Devyn and Wynn stood going over the list of supplies they needed to take with them on their journey. "We'll also want to talk to anyone who comes in to pick up supplies. Perhaps we should see who hasn't picked up their mail and pay them a visit to see how they are doing."

"I'd heard Lorana was bonded now. She's due back today," said the innkeeper, smiling at Devyn. "I didn't know she married the handsome young prince. He used to come through here all the time with his brother. Dax was quite a wild boy before he became king over in Mal Evol. Of course, we hear he's bonded now with a brand new son of his own. Devyn was always much better behaved." Her smile was fond as she gazed at Devyn, and she didn't see Rall's eyebrows rise at her words. "Lorana intended to return by this morning, but her schedule is frequently disrupted. She'll be back today, or tomorrow at the latest. If she's delayed beyond that, her guards will get a message out to us."

"I knew she might not be here when we arrived," said Devyn, when Rall told him Lorana was delayed. "We need to leave on Lunaday whether she's returned or not." His tone was matter-of-fact, but it was clear he was disappointed. "We both knew our timing might be off and we could miss seeing each other."

"Jules, you and Wynn were raised on farms not unlike these, so you might be able to get information from them we couldn't. Devyn and I will stay here and wait for Lorana and get the medicines and supplies we brought stored properly," said Rall. "You two take some horses and make some visits. Just go to a few of the nearer places so you can be back in time for supper."

"They may know more about what's actually going on," agreed Wynn. "The farms are isolated, so they'll think everyone already knows what they know. They won't make a special trip to tell anyone about something bad they might have seen or heard—they'll assume they were the last to find out."

Toward evening, Jules and Wynn returned with little more information than they had before. "No one knows anything for sure, but they're all upset," Wynn said as they sat by the fire in the common room. "It's really strange, because it's planting season. News should travel between the farms along with the roving field hands, but no itinerant workers have arrived this year. What could have happened to the laborers? They usually come up from Braden and Widge as soon as the ground thaws."

Lorana arrived just then, bringing news of another family's disappearance. After grabbing her and kissing her soundly, Devyn carried her kit up to their room. Now, the five of them sat before the fire in the tiny common room, and Lorana told them what she'd found on her rounds.

"We've had the occasional person go missing, ever since I've been a healer in this particular area. A person sometimes goes hunting and never returns, but this is different." Lorana was tired and full of worry. "Several entire families have disappeared since I was last here. I don't know what to think."

"Do you think they left voluntarily?" Rall took notes as she talked. "This is the most sparsely populated area in the North. Something about living in the shadow of the Escarpment keeps folks from settling here."

"No. I can't explain it, but I don't think they left of their own accord." Lorana's sadness was palpable. "I know in my heart Baron Hemsteck didn't leave voluntarily. Ivan would never have abandoned his valley, not even if he were reduced to living in a mud hut. The land has been his family's home since the founding of the Temple. The keep is in ruins, but it's all he has left, and he wouldn't consider leaving.

"And as for the others, I've been caring for these people since I left the novice barracks. I've delivered their babies. I've helped them bring much of their livestock into this world. They wouldn't abandon the land their families have farmed for so many generations. Never." A tear rolled down her cheek. "They aren't the sort of people who give up and go south to the cities. They've carved their lives out of the shadow of the Escarpment, and they love this place with every fiber of their being. The only reason any of them ever leave this land is if they're sent to the Temple to be a novice."

Devyn reached for her hand, squeezing it. "I'm so sorry, my love. We're going to get to the bottom of this and bring them back if possible. If any of them are alive, we'll try to find them and return them to their homes."

"I know you will," she said, worry and fear clear in her eyes. "If they're alive, you four will rescue them. I know it. But please be very careful. I think a mindbender is at work here in the lowlands, and he's mastered some skills battle-mages aren't able to protect themselves from. Please, avoid his notice at all cost. You absolutely must not let him seize your minds."

Wynn said, "It's true a strong mindbender can take a battle-mage by surprise and control him if he isn't wary. But I promise we won't let him. Soren did it to each of us at one time or another during training and wouldn't stop until we figured out how to break free from him." He shuddered, remembering the terror he'd felt. "We'll be vigilant." He shrugged. "You shouldn't worry, because both Soren and Mother Relynne badgered us and wouldn't let us leave Aeoven until they knew we could all break free. We never knew when Soren would attack."

"It's safe to say he'll never try to take over Wynn's mind again, that's for sure," laughed Jules. "Wynn panicked and visualized a hundred needles stabbing Soren's physical body. Trapped within Soren's empathy as he was, that was all it took. The poor man let Wynn go rather quickly, as he was bleeding profusely and required a healer himself!"

"I didn't know how a healer's empathy works. It didn't occur to me his body would be damaged," replied Wynn, red-faced. "I thought he'd gone mad. I was desperate to get control of my body. I promised I wouldn't do it to him again."

Rall laughed at the memory. "He *was* a bit unprepared for Wynn's gift of visualization. If I didn't know it was unethical, I'd say Mother Relynne set Soren up for a lesson in humility when she selected Wynn to be his first victim." Jules and Devyn both snickered as they agreed with him.

"See?" said Devyn, squeezing Lorana's hand again. "Wynn is right, my dear one. A mindbender might take one or another of us by surprise, but he'll have a hard time keeping us." Everyone laughed at that. "Mother Relynne is nothing if not thorough in her instruction!"

Chapter 25

After three days, Wynn and his companions bade goodbye to Lorana and began the trek up the steep Hemsteck Trail. The heavily fortified East Gate of the wooden stockade surrounding the town opened directly onto the road and was the only way to reach the mines from the west, though there was a path from the Valley of Mal Evol in the east, even more difficult than the western trail. The gate remained locked, and just as on the West Gate, a guard was mounted there at all times, armed with a bow. "There's nothing good coming down that road these days," said the grizzled woman on gate duty. "Now the old baron is gone, it's mostly just those strange creatures more like rats than people. They're mad, mindless things. We shoot them full of arrows."

Wynn heard the thunk of the heavy gate closing behind them. "This is pretty final. We're really on our way to fight this mage. I wonder if he'll be as bad to fight as Mother Relynne was. I'd hate to think of how evil she could be if she wanted to."

The others agreed and talked quietly as they walked. They'd traveled barely an hour when Rall said, "Something is stalking us. It feels like a fairly big water elemental."

"I'll see what it is," said Wynn, and he vanished into the underbrush. A few moments later he returned. "It's a water-wraith. I hate dealing with those things."

"It should be easy for you," said Rall, somewhat sarcastically. "Just shoot him full of magic arrows."

"Well, I can try," said Wynn, somewhat doubtfully. With that, he vanished again.

"Hey, wait! I didn't mean it! Oh, hell." Rall turned to follow Wynn and was nearly knocked off his feet by a loud explosion as foul globs of jelly began falling from the sky.

Dodging madly, the men attempted to avoid the stinking mess raining down on them, to no avail. Now covered in reeking, gelatinous goo, the three mages stared at each other, nonplussed.

"I used too much lightning, I think," Wynn said as he returned, his white armor pristine and shining in the morning sunlight. "I have to remember to use a little less next time, but it was only my second water-wraith, so I didn't know how much—oh, you guys are going to need a bath."

Devyn stared at Wynn and then his affronted companions. Slapping his thighs and howling, it was all he could do to remain standing. Jules hooted so hard his sides hurt. Rall muttered something incomprehensible as he too succumbed to manic laughter.

Wynn wasn't sure whether to join in or not.

As he undressed next to an icy stream, a rather chagrinned Rall simply nodded when Jules said, "Sarcasm is a deadly weapon in your hands. You might want to think carefully before you use it around you-know-who."

After bathing, they continued hiking. The path began fairly easily, but by evening, it became extremely steep. The four men were in excellent shape and negotiated the trail with only moderate trouble.

As they made camp, Devyn said, "Well, we now know for sure someone has been doing roadwork recently."

"How do you know?" Rall asked. "I've not been up this way in six years. I agree it's a lot worse than it was then. If it's like this all the way up to the mines, our journey will take longer than planned."

"The mage's signature feels quite recent to my earth-sense. This road was altered perhaps just since this last Harvest season. Besides, I traveled through here with my brother on business for our family three years ago, just before my father died. It was rough then, but the baron's cart could manage it," replied Devyn, shrugging. "Father wanted to get Dax away from some of his amusements and felt a complete survey of the trail was in order. The entrance to the east end of the trail is close to my family's summer house." He chuckled. "Dax was supposed to be learning how to be a vintner instead of a pleasure-boy. Temple approval is always required for anyone journeying up the trail, and Abbott Taj decided I should make the trip with him."

"Did you run into any of Ariend's children?" Jules thought about the encounters they'd had in the lowlands.

"We did, at High-Point shelter. Two of their warriors appeared at our fire." Devyn's expression was solemn. "Dax and I weren't surprised. We expected to see them there."

"What are they like, as people? The only ones I've met were completely mad, and we've always ended up having to kill them." Jules's dark eyes were sad. "I've never had the privilege of meeting them under better circumstances."

"They were intriguing, polite, and pleasant. They never let the males leave the village until the madness affects them so badly they're a danger, so it was only females we met," Devyn replied. "They are learned and know everything about our people and the Temple, divining much from observing the heavens and reading the stars. The two we met were elders, sages who told us the stars are the words of the Almighty Father and the Mother of All, written there for those who would look. We of the lowlands know very little of them as a people, save they are scholars who thrive in the heights where we can't and who've suffered terribly at the Dark God's hands." He fell silent, remembering the meeting. "They had a warning for Dax and me to bring to Mother Relynne. We didn't understand it, but we carried it to her nonetheless."

"What was it, if I may ask? I'll understand if it's a Temple secret and you can't say." Wynn was curious from a professional standpoint. "I've read about Ariend's children, of course, everything that is written. They invented both the printing press and the process of grinding lenses, which we use in making our eyeglasses and distance-viewers. In fact, most of our technology, like the waterwheel, was a gift from them. They were given to us at the founding of the Temple in Aeoven to aid us in our battle against the Bull God."

Rall said, "I didn't know that." His expression was thoughtful. "I'm not surprised, though. It's said they taught Aelfrid Firesword the way to make Temple armor."

Wynn nodded. "That's the reason I know about them. Journeyman armor smiths study this part of our history, and we're required to memorize it. To advance within the craft, we are tested on our knowledge of this and other mysteries you might consider obscure. This knowledge has no practical use outside my craft." He grinned, adding, "We each have to learn so much specific information when we settle on a craft that most mages don't have time to study outside their own area. The lore of Ariend's children is knowledge we smiths keep and pass down faithfully so it won't fade away. Despite the difficulty of getting to the meeting place where both people can still breathe and communicate, they have a great deal of mysterious and arcane knowledge that they share with us, always to our benefit."

The others nodded. Jules said, "I always wondered about that—we went from being nomadic barbarians to farming and living in villages rather quickly."

Devyn said, "What Ariend's children told us isn't a Temple secret, but it's a prophecy that makes no sense to me, even today. The elder, Aril, gave us a scroll on which was written: 'The worlds tremble in the starry void. The stolen child yearns for his mother's breast in the foreign land and is succored on despair. Vintages of unsurpassed sweetness will be the wines of the last days. Most faithful scion of the line of keepers, be not diverted by the burning city of old. Hold fast to the altar when the house of holiness is under siege. Your faith and resolve preserve the blood of the keepers. A place is prepared for you at my hearth.'

"Aril was a seer and was sent the prophecy only a week before we arrived at the meeting place." Devyn continued, "At the same time, she was told when my brother and I would be at High-Point and that the message was to be given to us. We know that the hearth referred to is Aeos's Great Hearth, so someone will die serving her. Of course, we would all die for her if it would preserve Neveyah, but beyond that, it makes no sense."

"I agree it's vague," said Jules. "But prophecies are obscure by their nature." He stirred the fire with a long stick, pondering the ambiguous foretelling.

"It's another dark prophecy. I don't like it." Rall shifted uneasily, mulling it over, trying to make sense of it. "It speaks of a burning city and a temple under siege. 'The city of old' must refer to Mal Evol City, and it's not the first terrible prophecy regarding that Temple. There are several others."

"I agree, but as you've said many times, prophecies are rarely clear or easy to understand," replied Jules. "The good thing is we'll be dead long before such a thing happens, Aeos willing."

"I leave the interpreting of prophecies to you three. You know much more about that sort of thing than I do," Wynn said. He checked on the birds he was roasting, finding they were done perfectly. "*My* interpretation is solely guided by my stomach. It says dinner is ready!" He took the pheasants off the spit and pulled the potatoes off their stones amidst the coals. "Let's eat!"

◆◆◆

During the night, a spring snowstorm set in, making travel the next day more difficult. Still, they were well prepared for the notoriously bad weather that occurred as one traveled higher.

The second night on the Escarpment, they found a place to stay in an old longhouse that once had sheltered teams of oxen and the drivers of the heavy ore wagons that traveled the road from the Hemsteck Mine. With every season that passed, it had fallen into disrepair a bit more. After a spate of vigorous housecleaning and some chimney mending on Wynn's part, they spent a warmer night than they'd expected.

"We'll need a place to hide while we're planning our assault," said Rall. "We won't be welcome at the keep, I'm sure."

"A good shelter would help since we'll have to set a cold camp once we're in Grakken's neighborhood," Jules said. "We don't want any smoke to give us away."

"I thought about that, so we have enough ration bars for two weeks if we're unable to hunt. Heaven forbid we have to depend on them for so long," Devyn said, stretching and yawning.

"You provisioned us well, Dev," said Rall. "I think you took every eventuality into consideration."

"I plan to have a long and illustrious career and end my days as an elderly, wise mage, so starving or freezing to death now isn't on my agenda." Devyn's comment elicited chuckles of agreement from the others. Devyn turned the quails that now roasted over the merrily burning fire, browning them evenly.

That night, they set a two-man watch again. During the night, the weather warmed to above freezing again, and by morning, the snow was slowly melting, making traveling both wet and difficult.

Chapter 26

The four mages began the climb to the next stop. "I think it will be at least a day or two before we arrive at the entrance to the Hemsteck Valley," said Rall. "We're high enough that there will be snow on the ground in most places for several more weeks. Some may still be here in sheltered places at Summer Solstice."

"Do you think it'll snow again? It's certainly cold enough." Wynn's breath misted as he walked. When he made the mistake of looking back at the longhouse, he was able to see just how steep the path really was.

"I'm sure it will," replied Rall. "The rain falls as snow up here most of the year. The baron has a large kitchen garden, but he grows mostly crops that can reach maturity in three months and that thrive in the cool weather he enjoys in the summer." They fell silent as they concentrated on keeping their footing.

"I find it difficult to imagine how an ox-drawn wagon full of iron ingots could negotiate this trail," said Wynn, after a while. They had been climbing for the better part of an hour. "I know a bit about those sorts of wagons, having offloaded enough of them at the armory." The others chuckled.

"They didn't," said Devyn, grinning. "This road was very different when I was here last, much smoother and wider. While it was in poor condition, it could easily have been repaired, and the old baron drove his oxcart down to market two or three times a year. Someone deliberately remade the trail in this fashion, although I can't imagine why."

"If so, it's been changed to keep folks from coming up here to check on things," said Jules. "If what we've heard is right, this rogue-mage has commandeered the Hemsteck Keep, but for what? I've thought long and hard on this, and I can find no reason why he would want a ruined pile of stones a person can't live in, mines that are all played out, and soil you can barely grow turnips in."

They came to a place where a wide, deep stream now crossed the road, cutting it in half. The water raced downhill over deep, boulder-strewn rapids and had carved a yawning chasm through the old trail. "That was never here before," said Rall.

"Now what? I certainly can't leap that far. The channel is cut too deeply and the water is running too swiftly to try crossing it here." Jules's dismay was echoed by the others.

"Rall, why don't you use your gift to search the water and see if you can locate a ford?" Wynn's question earned him surprised glances.

"What gave you the idea I can do something like that?" Rall's consternation made Jules grin. "I never thought to try. I suppose it's possible."

"I don't see why you can't. I've been trying to use my gift to sense the weather since we were surprised by the snowstorm yesterday. I'm not really good at it yet, but I can recognize some things."

Devyn and Jules stared at Wynn and then looked at each other and shrugged. The sky was the same overcast gray as everyday had been. Storms arrived with little warning on the Escarpment.

Rall's eyebrows rose into his knit cap. "What have you found? I don't think I ever heard of lightning-mages being able to sense the weather, but why not?"

Wynn extended his senses as far as he was able and said, "I probably can't sense it like a healer can, but there's a lot moisture gathering up there, and it'll fall soon, by this afternoon. I think it'll be snow, but I'm guessing that because of how cold the wind is. I can't feel the water exactly, but I know it's there, because when I send out my awareness as if I were searching for a mage, it makes my lightning-sense tingle the way it does in a rainstorm."

Rall had extended his senses to their limits too. "You're right…. I sense a lot of moisture building, so we should find a good camping place as soon as we can. When it does fall, it'll be a blizzard." He looked at Wynn, shook his head, and said, "That was a smart idea. I'll try checking the stream, but maybe Devyn should search for a ford too, because I can't really sense the earth the way he can."

Both Devyn and Jules had tried sensing the weather when Rall did. "I'll try searching the earth. I don't think I can detect anything about the weather other than what my eyes show me," said Devyn. "Old Hanse was able to feel the earth over a wide area. I'll see what I can do. I've done it before, following weaknesses in the earth to exploit for whatever project I was working on. Other than that, I never had a reason to try."

"I can't tell anything about the weather either, but I wonder how else we could use that skill." Jules sent his senses out as far as he could around him but came up with nothing. "Maybe there isn't anything a fire-mage could feel here. My lightning or water skills certainly aren't strong enough to pick up what you two do. I'll keep practicing that trick anyway because it could be useful."

Rall concentrated on the stream. Grinning, he realized he could sense it for nearly a furlong in any direction. "There seems to be a shallow area not too far to the south of us, but we'll have to leave the trail."

"I see what you mean." Devyn had his senses extended. "The terrain is fairly steep between here and that point. We can do it if we're careful to work our way along the edge of this small canyon. I don't think I should try to rearrange the earth to make the way easier, because we don't want to give ourselves away."

"I agree," said Jules, and the others nodded.

With some effort, they arrived at the place where the water crossed a shallow area on its way to the River Fleet. As quickly as possible, they forded the creek, ignoring the icy chill. The crossing was difficult and not just because of the cold—the rapidly running water concealed many rocks and small holes, making the footing treacherous.

"It'll be easier to make our way back to the road on this side than it was on the other." Devyn's words were somewhat obscured by the noise of the stream, but he didn't raise his voice. Something told him they needed to travel as quietly as they could now, and when he mentioned it, the others agreed.

Once they arrived back at the old road, they traveled as quickly as they could. After a while, they began looking for a place to make camp. Devyn found a spot set back in the forest, and they set about making a good-sized shelter. Rall made a small firepit in the center the way the people in his village did when they were out foraging. Once inside, they were snug and dry, the small amount of smoke escaping through the hole in the center of the roof of the rough lodge.

As expected, the storm when it came was long and intense. During the blizzard, the four retreated into silent prayer and meditation as a way to escape the crowded living conditions, and Rall's spirits improved accordingly.

♦♦♦

After three days, the storm lifted, and the four were able to continue traveling. They came to another old longhouse, one in serious disrepair. They made part of the old place livable and passed another night in moderate comfort. While they gathered about the fire, enjoying the hare Wynn had snared, Rall said, "This should probably be the last fire we have, unless we're forced into retreating for a while."

"I think you're right. Let's hope we're done and on our way back down within two weeks," agreed Jules. "I've had to subsist on ration bars before, and they lose their appeal after a day or two."

"Besides, we want to go unnoticed, so going back and forth is not an option," Devyn said, and everyone agreed. "The trail is the only route into the Hemsteck Valley, and I'm sure it'll be watched. If we enter at night and refrain from traveling during the day, there's less chance we'll be seen."

"Agreed. Once we reach the entrance to the valley, we'll wait until dark," Rall said. "And don't worry about food. You're traveling with a barbarian, and we were hunter-gatherers only a few generations ago. I've noticed quite a few plants with edible roots up here, even under the snow. If we can wash them, they will be safe to eat uncooked, and we can supplement the ration bars with them." He grinned at Jules's doubtful expression. "The world is usually full of food if you know where it is and how to fix it, Jules. I could even make you a nice salad if you'd like."

"No, thank you. Salad gives me nightmares," replied Jules, grinning. "Vegetables frighten me." The others laughed, and the evening was spent playing an impromptu game of stones, using light and dark pebbles they'd found along the way.

The next day was uneventful, though the going was rough. The trail had many gaps they had to leap across and several places where they had to find alternate routes, but they managed to find their way.

"Even as slow as we're traveling today, we should arrive at the entrance this afternoon," said Rall. "We'll have to be on our guard once we enter the pass."

They made a temporary camp in the shelter of the alpine forest, under the evergreens where the snow was scant. Well after dark, they entered the narrow gap that led into the Hemsteck Valley. In some places, the way was constricted. Only one wagon could have gone through at a time. The sheer walls of the Escarpment rose on either side as the gorge cut through to the valley. The trail rose sharply as it wound through the narrow canyon, making twists and turns, going around blind corners. The four traveled as silently as they could, and when they spoke, it was in low whispers.

"If I was going to set a trap, I would put it here because my victims would be funneled right into it." Wynn's comment was barely audible. They rounded a sharp bend, and he stopped short. The group came to a halt behind him. "What's this? I never heard that the road ran through a tunnel." A black passageway into the mountainside loomed ahead. The four retreated around the bend and stood in the shadows, quietly conferring. Periodically, Wynn crept back, peering through his spyglass in an attempt to make out details inside the dark and forbidding entrance.

"This road never passed through a tunnel before," said Rall. "I'm not going in there until we know more about it."

"It's quite recent," said Devyn, sending his senses out as far as they would reach. "Despite the deceptively fine-looking masonry on the entrance that makes it appear as if it's always been here, it's new and not that well done. It was built over the old cobbled road that used to go all the way to Arlen. The tunnel goes back a long way, further than I can sense. I don't know why they would make such an elaborate entrance when the road to this place is nearly impassable unless they're trying to lure people who don't know it shouldn't be here." He stood with his eyes closed, trying to sense the way the soil of the hillside felt. "There was a landslide here, closing off the gap. Someone either caused it or used it as a reason to make this tunnel."

"I wish you could tell us if it the road goes clear through or if it's a trap." Jules's apprehension was shared by all. "We either risk entering it and facing whatever is there, or we try to scale the Escarpment. If we decide to do that, we have to go back to Arlen and send to Braden Temple for climbing gear because we can't do that without it."

"We *know* it's a trap. What sort is the question. From the condition of the road up to this place, it's clear Grakken wants to keep people from entering the valley, at least from this side," agreed Rall. "I hate to say it, but I think we have to go forward. We won't be able to get back up here for at least a month if we go back now. I really don't think we should wait even a week. If any of the people who've disappeared are still alive, they may not be in a month."

"I think you're right," said Wynn. "This may be the only chance we have to rescue them."

"I don't know if we'll be able to save anyone. Even if we can free them, I don't know what state they'll be in. I only know what I've read about the things mindbenders do to their victims, and it may be they will be damaged forever." Devyn shrugged. "We may be able to free them, but *save* them? I don't know."

Rall understood what Devyn meant but said, "We have to make the effort anyway." He looked at his companions. "Are you ready to chance the tunnel?"

"As ready as I'll ever be," replied Jules. "We don't even know if it *is* a tunnel. It may be a cave. We only know it goes back too far for Devyn to sense. Aeos only knows what we're walking into here."

They checked that their weapons were easily accessible. "Let's go. Who wants to lead?" Wynn's comment elicited muffled chuckles from the others. Wynn usually traveled ahead.

"I'll go first. We'll need to put our cloaks in our kits in case we have to do any fighting. Grakken may have someone posted at the other end, waiting for visitors. Your armor is too white, so you trail behind and maybe it won't give us away." Rall turned to Jules. "Sometimes, the air is unbreathable in mines. Do you think we should light a candle? If noxious gasses lurk inside there, a candle would tell us."

"Perhaps explosively," said Wynn, grinning. "I can darken my white armor, but you can still go first." He scraped several handfuls of dirt over his legs and his body.

Jules said, "I don't know about a candle. If his armor is too white, then any light would be bad, don't you think? And there is the possibility of an explosion if we were to run into a pocket of bad air."

"I know, but…some bad air suffocates you, and the candle would tell us. And without it, we'll have to feel our way along the wall. That's the only way we could do it, and we will still require light at some point." Rall looked at Jules, his arms crossed.

"How can we possibly make any speed with no light?" Devyn's question was echoed by Wynn.

"We can't risk it. An explosion is no laughing matter, and these mines were notorious for that." Jules shrugged. "We must be careful in there, whatever we do, because even if we were to survive an explosion, the passageway would likely cave in on us."

After more discussion, they agreed to go without a light unless they absolutely needed one.

"We must have absolute silence until we are well out of this tunnel and on the other side. Agreed?" The others nodded and followed Rall into the black entrance.

Chapter 27

The four mages entered the tunnel, treading warily on the broad, paved road. Soon, they had passed beyond the light from the entrance. As they went deeper and more fully into the darkness, they stayed to the wall, walking in single file. Each man behind Rall kept one hand on the man in front of him, slowly feeling their way along the smooth masonry with the other. The tunnel seemed to follow the old trail, with many sharp turns and corners.

Time appeared to expand until they had no idea how long they had been inside. They stopped at one point and had a quick meal of ration bars and water, taking the risk of lighting a candle to do so. Everything looked normal, just an average tunnel made of large stone blocks. Still, after their meal, they extinguished the light, and continued.

They had been in the passageway long enough that they were getting hungry again, but at long last, a faint glow appeared ahead of them, emanating from around a distant corner. At first, it looked they might be coming to the end of the tunnel, but as they rounded the corner, they quickly saw how mistaken they were.

They had come to a cavern, and the glow emanated from the gelatinous hide of an immense waterdrake. Unfortunately, it saw them at the same time they saw it. With an ear-splitting shriek, the beast swung his massive head toward them. The four men scattered. The creature raced across the cavern, its giant maw filled with razor-sharp teeth snapping dreadfully close to Wynn's head.

Horrified, Wynn panicked. Before he could even think about it, his reflexes kicked in, and he called a massive lightning spell, a curtain-call. Thunder shook the cavern, and part of the tunnel collapsed as the lightning sheeted toward the waterdrake, temporarily blinding them.

"Shi-i-i-t...," Rall groaned. "You idiot—what are you thinking?" His armor was bespelled to protect him from lightning attacks, and he instantly tossed up a water-shield.

The waterdrake had shielded against lightning, and it promptly cast a massive water spell. When the water came back at the group, it was fully charged with a colossal amount of voltage.

The backlash just missed Devyn and Jules, who dodged to either side, reflected off Rall's shields, and washed right over him, catching Wynn full-on. In the confusion, Wynn couldn't decide which element to shield against and inadvertently raised two, one for water and one for lightning. Jules's eyes popped as he felt both shields briefly stick together.

Miraculously, the electrically charged water reflected off Wynn's shields at just the right angle and rebounded, still fully electrified. Because it was water, the drake didn't shield against it, taking the full brunt of Wynn's massive lightning spell. Held immobile, the waterdrake's immense body jerked and spasmed, then thrashed wildly, shaking the ground as if by an earthquake. The great creature shrieked in octaves that tore at the attackers' ears. The cavern shook with the thunderous noise, and the tunnel behind them caved in completely, trapping them. Unable to remain standing, the beast staggered backwards and fell, lying on its side, thrashing and alternately bellowing and keening.

"What the—Wynn, don't panic, and for the love of Aeos, don't use magic again! Spread out!" Rall barked orders. "We have to give it so many targets it can't concentrate on just one of us."

"We can't surround him. He's lying with his back to the wall, and he's not budging," shouted Jules, swinging his sword, trying unsuccessfully to get near the thing. At last, he got a good swipe at the long neck, dodging as the beast tried to crush him with his head, his blade glancing off the tough hide. "Be sure your blade is centered. His hide deflects it if you're the least bit off!"

Wynn's lightning spell had somehow hindered the drake's ability to cast magic, and the men swarmed it. It lay flailing and gnashing its teeth, trying to bite anyone who came near. All the while, its shrieks were deafening. Devyn managed to slice one of his eyes, and the wounded beast turned his attention to him, snapping at his tormentor. Nimbly leaping to one side and slashing again with his sword, Devyn evaded the drake's razor-sharp teeth, opening another long gash along the side of the creature's face.

Wynn used that moment to race up, dodging the flailing legs, and with his sword held firmly in both hands, he stabbed with all his strength at the soft underbelly. He evaded the claws and snapping jaws, driving down with all his strength. Suddenly, his feet slipped out from under him, and off balance, he fell face down. Driven by his momentum and his weight, his sword sliced the tough hide, tearing a gaping hole in the beast's abdomen.

The stench in the cavern was bad before, but it was indescribable as the creature's guts spilled out, partially burying Wynn under a reeking pile of entrails. Gasping for breath, he fought to get out from under the slimy offal. Once his head emerged, the odor had him puking. Frantically, he struggled in the filth.

The belly wound really got the beast's attention. With a terrible gurgling screech, the waterdrake desperately gnashed its teeth at Wynn, who couldn't get his footing and kept slipping in the muck. Twice, the slashing claws and snapping teeth nearly had him, but each time he slipped, and the enraged creature missed catching him.

Taking advantage of its preoccupation with trying to crush Wynn in his jaws, Devyn, Rall, and Jules managed to hack the enormous head off with three great blows of their swords.

The heavy splat of the massive head as it fell to the muck was almost anticlimactic. A deafening silence reigned in the cavern. As life left the creature, the glow of his body faded, leaving them once again in the dark.

"Now what?" They were each somewhat deafened by the terrible din of the battle, and Rall's voice sounded odd in the darkness.

"How are we going to get out of here?" Jules ask the question everyone was thinking.

"If I could just see even a little, I could use my magic to make a way out," came Devyn's reply.

"Give me a moment, and I'll have us some light. I don't want to waste our candles if we don't have to." Jules groped until he found a sturdy branch in the drake's nest. Casting a small fire spell, he made a little torch. "If we're going to blow ourselves up, we may well go in style."

"This place looked better in the dark." Wynn's comment was echoed by the others. They were covered in filth and gore, but Wynn was the worst by far.

"You know you did everything wrong there, don't you?" Rall regarded Wynn, who nodded sheepishly, clearly expecting to be lectured on his stupidity. Shaking his head in disbelief, Rall said, "I don't know why we're still alive, but I'm not going to question it. If you hadn't panicked and did whatever it was you did, we'd still be fighting the damned thing, and I guarantee we wouldn't be winning." He clasped Wynn's shoulder. "But do me a favor if you could."

Wynn nodded, uncertainly, waiting for the diatribe he knew he deserved.

"The next time you gut a waterdrake, you might try to be bit neater. You're a bloody mess." Rall's mimicry of the prissy senior healer, Soren Torsson, was perfect. The cavern echoed with hoots of laughter, and even Wynn found himself snickering.

Chapter 28

In the flickering light of the little torch, the four men saw a breastplate lodged in the debris. "This is Temple armor," said Wynn examining it. "It was made for Jode. He's...."

"I know who Jode is." Dismay was written on Rall's grimy face. "He and Bors disappeared months ago. Mother Relynne sent them to see why the baron had stopped coming down to Arlen. She thought he might be ill or even dead, as he is quite elderly. It was before anyone knew something was wrong up here."

Wynn picked up a leg guard, made with a black, light-absorbing finish. "This was made for Larsse Johansson. He was the man who frequently worked as our spy. This armor was unique, one of a kind. The making of it was a challenge, as it was like an assassin's armor, only it was created for a man gifted with no magic whatsoever. The spells woven into it were purely defensive. I finished it for him at the end of Harvest. Now we know why the spy Mother Relynne sent disappeared and who he was. I did my best, but his armor couldn't protect him from the waterdrake's jaws."

"No armor could protect a person from such a creature," said Rall, gazing at the immense corpse. "I can't imagine any lone warrior could survive an encounter with such a terrible thing."

Devyn leaned against the wall of the cavern, his ear pressed to the stone and his hands flat against it, straining to get the feel of the mountain that surrounded them. He'd been carefully examining the walls for some time. "I think it's thinnest here—there's a slight fracture, one I would exploit if I were going to create an irrigation channel. If I can open the fissure wide enough to crawl through, that will have to do, as it will be a larger working than I've ever done. The passage out will be long, and I can't tell exactly where it will emerge, but I think we'll be inside the Hemsteck Valley." His earth-senses were extended to their furthest limits. "The fracture will open a bit high on this end, so we'll have to climb up to it."

"What do you need us to do?" Jules stood next to him, holding the torch.

"Just raise your shields and pray to Aeos that the whole mountain doesn't come down on us." The grin didn't disguise Devyn's apprehension. "I've never done a working like this from underground before, and I don't know if shields would protect you if it goes badly."

"This place is pretty unstable. The fact that part of it collapsed earlier disturbs me," said Jules. Worry lines creased his forehead. "But we can't stay here. With the waterdrake decomposing and taking up half the cavern, the air isn't going to remain breathable for long."

"It's not really breathable now," agreed Devyn. "I'll try to be careful. Besides, I don't want to alert anyone who might be sensitive to magic that we've escaped the cave-in. Is everyone ready?"

The others raised their shields, and Devyn sent his senses out. Fully tranced, he found the place he wanted and began gently nudging the earth to either side, widening the crevice slowly so as not to cause a cave-in. Several times, the ground under their feet shifted slightly, and the watching mages braced themselves, but the cavern remained standing. As the minutes progressed to an hour and Devyn remained deeply entranced, the others gained a new respect for those mages who worked in what was considered the least glamorous of the elements.

"I've never seen an earth-mage working other than in the smithy, and what they do there is quite different, much more like what I do. We each add different strengths to the armor, but nothing fancy. Nothing like this," Wynn whispered. "It's interesting how he's doing this." He followed his cousin's magic with his senses as well as he could, learning some things that gave him ideas, though earth was his weakest element. "It's like Bertte said years ago. It's all about control, and Devyn's is amazing."

Jules agreed. "I've watched Aneka cutting stone at the quarry, and it boggles the mind how she is able to be so precise, but what he's doing here is quite different. Much more subtle."

At last, Devyn emerged from his trance and said, "It'll be tight in some places for you, Rall, but I think you'll fit through. And we'll have to shove our kits along in front of us." Exhausted and attempting to hide it, he sipped water from his canteen with trembling hands, trying to regain the physical strength he would need to make the escape.

"We can wait until you're able to do this," said Rall, handing him a ration bar. "Eat this so you don't faint on us. You've exhausted your chi on our behalf, and we appreciate it."

Numbly accepting the ration bar, Devyn leaned against the cavern wall.

Wynn's mind was still occupied with the delicate way Devyn had used his magic to encourage the earth to form the fissure, which would have grown there naturally over time, instead of using brute force to blast them out of the cavern. "I imagine the hard part wasn't making the path through the mountain. Any journeyman could have blown a hole, and we might have survived it. Maybe we could even have done something to that effect, but it would have been noisy and nothing like what you just did. The difficult part was making it unobtrusive and doing it quietly. You have incredible control over your ability, cousin. I learned a great deal from observing you just now."

Devyn looked at him, surprised. "I've developed a few skills. Folks don't like having the earth shake under their houses, even if you're doing it to improve the irrigation in their fields. But any of you could have opened a way out of this place. There are two earth-mages for every one of strength in another element, and most mages of other persuasions are just as strong in earth as they are in the others. It's the easiest of all the elements to master."

"No element is easy to master, so don't be ridiculous," Rall said. "Wynn's right. I don't know anyone else who could do such a large working in *any* element as quietly as you just did. I'd bet that no one sensitive to magic noticed you working when it was in progress. I could barely sense you doing it, and we were right here. Maybe not even Abbess Lera could do such a major working so quietly. That took finesse."

"Well, thanks, but we need to get out of here." Unused to receiving praise from his fellow mages, Devyn changed the subject. "Jules? Are you ready?"

"Yes, but you follow after me so that Wynn can follow behind Rall in case he needs help getting though some spots. Wynn is the strongest of us, and he'll be able to shove him while we pull, if needed." Jules settled his pack. "Okay, I'm ready." Lifting him by the legs, Wynn and Rall raised Jules to the ledge, and he scrambled into the opening. "Okay, Devyn, you're next."

They did the same with Devyn, and then Wynn boosted Rall up. Leaning down as far as he safely could, Rall pulled Wynn up. Just as he made it to the ledge, the small torch Jules had left burning guttered out, leaving them once again in the dark.

Now the four were jammed in the small tunnel, with Wynn perched on the ledge. It was an eerie feeling, not being able to see how close he was to falling.

After some wiggling and rearranging themselves, Jules and Devyn began moving forward. Crawling on their hands and knees and sometimes scooching on their bellies, they worked their way through the narrow crevice. It sloped upwards, and occasionally fresh air came in, alleviating the claustrophobic feeling somewhat. In several places, the fissure was just barely big enough for Rall to inch along on his belly, but though he was grazed and scraped by the sometimes frighteningly tight quarters, he was just able to squeeze through the narrowest part.

Time ceased to have any meaning. It was impossible to know how long they edged their way through the crack in the side of the mountain. The men knew only that each small inch forward was a step toward safety. Numbly, they crawled and occasionally slithered to freedom. After an eternity in the dark,

Wynn began to see occasional glimpses of daylight around the bodies of his companions.

At last, they came to a stop. "I'm at the edge. You'll have to lower me, Dev. It's going to be a bit of a drop for Wynn, but he can do it. I think it's about twelve feet, so be prepared to catch him." Jules's whisper floated back down the line. One by one, they lowered each other to the ground.

Finally, Wynn tossed his kit down to the others and lowered himself feet-first until he hung from the ledge and dropped. Rall and Jules caught him, setting him down beside the others. Wynn stood blinking in the light of the overcast day. "Thanks. Wow—the hillside is steep out here." The men stretched, working the kinks out of their muscles. "I see now why the relief map in Mother Relynne's study depicts this valley with walls like a bowl. Do you think it was made by a volcano?"

Devyn nodded. "An old one, long dead. While there's some residual activity, I sense no more than any other place I've been—and far less than those volcanos in the Barbarian North."

They had been underground all night and most of the morning. The passage Devyn made for them emerged high on the wall above the Hemsteck Valley, about half a league away from the road. Mists shrouded the hillside, and snow clung in patches wherever a rock or shrub stood.

Wynn had never been as filthy or as uncomfortable in his life as he'd been since the battle with the waterdrake, and it only got worse as time went on. Now in misery and feeling rather sheepish, Wynn asked, "Rall, can you sense if there's a creek or something nearby? I really…need to clean up. We also should tend to our injuries, right?" Sitting on the rocky ledge and sipping the last of his water, he savored the smell of the clean, fresh air. "If not, we can probably call enough water to get ourselves mostly cleaned up, but ah…I'm a little uncomfortable right now. I've got stuff down my back." It was an understatement.

The others just grinned at his misery. "I imagine you do, seeing as how you've got it everywhere else," said Rall. Closing his eyes, he tried to sense if there was water nearby. "I think there's a spring just down from here, but it feels odd to my senses. The hillside is steep but not impassable. We'll have to go carefully."

"It's going to be darned cold, trying to bathe in this weather." Jules's groans were muffled as he bent to shoulder his pack.

"I think it's a warm spring—I can't really tell until we get there, though." Devyn grinned at Rall. "I smell the faint scent of sulfur in the mists."

The way down was treacherous, with loose soil and rocks. The vegetation was much younger than in other places on the mountain, perhaps ten years old at the most, and the hillside appeared to have suffered an avalanche in recent years. The small trees and shrubs clinging to the slope kept the men from sliding downhill. The short trek down to the spring took nearly an hour, as they didn't dare hurry. By the time they arrived, Wynn was nearly weeping with relief at the thought of bathing and wouldn't have cared if the spring was warm or not.

They made camp on a small, nearly level place by the spring, thoroughly cleansing the grime and gore from their hair and clothes. It wasn't deep, but the temperature of the water was pleasant and definitely helped ease their misery. At last, their clothes and armor lay drying, and they took turns applying medicinal salves to their numerous wounds and wrapping bandages around the worst of the scrapes and other minor injuries.

Rall was relieved to see no one was hurt badly. "I'm amazed we survived that with no major injuries other than to our hearing."

"The noise was pretty horrendous," Jules agreed. "But now we have to figure out where we are, and then we have to scout the Hemsteck Keep to see what we're up against."

"We're going to have to wear damp leathers tomorrow," said Devyn. "Oh well. Once we have them on, they'll warm up."

"I can live with that," replied Wynn, shuddering at the memory of what he'd washed out of his clothes and hair. "In fact, I'll enjoy it."

"I've never seen anyone with the sort of luck you have, cousin." Devyn pulled a comb through his damp hair. "If you were to take up gambling, you'd be rich."

"It doesn't run to things I do on purpose. It seems to happen on its own, whether I want it to or not." Wynn felt better now he was in his spare clothes and wrapped in his cloak. "Usually, my luck happens when I wish it would just leave me alone."

"Well, I'm certainly not complaining about your luck anymore," said Rall. "I just hope it keeps on working in our favor."

◆◆◆

The next morning, they made their way down to the floor of the crater, where Jules found a tree that afforded him a perfect view of the entire Hemsteck Valley. Perched in its sheltering branches, he was able see the far, upper end where the mines lay, and he also had a good view of the village and the ruins of the old keep. The others were similarly situated in various trees, and now the four mages simply watched, waiting to see if the rather noisy death of the waterdrake had been noticed.

As the day progressed and Jules trained his spyglass on the old castle, he saw no activity. That no one had come to see what had happened perplexed him. *What does this mage do—staying indoors all the time? Where does he get his food if he doesn't go outside?* Jules trained his glass on the far side of the valley where the trail continued on up to the place known as High-Point camp. He knew that from there, it continued through the high passes and then down to the Valley of Mal Evol, emerging somewhere near the royal family's vineyard. He'd often thought about making such a journey, but now he wasn't so keen on the idea.

Later, the four men gathered to share what they'd learned. "It seems strange. Even if Grakken didn't sense Wynn's lightning spell yesterday, certainly his thralls should have if they have any strength of magic at all," Rall whispered. They camped in the shelter of a thick copse of evergreen trees near the old road but remained well out of sight, no longer traveling out in the open.

Jules stretched, cracking his back. "It troubles me. Grakken went to all the trouble of compelling his tame earth-mage to spend large amounts of magic destroying the road to this valley. That in itself was an achievement. Then this earth-mage caused a landslide and used the rubble to make a rather nice den for a waterdrake. That's a lot of work. Why didn't these mages come out to check on it when the den collapsed?" His question was echoed by the others.

Rall said, "Grakken succeeds in getting the nasty creature to make a den where he wanted it to, and now he ignores it. The records tell us waterdrakes normally live where there is ample large game such as deer, mountain goats, and upland bear for them to eat, and we've seen little of that here, unless they've been feeding it some other way."

A terrible thought struck Jules. "No! I must be wrong—my imagination is running wild. Surely not even an acolyte of Tauron would go so far as to kidnap people to feed to a waterdrake. Still, where could the people be?"

Wynn said, "Your gruesome notion does explain the complete disappearance of so many, Jules. I thought they would be at the keep being forced to serve this rogue-mage, but there's nothing other than the smoke from small fires in three chimneys to indicate that anyone is there." He saw the raised eyebrows on his companions' faces. "The weather is near freezing in this valley, even in the daytime. In a place that big, if there were a lot of people, there would be many more fires." He fell silent, his attention on the small knife he used to whittle a design on a walking stick.

"Go on. I'm interested in your ideas," said Rall. "You must have more to say. Why do you think this?"

"I counted twelve chimneys still standing at the keep. They're immense—each must serve many fireplaces on the various levels. From what I could see, six are in the part that's fallen in on itself, so they're not in use. In the wings that appear in fairly good repair, only three chimneys, one that I think is for the kitchen and two of the others are in use today, a single fire in each." He looked up, seeing disbelief in Rall's face. "I say that because only a thin stream of smoke issued from them, and there's plenty of wood here in this valley for fuel."

Devyn said, "I had a perfect view of the woodshed near the kitchen, and it's filled with cut and split wood, all stacked and seasoned. So you may be right—there must not be any need for more than two or three fires."

Wynn sat cross-legged, carving dragons along the length of the stick. Having a small task helped Wynn organize his thoughts and kept him from chattering nervously. "Perhaps Grakken knows the cavern collapsed but thinks it was natural. He may think the beast escaped or is dead. The place was terribly shaky, or it wouldn't have fallen apart the way it did from the noise of the fight."

"Well, your spell being cast in such close quarters nearly deafened me," said Rall, rolling his eyes. "My ears still ring sometimes. I disagree with you. I think Grakken must know something unnatural happened to his pet waterdrake. I *do* think you're right about the small number of people at the keep, though." He looked at Wynn thoughtfully. "I find it interesting that we all looked at the same place today and saw the same things, but you divined the most information from the least amount of clues."

"Where are the missing people? Where is their livestock?" Jules asked the questions on everyone's mind.

Devyn sat silently contemplating what they had *not* discovered in their long hours of observation. Now he said, "I think we'll have to get closer to the keep. There's a dense stand of firs just above it. They're thick and will hide us well enough, as well as being a good, dry place to camp. From there, we'll have a better view through the windows. We should make our move as soon as it's fully dark. In this weather, the moon won't give us away."

"Agreed. We'll know more about whom we're facing and what their capabilities are if we get closer. We should rest now if we can. It'll likely take us all night to get there safely." Rall closed his eyes and turned his thoughts inward, meditating.

"I'll pray for heavy snow to hide our tracks." Wynn set the stick aside and returned his knife to his pocket. "We want to remain hidden as long as we can."

◆◆◆

The journey to the other end of the valley and the stand of trees overlooking the keep was cold but uneventful. Making the trek slightly more difficult, Wynn's prayer had been answered, and they journeyed under the cover of a heavy snowfall. In the abandoned village, the few houses that still had walls were nothing but roofless, empty shells.

The four mages were camped and under shelter by dawn. From their perches high in the fir trees, they could see into many of the occupied rooms of the keep. Each man had a copy of the floor plan as Mother Relynne remembered it, marking his observations on it with a grease pencil.

By dark, the four mages had a better idea of how many people were in the keep, and they compared notes. "This room here seems to have the most activity, from what I could see." Rall pointed to a set of rooms on his map. Checking their own maps, the others agreed. "But what I *really* wonder about is the purple light glimmering on the fourth floor." He tapped his finger on the room in question. "It's the chapel. I don't like it."

"Maybe there's a purple lamp there," said Jules, doubtfully, "like the stained-glass one I made Aneka for Holy Day this year. Candlelight gleaming through it shines around the room in different colors, so if this one is purple, then the light would be too."

"No, this has something to do with the Bull God," said Rall, unwilling to name Tauron so close to the keep, though he didn't know why he felt so reluctant. "His color is amethyst, and so is that light. This Grakken is definitely an acolyte of his, so the chapel must be in use for some ritual purpose."

"You may be right. If that's so, we'll have to destroy any artifacts he may have infused with his god's magic," Jules agreed, feeling the same hesitancy. "You know what Mother Relynne said. Those objects are dangerous and can ensnare the unwary. Who knows who will stumble upon this place in the future? Random explorers won't have the protections of Aeos's vows. Every artifact must be destroyed."

"How many men did you count? I saw no women or children." Wynn was relieved that no children were in thrall to the rogue-mage. "I counted two, but I couldn't tell who was in charge. Perhaps one of them is Grakken."

"I think we'll have to get inside to find out anything more. Once we're in, we're committed and there's no turning back." The others all agreed with Rall's decision. He added, "If we somehow get separated while we're inside, we'll meet back here. Alone or together, we have to kill Grakken and his minions and destroy any magic artifacts." He tapped the map, thinking. Rall decided the time had come to make a statement that Taj had asked him to find a way to insert into a conversation, as it involved a delicate matter. "The chapel room is on the top floor. The kitchen is perhaps three levels or more below, in this area. A conservatory seems to be over here," he said, pointing to a place on the map. "The cellar must be below that if it is laid out like the Keep of Mal Evol."

Devyn looked up sharply. "How do you know how my family's summer home is laid out? I don't think you've ever seen it. We've let it get awfully rundown. We rarely entertain anyone there." Devyn was visibly disconcerted that Rall had brought up his family's old home and now wondered what he knew about it. "Our winery is out there in the back of beyond. The vines are the only reason we hang on to the old place."

"Apparently, a lot of folks have been guests at your summer home recently. Your mother frequently entertains there, holding special wine-tastings and the like. Taj drew a map of the layout of the public rooms for me," Rall said, unruffled by Devyn's dismay.

Judging by Devyn's sudden intake of breath, Rall's revelation had been taken the way Taj had hoped it would be. "Mother has had guests there? What the...." He stopped, nonplussed. The family never, under any circumstances, entertained anyone who was not of the Temple there. His father would never have allowed such a thing.

Only those in the direct line of succession understood the secret that lay deep within the keep.

Until the very recent birth of his nephew, Maxon, Devyn had been his brother's heir. His family had one rule that was enforced above all others, and it had been ingrained in him from birth. The few family members who understood what lay deep within *never* discussed the old keep in more than passing terms. They absolutely never mentioned the layout or the throne containing the bones of the god Ariend, concealed deep within to anyone, not even the Temple, though of course the higher clergy was aware of it. When the king sat on the throne, he had dominion over the soil of the valley and had some control over the weather. Generations of kings and queens had used the Throne of Stone and Bone with reverence for the god trapped within, using it to protect to the valley, and to ensure the prosperity of the people of Mal Evol.

But Tauron wanted nothing more than to regain control of Ariend's prison, which he'd lost when Aeos took it from him. If he gained control of Mal Evol, he would have the wedge he needed to take Neveyah.

The clergy of Aeos built the College of Warcraft and Magic and the holy city of Aeoven out in the wilds of the unpopulated West, as a deliberate ploy meant to draw unwanted attention away from the importance of the keep. They loudly and visibly proclaimed Aeoven as the center of the clergy of the goddess Aeos. Gradually over the years, the secret hidden deep within the Keep of Mal Evol was forgotten by all but the few who needed to know. Even the majority of the clergy was unaware of the truth—that the god Ariend still lived, trapped within the prison of Tauron's making. The abbacy of the Temple agreed the fewer who knew the secret, the easier it would be to keep.

That his mother was entertaining random guests there was inconceivable.

Reeling slightly from the blow Rall had so casually delivered, Devyn became aware he was still talking. "The Hemstecks are a distant branch of your family. Taj thought the map of your keep might be useful, as the same architect designed the two castles. There may be similarities in the two places." Rall looked knowingly at Devyn. "You *will* let us know what you find familiar about the floor plan when we get in there, won't you?"

"Of course I'll guide you if I can, but why didn't you tell me earlier you'd seen a map of my family home?" Devyn tried to hide his agitation. "From the outside, this place looks nothing like it. This keep has been added on to many more times than our drafty old barn. There are towers here, of course, but they're in different places. These ruins are much larger, so it will be quite different. Anyway, I was sent to Aeoven when I was nine. I inadvertently collapsed a toolshed in the gardens at our townhouse in Mal Evol City. That's where I was raised, you know, in Mal Evol City, not out in the country. I haven't got as much knowledge of the summer house as my brother would have. I haven't been there as often as he has."

Jules grinned at Devyn's obvious discomfort, knowing exactly why Devyn was being so evasive. "I find it humorous how you refer to that palace in Mal Evol City as your townhouse, as if your family were nothing but prosperous wine merchants."

"Well, the 'palace,' as you seem to want to refer to it, serves as the council chambers for the business of governing and also as a good place to entertain and encourage merchants from the far-flung reaches of Neveyah to purchase the wines of Mal Evol. We *are* nothing more than prosperous wine merchants, if you think about it," Devyn replied. "My family makes very fine wine, but someone has to be the figurehead for the country, small though it is. Yes, that's been my family's job for many generations, but be real, Jules. Only one of us can be king or queen at any given time, and the rest of us have to earn a living somehow. Ruling a valley isn't very lucrative unless you can sell the goods made there. We *are* rather good vintners, if I do say so."

His pride in the wine produced by his family was not feigned. "Besides, everyone knows Taj and the Temple really run the country—my brother is just the senior wine merchant in charge of promoting the fine goods produced there. He also sells dresses, if you're interested, Rall. The couturiers of Mal Evol City are the most respected in all of Neveyah."

Wynn burst out laughing, muffling his snickers in the folds of his cloak. "Do they make dresses that large, though? That's a lot of barbarian to cover in ruffles and lace!"

Devyn and Jules dissolved into muffled hoots at Rall's expense. "I'm not a ruffles sort of warrior. They don't go well with my war paint. I do like a bit of lace now and then, though." Rall struck a haughty pose, and the others howled with laughter.

◆◆◆

Devyn was unable to calm his mind and volunteered to stand the first watch. *What's been going on at home? Has my mother gone mad? Inviting guests out there...please, Aeos, tell me she hasn't actually shown anyone the Throne of Stone and Bone.* A sense of foreboding gripped him. *Mum's been odd ever since my father's death. But what can we do?* He decided he'd best get a message to Dax as soon as he could, suggesting his brother set their mother up in a nice country place close to the city. Maybe he could get Taj to authorize the healers to use their talents to encourage her to just forget about the throne. It was an improper use of empathy but would be for the good of Neveyah.

Chapter 29

Stashing their kits in the fir grove under the cover of branches, the four men entered the keep through a window in the abandoned wing, passing through the oldest parts of the castle. The glass that had once graced the window was gone, and the shutters too had long ago been blown off by the winter storms.

Rall warned Wynn not to use any magic until they found their quarry, unless they were discovered and had no choice. He agreed, saying, "I understand why you feel you have to tell me this after what happened with the waterdrake. But I've been thinking about what I did wrong there, and I know what not to do."

"It's just that I sometimes forget you were never trained the way we were, and some things weren't ingrained in you like they were in us." Rall clasped his shoulder. "Forgive me for being such a prat."

Surprised, Wynn nodded and followed the others.

Snow drifted and fell frequently as they made their way through the many roofless rooms and galleries toward the immense hall where generations of barons had entertained merchants and visitors from far away.

At last, they found themselves in what looked like a large courtyard, but which they knew was not. It was the old great hall, now roofless. Two decades before, the roof and two floors above had fallen in, leaving a rubble-filled shell. Immense mounds of broken beams and other wreckage lay where they had fallen. In places, great shards of splintered wood stood straight up like sentinels in the abandoned ruin.

Tattered rags, remnants of once-bright banners, hung on the walls, long unrecognizable and shifting in the winds that occasionally whistled through the cavernous space. The four mages carefully negotiated past strange lumps that were once the roof and floors above. The snow stopped momentarily, and the area brightened. Wynn looked up and saw the stars shining brilliantly, so clear they seemed to hang just above the open roof. With a pang, he wondered if Seri was looking at those same stars. Wind blew and swirled, lifting the powdery snow, forming miniature snowstorms and depositing it in corners and random drifts.

Devyn whispered, "From this room, we should be able to go upstairs to the second floor. This is the oldest part of the keep, and if it's like other places of this era that I've been, there's no direct entry from here to the newer wings. This was the great hall." His eyes searched, but only the central area was lit by the starlight shining through the open roof.

He peered into the shadows until he saw a deeper darkness and knew it was the opening he looked for. "The stairs should be—yes, that should be them there, but the floors from above have formed a wall of sorts, so we can't see them. The staircase should be a sweeping curve if they were built like the grand staircase in my family's townhouse. There should be a door at the top to the newer areas of the keep. We'll have to be careful. The ballroom has fallen in and the rooms above that, so who knows what else has collapsed? This is where the real danger begins, more than just the obvious enemy and his minions. This place is falling down, and when we're on the upper floors, we won't know which rooms are safe to enter."

Looking up, the others saw several stories of doors and gaping holes that appeared connected to parts of the place that was still standing.

"That would be a murderous drop," said Jules. "If the fall itself didn't kill you, impaling yourself on the rubble down here surely would. Let's be careful not to flee through doors without looking first, right?"

Everyone agreed, and they began making their way through the rubble to the dark opening at the foot of the wide staircase.

A slight pop sounded in the silence, followed by a loud crash, as debris fell from a pile. Several small forms emerged from the shadows, swarming the four mages, slashing with claws and teeth that gleamed briefly in the pale starlight. Swords flashed, and the four men struggled to keep their balance in the deep drifts of snow that concealed much of the fallen debris. The squeals of the wounded foes and grunts of the defenders sounded loudly in the dark until, at last, the bodies of their attackers lay in the bloodstained snow and the four mages cleaned their swords, relieved at having made quick work of it.

"Now what?" Wynn felt fear in the pit of his stomach. "We've just given away our presence here."

"Maybe not," replied Rall, his mind quickly running through all their options. "If these devolved people are lurking here, other creatures may also be here to take care of any who wish to use this way to gain entry. Grakken and his mates would hear occasional bursts of noise from them clashing with each other all the time. We aren't the first these have fought, see?" Indeed, the dead attackers did show signs of having survived several battles. "The sounds of things caving in and falling must happen all the time in this place," he said, looking at the snow-covered piles of rubble that surrounded them. Already the wind-blown snow had begun to cover the dead, hiding their tracks and the evidence of their battle.

Jules said, "We'll have to be doubly wary then. Who knows what sorts of guard dogs are hidden here, waiting for us." Turning, he started up the steps.

The further up they went, the glimmer of light from the great hall gradually diminished. The wide, curving staircase grew darker and darker until it was pitch-black. At last, Jules halted, unable find a way through the wreckage. Sighing, he said, "We have to go back and find a different way. We'll never make it this way without some light."

"We can't backtrack. We've spent too much time at this already," said Rall. "We'll have to risk a light." He handed the stub of a candle to Jules, who lit it with the merest breath of magic, one so small even Rall couldn't sense it. Jules shielded the tiny flame from the breeze and tried to keep the light focused near their feet. Slowly, they worked their way up the grand staircase. Piles of debris blocked their path in several places, forcing them to climb over the precariously balanced rubble.

At the top, faint starlight showed a landing that was relatively clear. Visible in the pool of light cast by the candle was the family crest of the Hemstecks, inlaid in the center of the beautiful ceramic tiles, a small glimpse of the beauty that once graced the keep. The frosty mosaic was treacherous, and the four men stepped carefully to avoid slipping.

To their left, a gaping hole that once held the enormous doors to a grand ballroom opened onto a sheer drop to the old great hall below, and an immense set of intricately carved doors stood to their right. Extinguishing the candle, Jules handed it back to Rall, who waited until it cooled in the icy air to slip it back into his pocket as they advanced by starlight to the wide, heavily carved doors. Quietly, Jules lifted the latch and pulled the right-hand door, hoping to open it with no trouble.

It was stuck.

Bracing himself on the slippery tiles, Jules pulled with all his might. With a faint creak that sounded as loud as a scream to the four nervous intruders, the door swung open on stiff hinges. As he pulled, the door moved more easily, at last swinging effortlessly, revealing a long, dark, empty passage.

The corridor was shadowy, but at irregular intervals, faint patches of grayish light spilled out of random open doors from rooms lit by starlight. A brisk breeze blew through the corridor, and now that it was moving easily on its substantial hinges, the door began swinging open in the wind. Catching it, Wynn carefully pulled the heavy door shut behind them so the breeze wouldn't bang it against the wall of the slick landing. The closed door cut off some of the starlight, but their eyes adjusted soon. The corridor was free of snow and ice, and their footing on the rotting carpet was solid once again.

"Now we'll travel by the light from the open doors." Jules's whisper floated back to Wynn as they began walking down the passageway.

Devyn also whispered, "The stairs to the family quarters should be at the end of this corridor."

They had gone halfway down the hall when the hair on Wynn's neck rose. "Something big is stalking us. It feels like a thunder-liz.... Gah!" His whisper broke off as a heavy, reptilian form slammed into them, knocking Rall, Jules, and Devyn down. It was the largest thunder-lizard Wynn had ever seen, at least fifteen feet long. Slashing wildly at the enormous shadow, Wynn looked for better footing or some room to fight.

As the others rolled away from the snapping, snarling jaws, Wynn backed up in the dark corridor, nimbly stepping over Devyn's rolling form while fending the creature off with his sword, back-pedaling until he was against the door and could go no further. Frantically slashing with his right hand, he searched for the latch with his left, intending to open the door, lead the creature through and then shut it out. Finding the latch, he lifted it, pushing on the heavy door with his shoulder. Once again, it was stuck. Now desperate to get the door open, he nudged harder. Still it was stuck.

"Come this way, my friend," Wynn urged the great beast as he rammed the door open with his shoulder, saying, "We can fight better out he...oops!" The gusting wind caught the door and slammed it against the wall of the landing with a resounding crash. Wynn fell backwards, landing hard on the tiles and skidding across the floor. At the same time, the creature rushed Wynn, leaping for where his face had been only a moment before. Barely catching the edge of the door and hanging on for dear life as he lost his balance, Wynn narrowly avoided being carried along with the lizard. Rolling to his belly, his boots vainly sought traction on the ice-encrusted mosaic of the landing.

Momentum kept the massive thunder-lizard traveling across the landing. Unable to find purchase for its enormous claws, the beast skidded over the ancient, frost-covered tiles and through the opening of the old ballroom, launching itself over the edge. The huge creature dropped to the jagged piles of rubble on the floor below with a horrible, squishy-sounding crash. Using the door to lever himself up, Wynn scrambled to his feet, slipping and sliding as he dragged the door closed again, latching it.

He stood with his heart pounding, panting and feeling the adrenaline coursing through his body. The distant sounds of something large thrashing and keening came through the door, but the muffled echoes soon dwindled away.

"That was quick. You were done and had the door shut before I even got my sword out." Devyn sounded as if he was struggling not to laugh. "I'm not sure how you thought of such a good plan so quickly, but it worked perfectly."

Rall's amused whisper came from Wynn's left. "Ahem. 'Come this way, my friend'? How very civilized of you."

As Wynn's eyes adjusted to the darkness, he recognized the silhouettes of his companions.

"Well, that was easy." Jules checked Wynn over, finding no serious injuries. "Was that your plan?"

"Not really, but I'll take it," replied Wynn, shuddering. "All I wanted to do was close the door between him and us and hope he didn't gnaw his way back in."

"I can't wait to see what else is lurking up here," whispered Rall, bitterly. "Grakken seems to have placed a watchdog of some kind everywhere. We can't even be sure that was the only one on this floor, although those things tend to eat everything else that lives and breathes."

"Yes, he's taking no chances. But are the watchdogs to stop intruders or prevent escapees?" Devyn's question met with silence. "Where are the missing people? Where is Baron Hemsteck? I've been asking myself this question since we began watching the place."

"That's what we've all been wondering," agreed Wynn. "I saw nothing in the fields that looked like graves, but maybe the snow hides them." His whisper sounded doubtful.

Warily, the four men continued down the hallway, coming at last to a door. Opening it, they saw a dark stairwell to the left, going up. At the top, a faint patch of grayish light filtered down. Closing the door again, they stood considering the problem silently. "There's starlight up there. But this stair only goes up from here," whispered Devyn. "Apparently, this passage is on the ground floor, even though we went up from the great hall to get here. I have no idea where we're going. We should be entering the private residence, but now I don't know."

"From my spying post yesterday, it looked to me like they built the keep into the side of the mountain," said Wynn. "I think they had to take advantage of the lay of the land to enlarge this place and still leave farmland and room to graze animals to support the old village. It's a small valley, and it would have supported a lot of people when the mines were open."

"Well, this means any knowledge I might have had of my family's summer home may not be accurate here." Devyn's whisper sounded smug. "I didn't actually think it would be."

"As you always say, nothing ventured, nothing gained," replied Rall, serenely. He'd made his point and rattled Devyn, which was really all he'd been told to do. Taj felt the security of the Keep of Mal Evol was not being taken seriously enough and wanted Rall to make a discreet point that would get back to King Daxyn. "I didn't really know if it would help or not, but why not use what knowledge we may have?"

"I don't know how you do it," muttered Devyn. "You get me all twisted around and then act so calm about it. You've always done that."

"He practices in front of a mirror," whispered Jules. Due to his nerves, his wicked sense of humor was reasserting itself, and he was hard-pressed to keep himself contained.

"Shh," whispered Wynn. "Let's be quiet now."

Somewhat chastened, the others complied. Opening the door again, they started up the stairs with Jules in the lead. At the top, they paused just inside the landing. The door was open, blocked by a small pile of debris. The stairwell opened into what appeared to be the center of a long, wide gallery. Windows ran along one side of the hall, dimly lighting the scene, and doors ran along the passage opposite. In the dark, the debris along either side of the corridor was hard to distinguish, but most of it appeared to be ancient, crumbling furniture.

"Left or right?" Jules's low whisper sounded in Devyn's ear.

"Right—left will take us back toward the ballroom. Some of these open doors were visible from downstairs. The floor has caved in at that end," replied Devyn.

Nodding, Jules advanced down the hall. The pervasive silence was eerie. They passed a shadowy form, seeing it was a low table set below the tattered remains of a once-pleasant oil painting, though the gray light from the window opposite made it appear ghostly. As they progressed, indistinguishable shadows along the sides of the passage gradually reformed into low tables and broken chairs placed between the windows and doors, sad soldiers standing guard.

This had been a home of great wealth and beauty. Now the decaying remains were depressing, once-beautiful courtesans holding onto their splendor with determination, fragile corpses rotting where they stood, refusing to admit they were dead. Oil paintings and tapestries hung above dark lumps, the frayed rags of their glorious past moving gently with the breeze that persistently wafted through the hallway.

A strange popping noise sounded behind them. Drawing their swords, they turned, meeting the attack. Three rat-like creatures launched themselves at Wynn, who trailed the others. His sword flashed, and in seconds, the three attackers lay dead at his feet. Shaking his head, Wynn pulled out his bandanna and wiped his blade clean before sheathing it. He motioned the others to continue forward.

At the end of the hall, they came to a door that opened onto a small, narrow stairwell. Now, they had to choose whether to go up or down.

"This looks like it could be the servants' stairs," whispered Devyn. "They should give us access to every floor in the place and will take us to the kitchen." He turned, just as popping noises sounded again, this time both from in front of and behind them.

Drawing their swords, Jules and Rall met the attackers in the stairwell. The door closed, cutting Wynn and Devyn off from them.

Wynn tried to keep the noise down as he and Devyn battled the five rat-like creatures that had appeared behind them. Defending themselves quietly took some doing. Wynn cringed as he stumbled against a table that fell over and then knocked a painting off the wall. The squealing of their attackers couldn't be muffled, and he was terrified their noise would be overheard.

The conflict was difficult, as the furniture and close quarters hampered Wynn and Devyn, restricting their movements as the fight traveled back the way they had come. At last, near where they entered the hall, they prevailed, and once again, Wynn surveyed the mess. Counting the corpses from the previous battle, eight small bodies now littered the hallway.

Rall and Jules were not having much luck at being silent either, as squeals and heavy thuds sounded through the closed door.

"You were right. Remember what you said when we were down in the hill country near Arlen? They do appear out of nowhere." Devyn's whisper echoed Wynn's thoughts as they walked back toward the door. "Here in the silence, we can hear them when they emerge from wherever. Out in the fields, the ambient noises mask the sound."

"I believe they do arrive from nowhere we can go, but *how* they do it is what I really want to know. That popping noise we've noticed is the only warning we've gotten." Suddenly, Wynn noticed how silent the corridor was. "Where are Rall and Jules? They should be back by now. They only had three to deal with." His whisper was barely audible.

Sword in hand, he opened the stairwell door.

The windows illuminating the stairwell showed the gray of dawn just beginning to lighten the sky. There was no sign of Jules or Rall. Footprints and scrapes in the dust gave testament to the fact they had been there at the landing. Two distinct sets of enormous boot prints indicated to Wynn that two very large people had approached from the floor above, people bigger than Rall. The prints were made by boots with soles and heels whose nail-patterns Wynn didn't recognize. "These weren't made by Temple boots," he whispered. Devyn just nodded.

Three small corpses with rat-like features lay just off the small landing, somewhat blocking the stairs down from the upper floors. None of the footprints that came from above could have been made by the bodies that lay in the stairwell. The tracks continued down the stairs, along with scrapes in the dust indicating two large things had been hauled away.

Odd sliding noises, as if heavy objects were being dragged across a hard surface, emanated from far below.

Wynn felt sick as his eyes met Devyn's. Without a word, the two men closed the door behind them and silently followed the tracks down the stairs.

Chapter 30

The door shut, cutting Jules and Rall off. Dimly, the sounds of the scuffle behind them came through and then faded. Hindered by the close quarters of the steep, narrow stairwell, the two had some trouble dispatching their attackers. It was more of a struggle than was optimal, but they prevailed.

Rall turned to open the door to reenter the hallway. Suddenly, his head rang as an immense mail-clad fist knocked him into the wall. Sliding to the floor, bleeding from his ears and nose, the last thing he saw was an equally immense boot kicking Jules's unconscious body down the stairs.

Two massive minotaurs stood looking down at their unconscious foes. One minotaur was well over seven and a half feet tall, the other only slightly shorter.

"I wondered what was making all that noise. Looky here!" The hoarse whisper sounded odd coming from such a grotesque face. "This place is full of doors we've never opened. What should we do with 'em? They got them horrible ugly tattoos all over. Mean's they're magic wielders, priests of the goddess."

The larger of the two minotaurs looked at Rall. "I think this one is one of them bar-bar-ee-ans they got up north. Tauron's golden horns! He's an ugly brute, all white and pasty like that. I think he's an old man. His hair's all white, but he's a strong, old thing, a good fighter. Too bad for him, ending his days here."

The smaller of the two minotaurs took Jules's unconscious form by the arms, saying, "We should give 'em to Grakken. He'll probably give 'em to Kandek for a sacrifice, an' we'll benefit for finding 'em. If nothing else, maybe he'll heal 'em for us to have some sport with." He started down the stairs, dragging Jules's limp form.

"Yeah. Be more fun than trying to get one of them wimmen that was in the pens to treat us right. These boys made quick work of them rats. I hate fighting those little buggers. This place is crawling with 'em. Can't even shit without 'em popping up while you're doing your business," said the bigger of the two, his whisper a low rumble. Taking Rall by his arms, he dragged him off, following the first minotaur.

They entered a long hall lit by a lone lamp and turned down another with storerooms on either side of the corridor.

"I don't get it, Bek. These wimmen start out fighting like they ought, but then they go an' faint soon as they get a good look at me. An' they're delicate. One good love tap an' they're dead. Not like the ones from home." The smaller soldier's bovine face broke into a grin, showing many teeth filed to sharp points. "Kulda near on kilt me night before I left home last week. Scratched my face bloody an' made me recite ten poems afore she let me up her dress. That's a proper wommun for you."

"These wimmen don't like a man reciting a good, bloody poem, Luk. Where's the romance? How do you woo one of these if they won't hit you no matter how hard you shake 'em, an' you can't show 'em yer face?" Bek shook his immense, horned head in wonder. "We're Tauron's warriors. We've been through the remaking, so it's our right to mate with anyone who'll have us, but these wimmen act like it's rape instead of an honest invitation. I don't get it."

"There ain't no wimmen left in the pens nor men or even the babies, 'cept that one we talked to last night, and she's too delicate for my taste. It's cruel what Grakken did to 'em." Luk slowed, speaking softly now. "Yeah, they was gorms, an' those boys wouldn't of survived the remaking, but still. There was no reason for it."

"Don't get caught talking about that, or you'll end up like Jelk and Werk. I'd rather die clean than go such a disgusting way," Bek cautioned. "Besides, once Grakken gets these boys healed up, maybe we'll see if the rumors are true about how good these priests of Aeos are at fighting."

The smaller minotaur brightened up. "Yeah. Let's get 'em down to the kitchen an' see if the old baron will sort of heal 'em up before Grakken finds out we got 'em."

"He won't do anything unless Grakken or Jenner tells him to do it. He's under their spell, an' he don't do nothing *we* say. I been here off an' on for two months now, an' that's how it is."

The two minotaurs continued dragging their captives down the narrow hallway. A smaller shadow filled a doorway, a blond man who would have been large if not compared to the immense soldiers.

"What have you two got there? Well, well. I wondered when the bloody Temple would send their finest to see what was going on." The man stood with his arms crossed. "Shackle them, and I'll get them dosed with silf. Even you won't be able to contain them if they wake with all their abilities." He opened the door to an unoccupied storeroom. "This will have to do for them. Put them in here and chain them up. Then go find something constructive to do."

"Sure, earth-mage. Then we'll have some fun with 'em." Luk glared at him with naked hatred.

"Oh, no, you don't. As soon as Grakken is awake, he's going to want to see these two. They're for Kandek. Make no mistake about that. They're exactly what he's been waiting for. We thought they'd only send one priest of Aeos, but they sent two. Tauron will be pleased with our offering tonight."

◆◆◆

Jules gradually regained consciousness with a raging headache and a foul taste in his mouth. His ribs felt as if he'd been kicked by a horse. As his sense of awareness returned, he realized he was bound and gagged. He was in some sort of storeroom with a tiny window high up on the wall through which a small amount of light shone. Heavy chains shackled his wrists and ankles. As he slowly turned his aching head, the dim light revealed Rall, battered, bloody, unconscious, similarly bound.

Jules tried to sense his magic and failed, thinking *This is just bloody wonderful. Now what?* He settled himself, trying to quell the panic that kept rising.

He found he could sit up. His hands were shackled in front of him, allowing him some movement. His ankles had enough slack in the chains that he would be able to shuffle once he was on his feet. His captor had made sure he could tend to his own basic needs and perhaps hobble along, if he'd felt capable of standing up.

Rall's eyes opened, and for a moment, he stared unseeing. As his situation became clear to him, stark panic appeared on his swollen face, followed by intense rage. Jules grimaced inwardly, meeting Rall's eyes. He saw his own thoughts reflected there and nodded.

As he grew more aware of his surroundings, Jules realized his mouth was full. *That's what the taste must be. They dosed us with something and used the gags so we wouldn't vomit it up.* He raised his shackled hands and pulled the gag off, using his fingers to clear his mouth, spitting the disgusting remains of a foul-tasting, leafy paste to one side.

Rall did the same.

Something told Jules not to speak. Raising his hands, he held one finger up to his cracked lips, and Rall nodded. Leaning back against a barrel, Jules closed his eyes and ran through his grounding and centering exercises.

The sound of a bar being lifted was followed by the door creaking open. A gaunt, raggedly dressed old man entered. He bore a tray with two cups of soup and a loaf of bread. A jug of water also sat on the tray, which he placed between Rall and Jules.

"I'm sorry you're here, more sorry than I can say," said the old man, in a dry whisper. "I'm under a geas to serve these brutes, but they let my mind run free, since the rest of me does their bidding despite my wishes to the contrary. They consider me too senile to be capable of plotting sedition. There's a bucket in the corner for your personal needs." He reached up on a shelf and set down two earthenware mugs that he filled with water for them.

"You must be the Baron Ivan Hemsteck," whispered Jules. His breath came in short gasps. It hurt to breathe too deeply.

"Yes, I am. I recognize young Rall there, but you're new to me." Ivan reached for the door.

"Jules." He met the old man's eyes. "I'm Jules Brendsson. Thank you."

"Jenner dosed you with silf so you can't sense your magic. Your meals will be dosed with it also," whispered the baron. "Eat this food and regain your strength. The silf may take away your powers, yes, but it will also ease your pains a bit, and it won't dull your wits. Use what you have to plan your escape, and don't mourn the loss of what you have not." He shut the door.

The two prisoners heard heavy footsteps approaching, sounds that seemed to echo down a long passageway and stopped outside the door. A tired sounding voice said, "Well, your lordship. Did you feed them and give them water?"

"Of course I did," replied the baron, in a quavering tenor. "I live, Jenner, but only because I serve. I understand that well."

"They're awake then. Those two soldiers of Tauron roughed them up pretty bad. Should I call Grakken to heal them now?"

The old man's tones were sardonic. "Yes, you should. Your tame minotaurs were far gentler on them than they've been on some of the others, which isn't saying much. At least these two big fellows have enough slack in their chains to be able to feed themselves and piss in a bucket." His tones were scathing.

"They'd better not have hurt them too badly. These two must be in good health for the ceremony tonight," muttered the earth-mage. "Grakken is expecting a visit from High Priest Kandek today. The high priest will be pleased to have a real sacrifice to offer up on his new altar tonight instead of the usual miserable rabble."

"I'm sure 'the miserable rabble' would have been glad to hear that if they'd survived your boss's little frenzy the other day," replied the old man. "Speaking of which, if we're done here, I have to go and check on the one that does remain. I'm sure despite the ruckus of the other day, Grakken still has plans for her and wants to keep her alive even though he has these two fine specimens for tonight's festivities, so...."

"Well, go about your duties then. I'm going to sit here just to keep those freaks from Serende from getting any ideas about using these two for sport. As soon as he's awake, I'll let Grakken know they're here, through our link. He'll be worried about their safety."

"He *should* be worried about those soldiers, Jenner. They're bored, and there's nothing worse than a bored minotaur. Just so you're aware, the woman likely won't live through the day after their gentle courtship of her. You only have your minotaurs to blame for that. But it's not my job to worry about the health of his sacrifices, especially since Grakken himself seems to be so careless with them."

"How dare you criticize him for what happened in the pens?" Jenner's outrage was palpable, even to the two prisoners who listened through the door. "When Ander was killed, Grakken went mad, it's true, but that was because the link was broken. He's the gentlest of

380

men, and he's a healer. What happened was horrible, but it wasn't his fault. He had no idea what he was doing."

"Nevertheless, you're down from nine to three now, counting these two. Probably only two. The woman's most likely dead by now," the old man replied coolly. "My task is to see that everyone is fed, and these two prisoners have their food now, so if you're done with me, I have to serve breakfast to the poor woman if she is alive, even if she doesn't survive the day. Too bad your ever-so-gentle healer can't heal her."

"You know he doesn't dare go near her. The memory of what happened eats at him. With only me holding the link, it will take little for him to break loose again." Jenner exhaled heavily. "I'll do what I can for her, but I doubt she will survive. Those soldiers are animals."

The baron turned and began shuffling away. Pausing, he turned back to the man who guarded the door. "Those rat-people Grakken's boss is so fond of have gotten into the chicken coop again. They nearly decimated the whole flock. If you intend to eat meat, we need replacements. Of course, with your prisoners dying right and left, there's not too many to feed." Once again, he began shuffling down the hallway.

As the baron's steps faded, the captives looked at each other. Jules was about to speak, but Rall held a finger to his swollen and bruised lips. They heard sounds of a chair creaking as a heavy body settled on it. "Just so you two know, I can hear everything you say. But feel free to chatter all you want. I'm not going anywhere."

"Thank you," said Rall, his voice coming out with a croak. "It's good to know we're safe. And what's your name, just so we know who to thank?" His eyes were murderous, hard as the stone floor the two prisoners sat on.

"Keeping you safe?" An evil chuckle sounded from outside the door. "You have no idea. I'm here to do exactly that, but you may not appreciate my efforts on your behalf once Kandek arrives. You two have the dubious honor of being the first priests of Aeos ever to be offered up on Tauron's holy altar. Tonight will be the big event. You may as well eat and rest up a bit. It's your last day. The sacrificial ritual is drawn out and gruesome and not something I envy you two for. But on the positive side, Grakken will be down to meet you soon, and he'll heal your injuries. Those minotaurs are brutes."

"Well, it looks like a fine meal, so again, thank you for your efforts. We'll just busy ourselves with enjoying it in peace then." Rall spoke with the utmost politeness, and his voice dripped with sincerity. It sounded incongruous, coming out of such a swollen, battered face.

Jules looked at Rall and nodded, a grim smile on his bloodied face. Their chains rattled as the two prisoners set to eating their meal. The soup was good and the bread was fresh, so the two men silently ate.

Chapter 32

Jules and Rall shifted restlessly, trying not to rattle their chains any more than they had to, unable to ease the pain of their more serious injuries. Jules thought Rall must be severely injured, as swollen as his face was. The big man made no complaint, but it was easy to see he was suffering.

Jules's own back was a mass of bruises, and he thought one of his kidneys might be damaged. His ribs were sore, and judging from the way it felt when he breathed, at least one was broken.

"Grakken is awake now and will be here to tend to your injuries soon." The gruff voice held a sneering note. "You mages have grown soft, getting caught by two of the stupidest minotaurs Tauron's legions had to spare. I expected more out of the Temple than you two."

"Could I have a firmer pillow?" Jules couldn't stop himself. "I'm not used to such a soft bed. I'm going to be a bit stiff for the big ceremony tonight. Do you think Kandek will mind?"

"You'll be stiff all right." Their guard guffawed. "You just get your beauty rest, priest. You'll need it!"

Heavy footsteps approached. "Oh no, you don't. These two are for Kandek."

The two captives listened as an oddly deep and yet nasal voice said, "They're good fighters. You should of seen 'em kill those rats. We just want to fight 'em for a bit of exercise. They need to exercise or they'll get soft." The strange accent was difficult to follow, but the voice held a wheedling tone to it. "We won't hurt 'em."

"I've seen how you boys play with folks. These two are not to be touched. Go away or I'll bury you here and now. Your toys rarely survive the night after you're done with them."

"We could play with you instead, Jenner." A second, raspier voice held a threatening tone. "There's naught to do here. We're bored with this place."

"Yeah. We could play with a scrawny gorm earth-mage." First Voice sounded hopeful. "Maybe bite his head off an' spit in his neck hole."

"Could you, Luk?" A rumbling noise emanated from the passage, rattling the dusty objects in the storeroom. Jules and Rall looked at each other and then up at the shelves, fearful that things might fall on them.

"Holah! My feet are stuck!" Luk sounded surprised. "That's not fair, Jenner. Using yer filthy gorm magic is cheating. Turn me loose."

"Yeah, using magic is cheating, gorm. Let him go or I'll be ripping yer arms off and beating you with 'em." Second Voice also sounded quite offended. "You gorms have no honor."

"I don't play fair, Bek. I don't have to. Your head is going to be stuck in this stone wall next unless you behave. These two prisoners are for Kandek, and you aren't getting them." Jenner stood his ground. "If you want Luk freed, do it yourself. You can amputate his feet now, or he can starve to death."

"Well, I'd have to cut 'em off at the ankles, deep as he's sunk into the stones. He wouldn't be much use if I did that." Bek's deep voice sounded doubtful. "Can't you just let him go? I don't wanna dull my sword on his leg-guards."

384

"I'm tired of his constant whining. He's worse than a two-year-old. Cut him out of the stone yourself or cut him off at the ankles. I don't care which." Jenner sounded fed up.

Luk set up a wail. "No! Don't do it! Don't cut off my feet! Bek, make him let me loose of the stone. They're going to sleep on me."

Rall and Jules stared at each other in disbelief.

"What's going on down here?" Another voice sounded in the passage. "Oh, hell. I should have known. Jenner, stop teasing the minotaurs. You know they can't think their way out of a wet sack with their brains all mashed around in their heads like that. Turn Luk loose—now! He and Bek need to go hunting for their dinner. You two get out there and get a good-sized buck. Kandek will be here early this afternoon to welcome our guests properly, and you'll want to have plenty to share with him."

Luk whined, "C'mon, Jenner. Grakken said let me loose."

"All you would have had to do was pull your feet out of your boots, you stupid minotaur. You need to look beyond the obvious." Jenner's voice was amused. There was a slight rattling of the walls and shelves again. "There. Go hunt up some dinner for your boss like the good dogs you are."

"This place is so cold yer blood freezes. Makes hunting a misery," Luk said. "Kandek's gonna get his someday, same as you, Jenner. I'll eat his heart. Then I'll eat me some earth-mage heart and see if it tastes as puny as he looks on the outside." He stamped his boots, getting the feeling back in his feet. "I'll eat it roasted."

Jenner snorted. "Sure you will."

"I hate hunting for Kandek," Bek said. "It's bad enough hunting for myself. The waterdrake hunted this valley out. There's nuthing of any size left. Even yer tame waterdrake up an' left 'cause the food's so scarce."

"Is he gone? I'm not so sure he left on his own accord. I think he had some encouragement," replied Grakken. "But I'll be sure to tell Kandek how you boys feel."

"Do that," said Bek. "He knows how we feel, but it don't hurt to remind him. Still, Kandek's stronger'n me, so we'll hunt for him. We don't like it, but we'll do it." The sounds of Bek and Luk's heavy footsteps dwindled, and the door to the storeroom swung open.

A slightly-built man with mousey blond hair and a studious demeanor stood silhouetted in the doorway. "Priests of Aeos, I know the soldiers of Tauron were rough when they captured you, and I'm sorry. It's their nature. I'll heal you now. I know you won't thank me because you'll die tonight, and I do regret that. Still, I need to heal you as you must be in perfect health to be a worthy offering to the Bull God." Holding one hand out toward each mage, Grakken healed both Rall and Jules simultaneously.

The familiar warmth of the healing magic settled over both of them, bringing blessed relief. Grakken had healed their internal injuries without even touching them. No healer of their acquaintance could have done such a feat, not even Soren Torsson. The two mages were dumbfounded at the effortlessness of the healing, sensing the man hadn't used much chi to do so major a working.

"Now, do you want to tell me what you did with my waterdrake? I hear he's gone now." Grakken stood there looking at Jules with a slight quizzical expression, as if he didn't really care if Jules answered or not. The compulsion he applied so heavily, though, indicated that, indeed, he did care quite a lot.

Jules felt the tug of coercion and, as he'd been taught, he went along with it, telling the literal truth. "I didn't make it leave, if that's what you're wondering. When I saw it last, it was in its lair. I'm sure you can understand that I had absolutely no intention of disturbing the creature." Jules's sincerity rang absolutely true to the mindbender, who now turned his attention to Rall.

"What about you, barbarian? What do you know that this man doesn't?"

"I know nothing about your waterdrake that he doesn't. However, since you're asking what I know that he doesn't, I burned his dirty laundry when he went on his first away-posting." Rall shrugged. "It made the house smell bad."

Surprised and hurt by the suddenness of that revelation, Jules's eyes widened. "That's unfair. Why would you bring that up now?" An intense feeling of betrayal that his friend had never told him surprised him. "What gives you the right to be such a smug git?"

"You were a pig, Jules." Remembering what Arne had said, Rall stirred his long-buried emotions as much as he could in an effort to confuse the empath. He focused on visualizing his anger and disgust as clearly if he were casting a spell, remembering the morning he had emptied Jules's sty of a room. "Living with you was hell. Do you have any idea how revolting it is to have to muck out after you? To top it off, the window had to be left open for two days to rid the place of the stench of your dirty socks, half of which, it turned out, were mine!"

"I wasn't that bad! You're worse than an old woman. You have no sense of humor." It hurt, even if it was true. "All you ever wanted to do was sit around reading. I enjoy a good book once in a while, but really—there's more to life than that. When we moved in together, I thought we'd have a little fun in the common rooms, but no, not you. You were too busy following me around all the time, constantly shoving coasters under every teacup and straightening the damned doilies like some barbarian grandmother!"

"We didn't 'move in together.' Don't even suggest that. I didn't ask to have you as a roommate. I was content with Arne, thank you, until you screwed your own situation up and they forced you on me."

With each of Rall's words, Jules became more enraged. "Oh, great. Just what I need—you kicking me when I'm down."

"When you went to Armat, I would have celebrated, but I was too busy cleaning. Your sheets hadn't been changed since the day you moved in." Rall rolled his eyes. "And don't even get me started on what it's like to share a bath chamber with you."

"Why are you such a prat? Goddess help me, but you're the most arrogant jackass I've ever known." For a moment, Jules was so angry he forgot where they were and what their situation was.

Unable to cope with the intensity of their quarrel, Grakken pressed his hand to his forehead. "This is ridiculous. You two are as bad as my minotaurs. You both need to rest." He walked out, closing the door behind him.

Frustrated and red-faced with anger, Jules leaned his head against the barrel. Forcefully, he tried to clear his mind, knowing why Rall had brought up such a sensitive subject but feeling as if he had been ambushed, nonetheless.

"Forgive me—that was completely unfair." Rall smiled uncertainly at Jules, who grinned back crookedly. "One has to wonder how this minotaur priest they're talking about comes and goes, when this climate is so hostile to them." Rall's whisper drew a nod from Jules.

They heard Grakken speaking to Jenner. "You're doing well—I know this is hard for you. Bury those minotaurs if you must, but protect these two. Their sacrifice on the altar of the Bull God will mark the beginning of Tauron's liberation of Neveyah." The sounds of Grakken pacing back and forth came through the door. "The power he will gain over Aeos with the harvesting of two of her own will give him the edge in his battle to take her as his wife. Kandek will be beholden to us once again. We will regain the ground we lost after Ander died and I...decimated the pens in my madness." The sound of utter emotional devastation in Grakken's voice as he made that comment made Rall and Jules look at each other in surprise.

The chair scraped as Jenner suddenly stood, and then the prisoners heard muffled sounds, as if the two embraced. "You didn't know what you were doing, my love." Jenner's voice was tender, soothing him. "Those rat-people are a plague, and Ander never should have died. But it's not my place to second guess our god or his most holy servant. If Tauron feels the rats will cripple Aeos's clergy, then fine. They've certainly crippled us."

"But the blood...I can't get it out of my mind...the poor children...oh god...."

"It wasn't you, Rafe. You would never have done such a thing if the link to Ander hadn't been broken." The sounds of Grakken's weeping came through the door, muffled possibly by Jenner's shoulder. "Besides, I *was* able to get you to hear me eventually, and that's what matters. Think of the positive. We have these two, and they'll make up for the ones we...lost."

Rall and Jules listened to the conversation in amazement. "His real name is Rafe...but that explains why no one noticed the cave-in and the death of you-know-what. It must have been chaos here." Rall's quiet whisper drew an answering nod from Jules.

Grakken spoke again, sounding reassured. "You're a rock to me. You're right—we must think of what we have accomplished. We're the ones who took the chosen child of royal blood to Serende, Jenner. It was we—you, Ander, Margot, and I—who handed the infant to the priests. Now, thanks to the wisdom of those who unleashed the rats on us, only you and I are left. But, incomplete as we are, it is *we* who will give Tauron the clergy of Aeos.

"Our rise to power depends on this, and power is everything. The people of Neveyah must be led to the Bull God, and we must be their shepherds. *We* must rule because Kandek and any of his minions will treat our people harshly. The minotaurs don't understand how to rule without violence and are unable to adapt to our ways as Tauron wishes them to. You've seen the petty squabbling among the warlords in Serende. Even among the Circle of Six, no agreement can be reached regarding how to bring about the change."

Jenner's voice was soft, tender. "As you frequently tell me, it's their way. They treat each other harshly, and right now, we must be stronger than they. I know you don't want to be a king, but Neveyah will benefit. It's for our world, Rafe. It's for our people. We can't let these minotaurs be our rulers until they've been taught a gentler way of life. Their way is too severe for our people, and though Tauron wishes them to change, they fight it every step of the way. *You* are the child of Aeos that was foretold, the one who will lead Serende to greatness and lead Neveyah to the one true God. You will lead us, and with the sacrifice of a few, the rest will prosper."

"I'm comforted by how strong your faith in me is. It sustains me through the bond that links us. Thank you for that."

Grakken's footsteps faded as he walked down the hall.

Rall looked at Jules, mystified. He mouthed the words, "Chosen child? Infant?" His eyebrows rose.

Jules was as perplexed by the whole exchange as Rall was, shrugging and shaking his head. He leaned back, attempting to get some rest. He felt sure Wynn and Devyn knew by now they'd been captured. As the baron had said, there would be a chance to escape, and he and Rall needed to be ready when it happened. Soon Jules slept, fitfully.

Rall's mind turned around the mystery of what infant Grakken could have given to the priesthood of Tauron and what it could mean. The words were familiar and nagged at him. Then it struck him. They had just left the town of Arlen, and Devyn was speaking about the time he'd traveled with his brother Dax, who was now king of Mal Evol. A prophecy had been handed to the brothers, one that mentioned a child. Now, Rall's mind focused on remembering it. *The worlds tremble in the starry void. The stolen child yearns for his mother's breast in the foreign land and is succored on despair.* His heart sank as he realized it would be years before the prophecy would be made clear.

The prophecy must refer to the baby Grakken is talking about. If he was an infant when he was stolen, he would be about two years old now. This is bad. What is it about this boy that causes the worlds to tremble? Still, I don't know of any children of significant bloodlines who are missing, other than the people from around Arlen. This is another sign that the end-days are approaching. Aeos, help us. We have to get this information to Mother Relynne.

Settling himself as well as he could, Rall prayed and meditated. He had to have faith that when Wynn and Devyn managed to spring him and Jules, he would be rested and ready to do whatever he had to, despite having no access to his magic.

Chapter 33

Wynn and Devyn located a place large enough for them to stretch out and sleep later, tucked behind the sturdy shelves that held many different types of weapons, some so ancient that Wynn had no idea what they were for. After carefully inspecting every item there, he chose two fine swords and immediately returned to the secret passage, closing the door and sitting on the landing. There he cleaned and honed the blades as well as he could, muffling the sounds under one of the heavy woolen blankets he'd found in the crowded storeroom. A lamp halfway down the steep stairs cast enough light for him to work.

While Wynn labored on the swords, Devyn quietly inspected the layout of the top level of the keep. The storeroom where the two mages hid opened into an alcove just off one end of the long gallery that ended in the chapel. If one didn't know the storeroom was there, it could easily be missed. In the old days, when the keep was full of life and people, the servants would have been able to traverse the important areas with no trouble and would have been discreetly available whenever they were needed. The servants' passage was a real shortcut connecting the kitchen, four stories below, and the workrooms with the rest of the residence. To walk the same distance through the main halls would have taken far longer.

If one did happen to notice the alcove in the far corner of the gallery and open the door to the upper storeroom, all one saw was an attic room no different than any other. It was an immense room of no importance, where once long ago, many seamstresses sewed for the entire mining community that was the backbone of the Hemstecks' fortunes. Now, it was impossible to gauge the room's true size, as it was filled floor to ceiling with row upon row of countless, dusty shelves loaded with the debris of generations, everything from moldering bed linens and vast quantities of old crockery to crumbling plate-armor and rusty, deteriorating weapons.

Tucked in a corner was the small, unimportant door that opened into a dark broom closet. The wall at the rear was actually the old door that opened to the abandoned servants' passages. When the sewing room fell into disuse and the passage was no longer needed, the door was nailed shut, but Devyn could see where the nails had been removed very recently.

The main stairwell that served the living areas was still in use by those who now occupied the keep and was located toward the center of a long, beautiful gallery that ran the length of the occupied wing. Pausing next to the top of the elegantly curving stairwell, Devyn listened. Muffled voices rose from the floors below, and doors opened and closed. Nervously, he slipped back to the alcove and waited with the door cracked open, listening. No one came up, but someone did go down. The carpeted stairs creaked slightly with each step.

When he could hear no more noises, Devyn stepped back out to the gallery and observed the beauty and architecture of the wide, graceful hall. For the first time, he had a glimpse of the true grandeur the Hemsteck Keep had once boasted, and a sense of familiarity swept over him, momentarily feeling as if he'd stumbled into the chapel wing of his own family's home in Mal Evol City.

All manors had a chapel, as a typical home might have a hundred people living in it at any given time when one counted the family, servants, and guests. This old wing was built in the same way as all the manor homes Devyn had ever stayed in, with the Chapel of Aeos taking up half of the attic. The chapel was always built at the top as there must be an opening in the roof over the altar to allow the smoke from the sweet herbs burned as offerings to rise to heaven, along with the prayers of the devoted. Weather never entered a consecrated chapel, and despite the grandeur of the rest of the home, the interior of the sanctuary itself was always very simple.

The worship of Aeos was as unlike the worship of Tauron as it could possibly be. No priests were required to serve in her chapel. All established rituals were family-oriented and led by the father or mother, in a rich family's home just as in a poor family's home. Aeos did not demand sacrifices and abject worship. Instead, her chapel was a place where people would go to reflect and pray. In a large manor, the servants and guests, as well as the family, would be found in the chapel at any time of the day and night, seeking solitude, meditating, and offering their prayers to the Goddess Aeos.

From the alcove, Devyn stepped out and faced the ornately carved doors of the chapel. Along the east-facing side of the upper gallery, light entered in through tall diamond-paned windows, enough that the hall was illuminated cheerily, despite the grey, overcast skies. Every inch of the wide hall was immaculately clean, and the tapestries and oil paintings that graced the walls opposite the windows were in perfect condition, lovingly maintained by the baron during the years the rest of his home fell to ruin. The thick carpet running down the center of the gallery was worn from the footsteps of countless generations of worshippers, but still colorful. The doors to the chapel gleamed with a fresh coat of polish.

Devyn silently observed the beauty of the upper gallery. That the chapel was an important place to the old baron was clear. One could see the love and attention with which he'd preserved the place.

Moving to stand before the chapel doors, Devyn's hand hovered near the latch and then dropped to his side. With his ear pressed to the wood, he could hear nothing out of the ordinary, but something told him to heed the baron's words and not enter until the ritual was in motion, after night had fallen and it was fully dark. Since the high priest of Tauron had turned the chapel to his purposes, he would have set magical traps to catch the unwary trespasser when it was unoccupied. Devyn thought it probable that the only time it might be safe for the uninitiated to enter would be when the high priest himself was there.

He returned to the storeroom, closing the door silently behind him, and went back through the broom closet, sitting on the landing of the servants' stairs next to Wynn. He told Wynn his findings and his feelings about the chapel.

Wynn nodded. "Only the strongest of their society survive, and the stupid ones are soon weeded out. I suspect spying on Tauron's sacred rituals qualifies as stupid." He held the two blades up. "These are as good as I can get them. I didn't bring a proper sharpening kit, so this will have to do. They're sharp, but nothing like what I could do at home."

"They'll do. They're sharp enough to kill a minotaur, and that's all we need." Devyn leaned back, closing his eyes and listening to their surroundings. Faintly, the creaking of floors and occasionally, distant, heavy footsteps sounded through the walls around them. Opening his eyes, he looked at Wynn, saying, "You look knackered, cousin. You need to rest. Let's get settled in the storeroom. I found a rare book there that I want to read while I have the opportunity. I can do that by the light from the window while you sleep."

"I could use some shuteye, now you mention it." Wynn's wry grin lit up his face. "I've been trying to figure out how we're going to rescue them, and I'm coming up with nothing."

"I'll tell you how we're going to do it as soon as I figure it out." Devyn clasped Wynn's shoulder. "Don't worry. We'll manage somehow."

Chapter 34

Rall and Jules were startled into wakefulness by the door opening as Grakken entered and sat on the floor opposite them.

"If we had a campfire, this would be cozy," said Jules.

"Yes, it would. I like you," Grakken's genuine smile gave him the appearance of any healer of their acquaintance. "It's too bad I didn't find you before the Temple of Aeos did, because there's no chance for you now. The only way to break the geas on you is for you to be broken on the altar."

"I can't speak for Rall, but I'm quite happy in my religious beliefs." Jules's chains rattled as he shrugged. "If I must die, then so be it."

"You say this now, but you have no idea what lies ahead. You will be tortured, kept alive for as long as is possible for me to do so, and you will die in the most horrendous way possible." Grakken's face paled as he spoke. "I must keep you alive as long as I can while the High Priest Kandek ritually tortures you to the brink of death again and again."

Jules said, "If it ends that way, that's too bad, but I knew this was a possibility when I came here."

"And you, Rall? Do you feel the same way?" His smile was kind, and Rall grinned back.

Rall's answering smile was gentle, as if he spoke to a dear friend. "Of course I do, Rafe," he replied, deliberately using Grakken's given name. "I'm not the strongest priest or the best warrior, but I live for Aeos and will die for her if I must and am proud to do so." Grakken's eyes flickered at the mention of his true name. Rall thought, *Take that for presuming to be on a first-name basis with me, asshole.*

"Since we're all being honest here, I've been told to let you know what to expect tonight. It will be agonizing and drawn out, as a good offering should be. Once the ritual begins, I won't be allowed to alleviate your pain, although I will experience it with you because of my empathy." Grakken looked at Jules, sensing he was the weaker of the two. "First, you'll be stripped naked, as no one can enter the sanctuary of Tauron wearing clothing. It's an abomination in his eyes. You must be seen as having nothing to hide. Everyone will be unclothed."

"That sounds frosty," said Jules, with a mocking tone to his voice. "Will there be a fire there to warm the place up? I'd hate to get a cold or something from this." A sly look passed across his face, and leaning forward, he whispered, "And just between you and me, Rall's not all that manly when things get too chilly." He winked knowingly at their visitor. "The big barbarian has a rather small package for a man his size, know what I mean?" He grinned.

Ignoring Jules's attempt at diverting him, Grakken said, "Once your clothes have been stripped, you'll walk to the altar where you will lie down and offer up your lives to the one true god, Tauron. This is the first part of your long journey to his arms."

"I probably won't do that voluntarily, but I've no doubt you can wiggle your fingers or wave your hand, whatever you people do," replied Jules, his tone slightly insulting. "After all, you're a mindbender. From what I hear, coercion is your strongest skill." Jules's smile was as innocent as it was bright, barely disguising his contempt. "What does Grakken mean? Oh, yes, I remember. It's a minotaur name. It means 'he who bends minds.'"

"Yes, that's exactly how it'll be done." Grakken's smile became less friendly. "Mindbender—how appropriate. Your body will do as I command, and your mind will watch as it happens. I like that term, though it was no doubt meant to be an insult."

Rall burst out, "Damned right it was an insult, and I'm not taking it!" His outburst startled Grakken. "What do you mean, saying I'm not manly in the cold? I was born in the cold, you soft wetlander. Your package is notoriously *short* on delivery, or so we hear."

"Took you long enough, barbarian. Are your wits as shriveled as your nuts?" Jules sneered at him. "You're too damned slow. Always have been and always will be."

"I'll show you shriveled. Stand next to me naked, jackass, and we'll see who's the manly one." All through their novice years, Rall had been the butt of jokes that were at times exceedingly insulting and baseless, all because he was too tall compared to the others. He'd been harassed, referred to as a giant, and his heavy accent had made his detractors allude to him as stupid and barbaric. The fact he'd matured a year or so later than the others was also an issue—boys being boys, they'd made rude remarks, teasing him in the dressing room, unaware their casual cruelty had struck home.

Thus, Rall had struggled to erase his northern accent from his speech and strove never to appear less than the most cultivated of Aeos's clergy, at times warring with his own nature in that effort. "Your jealousy is offensive in a priest, little man. You're an embarrassment."

"Stop it!" Grakken pressed his hands against his temples. "I'm not here to listen to you two squabble." With some difficulty, he calmed himself. "In the ritual, the next thing that will happen is Tauron will enter the physical vessel of the high priest, Kandek. He will test you and accept your sacrifice—the god will perform the entire ritual himself."

Curious, Jules said, "You mean Tauron will really be inside this minotaur? That sounds uncomfortable. Where does the real minotaur go when your dark god is in his head? And how does he fit inside this person's body?"

"He doesn't go anywhere. Look, I want to help you, don't you see? If you know what you're facing, you'll see that I can help you by inserting a pain-block in your minds. But you have to allow me to do it. The geas you're under won't let me without your permission." Grakken's face became flustered. "Why can't you just listen?"

"Don't pay any attention to him, Rafe. He's always been an idiot." Rall smirked at Jules. "Please, continue telling us how we're going to die. I'm interested from a professional standpoint, priest to priest. But the jackass does raise a good point. Exactly where does the high priest's mind go? Is he still there, or is he unconscious?"

"God, help me. Educating you fools is going to take all day," muttered Grakken. "Okay, *Rall*, since you want to talk theology, Kandek will still be there when the god enters his body, but it'll be as if he were in a corner of his own mind, observing everything, unable to affect anything. He's called the First Observer and is most fortunate to be allowed to watch the sacred ritual from such a privileged position." He took a deep breath. "Now shut up so I can explain the rest of this to you.

"Once Tauron enters Kandek's body, he will question you, using both pain and pleasure to encourage your answers, and believe me, no matter what you think now, you *will* tell him everything. You'll be eager to tell him the minutest of things, right down to what your mother ate for breakfast the day you were born. The Bull God yearns to know you, what sort of person you are, how you think, your deepest secrets—everything. At first, you'll struggle, but very quickly, you'll be volunteering to give him any scrap of information you can think of. By the end of this phase, you will abjectly worship Tauron, and he'll know you better than you know yourself. That is the first part of the ritual and is called The Knowing.

"During the second phase, Tauron becomes your lover. He will share a kiss with you. You will know pleasure beyond anything you've ever known. There is no way to describe it. This is called The Sharing, and it's where the god experiences and tastes *your* ecstasy. If you're very fortunate, he will make carnal love to you, an experience only the most privileged and valued of sacrifices are chosen for. Because you're the first priests of Aeos to go to his altar, I'm sure you'll both be selected for this honor."

Grakken was about to explain more when Jules interrupted him. "Um, Tauron will be wearing this minotaur's body still, won't he? I don't think that's going to work well for me. I don't have a problem with you fellows kissing boys or minotaurs, if that's what you like, but I'm a bonded man now, and my wife would kill me if I kissed anyone else."

Nonplussed, Grakken stared at him.

"Surely you can understand my position. You don't even want to know what my wife would do if she ever found out there was sex involved." Jules shuddered. "It won't matter that I'm dead. She'll hunt me down to the furthest corners of hell. She'll never understand, not even if I tell her your Bull God made me do it."

Rall agreed. "Oh my, yes. His wife's a jealous thing, and rightfully so. She'll gut him for sure once she finds out he's been kissing minotaurs and making love to strange gods. I have to question your god's taste in lovers, though. Jules here behaves like a slimy, cheating pleasure-boy every chance he gets. He's slept with every friendly-girl in Neveyah and who knows how many others. His wife has good reason to be jealous, poor woman. He can't keep his pants buttoned to save his life."

"What do you mean 'slimy'? At least I had a good time when I was a bachelor, unlike you, you pompous prig. You were no virgin yourself—don't pretend you were. Of course, you always had to get so drunk that you could barely perform before you loosened up enough to stagger off to bed with a willing woman." Stung, Jules stuck his tongue out at Rall. "You're pathetic. You've been nothing but a gelded pony since you bonded that impossible woman."

"Shut it, Jules," Rall snapped. "Don't you dare bring Feia into this. You're just jealous of her place in my life. You've always been jealous of her." For a brief moment, he wanted nothing more than to feel his fist striking Jules in the face. "Admit it, you wanted me for yourself. And there's no pony in Aeoven more gelded than *you,* Jules. You constantly grovel at Aneka's feet, begging her forgiveness for your sleazy sins, terrified she's going to dump your untrustworthy ass. It's nauseating."

"Jealous? Oh, don't you wish. Feia's twice the man you are, and she's destroyed you. You can't decide what sock to put on first without her guidance." Jules's red face blatantly showed his scorn. "You're less than a mouse. Your career is over. No one wants to work under a man who needs to be told when to fart." Ruthlessly, he mimicked Feia at her worst. "Rall—the baby's nappy needs changing. Rall—take the trash out. Rall! Rall! Rall! You're a eunuch, not a man."

"You're a dead man, Jules. When these chains come off, I'm going to kill you."

"Stop it, you two!" Grakken shook his head, trying to clear it of his prisoners' emotions. "Look, I'm just supposed to tell you what to expect, and then you two can bicker to your hearts' content. I'd hoped to put a pain-block in your mind to help you get through the torture, but with your stupid quarreling, I can't concentrate, so you're on your own. Here's what to expect." Grakken spoke quickly, just wanting to get it over with. "The third and final part is called The Offering. Most Holy Kandek will slowly and ritually gut you, and your bones will burn in the holy fire, while the Dark God weighs your soul. Your screams of agony will be as music to him, because with your deaths, Tauron will have achieved a victory over Aeos."

"Well, that's a relief," said Jules, leaning back against a barrel. "At least Aneka won't find out I've become Tauron's newest pleasure-boy." His anger at their situation boiled. "And at least Rall will be as dead as me, the arrogant bastard. His clumsiness is the reason I'm in this fix in the first place. Can he please go to the altar first? He's always had to be first in everything else."

"*My* clumsiness...!" Rall raised his bound hands and made a rude gesture, accompanied by an equally rude noise.

Abruptly, Grakken stood up. "I have to go now." He pressed his hand against his forehead. "All in all, each part of the ritual takes about four hours, perhaps longer if I can keep you alive, so now you're prepared. Good grief—you people have given me a headache. How you managed to get all the way here without killing each other is beyond me." The door closed, leaving the two mages in the dimly lit silence of the storeroom. "Jenner, we need to make sure everything is ready for Kandek's arrival."

Jules and Rall heard the chair creak as their guard stood and followed Grakken down the hall. The sounds of the two men speaking drifted into the storeroom, the words muffled and indistinct.

"We're in deep trouble, my friend. We may not make it out of this." Jules's whisper was raw, and his dark eyes betrayed his fear. "Rall—please believe me when I say I have nothing but respect for you and for Feia."

"I know why you said it, and it stung because there *is* some truth to it. We have Rafe off balance and need to keep him that way. Arne might have saved us. Rafe doesn't appear to have good barriers, so we need to stay angry, and that means we'll have to air the things that lie festering between us. He has no way of defending against strong emotions." Rall's whisper was fierce. "We have to take the first opportunity to escape that we get. And we *will* get one at some point. We just have to recognize it when we see it."

They fell silent as footsteps approached down the hall. The door scraped open, and Jenner stood silhouetted in it. "You two should have paid attention to Grakken. He's a great man, and he could have helped you by simply inserting a small loop in your mind. He can't do it without your permission because of the geas that ties you to your goddess. You'll wish you'd let him help you, believe me, about the time Tauron's pulling your guts out of your assholes and stuffing your idiotic mouths up with them." Jenner's scorn was clear. "You're a pair of bloody fools if you're really as stupid as you sound. You still have time to let him insert a pain-block into your minds. You'll die anyway, but it won't bother you so much. If you wait until Kandek gets here, you're done for because he won't allow Grakken to ease your pain. You've been accorded a great honor. Kandek is the highest priest of Tauron in Serende."

"Thank you ever so kindly," replied Jules, rolling his eyes. "We recognize what a privilege it is."

"You just don't get it, do you? The priesthood of Tauron thrives on the suffering of others. It's pleasurable to Most Holy Kandek that Grakken must be linked to you to keep you alive and that he'll suffer every agony with you *through that link*—he relishes that aspect of it. Kandek will rob you of your life slowly and use your agony to fuel his connection to the one god. For a proper sacrifice, you must be kept alive as long as possible, and every time Grakken goes through this ritual, it destroys him a little more, but that means nothing to you noble sons of Aeos. The minute Kandek opens this door, your life in this world is over and your existence in a world of endless misery begins." Jenner stepped back and closed the door, and the chair creaked as he once more sat in it. His voice drifted through the thin door. "If you two idiots change your godforsaken minds, let me know. Please, let Grakken insert the pain-block."

Jenner's plea was met with stony silence. There was no way either man would allow Grakken to break the geas that bound them to Aeos.

The two prisoners' eyes met, and Jules nodded with grim determination. He knew Rall was thinking the same thing. If Wynn and Devyn had avoided capture, they'd be planning a way to rescue them. Fervently, Jules prayed they were safe. *Heaven help us if they were taken too.*

Chapter 35

Wynn had immediately fallen asleep as soon as he and Devyn were concealed in their hiding place. But now, he wandered in a lush, fertile green field under beautiful blue skies. He was overcome by a sense of urgency, a feeling there was something he had to do.

Cresting a rise, he came upon a scene of terrible carnage. A battle had taken place, a bloody massacre ending perhaps only moments before his arrival. A company of Temple soldiers lay dead, cut down among the bodies of countless old men and young boys armed with bloody scythes and farm implements. Shocked, Wynn wandered among the corpses of both sides, fearing he would find a friend, but he recognized none of them. *I'm dreaming. It's only a dream.* The mantra didn't comfort him as it usually did. There was something different about this dream, something too real and solid.

At last, he came to the center of the battlefield. There, a young water-mage clad in turquoise blue knelt in the grass. Except for his hairstyle, he looked exactly like Wynn's father must have as a young man. The mage was flanked by two others, a man and woman who were unfamiliar to Wynn. All three were covered with dried blood and gore, and desperation was clear on their faces.

The water-mage had no sword but held his hands as if he gripped one before him by the pommel, pointed straight down, the tip grounded. The two others, a male fire-mage and the other, a pretty female earth-mage, knelt on either side with their swords crossing in front of him in an X, points to the ground. All three mages were tranced, and the water-mage appeared to be guiding them in creating a powerful spell. A great working, larger than anything Wynn had ever before witnessed, was in progress, and the water-mage was the focus of the power—potent energies swirled around him.

"This is your son as he will one day be." Hearing a voice, Wynn glanced up and saw a woman standing behind the three mages. She had his mother's features, but her eyes were a brilliant sapphire-blue, and her simple dress matched the blue of her eyes. "The war goes badly. The stolen child has taken the city of old, and my holy house has been desecrated. My most faithful servant has been foully murdered on Tauron's unholy altar, the first of my beloved clergy to go to the great slaughter. These three will save Neveyah from the madman's mind-magic, but mighty though their feat will be, it is only a temporary measure. Your son will save Neveyah twice. The first time will break him and drive him away, but he will follow his son and return. The second time will be the saving of him."

Wynn blinked, and the scene changed. The landscape was familiar but different, barren and dotted with clumps of brown, thorny bushes Wynn had never seen before. It was Neveyah, but greatly changed. Now, his son was much older and deeply marked with grief, as were the three younger mages seated on the ground with him. One was crippled; he wore a unique brace on one leg. A most unusual healer's staff lay on the ground next to him. All three of the unfamiliar mages were fully augmented as both healers and battle-mages—an impossibility Wynn laid down to the fact he was dreaming.

The four sat, silent and unmoving. Though at first glance they appeared simply to be camping, on looking closer, he saw they were entranced, much the same way healers were when they worked. The three strangers held swords before them, both hands gripping the pommels with the points grounded. The strange blades appeared very like his father's ensorcelled sword, Scorpion. Again, Wynn's son, Johnny, had no weapon, though he held his hands before him as if he did. The four men channeled the elements through the swords, and a wall rose behind them, borne of magic, smooth and dark, twenty meters tall.

Colossal energies joined the three blades, even connecting Johnny through the sword that was not there, focused and guided by the young mage who wore armor of such a dark blue it was nearly black. His armor was embossed with green and gold leaves, a thing Wynn had never heard of. Except for his strange augmentations, this mage looked so much like Wynn himself that for a moment he was confused. Then he realized he was looking at his grandson-to-be. *His augmentations...the assassin's rune, the healer's crescent...healer's vines and warrior's thorns. Green on his armor.... What could be the meaning of this? It's not possible.... The two magics can't exist with strength in one mage.*

He saw Johnny too was fully tranced as if he was a healer. Of the four, only John wasn't marked as a full healer, but he now bore *blue* stars, a color no healer would have. All of these strange things perplexed Wynn, but one thing puzzled him most of all. "Where is my son's sword? Why does he alone not have one?"

"You must create it, mighty smith. When you return to Aeoven, you must make your son a blade that is in appearance like unto these three swords. The blade you will forge is the older brother to these. This circle will only be complete once your masterwork joins with the others for the great task. Your creation will be the lynchpin, the key that will enable your grandson's magic when it is *his* time, and he attempts to complete his greatest work. I will guide you in its making." Wynn felt something in his hands, and looking down, he saw he held the weapon-to-be. "When you have finished the sword, you must take your family and return to your home in Ariend for your son's safety. When it is time, he will be called to return to Neveyah. You must bestow the blade on him at that time, binding him to it using the ritual geas. The sword's name will be given to you then."

Intricate engravings marked the sword, with runes for water, stealth, and healing. Wynn held the slender, graceful blade up to the light, admiring the shape of it, feeling the magics that lay banked within it, just beyond his grasp. The creation of this magic-enhanced weapon was the true task for which he'd been brought to Neveyah, and that realization overwhelmed him. With deep reverence, Wynn committed every aspect of the sword to his memory. "I'll do as you say, Lady of Heaven, though I don't understand all you've shown me. That field of battle…. I fear for my son, but now I know you'll have him in your hand."

The dream faded, and Wynn was left to ponder what he'd seen.

Wynn's eyes opened, and he sat up. "I've had a true dream. I know what I must do when I get back to Aeoven, but little else makes any sense."

"Tell me." Devyn closed his book, his sharp, brown eyes taking in his cousin's confused expression. "I'm fairly good at sorting these things, and if we can't figure it out, it's best we both know what occurred so Mother Relynne can deal with it."

"I'm supposed to make my son a sword. That much I understand, and when we return to Aeoven, I'll do it. I know what the Goddess wants. It's the rest of the dream that worries me."

"I'm listening." Devyn settled himself, and Wynn told him what he'd seen, the strange augmentations, what the Goddess said in regard to a war and her clergy, and what he feared loomed in the future for Neveyah.

"My cousin, you have indeed had a true dream," Devyn said, clasping Wynn's shoulder in sympathy. "It's as they always are, full of portents, omens, and impossibilities. That you must make a special sword for your son is clear. The rest of it, not so much. We'll carry this information to Mother Relynne, and she'll deal with the future, she or whoever succeeds her in the Holy Seat. In the meantime, we must concentrate on surviving what lies before us tonight. I've developed a plan I think will take care of getting us into the chapel at the right time. If we can, we have to ambush the guards as they actually enter the chapel. That way we'll be inside. We'll have to take out the high priest and the earth-mage first, if we can."

Wynn stared at him.

"You must cut Rall and Jules's bonds as quickly as possible and give them the swords. I'll keep the minotaurs occupied until you can help me." He grinned at Wynn's expression. "What? It's a good plan."

"If you say so. The baron said their food was dosed with silf. You and I will be the only ones on our side who can use magic, so we'll just have to hope I can free them from their chains. If we can't spring them first thing, I don't know if we can beat three minotaurs helped along by a mindbender with his earth-mage in thrall to him."

"Then you'd best try to get some more rest, cousin." Devyn opened his book again, and Wynn settled back down to sleep, this time undisturbed by dreams.

◆◆◆

The afternoon had begun to grow late. Devyn and Wynn loitered just inside the storeroom, listening for movement in the hall. Both had rested as well as possible, and now they simply observed, waiting for some change in the general routine. Eventually, they heard the door to the chapel open. Through the tiny crack in the doorway, they saw an immense, horned shadow pass and heard heavy footsteps receding down the grand staircase.

"I lingered just outside that door this morning. As near as I could tell without opening, the chapel was vacant," Devyn whispered to Wynn. "I swear no one was in there—I would have heard them."

"It's a puzzle," agreed Wynn. "The baron said this high priest comes and goes freely and never uses the front door. There must be a logical explanation for it." His blue eyes were thoughtful. "We'll find out soon, I suspect. The baron said the ritual would begin well after dark. We still have at least an hour or so to wait."

Chapter 36

Night had fallen, and the storeroom where Jules and Rall were held prisoner was dark except for the light that filtered through the cracks around the doorjamb. The door opened, and an immense form stood silhouetted in the light. A harsh, deep voice said, "You will rise and prepare yourselves for the journey before you." The figure stepped into the room. The minotaur was at least eight feet tall and wore a gaudy, purple robe worked with silver stars over scratched and dented armor.

Jules and Rall felt their hearts nearly stop when they first saw his features in the light from the open door. It was by far the most hideous face they had ever seen. Red eyes burned in a face that was a cruel parody of a melding between a human and a bull. Tip-to-tip, the priest's horns spanned nearly four feet, and he had to duck and turn sideways to enter the room.

Grimly determined to show no terror until he was actually on the altar being cut open, Jules said, "So soon?" He yawned. "I just fell asleep. Tell me it's not morning already."

A huge fist reached down and yanked the chains that bound Jules's wrists, picking him up, holding him dangling off the floor. The manacles bit deeply into his flesh, but Jules said nothing, simply hanging there, waiting for whatever was going to happen next. Shaking him violently twice, the high priest looked intently into Jules's eyes. In that brief gaze, he felt the priest had weighed and measured him as a man.

Speaking to himself, Kandek said, "Good strength of magic. Knows how to fight and controls his fear well. This one would have survived the Remaking with most of his wits had he been born in Serende. He could have risen high in the priesthood, but not so high as to challenge me. A good sacrifice. Tauron will be pleased." Closing his eyes, Kandek used his foreign magic to shred Jules's clothes and boots and set him down. Stark naked, except for his shackles, Jules stood on the cold stones. Tufts of rags and bits of leather lay scattered on the floor, giving testament to the force of the priest's magic.

"You're good," said Jules. Rall, however, recognized the shock and horror in his voice, feeling those same emotions himself. "An efficient use of magic. I can see how it saves time, although it's a bit hard on one's clothing. You must be Kandek. Nice to meet you. Perhaps we could have tea and talk shop sometime. I've always wondered how the dark god's magic works."

Kandek ignored Jules as if he were a piece of furniture. His evil gaze fell on Rall, who was calm under the scrutiny of the walking nightmare that was the high priest. "Now, for the barbarian. This gorm interests me." Picking Rall up by the chains that bound him, Kandek shook him violently, as he'd done Jules. "I sense exceptional strength of magic. Deadly reflexes held under great restraint." Glowing, red eyes peered closely into Rall's, looking into his soul. "Yes…you would have survived the Remaking with all your intelligence and wits intact. That's a rare thing, gorm." The great maw stretched into a grin, showing yellow, sharply filed teeth. "You would have reached to take my place had you been born in Serende, barbarian, and you might have achieved it. I will gain much strength by eating your heart." Still holding Rall dangling by his chains, Kandek unclothed him in the same way as Jules, and the two men stood shivering before the priest.

Kandek turned to the two minotaurs who loomed outside the door. "The meal you provided was barely adequate for my needs. If it hadn't been the full half of the smallest buck I've ever seen, I would have thought you two had forgotten your manners."

"This valley be hunted out, Holy Kandek. We would do better if we could hunt in the lower valleys where it be warmer." Bek managed to sound both aggressive and subservient, a trick that made Rall repress a grin. "We could bring you many slaves for the altar if we could go lower. Grakken don't take as many gorms as he could."

"We could breathe better, and it's warm enough to live down lower. We're penned up here as much as the slaves," Luk said. "Grakken's dangerous. He uses his gorm mind tricks to make us do his bidding, and what he done to Phak and Gerk was disgusting. What he done to those slaves was unnatural. Even gorms don't deserve that."

"Grakken's mad, yes, and he's dangerous. But he does as he's told, and he controls you, so that makes him far more valuable to me than you ever were." The immense priest chuckled, a rumbling, grating sound. "You will escort my guests to the altar. Gently. They will arrive there healthy and unharmed, or you will take their places." Kandek stepped through the door, and the two minotaurs backed away from him, terror stark on their bovine faces. "Prepare yourselves now for entering the sacred temple."

They began to protest. Kandek said, "Oh, yes. Your presence is required. You will attend the ritual. I may need to harvest your chi as well as theirs, and you'd better not whine about the cold or you'll find yourselves on Tauron's altar where it gets nice and warm. That may happen anyway if the god requires it. I'll be waiting."

"Those other two don't seem so frightening now, do they?" Jules's whisper sounded in Rall's ear. "They seem rather pleasant in comparison." The sounds of the two minotaur soldiers slowly divesting themselves of the many layers of their clothes came through the door. "I guess once you've seen a megalomaniac high priest of Tauron, the other minotaurs don't seem so bad." Jules shuddered. "You know, I'm not looking forward to kissing this priest quite as much as I thought I would, now that I've met him. He's not really my type."

"Huh. And you've slept with the ugliest friendly-girls in Neveyah, so that's saying something. Perhaps being the earthly vessel for a god of evil changes one for the worse." Both men felt nauseated at the thought of what they were facing, and kissing the priest was the least of their worries. Doggedly putting their fate in the hands of Aeos, the two prisoners buried their fear.

Just outside the door, Kandek said, "Grakken, these two priests of Aeos are strong, both physically and in life force. However, the geas that ties them to their goddess will require more effort to break than we thought. You must work most diligently to sustain them through the second stage of the ritual, or they will die before they're broken, especially the barbarian. They have the ability to will themselves to die before the ritual is complete, so you must keep them from doing so. Your thrall will follow and observe us, as this will require his strength also. Go now and prepare yourselves."

"But the pain…. Jenner may die of it. He's not empathic, but we're linked through the geas that binds us. As it is, even outside the door, he'll feel everything I suffer. If you bleed him of life-chi, he may die." Grakken's voice was filled with dismay. "He's all that's left of my coven since the rat-people killed Ander. I've found no others in the local population with the talent."

"No great matter. The thrall is disposable. Tauron may require his sacrifice. Would you withhold him if our god requires him?"

"No! Of course not. He is dear to me on a personal level, yes, and it would be a terrible personal sacrifice for me to lose him, but there's another reason, one you discount too readily," Grakken replied. "You clearly don't understand the link and why it must remain unbroken. I and my thralls are of one mind, and it is essential we remain so. When Ander was killed, we were incapacitated for two days. Jenner was alone, so it took him that long to get through to me enough so I could reestablish the link. Two days, Kandek! Two days before I regained control of my mind, don't you see? You know what happened before Jenner was able to get through to me. Two of your guards are dead. The children…the slaves…. Jenner is the last link holding my sanity, and it requires every bit of his attention to keep the madness at bay. Yes, I have great empathic ability and I can do what you ask, but it comes at a great cost. If Jenner dies or is cut off from me, I'll most certainly go mad. You'll have no one to protect you

418

from Bek and Luk while you're in the trance. No one to protect you from…me."

"Yes, two of my guards were rather artfully dealt with, it's true. They shouldn't have been so stupid as to get in your way. Regrettably, the slaves were squandered, but now we have much better gifts to offer up on the holy altar. I doubt you're capable of doing *me* any damage, little man." Kandek dismissed Grakken's concerns. "My two remaining oh-so-devoted guards are quite expendable. Their life-chi will be harvested first unless they are *very* good to me." His horrific face broke into a grin as the sounds of the two soldiers disrobing stopped for a moment and then resumed with more enthusiasm.

Kandek's rasping voice took on a reverent tone. "With this offering, we'll break down one more of the goddess's few remaining defenses. The most recent prophecy says that when the treasured servant of the Bride is broken on the altar of the One True God, Neveyah will fall, and the Bride of Heaven will kneel before her rightful husband. I tell you now, this barbarian is most surely that man. His strength is easily twice that of his companion, and the other one is a worthy foe. Surely, the goddess places a high value on such a man as this. Surely she treasures him. This priest is a servant whose strength of magic is equal to mine, as is his ambition to rule and his strength of will." Kandek smiled in anticipation, his red eyes gleaming. "He'll require much effort to break, but it can be done. Tonight, with the gift of this barbarian's broken body, Tauron will receive Neveyah as was promised. I will have given it to him."

Disbelief was starkly written on Grakken's face. "You must be mistaken." The words trembled on his lips; contradicting Kandek was dangerous. "These two are the most asinine of men, squabbling incessantly over inconsequential nothings. It's impossible to be in the same room as them."

"You're an idiot, Grakken. They've played you well and kept you from reading their true motives. They prevented you from using your little manipulations and mind-tricks to free them of their geas voluntarily. But no worry, the ritual of sacrifice will break it and be a pleasant diversion that will generate more chi than you can imagine. This barbarian is the one spoken of in the prophecy. Don't presume to doubt me. You and your thrall will be ready and waiting when I arrive at the altar, or you will pay the price along with Bek and Luk."

"As you wish, Holy Kandek." Their footsteps dwindled, Grakken's light steps scurrying and Kandek's measured and heavy.

The two rather subdued minotaur soldiers entered the storeroom, naked except for their weapons.

Now, Jules and Rall found themselves shuffling down long corridors, wearing nothing but chains that jangled with their every movement. Their bare feet felt strange on the icy stone floors, and their skin pebbled with goose bumps in the chill of the unheated keep. It was a most peculiar procession that slowly moved through the hallways. The minotaurs obviously felt the cold quite keenly, as the chattering of their sharply filed teeth proclaimed.

At the end of the service corridor, they passed through a pair of heavy doors and entered a long, parquet-floored hall that felt smooth on their bare feet. This led to an immense, strangely abandoned-feeling reception room. There they began climbing a carpeted, spiral staircase to another long passageway. As the two prisoners hobbled through the inhabited areas of the keep, it became apparent that "inhabited" was too strong a word.

The prisoners shambled along as fast as their shackles would allow, and the curious parade wound its way through endless, poorly lit hallways lined with priceless antique furnishings, crumbling and useless. Slowly, they passed darkened rooms, empty of occupants but filled with the accumulated detritus of generations of habitation. Another set of wide, graceful stairs opened onto more grand corridors, long empty of noble domesticity, stately and cold, frigid in their abandonment. Frost covered the windows inside and out. Icy floors at first burned and then numbed bare toes as the procession slowly made its way to the top of the keep.

With difficulty, Rall and Jules climbed the last, long flight of carpeted stairs to the chapel above and the horror that awaited them.

Chapter 37

The sounds of two people rapidly ascending the main stairwell alerted Wynn and Devyn that the time had come. Opening the door a crack, they saw two men, stark naked, entering the fourth floor at a run. The smaller of the two produced a key and unlocked the doors of the chapel, pushing one open and holding it for his companion. Once they were both inside, the door swung closed.

"What the...." Wynn looked at Devyn, scandalized. "What are those two thinking, trysting in the chapel when so many rooms are empty? They're going to be interrupted when this ceremony begins."

"That's not what they're doing. I forgot to warn you. It's rumored all rituals in the cult of the Bull God are performed in the nude." Devyn grinned at his cousin's expression. "Now we know it's true."

Wynn's response was cut off as an immense shadow loomed on the stairwell and formed itself into the shape of a gigantic minotaur, completely naked and fully male. As Kandek passed their view, Wynn was rendered speechless by the brief glimpse of the horrifically misshapen head crowned by two long horns, a being so tall and with a rack of horns so wide the creature would most likely have to stoop and turn sideways to enter most rooms. The minotaur's muscular neck was so thick, Wynn wondered if his head could turn as readily from side to side as a human's could. He was much larger than Wynn had expected. The deep scars crisscrossing his body demonstrated he had survived many battles. He was a being who radiated authority and power even when naked.

With a gesture from the minotaur, the doors of the chapel swung open. Once the massive creature had entered, they closed behind him.

Even though only a short time had passed, Wynn began to get nervous. "What if they're already in there? What if the priest is already in the trance? What...." Wynn stopped as Devyn held a finger to his lips.

"Shh. They're not. Listen...." Devyn cocked his head, a puzzled look on his face.

Faintly, from several floors below, the sounds of chains clanking, interspersed with a strange, dragging sound, drifted up the stairwell.

Devyn looked at Wynn. "Be ready. The minute those doors open and they pass through, we're going to charge them. Where are the swords for Rall and Jules?"

"I put them in this." Wynn turned, shrugging into a shoulder sheath he'd rigged. "It's for a much broader sword, but it works well enough for me to carry them both."

"Good." Devyn pressed his ear to the crack in the door. "Shh, they're on the floor below us. Be ready."

The dragging, sliding sound and the jangling of chains grew closer. Shadows loomed, forming into the silhouettes of two minotaurs and two much smaller men. At last, they emerged from the stairwell. Leading the way was a minotaur Wynn would have considered huge had he not seen the high priest. He was followed by Jules and Rall, both shackled at the wrists and the ankles, followed by another guard. All four were nude. The strange, sliding sound was made by the prisoners' chains scraping along between their feet as they walked.

Watching them, all Wynn could think of was how badly this was going to go since Jules and Rall were going to have to fight stark naked.

Under the cover of the rattling noises, Devyn and Wynn eased out of the storeroom to the alcove. Still hidden in the shadows, they stood poised, ready to launch themselves through the chapel doorway as soon as Rall and Jules had passed through.

◆◆◆

Grakken and Jenner knelt before the altar, their foreheads pressed to the floor. The doors to the chapel opened, and the surge of malevolence that was the mind of the high priest announced his presence. Safely cocooned within the stability of Jenner's mind, Grakken was unaffected, even when Kandek knelt beside him.

Chanting the ritual prayers and performing the grounding and centering exercises, the priest and his two acolytes entered a state of heightened awareness, preparing to give the ritual gifts to the Bull God.

The doors swung open, and Rall and Jules were ushered in. Stunned, the two prisoners saw a remarkable doorway that bathed the chapel in a purple light. Freestanding and set in the far corner of the room, the frame was immense, made entirely of amethyst. A liquid sheen rippled across the opening as if upon a pool. Yet, though it shimmered, it wasn't water. The portal opened into a room hung with rich tapestries and filled with ornate, lavishly gilded furniture, obviously made for much larger people.

"A portal…." Rall breathed the words as two huge fists forced the prisoners to kneel, pushing their foreheads to the floor.

"In the name of Holy Tauron, I accept the gifts of your lives, which you now offer up." Kandek yanked Jules to his feet by his chains.

"It's not really a gift, right? I mean, it's not my idea, so it's more of a theft." Jules's head snapped back as the priest casually backhanded him. With blood flowing from his nose, he said, "You can force me to do anything you want, and you can take my life, but it's not a gift. It's a theft. We need to have that clear." From out of the corner of his eye, Jules saw Devyn and Wynn slipping into the chapel just as the doors swung shut.

Kandek's fist swung back, preparing to hit Jules again. In mid-strike, the immense high priest was transfixed by a bolt of lightning.

Jules said, "Holy shit, Wynn! You scared the hell out of me with tha...Aaugh!" A second bolt struck beside Jules, and Jenner fell unconscious.

With a cry, Grakken leapt to his feet and then fell back to his knees beside Jenner, clutching him in his arms, sobbing. "No...live...you must live. Oh god! Don't die on me. Please don't die." Desperately, he poured healing spells into Jenner's inert body, completely uncaring of the chaos now raging around him.

The lightning spell that should have killed him caused Kandek to stagger and fall, twitching and foaming at the mouth. Quickly, Wynn dropped the swords to the floor before Rall and Jules. Using his steel-cutting lightning-magic, he cut Jules free of his chains, while Grakken sobbed over Jenner's prostrate form.

"Oh no...."Jules said when Wynn produced his white-hot steel-cutting magic. The whites of Jules's eyes showed, and hysteria tinged his voice. "Oh, Goddess…. That's awfully close to my hands…Gah! Oh, Goddess…my feet…be careful with that lightning, you bloody idiot…. Thanks!"

As soon as his chains were cut, Wynn turned to Rall. Devyn had engaged the two minotaur guards in battle. "Hurry! I need some help here!" The sounds of Devyn nimbly parrying and blocking spurred Wynn on.

Unfortunately, he didn't have time to cut Rall free.

With an unearthly roar, Kandek rose to his feet. A massive shield went up, and he focused his attention on Wynn. A sword of fire appeared in his hand. "Blasphemer! You have defiled this holy place!" The fiery sword swung, missing him. "Now you will die."

All of Wynn's strongest spells sheeted off the priest's shield. Wynn fought with all his might against an adversary stronger and more adept than any he'd ever faced. The priest was fast with his sword, and his spells were delivered just as rapidly as Wynn's. The two battled back and forth before the altar, while Grakken desperately tried to shield Jenner. Once again, the earth-mage's body arched as one of Kandek's lightning spells sheeted off Wynn's shield.

"Kandek, no—Kandek—you're killing him…for the love of god, stop this madness!" Terrified, Grakken grabbed Jenner's arms, trying to pull the large man to safety. "Don't die…please don't die…."

Wynn relentlessly probed the shield the priest had thrown up but couldn't find a weak spot. He tried his steel-cutting spell but couldn't sense where it was tied off. Still, his own shield held solid against Kandek's assaults, which appeared to puzzle the priest. As the fight wore on, Wynn's world narrowed. At last, he was able to use every trick he'd ever wanted to try on an adversary.

Devyn struggled against Bek. Still kneeling, Rall desperately blocked Luk's blows as well as he could, cursing loudly as Jules alternately blocked Luk's swings and hacked away at Rall's chains, trying to cut him free. Hearing his shouts, Luk turned to assisting Bek, and Rall said, "Forget it. I'll just have to manage. You two keep these bastards off my back while I deal with the bloody portal to Serende. Help me up."

Jules pulled Rall to his feet and said, "Bust it up, my brother. Destroy that portal so it can't be used again." He turned his attention to Luk, who now retreated before Jules's vicious attack.

The battles shifted back and forth as the various combatants traveled all over the chapel. Gripping his sword in both hands and shuffling along as fast as he could, Rall was hard-pressed to avoid being killed as he struggled to cross the room. "Shi-i-t...Gah! Oh no...." Ducking and weaving crazily amid the mayhem, Rall at last managed to hobble over to the portal, mostly unscathed. Hacking with all his strength, he beat at the glowing doorframe of amethyst crystal, which began throbbing eerily like a heartbeat.

Devyn sliced Bek's belly wide open, and the minotaur knelt shrieking, trying to keep his guts inside. Seeing his mate in trouble, Luk turned, but Devyn forced him to backpedal toward Jules, who thrust his sword into Luk's back, getting his attention. Taking that opportunity, Devyn spun around with a mighty swing, and Bek's screeches were cut off as his head hit the floor with a squishy thud.

Despite the stab wound in his back, Luk battled both Jules and Devyn with almost no sign of pain, fending them both off until he suddenly realized what Rall was doing.

"Oh no, you don't, gorm. That's my road home, and you ain't takin' it from me!" Still battling Devyn and Jules, Luk tried to work his way over to Rall, who grimly stayed on his task, chopping at the gateway with all his might. Cracks appeared in the right-hand side of the frame, and the view inside the portal muddied. Lightning began crackling as if across the surface of water. Now, the doorway began to hum, a low vibration. Blocked and unable to get to the portal, Luk bellowed, "Stop him, Kandek! Kandek, look to the portal!"

Jules took advantage of Luk's distraction, slicing off his hand, and the minotaur shrieked, clutching the bloody stump. Devyn ran his sword through his heart. As Luk sank to the floor, Jules raced to Rall's side and began hacking away at the other side of portal. A sharp, burning scent filled the air, and smoke began to rise from the crystal doorway.

Devyn joined Wynn, both of them battling Kandek. The gigantic minotaur produced a second fiery sword, and the two mages now fought desperately, casting spells and trying to break the high priest's shields. His spells became wild, bouncing all over the room, as if he were becoming desperate.

A ball of lightning flew at Devyn, rolled off his shield, struck the altar, and rebounded again. It struck Jenner full on and caused Grakken to drop him. The earth-mage arched once more and went limp.

"No...no...Jenner, why?" Grakken raised his face to the opening above the altar. "Why, God? Why?" He crushed Jenner's body to him, burying his face in the man's hair. "Oh, my darling...What did you ever do to deserve this? Dead! He's dead!" Clutching his head, Grakken screamed, a long, agonized wail that pierced even Kandek's ears. Everything seemed to pause as Grakken's shrieks reached a crescendo. He turned to Kandek, and his eyes glittered with madness. "You! You murdered him with your obscene lust for power!" He advanced toward the priest, his eyes alight with mad hatred.

Kandek paused as lines of force left Grakken's hands, and a visible shield formed around the high priest. Grakken's mad voice was chilling. "You want power? I'll give you power!"

The Temple mages scuttled back, not sure what was going to happen.

Kandek spasmed, and a look of dismay crossed his grotesque face. Locked in Grakken's thrall, the high priest's two fiery swords vanished. "I warned you, Holy Kandek." The mindbender giggled. "Don't say I didn't warn you. Now you understand real power!"

As if he were a puppet, the minotaur rose to his full height, jerking and wild-eyed. A thin, high scream was torn from his throat, and a fine, red mist formed around him. Horror-stricken, the four temple mages watched as Kandek's skin first loosened and then detached from him in a long strip as if he were a gigantic apple being peeled. The high priest's screams rose, and Grakken laughed and danced. "I tried to tell you! No one to protect you," he said, his voice bright, almost a singsong, as the priest's skin lifted in a bloody haze and floated in the air like a ghastly rope. "No one to protect you from me!"

In moments, the blood-soaked remains of the high priest lay quivering on the floor, a peculiar moaning sound rising from him. Overwhelmed by compassion, Wynn stabbed Kandek through the heart, killing him. Then he and Devyn warily faced Grakken.

Shaken at what they had witnessed, Rall and Jules redoubled their efforts, slamming their swords into the crystal as it vibrated and sparked. More cracks formed, and the portal pulsated as if it were breathing.

Grakken turned toward Wynn, his eyes glittering. "Don't worry—punishing him has taken most of my strength. But...I'm the chosen one. I have killed the highest, so *I* am now their ruler. I must go to Serende. They...but I've no magic...I need a weapon...." His eyes had become wild and unseeing. "Give me your sword, soldier." Grakken reached out, and Wynn's blade tried to pull itself out of his hand. "I have both the healing magic of Aeos and the mind-magic of Tauron. I have no elements, but you can't break my shield. No one can break my shield. Give me your sword."

"No, sir. I like this blade," said Wynn, holding onto his sword with the steely grip strong from pounding metal all day long. "Get your own."

"Give it to me." Grakken gestured again and this time put all his effort into magically snatching the sword, and once again, Wynn held on to it. "Shall I make you suffer for it? I will, you know. Don't make me do it."

"All right, then. Take it," replied Wynn and, closing his eyes, he visualized his sword as a bolt of lightning. When Grakken's magic yanked at it a third time, Wynn threw it at him as if it were a knife.

The lightning-charged sword lodged to its hilt in Grakken's chest. His hands closed around it and, falling backwards against the altar, he jerked wildly, frothing at the mouth, his eyes rolled up in his head. Yanking the sword from his chest, Grakken stumbled forward, clutching his bloody chest as the sword clattered to the floor.

Aghast, the four mages watched as Grakken continued to stagger forward, falling partway into the damaged threshold. The gateway began twisting and chattering, and Grakken's body stretched to an extraordinary thinness.

Abruptly, he vanished, sucked through the portal.

A loud popping, followed by a low rumbling, emanated from the doorway, and the entire room began shaking. Black flames shot from the crystal frame, forcing Jules and Rall to fall back. "Um, let's get out of here," said Jules. "I think it's pretty well broken now."

Jules tried to drag Rall away from the portal, but shackled as he was, Rall was unable to move fast enough. The floor gave a shudder.

"Run! Leave me! I'll just hold you bac...uff!" Wynn had circled back and picked Rall up, throwing him over his shoulder, before Rall even realized what had happened.

The three mages raced toward the exit as fast as they could, leaping over the bodies of their foes, desperate to get away from the sizzling, black fire now consuming the portal. Wynn went as fast as he could, staggering behind under the weight of the heavier man.

The floor undulated and gave a tremendous lurch. Suddenly, a loud explosion knocked them to their knees.

As Wynn struggled to save Rall, the floor gave way beneath him. The four mages fell, tumbling to the room below, Devyn and Jules sliding down the ramp-like floor. Wynn and Rall weren't so lucky. As he fell, Wynn lost his grip on his friend, tumbling into the wreckage.

Rall flew head over heels. Abruptly, the chains binding his ankles were caught and trapped by two beams, stopping his downward momentum.

As soon as they landed and were able to find him, Devyn and Jules dragged Wynn out of the rubble, injured and unconscious. "He's breathing. Where's Rall?" A moan sounded from above. They looked up, seeing Rall hanging by his ankles and in terrible pain. The chain that bound his feet was firmly wedged between two beams, and he now dangled upside down, hanging from his shackled ankles. Jules said, "Oh Goddess. Now what?"

Pulling debris around until they could stand on it, the two tried desperately to get Rall free, to no avail. Jules said, "Help me try to lift this beam. If we can lift it, we can get him out."

◆◆◆

Ivan Hemsteck felt his geas break and knew Grakken was dead. Then he heard the collapse of the chapel and hurried as fast as he could to see if there were any survivors. Seeing the predicament Rall was in, he quickly found some tools for Jules.

For half an hour, they tried the prying bar, to no avail. With Wynn unconscious, they had no other choice. The beams were just too tightly wedged under the weight of the collapsed floor, and there was no way to apply enough leverage. When that failed, they attempted to break the chains with a chisel.

The baron checked Wynn over, finding his left arm was broken, but he would live. He then bathed his wounds with cool water and applied healing balm to Wynn's bloody head and splinted his arm. He could do no more for him until he woke.

After tending to Wynn's wounds, Ivan turned to trying to ease Rall's misery. He did what he could, but until they got him down, all the old man could do was clean the wounds within reach and give him a cloth dipped in water to ease his thirst.

Both Rall and Jules were covered in bloody scrapes. Very little of their skin was unscathed. As Jules worked, the baron staunched the blood and cleaned his many abrasions and wounds and then did the same for Devyn.

An hour passed. Rall hung naked and bloody, with Devyn underneath his shoulders, supporting his weight, while Jules tried vainly to break the chains. The two mages alternated to avoid exhaustion.

Wynn became aware of the familiar sounds of a hammer on metal. Opening his eyes, he saw Jules trying to strike the chains off Rall, who was clearly in a terrible fix. Pushing up with his good arm, Wynn tried to stand but couldn't. "Someone help me. I've got the chi to cut him free, but I need help to get up there. My knee doesn't want to work right. I think I twisted it."

"Ordinarily, I would say no because of your head injuries, but we have to get him down somehow, and this isn't working. You're his only hope." Jules climbed down and helped Wynn to his feet, finding a long board he could use to help himself walk.

After some effort, Wynn had climbed to where he could see the chain, and in a few minutes, he cut through it, freeing first one ankle and then the other from the beams. The others lowered Rall to the floor. Working quickly, Wynn's magic soon cut through the manacles binding Rall's ankles and wrists, enabling the baron to tend his wounds. It was a measure of his pain that Rall made no complaint while Wynn used his lightning to cut the steel that held him trapped.

As the last shackle fell to the floor, Rall said, "Thank you, my brother." Wynn was startled when Rall grabbed him in a rough hug, wincing from the pain of his broken arm. "Thank you for not leaving me behind. Thank you for being the madman you are. But you should have left me." His ankles were a swollen, bruised mess, and he was unable to stand.

"How would I explain that to Feia?" asked Wynn, grinning. "I think we're going to make it home after all. When the crystal door exploded and the floor fell in, I had my doubts, but here we all are."

"Yes, here we all are," Jules interjected, with a hint of his old sarcasm. "Some of us are naked and could really use a nice, warm fire and maybe some clothes. If you have a spare pair of socks, Ivan, my feet are freezing."

"Of course, you'll have to burn them once he's done with them," said Rall, grinning wickedly. "He's a bit of a slob."

"Cruel, Rall." Jules stood up, grinning. "Cruel but true. But now, since Wynn is wounded, Dev and I have to carry *your* carcass to wherever there may be warmth and clothing." He gestured at Rall. "And you're no lightweight."

Chapter 38

Two weeks after the battle with Tauron's priests, the baron's heavily laden oxcart rolled into Arlen, entering the gate just before noon. Ivan Hemsteck had decided to leave the valley. The trip was long, taking more than a week, as Devyn had to restore the road through the waterdrake's lair and rebuild it all the way down. After they passed through, Wynn and Jules reworked the trail so that only people on foot could travel the road.

A young journeyman named Morgan had arrived a week before to take Lorana's place. Since she was now bonded, and many healers hoped for good positions, Soren had shortened her stay in Arlen. But she had voluntarily delayed going back to Aeoven until her husband's return, shepherding the young journeyman as he gradually gained more self-confidence. When the gate-bell rang, signaling the approach of travelers from the Hemsteck trail, she ran to meet them, throwing herself into Devyn's arms, incoherent with relief and joy.

The innkeeper, Merylee, and her son led the baron around to the barn, insisting he stay in her father's old cottage. "My dad's place is lying empty now he's gone. No one will bother you there, and you'll have your bit of garden, just the way you like. We'll feel better knowing you're with us."

Devyn and Jules carried Rall into the common room where Lorana and Morgan immediately began working on healing his still swollen feet and badly bruised ankles. "What happened to you that could have caused such terrible injuries? Your ankles aren't broken, but they're twisted so badly you'd almost be better off if they were." Lorana examined his many wounds. "Two weeks of healing naturally and your feet and ankles are a little improved, but it would have taken months if you hadn't finally made your way down here." When they told her how he'd received the injuries, she was silent, tears filling her eyes. "Well," she said at last, "you're lucky. Your feet could have been trapped between those beams, and if that had happened, I don't think you'd be here at all."

When they were done with Rall, the two healers turned to Wynn's broken arm and his still painfully tender knee.

That evening, the four mages and Baron Hemsteck told their story to the assembled people of Arlen. As the truth of what had happened to the missing members of their community sank in, the shocked, horrified people, who gathered in front of the inn eager for information, stood stunned. Tears flowed freely as the tiny community began mourning the loss of so many. "Still, we now know what happened. May Aeos keep their poor souls forever."

The next day, the five mages rode the mail coach back to Aeoven.

◆◆◆

The coach left them at the end of the alley behind their houses, while Devyn and Lorana stayed on the coach to the Temple. Wynn paused at his back gate, disoriented at being home. The others noticed that he had been silent since the battle, and he admitted he couldn't stop thinking about his true-dream.

Even so, his heart was troubled by what he'd seen and done. At the strangest times, the horrific memory of

Kandek's flayed body would rise up in his mind's eye. After the chaos of the previous weeks, the calm of Aeoven was bewildering.

As he lifted his hand to the doorlatch, Wynn paused, fearing he would never be the same. The battles he'd fought had affected him. That much was true. But even more than those experiences, the true-dream, that message from Aeos herself, remained sharp and clear in his mind, and knowing what lay ahead for his son had changed him. He would never be able to live in peace knowing what he now knew about the threat Tauron posed to Neveyah. Still, he knew he had to put on a brave face for Seri and Johnny.

The door flew open, and his wife stood there, joy in her eyes. The world righted itself, and the weariness and pain of the last two months melted away as he held her in his arms. The warmth of the familiar kitchen eased his heart, making his vague fears fade.

Looking up, he saw his father holding Johnny. When he met his father's eyes, he saw compassion and understanding reflected there. "Welcome home, Son."

Home. Peace and contentment suffused Wynn, and the feeling of not belonging vanished as if it had never been. *I really am home, and I'll never have to leave my family again.*

Epilogue—Two Years Later

The wagon stood in front of Wynn's house on Rose Street. Liam sat in the driver's seat as Jules, Devyn, and Wynn finished loading the last baskets. Johnny ran wild while Kalen and Gayla chased him, laughing gleefully as they caught up to him. The children played the games they always had, not realizing Johnny's family was leaving Aeoven to return to Markett.

Once again, Rall picked up the unique sword Wynn had made for Johnny, sliding it out of the sheath, trying to sense the magics that lay dormant within it. That Wynn believed John would be a water-mage was evident in the designs etched with gold, the turquoise enamel of the scabbard, and the blue tooled-leather of the sword-belt.

He considered the blade, holding it up to the light so the engravings stood out clearly. The mystery of what it could possibly mean perplexed and worried him. Runes for stealth and for healing were reflected there, visible only when held at a certain angle. Rall returned the sword to its sheath, feeling left with more questions than answers. He knew Wynn had been led by the Goddess in the making of it and believed it meant misfortune loomed for Neveyah.

Birds sang and bees hummed in the warm, spring morning, and the voices of the others drifted to Rall, conversations meant to cover up the loss they all felt as they made their goodbyes to Wynn and his family.

"I'm sorry you have to leave." Feia stood chatting with Seri, Aneka, and Lorana. "I know you have to obey the wishes of the Goddess, though. We'll miss you so much. Aneka and I will be lonely, but at least Devyn and Lorana are going with you for a while."

"Yes. We'll miss you and Johnny, more than you know." Aneka wiped a tear away. "I thought we'd always be together, the four of us girls, but now you'll be gone for who knows how long. Abbess Lera's dream wasn't specific. It only said it was time for you to take Johnny away for his safety."

"I know, but Wynn wants Johnny to have at least one year as a novice since he missed out on that himself, so I promise we'll be back by then. We'll be gone twelve years at most. We aren't really farm people, you know, even though Wynn feeds half of Aeoven with our garden here." Seri grinned and said, "But if the Goddess says it's time to leave Neveyah, then we must go. It'll be an adventure. I can have my own horse, which I've always wanted, and it'll be good for Johnny to grow up on a farm."

"But it's hard losing you and Lorana at the same time." Feia fidgeted with the hem of her shirt, trying not to show how upset she was. Her eyes flickered to Lorana. "You and Devyn will be back after the baby's born, right?"

"Yes," laughed Lorana. "I want Seri to deliver this child, and if she's to do that, we need to be where she is. Once the baby can travel safely, we'll return. We should be back by Summer Solstice."

"But then when the Harvest conclave meets, Devyn is to be posted to Mal Evol Temple with Taj, and that means we'll never see you two again except when there's a conclave." Feia surreptitiously wiped a tear away. "Nothing's going to be the same."

Lorana hugged Feia, comforting her. "Feia, this is unlike you. You and Rall will go to Widge Temple, and he'll be the abbott there. That's a high honor, and you'll have the Temple school there all to yourself. You'll be in charge of the curriculum."

Seri tried to cheer Feia up too. "With the sort of training you'll be getting there, you'll be qualified to do anything you want. When Mother Relynne retires, I'll bet Abbess Lera is chosen to replace her. Rall is the logical choice to take Abbess Lera's place here in Aeoven, and you'll surely be the Mistress of Novices here at the college."

"I hope so. I'd like to have that position, and Rall would do well as abbott here," Feia replied, perking up. "Besides, Aneka is to be the abbess in Nola, so we'll be close to her and Jules." Aneka grinned, squeezing Feia's arm, and Seri hugged her.

With the cart loaded, Wynn and Jules sat on the steps, watching the children playing in the sunshine. "Johnny's going to miss them," Jules said. "The three of them are like siblings." They laughed as Gayla pointed at a squirrel, and the three children ran to look at it.

"I was pretty lonely as a child, but maybe the folks on the neighboring farm will have some children. Besides, I hope the Goddess calls Johnny back here while he's still young enough to be in the novice barracks. If she doesn't, I'm bringing him back when he turns fifteen so he can have that last year," said Wynn. "I missed out on a lot by not being a part of that." He sighed. "I'm going to hate being a farmer again. But I'll do it because we have to keep Johnny safe."

"Being a novice was fun, and you'd have loved it. And don't worry. Rall and I will visit regularly just to make sure you know which end of the sheep to milk," said Jules. "We can't wait to see how you apply your love of machinery to your farm."

"Well, I probably won't have time to do too much tinkering. The work is pretty time-consuming," said Wynn. "At least Bran has some sheep for me, so I don't have to buy any. Have they decided to let him be Dorn's replacement since you turned it down? They should. He's good at it."

"Yes, I think Bran will be the abbott there, for a while anyway," agreed Jules. "With Aneka having the chance to be the abbess in charge of the new Temple at Nola while it's being built, I've put my own career on hold for a while. Her plans for the architecture there are amazing, and I want her to have the opportunity to be a part of something grand and important. I'll be the armsmaster for both Nola and Widge, so I'll stay busy. I've got plans for beefing up the local militia so we can deal with the incursions by Ariend's children more efficiently. But I admit that in a few years, I'd like the chance to have my own Temple. I've a lot of ideas I'd like to put into place, and I had hoped...but never mind. I don't want our family to be apart for any reason."

"Don't worry, Jules," said Wynn. "I know you'll have your own Temple. We're still young, so I'm sure you'll have many great opportunities ahead of you."

"Wynn, I think we should get going so we can get to Wister before dark. We don't want to camp if we don't have to," Liam called from the wagon.

"Okay, Dad. Let me get Johnny, and we'll get going." Wynn stood up and called, "Johnny! It's time for us to leave."

"No, Dad! I don't wanna go!" Johnny turned and ran in the opposite direction. Wynn chased him, but the boy was fast and was nearly to the end of the street by the time Wynn caught him. Wynn carried his son back to the wagon, with Johnny flailing and howling his misery.

"Thank Aeos you're going to be helping to raise that child," Feia said to Liam. "I love those two dearly, but they aren't good at making that boy behave. They aren't consistent with him. He's a little beast at times."

"They mean well, and they love him," replied Liam. "He behaves well for me, it's true, but I've had more experience with children, so...."

"Dad, no! I want to stay." Johnny's screams had turned to pathetic sobs. "Please?"

"Settle down, Johnny. We have to go, and that's final," replied Wynn, handing the boy up to Liam.

"John. My name is John," said the boy stubbornly. "Johnny's a baby name. I'm a big boy now."

"Okay, John, have it your way," replied Wynn, climbing up and settling himself next to Seri. "But big boys don't have tantrums when they're about to go on grand adventures."

"Are we really going to have our own sheep?" John was already diverted.

Soon, the wagon rolled away, everyone waving. John bounced up and down despite Seri's demand that he sit still. Rather than argue with the child, Wynn produced a long scarf and tied him securely to the wagon bench, causing him to sob heartbrokenly again.

Devyn leaned over and whispered something to him, and the child quieted down, waving cheerfully to his friends.

Gayla and Kalen held hands, solemnly waving as the wagon disappeared around the corner. "Mama? Is John coming back?" Kalen asked.

"Not today, but someday." Feia answered. She and Aneka took the children and walked through the now empty-house, making sure everything was spotless for the next occupants. Closing up the house, they went out the backdoor.

"That child is a real handful," said Jules. He and Rall had watched John's antics, shaking their heads. "He's going to be something else when he comes back, don't you think?"

"Oh, he might have settled down a bit by then," said Rall, doubtfully. "Wynn's doing his best with him, and that's what matters."

They watched in silence, and then they turned and went to Jules's house. They sat at the table in the kitchen. "It's already boring without Wynn, isn't it," said Jules, staring glumly out of the sunlit window.

"It sure is," agreed Rall. He cringed, hearing Feia's waspish voice calling him to come home. "It's certainly not going to be the same now he's gone." Rall stood up and left.

The backdoor closed softly behind him, leaving Jules sitting in his kitchen, remembering the day he'd met Wynn Farmer. *That was the day my life changed forever. That was the day my life really began, if I'd only known it then.* In his mind's eye, Jules saw the young man emerge from the mist, bedraggled and confused, uncertain of where he was or how he'd gotten there.

"Oh, it's you, farm boy. Good. We can get out of here and reach the inn at Armat before they close the gates tonight...."

Lost in his memories, Jules smiled. Wynn would raise Johnny with his own brand of parenting, and when it was time, they would be back and everything would be good again. He grinned even wider, thinking about some of Wynn's more outrageous inventions. *Wynn's about to settle down and be a farmer for a while, but is the farm ready for Wynn?*

His reverie was broken as Aneka called, "Jules! Feia wants to go on a picnic by the river. Can you get that big basket from the kitchen? Rall's making the food."

Life goes on, Jules, but Rall's right—it won't be the same. Reaching up and getting the basket down from the shelf, Jules called, "Coming, dear." The backdoor slammed behind him as he raced down the steps.

APPENDICES

EXCERPT FROM THE BOOK OF LIFE

In the beginning, there was only the void, and the void was barren of life. Nor did any element exist there no fire, no lightning, no earth, and no water. All was as it should be, and the void waited.

Two spheres from beyond the void approached each other, as gently as bubbles blown in the breeze. When they touched, a new sphere was born. And in the void, new spheres appeared until ten new worlds had been born.

The Father and Mother were pleased and admired their work. Then began the great unraveling, and they surrounded the spheres of their children in a protective cocoon that they called the universe.

In the center of the universe, a star flared into existence. The day glowed with the light of the star, the physical manifestation of the Almighty Father. The ten worlds revolved around Him, one touching the other, and all was well in the universe.

The universe grew strong. In the night sky, the Mother cast a myriad of stars and set the moon to illuminate the dark. The moon was the physical manifestation of the Mother of All.

No longer did the spheres create new worlds when they touched. Instead, where they touched, gods were born. Upon awakening, each god made the choice to be male or female, and in this way, the spheres were divided, five worlds for the gods and five worlds for the goddesses.

For the long time of their childhoods, the gods and goddesses shaped their worlds, creating the lands and waters. Each world was different and yet similar, as were the deities who formed them, and each admired the handiwork of the others.

As they grew to adulthood, the deities began to populate their worlds with diverse peoples, whom they considered to be their children, and all were content to live in their worlds, and the universe was at peace.

And the gods and goddesses were five each, and these were their names in the order in which they came into existence:

Meren, god of the Water World Aquas, and his wife Grete, goddess of the Woodland World Alrunne.

Olod, god of the Sky World Geminis, and his wife Oriane, goddess of the River World Danus.

Priscis, god of the Winter World Morovi, and his wife Delhine, goddess of the Summer World Erendi.

Berrin, god of the Grasslands World Sanuvyr, and his wife Feylyn, goddess of the Ice World Chysat.

Ariend, god of the Mountain World Cascadia, and his wife Aeos, goddess of the Verdant World Neveyah.

All was as it should be. Eons passed in harmony until once again, a sphere appeared. From whence came this sphere, none of the deities knew, nor did the universe. Nonetheless, they welcomed this new world, and when the new god was born, he chose to be male. They called him Tauron, and in his childhood, he created the Arid World of Serende. All was well until Tauron grew into his adulthood and realized he alone of the gods had no mate.

At first, all the deities agreed if he had come into existence, then surely another goddess would come to be his wife. Tauron listened to their counsel and was patient. But as the eons passed and no new goddess was born for him, he became miserable in his loneliness.

"Why did you create me only to leave me alone?" Tauron often asked of the universe, but he received no answer, for the universe had not created him. Yet he was beloved, and the other deities made much effort to ease his loneliness, to no avail.

And the eons passed.

With the passage of time, Tauron became ever stranger, jealous, and cruel. The other deities began to fear and avoid him. He became even lonelier, and eventually, he descended into madness. He demanded abject worship from his people to ease his pain. As the eons passed, he realized he was alone and would always be so unless he could find a wife worthy of him.

In his obsession, he decided Aeos should be his wife. "She is the youngest of the gods other than me. She should have been mine."

Thus, it was in the guise of seeking counsel, he went to Ariend's mountain home of Cascadia and sought him out. During the feast Ariend set before him, Tauron took him by stealth and surprise. Tauron sealed Ariend alive into the haft of a spear carved from Ariend's own mountains and thrust the spear deep into the earth of the world of Cascadia.

Aeos, seeking her husband, could find him nowhere. She was distraught and sought the help of the other deities. The other gods and goddesses did not know where Ariend could be and knew something had happened to him, for he would never have abandoned his wife or his world and his children. They searched for a thousand years but did not find him.

Though all the deities came to Aeos's aid, one only pretended to search. Tauron was occupied in a different way. He added league after league of Cascadia to his own world and at last took Ariend's own beloved people, subverting them and making them into creatures lower than beasts. What once had been a gentle, clever, and scholarly people now were voracious and filled with an unquenchable hunger, mindless and violent. Tauron was filled with joy as he looked at his improvements to Ariend's people. "They were too full of pride before. Now they are as they should have been."

When Aeos saw what Tauron had done to Ariend's people, she knew he was responsible for the disappearance of her husband, and she searched the land. At last, she came upon the crystal and marble spear that had been thrust into the ground, creating an immense crater. There she found the skeleton of her husband Ariend embedded in the haft, arms outstretched and face raised to the heavens. Upon touching the crystal, she felt his heart beating and knew him to be alive. "Mother, Father, see what Tauron has done to my husband! Help me to save him, I beg of you!"

The Mother of All wept to see her son in so terrible a place. "My daughter, I must remain to hold up the sky, but the Almighty Father hastens to your side. Though many long years will pass, this evil deed will be made right. I have foreseen it."

Her father came to her side and wept upon seeing Ariend. "My daughter, it pains me, but I cannot interfere in this, though I wish it were not so. This tragedy must play itself out."

The other deities counseled Aeos to take the valley for her world and thus protect her husband until she could find a way to free him from his prison. The oldest brother, Meren, said, "Ariend still lives. There must be eleven worlds and one God for each. Tauron has added half of Cascadia to Serende and still attempts to take it all. He has subverted Ariend's people and made them into less than beasts. We must seal our worlds so none can cross the barriers, else Tauron will be the only god in the universe and our people will be abused in the same, cruel way." And the eight gods and goddesses sealed away their worlds.

Aeos did take all of Cascadia that Tauron had not yet gained and sealed the world of Neveyah from him. Then she ceded half of the combined worlds to her Father to ensure the balance would not be disturbed, and he guarded the land and people most carefully, for there must be eleven worlds, one for each of the eleven deities. Together, they nurtured the two worlds, weeping with sorrow over the fate of Ariend's people at the hands of Tauron. Each did what they could to mitigate the peoples' suffering, though they were not able to completely undo Tauron's work.

Aeos named the crater Mal Evol, which means Valley of Sorrow. For three thousand years, she guarded her husband and the spear that entombed him, ruling Neveyah and Mal Evol with love and a gentle hand. Aeos bequeathed great magic to a few of her people so they could withstand Tauron's hordes. She also gave the valley to one of her most trusted servants and instructed him to build a castle around the haft of the spear, saying, "When the blood of your blood sits upon the throne, you will have knowledge of everything that lives in the land of Mal Evol. Ariend will accept you and the blood of your blood to guard the remains of his world."

Thus, the trusted servant and his sons gave their lives to the carving of the throne.

Once more, Tauron began pressing Aeos, saying her husband was surely dead, and she must wed him and cede the other half of Cascadia to him to right the balance, as there must be one god for each world. She refused saying, "My husband lives. The Almighty Father is a god and worthy of the care and keeping of the eleventh world until my husband can be freed from the prison of your making." Tauron at last went away, weeping and descending ever deeper into madness.

Thus was born the enmity between Neveyah and Serende, the land of Tauron, the Bull God.

And in the world that he named Ariend, the Almighty Father planted the seed of the vine from whose line will come the Hero Foretold, the One Who Takes Back All.

Time and Calendar of Neveyah

Each year consists of 365 days and is divided into four seasons: Winter, Spring, Summer, Harvest, and one Holy Month.

Each season consists of three months, making twelve months that equal 28 days each, plus a Holy Month. Harvest (Autumn) and Winter are separated by the Holy Month of 29 days. The actual winter solstice falls on the first day of the month following (on the first day of Caprica). This is a month sacred to the Goddess Aeos, Goddess of Harvest, Hearth, and Home. It is a time when people travel to visit family and simply take time off for a small vacation, often taking two weeks to do it. On the day that falls between last day of the Holy Month and the first day of Caprica (called Holy Day,) each family holds a ritual feast in their home. It is a feast of thanksgiving and prayers for the New Year. Every four years, an extra Holy Day is added to the calendar and the day is a festival day all across Neveyah. Such a year is called a Long Year, though it is really only one day longer.

The months and seasons are as follows:
Caprica, Aquas, Piscus   (Winter) Begins on actual day of Winter Solstice
Arese, Taura, Geminis   (Spring)
Lunne, Leonid, Virga   (Summer)
Libre, Scorpius, Saggitus   (Harvest)
Holy Month   thirteenth month, stands alone on calendar, ends day before the winter solstice
Holy Day   Bridge between old year and new, belongs to no month, a day of celebration

Days of the Week -

1. Sunnaday—Minimal business is conducted; each family's tasks for the Temple as a whole are completed, such as chopping firewood, quilting, making clothes, and preserving food. The members of the temple clergy assemble in work gangs to accomplish these tasks from which they all benefit.
2. Lunaday
3. Tyrsday
4. Odensday
5. Torsday
6. Frosday
7. Restday – no business is conducted, and only minimal work is done on farms and other places where some work must be done seven days a week. This is a day for people to spend with their families or to pursue their personal interests.

Prominent members of Edwin Farmer's Family Tree

Aelfrid Firesword, founder of College of Warcraft and Magic

Biann D'Braden – 1st abbess and founder of Braden Temple

Iain Farmer

Liam Farmer

Wynn Farmer - *Mountains of the Moon*

John Farmer – *Forbidden Road,*

Edwin Farmer–*Tower of Bones, Forbidden Road*

Son – Jon Farmer

The Prophecies of Neveyah

Abbot Devyn D'Mal to the assembled clergy at Mal Evol Temple in the year 3215

"Keeper, you must save the remnant of my children, for when the end-times are upon you, you shall be barred from the valley of poison and beauty. The wall shall stretch from Horn to Horn and shall be the sign that none from the Valley of Shadows can enter the golden land. The eternal youth, the Lost One, will take the City of Gloom and those of my children left behind will suffer unto the third generation. He stands on the wall and gazes on the golden land, unable to enter."

Mother Lera to the assembled Clergy at Aeoven in the year 3229

"Hark now! The advent of the Bull God is upon us - he comes to claim his bride. She rejects him, and his mad desire is thwarted. Still he claims the dowry as was promised. The verdant lands shall fall to the Bull God and shall become a wilderness of thorns. Seek the hero who will hold safe the Heart of Neveyah. Take the Heir down the Forbidden Road and shroud him with the light of truth. Now comes the Hero from the lands of the Almighty Father; from his line shall come the one who will take back all. From him shall come the Hero Foretold who will triumph on the day of redemption."

Father Rall to the assembled clergy at Aeoven in the year 3254

"The storm rises in the lands of Neveyah, though it does not bring its wrath fully for yet awhile...when falls

the Beloved Hero into darkness, then will the storm's wrath fall upon Neveyah. The children of the Bull-God answer the call that rides on the wind. The light of truth remains shrouded beneath the Throne of Stone and Bone. The cradle of the rightful heir lies obscured by the truth. Let the Hero go to the Shadow Castle to seek the hand of her whom darkness has claimed. The moon is dark - In stealth seeks the hero for the window to the Tower of Roses; in stealth he unbars the door to the forbidden room. Four heroes depart and five return; yet the battle is not won, but only the first skirmish. The Beloved must fall to darkness ere the light of truth is restored to the Shadow Castle! Blood and tears reign in the Shadow Castle until the Hero Foretold comes to restore the scion to the throne."

Edwin Farmer to his companions on the Holy Quest in the year 3254

"The verdant springtime lies coiled beneath the surface of the shattered lands, waiting for the call of the Beloved, to set it free. The Beloved Hero falls to darkness; he sows the poisoned seed across the shadowed land, yet will he rise up to set free the land of Mal Evol on the day the land takes him home. All will see the fruiting of the land of the Living Shades. This will be the sign; the day of redemption is at hand."

"The Dark God laments his betrothed, she chooses him not. The hordes of the broken lands despoil verdant Mal Evol. Now send the heroes four into the land ruled by the Throne of Stone and Bone. Should the treasured one be lost to darkness, those left to walk in the light must flee down the Forbidden Road. Treasured and Beloved, beware the voice of reason. Long days of darkness shadow the realm. The poisoned land flowers, but death walks amidst poison and thorn. When blooms the land again, the day of redemption is at hand. Four heroes journey to bring forth the spring, but balanced on the edge of reason is the outcome.

Edwin Farmer to the assembled Clergy in the year 3260

"Now begins the quest in earnest. Send now the heroes four to the Shadowed Land. Beware! Beloved, the true task for which you were born begins. The storm rages, the door opens upon the field of battle, in grief recall the Forbidden Road. The Beloved Hero will rise on the day of redemption. Mist and shadows shroud the truth, but the Hero Foretold shall one day set them free."

Edwin Farmer to the assembled on the battlefield in Mal Evol in the year 3260

"My Beloved Hero has fallen. As has been foretold, he shall sow the poisoned seed, and the garden city will fall to him. Darkness falls upon the shadowed land. Long years of suffering and pain lie before us at his

dread hand. Yet, when comes the Hero Foretold, the Beloved will rise up and free the land. On the day of redemption, you will know deliverance is at hand when poison gives way to spring. Seek now the Forbidden Road, lest you be lost also."

<u>Zander Christophson to the assembled at Braden Temple in the year 3260</u>

"The end days are upon us. As has been written in the stars the Garden City must fall. Let your heart be eased, Dark Knight. Your beloved rests at my Hearth. He has earned his place in heaven. Now must the Companions aid the Father and the Son in building the wall which cannot be breached from Horn to Horn. The Elder Warrior and the Dark Knight must gather my people and lead them to the Holy City, all lies ready for them there. In less than two seasons the Lost One will lead the hordes of Tauron to the gates of the Garden City. He stands on the walls unable to enter the golden land, and the broken children of Mal Evol stand behind him. In his grief he sows the poisoned seed, a vain effort to recreate the verdant land. This must happen before the Throne of Stone and Bone lies broken and the Mountain God is free of his prison. The One Who Takes Back All shall right the balance of the worlds."

Connie J. Jasperson lives in Olympia, Washington. A vegan, she and her husband share five children, a love of good food and great music. She is active in local writing groups, an editor for Myrddin Publishing Group, and is a writing coach. She is an active member of the both the Northwest Independent Writers Association and Pacific Northwest Writers Association, and is a founding member of Myrddin Publishing Group. Music and food dominate her waking moments.

When not writing or blogging, she can be found with her Kindle, reading avidly.

You can find her blogging on her writing life at:

Life in the Realm of Fantasy
http://conniejjasperson.wordpress.com

Myrddin Publishing Group
www.myrddinpublishing.com

~~~

More great books from every genre await your reading pleasure!

~~~

MYRDDIN PUBLISHING GROUP BOOK LIST

WWW.MYRDDINPUBLISHING.COM

URBAN FANTASY ~ PARANORMAL ~ ROMANCE

GIRLS CAN'T BE KNIGHTS by Lee French (New Adult)
Everyone knows girls can't be knights.

YUM by Nicole Antonia Carson (YA)
Can Jim and his great-granddaughter Emily stop the carnage?

Brawn Stroker's Dragula: The Journal of Dee Flaytable by Nicole Antonia Carro (Mature Readers)
When the Vampire Queens battle, who will win?
Dragula is pure smut. Enjoy!

HEART SEARCH SERIES by Carlie M.A. Cullen (New Adult)
HEART SEARCH, book one: Lost, HEART SEARCH, book two: Found

One bite starts it all. . .Fate toys with mortals and immortals alike, as two hearts torn apart by darkness face ordeals which test them to their limits.

THE GUARDIAN SERIES by Joan Hazel (New Adult)
Book I THE LAST GUARDIAN, Book II BURDENS OF A SAINT
Delta Pack is an elite force of shape-shifters charged with maintaining order in both the shifter and human communities. High adventure and sizzling romance!

HIRED BY A DEMON by Gypsy Madden (YA)
A simple babysitting position goes terribly awry for Vara...Urban fantasy at its best!

GIRLS CAN'T BE KNIGHTS by Lee French (YA urban paranormal)

~~~

SCIENCE FICTION
LAND OF NOD SERIES by Gary Hoover
(Appropriate for all ages)
Book I—The Artifact,
Book II - The Prophet
Jeff Browning has been haunted by terrifying dreams since the mysterious disappearance of his father (a renowned physicist). But when he finds a portal in his father's office, he must overcome his fears in an attempt to find him.

THE DREAM LAND Series BY Stephen Swartz
Book I Long Distance Voyager,
The Dream Land 2 - Dreams of Futures Past,
 The Dream Land 3 - Diaspora
An epic of interdimensional intrigue, alien romance, and world domination by a couple of high school nerds mashed with psychological thriller and time travel.

MAZE BESET TRILOGY by Lee French (Superhero science fiction)
Dragons In Pieces
Dragons In Chains
Dragons In Flight
Superheroes in denim.

~~~

STEAMPUNK
THE CROWN PHOENIX SERIES by Alison DeLuca (Teen)
The Night Watchman Express
Devil's Kitchen
The Lamplighter's Special
The South Sea Bubble
A magic typewriter, time-travel, a mysterious train—high adventure written with Edwardian flair!

The Infinity Bridge (The Nu-Knights) by Ross M. Kitson (Teen)

Three teenagers are propelled into an action-packed race against time, involving alternate realities, airships, clockwork killers.... and Merlin.

~~~

LITERARY FICTION

AFTER ILIUM by Stephen Swartz (Mature readers)
Seduction and betrayal on the road to Ilium. An epic of interdimensional intrigue, alien romance, and world domination by a couple of high school nerds mashed with psychological thriller and time travel.

TALES FROM THE DREAMTIME by Connie J. Jasperson (Literary Fantasy, Mature Readers)
Three grownup Tales from the Dreamtime in one novella....A conversation with Galahad, a prince on a quest and a goddess in mourning, a stolen kingdom and the Fractal Mirror. Three tales of wonder and great deeds, three tales of heroes and villains.

HUW THE BARD by Connie J. Jasperson (Medieval Fantasy, Mature Readers)
Fleeing a burning city, everything he ever loved in ashes behind him, penniless and hunted, no place is safe. Abandoned and alone, Huw the Bard must somehow survive.

~~~

EPIC FANTASY

TOWER OF BONES SERIES by Connie J Jasperson
Published by Bard Books (Epic Fantasy, Mature
Readers)
Book I, Tower of Bones
Book II Forbidden Road
The Gods are at war, and Neveyah is the battleground.

DAMSEL IN DISTRESS by Lee French under
Tangled Sky Press (Dark fantasy)
Even cut flowers can bloom.

PRISM SERIES by Ross M. Kitson (Epic Fantasy,
Mature Readers)
Darkness Rising 1 – Chained
Darkness Rising 2 – Quest
Darkness Rising 3 – Secrets
Darkness Rising 4 – Loss
Darkness Rising 5 - Broken
Bravery is measured in moments. The forces of
darkness are rising—and tragedy awaits even the most
heroic.

THE GREATEST SIN SERIES by Lee French and
Erik Kort under Tangled Sky Press (Epic fantasy)
   The Fallen
   Harbinger
   Moon Shades
Prophecy. Secrets. Lies. It's all an illusion

Bard Books

A proud member of Myrddin Publishing Group.